Praise for *All*

'Both glittering with magic and drenched in blood, *All of Us Villains* kept me up at night with its heart-pounding pace and layered mysteries. I'll be waiting for book two with bated breath and bitten nails'
Sara Holland, *New York Times* bestselling author of *Everless*

'Dark, luscious, and brutally smart, *All of Us Villains* is a fresh but unforgiving look at the legacy of abusive families and community-sanctioned violence. Foody and Herman have created a thrilling story that is impossible to put down; I stayed up all night to finish this book'
Victoria Lee, author of *A Lesson in Vengeance* and *The Fever King*

'A blood-soaked modern fairytale brimming with magic, spectacle, and unforgettable characters'
Katy Rose Pool, author of *There Will Come A Darkness*

'Foody and Herman's collaboration offers a fun yet brutal tale of sacrifice, betrayal, and ever-shifting loyalties. From twists that'll make you gasp to believably flawed characters you can't help but cheer for and curse in the same breath, this one will keep readers on the edge of their seats'
Tara Sim, author of *Scavenge the Stars*

'Positively wicked in all the right ways. This series is my new obsession, and I cannot wait to devour the next one. With its innovative magic system, a twisted cast of characters you somehow can't help but love, and a plot that will leave you on the edge of your seat, *All of Us Villains* is addicting from start to finish. I'm obsessed'
Adalyn Grace, New York Times bestselling author of
All the Stars and Teeth

'Magical, clever and cutthroat, *All of Us Villains* sets out to make it impossible to know who to root for . . . A fun, twisty ride through a world full of spells and family secrets'
Kendare Blake, *New York Times* bestselling author of
the Three Dark Crowns series

ALL OF US VILLAINS

CHRISTINE HERMAN and
AMANDA FOODY

This edition first published in 2022
First published in Great Britain in 2021 by Gollancz
an imprint of The Orion Publishing Group Ltd
Carmelite House, 50 Victoria Embankment
London EC4Y 0DZ

An Hachette UK Company

9 10 8

ISBN (Mass Market Paperback) 978 1 473 23387 4
ISBN (eBook) 978 1 47323 388 1

Printed in Great Britain by Clays Ltd, Elcograph S.p.A

www.gollancz.co.uk

For Trevor and Ben,
HAGS

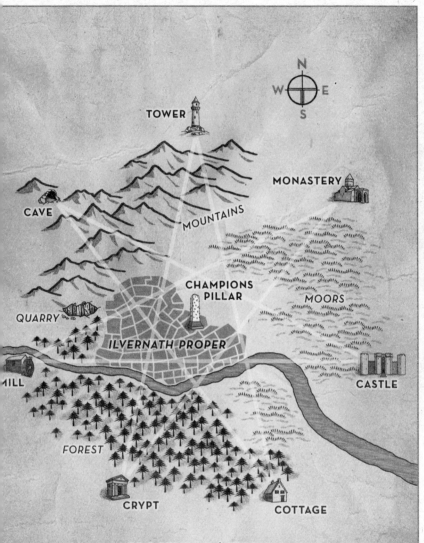

TOWER

MONASTERY

CAVE

MOUNTAINS

CHAMPIONS
PILLAR

MOORS

QUARRY

ILVERNATH PROPER

MILL

CASTLE

FOREST

CRYPT

COTTAGE

ILVERNATH

ALL OF US
VILLAINS

ALISTAIR LOWE

The Lowes shaped cruelty into a crown, and oh, they wear it well.

A Tradition of Tragedy: The True Story of the Town
that Sends its Children to Die

The Lowe family had always been the undisputed villains of their town's ancient, bloodstained story, and no one understood that better than the Lowe brothers.

The family lived on an isolated estate of centuries-worn stone, swathed in moss and shadowed in weeping trees. On mischief nights, children from Ilvernath sometimes crept up to its towering wrought iron fence, daring their friends to touch the famous padlock chained around the gate—the one engraved with a scythe.

Grins like goblins, the children murmured, because the children in Ilvernath loved fairy tales—especially real ones. *Pale as plague and silent as spirits. They'll tear your throat and drink your soul.*

All these tales were deserved.

These days, the Lowe brothers knew better than to tempt the town's wrath, but that didn't stop them from sneaking over the fence in the throes of night, relishing the taste of some reckless thrill.

"Do you hear that?" The older one, Hendry Lowe, stood up, brushed the forest floor off his gray T-shirt, and cracked each of his knuckles, one by one. "That's the sound of rules breaking."

Hendry Lowe was too pretty to worry about rules. His nose was freckled from afternoons napping in sunshine. His dark curls kissed his ears and cheekbones, overgrown from months between haircuts.

His clothes smelled sweet from morning pastries often stuffed in his pockets.

Hendry Lowe was also too charming to play a villain.

The younger brother, Alistair, leaped from the fence and crashed gracelessly to the ground. He didn't like forgoing the use of magick, because without it he was never very good at anything—even an action as simple as landing. But tonight he had no magick to waste.

"Do you hear that?" Alistair echoed, smirking as he rose to his feet. "That's the sound of bones breaking."

Although the two brothers looked alike, Alistair wore the Lowe features far differently than Hendry. Pale skin from a lifetime spent indoors, eyes the color of cigarette ashes, a widow's peak as sharp as a blade. He wore a wool sweater in September because he was perpetually cold. He carried the Sunday crossword in his pocket because he was perpetually bored. He was one year younger than Hendry, a good deal more powerful, and a great deal more wicked.

Alistair Lowe played a perfect villain. Not because he was instinctively cruel or openly proud, but because, sometimes, he liked to. Many of the stories whispered by the children of Ilvernath came from him.

"This is a shitty idea," Alistair told his brother. "You know that, right?"

"You say that every time."

Alistair shivered and shoved his hands in his pockets. "This time it's different."

Two weeks ago, the moon in Ilvernath had turned crimson, piercing and bright like a fresh wound in the sky. It was called the Blood Moon, the sign that, after twenty years of peace, the tournament was approaching once more. Only a fortnight remained until the fall of the Blood Veil, and neither brother wanted to spend it in the hushed, sinister halls of their home.

The walk downtown was long—it was a waste of magick to drain a Here to There spellring this close to the tournament, and they couldn't drive. Both were lost in their thoughts. Hendry looked like he was fantasizing about meeting a cute girl, judging from how he kept fiddling with his curls and smoothing the wrinkles in his sleeves.

Alistair was thinking about death. More specifically, about causing it.

The gloomy stone architecture of Ilvernath had stood for over sixteen hundred years, but in the last few decades, it had been renovated with sleek glass storefronts and trendy outdoor restaurants. Despite its disorienting maze of cobbled, one-way streets, questionable amenities, and minimal parking, the small city was considered an up-and-coming spot for the art and magick scene.

Not that the seven cursed families of Ilvernath paid much attention to the modern world, even if the world had recently begun paying attention to *them*.

The Magpie was the boys' favorite pub, although no one would guess that from how infrequently they visited. Determined to keep their identities concealed and their photographs out of the papers, Alistair insisted they vary the location for their nighttime excursions. They couldn't afford to become familiar faces—they'd been homeschooled for that very reason. The way their grandmother talked, one whisper of their names and the city would be raising their pitchforks.

Alistair looked grimly upon the Magpie, its sign a dark shadow in the red moonlight, and wondered if the trouble was worth it.

"You don't have to come inside," Hendry told him.

"Someone needs to watch out for you."

Hendry reached underneath his T-shirt and pulled out a piece of quartz dangling on a chain. The inside pulsed with scarlet light— the color of a spellstone fully charged with high magick.

Alistair grabbed Hendry by the wrist and shoved the stone back beneath his shirt before someone noticed. "You're asking for trouble."

Hendry only winked at him. "I'm asking for a drink."

Magick was a valuable resource throughout the world—something to be found, collected, and then crafted into specific spells or curses.

Once upon a time, there had been two types of magick: frighteningly powerful high magick and plentiful, weaker common magick. Throughout history, empires had greedily fought for control of the high magick supply, and by the time humanity invented the telescope and learned to bottle beer, they had depleted it entirely.

Or so they'd believed.

Hundreds of years ago, seven families had clashed over who would control Ilvernath's high magick. And so a terrible compromise was reached—a curse the families cast upon themselves. A curse that had remained a secret . . . until one year ago.

Every generation, each of the seven families was required to put forth a champion to compete in a tournament to the death. The victor would award their family exclusive claim over Ilvernath's high magick, a claim that expired upon the beginning of the next cycle, when the tournament began anew.

Historically, the Lowes dominated. For every three tournaments, they won two. The last cycle, twenty years ago, Alistair's aunt had murdered all the other competitors within four days.

Before they'd learned about the tournament, the rest of Ilvernath could only point to the Lowes' wealth and cruelty as the reasons an otherwise mysterious, reclusive family commanded such respect from lawmakers and spellmakers. Now they knew exactly how dangerous that family truly was.

So with the foreboding Blood Moon gleaming overhead, tonight was a risky time for the only two Lowes of tournament age to crave live music and a pint of ale.

"It's one drink," Hendry said, giving Alistair a weak smile.

Although the Lowe family hadn't formally chosen their champion yet, the boys had always known it would be Alistair. Tonight meant far more to either of them than a simple drink.

"Fine." Alistair threw open the door.

The pub was a cramped, slovenly place. The air was thick from tobacco smoke; rock music blared from a jukebox in the corner. Red-

and-white checkered cloths draped over every booth. For the sociable, there were billiards. For those keeping a lower profile, there was a pinball machine, its buttons sticky from whisky fingers.

The Magpie was flooded with cursechasers. They traveled the world to gawk at magickal anomalies like Ilvernath's, such as the curse in Oxacota that left a whole town asleep for nearly a century, or the curse on the ruins in Môlier-sur-Olenne that doomed trespassers with a violent death in exactly nine days' time. Now, the tourists clustered in groups, whispering over well-worn copies of *A Tradition of Tragedy*. The recent bestseller had exposed the death tournament and Ilvernath's surviving vein of high magick . . . and had catapulted their remote city into the international spotlight.

"I didn't believe that the Blood Moon was *actually* scarlet," Alistair overheard one of them whispering. "I thought it was just a name."

"The tournament is a high magick curse. High magick is always red," another answered.

"Or maybe," drawled a third voice, "it's called the Blood Moon because a bunch of kids spend three months murdering each other under it. Ever think of that?"

Alistair and Hendry avoided the tourists as they shuffled through the pub. "Do you think Grandma will start getting fan mail?" asked Hendry, snickering. "I heard there's a photograph of our whole family in the first chapter. I hope I look good."

"Sorry to break it to you, but that picture is from ten years ago," Alistair said flatly.

Hendry looked momentarily disappointed, then delighted. "So the entire world knows you had a bowl cut?"

Alistair rolled his eyes and headed toward the bar. Even though he was a year younger than Hendry, his hollow stare always made him look older—old enough to avoid being carded.

After he ordered, Alistair found himself waiting beside a pair of girls bickering with each other.

"Did you honestly come here alone?" the first girl asked. She smelled strongly of cheap beer, and like all the patrons here, she wore crystal spellrings on each finger that glowed white with common magick. Alistair guessed they were filled with simple spells: Hangover Cure, Zit Zapper, Matchstick . . . whatever suited a Friday night pub crawl.

"Of course not," the second girl said, smoothing down her violently red curls. "My friends are over there." She gestured vaguely at the entire bar.

"I thought so," sneered the tipsy girl. "You're famous now, you know. There's a picture of you on the cover of one of my mum's magazines. You're wearing sweatpants."

"It's been known to happen on occasion," the redheaded girl grumbled.

"I heard the Darrows have chosen now, too. That makes three champions so far—Carbry Darrow, Elionor Payne, and *you*." The first girl smiled viciously, in the kind of way that made Alistair guess the girls had once been friends. "But no one wants the Macaslans to win."

Alistair realized it now—he *recognized* the redheaded girl. She was the Macaslan who'd been announced as champion months and months before the Blood Moon had appeared, and the paparazzi had branded her the face of the tournament ever since. Alistair wasn't surprised that the Macaslans would stoop to such desperate grabs for attention. His grandmother had always described them as the bottom-feeders of the seven families, willing to use unsavory methods for even a taste of power. But the Macaslan girl's designer handbag and pretty face didn't give the impression of someone who would have to fight for attention.

At their words, several of the cursechasers stared, and the Macaslan girl cleared her throat and turned her back to them.

"Well, I don't care what people think of me," she said. But Alistair disagreed. No one wore heels to a dive bar if they didn't care about their reputation. "The evening news already called me and the Lowe champion rivals. Because I'm the one who's going to win."

The tipsy girl rolled her eyes. "The Lowes haven't even announced their champion yet. Whoever they are, they mustn't be that impressive."

As the bartender slid Alistair his drinks, Alistair fantasized about how quickly the Macaslan champion's confident expression would fall when he held out his hand, a ring glowing on his knuckles and charged with a curse, and showed her exactly how impressive he was.

But there would be time for that once the tournament began.

Still, as he turned around, pints in both hands, he met the Macaslan girl's eyes. They held gazes for a moment, assessing each other. But not wanting to be recognized, he walked away.

At the pinball machine, Hendry took the offered glass and shook his head. "I thought you'd start something." A spell shimmered around his ears—a Listen In, probably. "I'm glad you didn't."

"Maybe I should've." Alistair took a sip and smiled despite himself. He shouldn't be excited for the tournament, but he'd been groomed for it since his childhood. And he was ready to win.

"No, definitely not. What is it you say about our family? 'Grins like goblins. They'll tear your throat and drink your soul'? You can't help yourself. You have no restraint." Although it sounded like Hendry was scolding him, his smirk said otherwise.

"Says the one who brought a high magick spellstone to a dive bar."

"Someone has to watch out for you," Hendry murmured, repeating Alistair's exact words from earlier.

Alistair scoffed and turned his attention to the pinball machine. Its artwork resembled the fairy tales he'd grown up with: A prince rescuing a princess from a castle, a knight riding into battle, a witch laughing over a cauldron. And Alistair's favorite, the dragon, its mouth open in a snarl—worth one hundred points if the pinball struck its fangs.

While Alistair inserted a coin into the slot, Hendry sighed and changed the subject. "I had a dream today—"

"Typically, one has them at night—"

"—while napping in the graveyard." Despite his charm and freckled nose, Hendry was still a Lowe. He had a little villain in him. The Lowe family graveyard was his favorite place, full of vague, unnerving epitaphs for those who'd died young—even excluding the tournament, their family had a surprisingly large amount of tragedy in its history. "In the dream, you really were a monster."

Alistair snorted and mashed the game's buttons. "What did I look like?"

"Oh, you looked the same."

"Then what made me a monster?"

"You were collecting the spellrings of dead children and hiding them in your wardrobe, cackling about souls trapped inside them."

"Don't be ridiculous," Alistair said. "I'd do something like that now."

"You know, you should take a page out of that Macaslan girl's book and try to seem more likable. This tournament is different—the curse isn't a secret anymore. I mean, look at all these tourists! In *Ilvernath*! If you plan to survive, you'll need alliances with other champions. Partnerships with spellmakers. You'll need the world's favor."

Alistair looked at his brother intensely. Hendry was breaking their unspoken rule not to discuss the tournament, and it wasn't like him to be so serious. Besides, it didn't matter that *A Tradition of Tragedy* had turned Ilvernath's peculiar red moon and its bloody history into a global scandal. The Lowes had their pick of spellmakers lining up to offer Alistair their wares. Misfortune had a way of finding those who defied the Lowe family—their grandmother's notorious curses made certain of that.

"Are you worried about me?" Alistair asked.

"Of course."

"The family isn't."

"I'm your big brother. I have to worry about you."

Alistair's first instinct, as always, was to crack a joke. But confident or not, it was difficult to find humor in the tournament.

Kill or be killed. It was a somber affair.

Alistair's fear wasn't for his life, but for his mind. Even the most villainous Lowe victors left the tournament changed, broken. But Alistair refused to accept such a fate. No matter how brutal, how terrible he'd need to be, he couldn't let himself care. Not about the other champions. Not about his soul.

He needed to become the most villainous of them all.

He was still debating how to respond to Hendry when he was tapped on the shoulder.

"We've never met before," said the Macaslan girl as Alistair abandoned his game and turned around. Her words weren't a statement—they were an accusation. The other townies and cursechasers behind her whispered, their wide eyes fixed on the two boys who'd drawn the local Macaslan celebrity's attention.

Hendry flashed his sunlight smile and held out his hand. "We're not from here. We came to see if the book was true. That Blood Moon really is something."

His smile proved ineffective against the girl, who didn't return it. Her gaze dropped to his outstretched hand, to the rings with crystal spellstones dotting his fingers. "Sharma, Aleshire, Walsh, Wen," she said. "How impressive that, as a tourist, you've managed to purchase from half the spellmakers in town."

Hendry withdrew his hand and laughed awkwardly. "Impressive you can identify a spellring's maker simply by looking at it."

He elbowed Alistair in the side for him to say something. Unfortunately, despite their grandmother's warnings about exposing themselves, Alistair had little desire to keep up the charade. The cursechasers were going to stare anyway—he might as well give them something to look at.

Grins like goblins. Alistair smiled.

"What would it take for you to leave us alone?" he asked, even though he hoped she'd do the opposite.

The girl crossed her arms. "Your names."

Pale as plague and silent as spirits.

Alistair took a threatening step closer, though she stood taller than him in her heels. He liked that. "I'd like to know yours."

He held out his hand.

"I'm Isobel Macaslan," she told him firmly.

They'll tear your throat and drink your soul.

She grabbed his hand and shook. Her touch was cold, but his was colder.

"I believe you called me your rival."

A curse shot from one of his rings to her wrist, twisting and slithering its way up her arm like a snake. Its teeth sank into her neck, leaving two puncture marks above her collarbone. Her ivory skin instantly swelled violet.

She gasped and jolted back, her hand covering her wound. But rather than shout at him, Isobel regained her composure in moments, turning discomfort into a wicked smile. It made her look unfairly attractive. "Then it's my pleasure, Alistair Lowe."

Alistair felt a pinch on his wrist. He frowned down at the mark over his pulse point: white lips. The mark of the Divining Kiss.

It wasn't a curse, like what he'd placed on her. It was worse. She'd looked into his mind and plucked out his name. A cunning, clever spell. What else had she learned? A twinge of embarrassment gripped his chest, but he quickly swallowed that feeling down.

She can't have learned much, he thought. *Otherwise, she'd be afraid.*

Isobel smiled smugly. "Maybe it's *you* who should be afraid of *me*."

Alistair swore silently. Of course the spell hadn't ended yet.

And with that, she left, heels clicking on the tiled floor. Alistair stared as she disappeared out the door, strangely disappointed to see her go. Their nighttime excursions were rarely so entertaining.

Once she left, Alistair felt the gazes of the room hot against his skin, and he suddenly wished he hadn't worn such a heavy sweater. He heard a few of their whispers: "terrible," "heartless," "cruel." Beneath the smoke-hazy neon lights, those words felt more real than their family's usual bedtime stories. Harsher. He tried not to flinch.

Hendry pursed his lips. "The Asp's Fang? She'll be unwell for days, and she's another champion." His brother shot him a wary look. "Some might call that cheating."

Alistair shrugged and finished his beer. Unlike Isobel, he genuinely didn't care what the world thought of him. "She saw it coming, otherwise she wouldn't have shaken my hand." He tugged his sleeve to conceal the spellmark she'd left on him. Though he'd never have dreamed it, there might be another champion as cunning as he was. Almost.

"You *are* a monster." Hendry swallowed the dregs of his glass and hiccuped. "Rotten to the core."

Even though Alistair knew his brother was joking, he suddenly was no longer in the mood to laugh. "I'm blushing."

"You're absurd."

"You're drunk." And from one pint of ale, no less.

When Alistair turned, he came face-to-face with the bright flash of a disposable camera clutched in the greasy fingers of a cursechaser.

Rage surged through him. The world hadn't paid Ilvernath a passing thought for hundreds of years. Not its bizarre natural phenomena. Not its whispered fairy tales. Not the blood splattered across the secret pages of its history.

Until now.

"I hate that fucking book," Alistair growled. Then he seized Hendry by the shoulders and steered him out of the bar. If that photo was in the papers tomorrow, his grandmother would kill him.

It must've been the fury in Alistair's tone that made Hendry stop once they were outside.

"Al," he said in a low voice. "If you ever want to talk about the tournament—really talk about it—I'm here. I'll listen."

Alistair swallowed. The Lowes had prepared Alistair for this tournament his entire life, cultivated fear and fostered ruthlessness, teaching a child to twist the stories that scared him into ones he told about himself. They didn't accept weakness from a champion. Hendry was—and had always been—Alistair's only confidante.

Alistair wanted to win the tournament for many reasons. He wanted to survive, of course. He wanted to make his family proud. He wanted to return to his brother for nights like this one, drunken pinball and shared secrets at a local pub, pretending to live the life of normalcy they'd never had.

But most of all, he hated to imagine his brother grieving him. They had never been without each other.

"I will talk to you," Alistair murmured. "But not tonight." There was no need to spoil a rare night of freedom. Especially when it could be their last.

"If that's what you want," Hendry answered.

Alistair grinned mischievously. "What I want is another round. Let's find another pub, with fewer tourists."

And so, two hours later, their heads buzzing, the white kiss still stained on Alistair's wrist, the Lowe brothers returned home to their bleak estate.

Each one, in very different ways, dreamed of death.

|SOBEL MACASLAN

Though it was seven great families who originally founded the tournament, it's important to remember—that was a long time ago. Not all of them have remained great.

A Tradition of Tragedy

The funeral party flocked around the grave as the pallbearers lowered the casket into the earth. The weather was dreary and damp, heeled shoes sinking into mud, the grass field trodden and flooded, black umbrellas raised skyward. Funerals in Ilvernath were solemn, traditional affairs of veils and pearls and handkerchiefs. Families had lived here so long that many had designated burial grounds, where descendants could be entombed beside their ancestors.

Atop the hill overlooking the graveyard, the Macaslan family watched, licking their lips.

The Macaslans were a vile lot—stringy red hair, bulging purple veins, reeking of the most expensive yet repulsive cologne money could buy. There was no funeral in Ilvernath they didn't attend, but it wasn't to pay their respects.

They came to collect.

Before common or high magick was sealed in a spellring or a cursering, it was considered raw. And raw magick was a tricky thing to find. It could appear at random: in the accidental shattering of a mirror, tucked into the pages of dusty books, dancing in a clover patch the hour after dawn. Nowadays, much of it was mass produced, farmed and bottled like high-fructose corn syrup, sprinkled as a primary ingredient in everything from lipstick to household cleaners. But not so much in Ilvernath, where the old ways stubbornly continued on.

Isobel Macaslan examined the raw common magick shimmering white across the graveyard, like glitter caught in rain. People had magick inside them, too. And when someone was laid to rest, that life magick dispersed. If left uncollected, the wind picked it up and carried it away, where it would later nestle itself into forgotten places.

It was a beautiful scene.

Isobel was trying her hardest not to vomit.

She rubbed the two puncture marks at the base of her neck, where the Asp's Fang had bitten her. Her stomach had quaked all morning. A healing spell would cure her, but she refused to waste magick on Alistair Lowe.

She smiled, remembering the frowning, irritated photo of Alistair in this morning's edition of the *Ilvernath Eclipse*. Or even better: the fury on his face when she'd peeked into his mind. He had no idea how much she'd uncovered.

She knew about the crossword kept in his pocket, about the single word he couldn't guess that had irritated him all day (the word was "elixir," Isobel had realized almost instantly). He compared himself to a monster because of the stories his mother had told him as a child, the ones that still made him shiver. He'd found her attractive, and she wondered what he must've thought of the white kiss her spell had left on his skin, in the shape of her own lips.

Not that she'd uncovered his every mystery, only his thoughts floating at the surface.

But even if Isobel wanted to call last night a victory, there was only one victory that mattered. A victory the whole world expected the Lowe champion to claim.

And she had made herself his target.

"You look nervous," her father commented from beside her. He had a coarse, raspy voice from decades of smoking, and his brittle fingernails dug into her skin as he placed his hand on her shoulder. "You have nothing to be nervous about."

"I know," Isobel said, forcing false confidence into her tone. She was good at that.

"You're the most powerful champion our family has seen in generations," he reminded her for what felt like the thousandth time. "And this afternoon, you'll secure an alliance with the town's most respected cursemaker."

Isobel wished she shared her father's optimism. But ever since *A Tradition of Tragedy* was published last year, her life had crumbled. Isobel had never wanted to be champion. Yet the newspapers had named her one eleven months ago without her family's knowledge, and long before any of the other competitors. Seemingly overnight, Isobel was crowned Ilvernath's murderous sweetheart. Reporters started camping outside both of her parents' houses for the chance of a scandalous photograph. Her prep school classmates had dumped her like she was last season's trend. And the one friend she'd thought would understand more than anyone had betrayed her, then transferred schools just to get away from her Macaslan stench.

At the funeral, the white shimmering of raw common magick grew brighter in the air surrounding the grave, dissipating like a sigh across the field.

The Macaslans waited until the mourners had scattered before scuttling down the hill. A few stragglers watched them angrily as they worked—most of them the deceased's loved ones. One woman in a sleek black pantsuit hovered away from the crowd, assessing Isobel in particular. Maybe it was because of the contrast between her family's gaudy clothes and Isobel's patent leather miniskirt. Or maybe the woman was a reporter.

Isobel ignored them all as she coaxed a twinkling of magick into a flask. She sealed it inside, warm and humming.

"You shouldn't be here," another woman growled behind her.

Isobel turned to face one of the mourners. The woman hugged her arms to herself and glared at Isobel. Mascara ran down her cheeks.

Isobel pursed her lips. Of all the unpleasant methods her family employed to collect magick, funerals were by far the worst. Most considered the collection of raw magick from a burial unthinkable, but to the Macaslans, it was simply pragmatic. It wasn't as though the dead were using it anymore.

Isobel glanced at her relatives, hoping they might intercede for her. Truthfully, Isobel had rarely attended these family gatherings until recently. But they were all too busy to notice the confrontation.

"I'm sorry," Isobel told her, "but—"

"You're a bloody scavenger is what you are. All of you."

At that, the woman stormed away, and Isobel squeezed her silver locket in her fist, the one she always wore tucked beneath her blouse. Beneath her primer and long-wear foundation, Isobel's skin remained painfully thin.

The town's scorn had been easier to swallow before that book. Before strangers spray-painted obscenities on Isobel's front doors. Before photographs of her taking out the rubbish became tabloid fodder.

But Isobel *was* the strongest champion the Macaslans had raised in hundreds of years.

And she wouldn't be ashamed of doing what it took to survive.

To win.

The MacTavish cursemaker shop was in the roughest part of town, full of repurposed factories and condemned tenement complexes. Isobel's heels slipped awkwardly between the cobblestones as she walked beside her father to the door. The store had nothing to mark its name, only an orange neon sign of a dragonfly in the window, dull in the afternoon light.

"Are you sure this is it?" she asked. The other spellmakers in town had cleaner, more fashionable storefronts, with spellstones glittering in elegant displays in their windows.

Everyone in the world used magick, but the average person typically bought brand-name spells at department stores or patronized local spellmakers rather than craft enchantments themselves. Spellmaking families had their own dynasties and secrets, passed down from parent to child for centuries, bits of knowledge collected from all over the world. The spellmakers in Ilvernath might not directly participate, but they, too, played a vital role in the tournament.

The *Glamour Inquirer* called them the arms dealers.

Since Isobel's mother was a respected spellmaker herself, she'd already volunteered to supply Isobel with all her spells for the tournament. But to secure victory, Isobel would also need curses—enchantments designed to do harm. And her mother had no specialty in those.

The MacTavishes, however, were the best cursemakers in Ilvernath.

"This shop has been here for over six hundred years," her father answered.

"Yes." Isobel eyed the splintered doorframe. "It looks it."

Before they could enter, a van pulled up behind them. The window rolled down, revealing a man with a video camera. Isobel swore under her breath. She was never free.

"Isobel!" he called. "I'm with *SpellBC News*. Securing Reid MacTavish as a sponsor would be a big win for any champion. Is that why you're here today?"

"This isn't a good time," she said.

"Oh, come on," her father told her, smoothing down the lapels of his imported pin-striped suit. "Smile for the camera. Give the man his story."

When Isobel had accidentally found herself in the spotlight last year, her family had seized on it, hoping that her fame would garner her more spellmaker support. And so Isobel grinned through gritted teeth.

"I'm visiting the MacTavishes today to discuss a sponsorship, yes," she told the reporter. "And I hope I'll earn it. That's all—"

"Don't be modest," her father cut in. "You'll earn it."

"Do you have any comment on Alistair Lowe's picture in the papers this morning? For months, he's been called your rival, but with only thirteen days remaining until your face-off, what do you—"

"My daughter doesn't have anything to fear from him, or anyone else," her dad said. "Put that in your story."

Ready to be done with the interview, Isobel swiveled on her heel and entered the store. Inside, too, it was unlike most other spellshops, where counters gleamed, petty class one and two stones were heaped high in porcelain bowls and last season's spells were discarded to the clearance section. This place was so dimly lit she needed to squint, and everywhere was cluttered with scrolls, quills, trinkets, and dust. She hugged her purse to herself to keep it from scraping any surfaces and spritzed some peony perfume in the air to help conceal the smell of moldy paper.

A fair-skinned young man sat at the desk, poring over a leather-bound grimoire of divination spells. He wore more than a dozen necklaces, each covered with oval-cut spellrings whose stones had cracked, leaving them unglowing and empty. His clothes were black and looked thrifted, matching his dark and unwashed, unstyled hair. He would've been attractive if he wore less eyeliner.

Isobel cleared her throat. "Do you work here? We're looking for Reid MacTavish."

He lifted his head and smiled insincerely. "That would be me."

She hadn't expected him to be so young, only a couple years older than herself. He didn't look like any of her mother's spellmaker colleagues, and she wasn't embarrassed by her mistake. If he wanted people to take him seriously, he should've removed his tongue piercing.

"You must be Cormac Macaslan." He reached out an ink-stained hand to her father, who shook it a bit too eagerly. "And you must be the famous Isobel."

"The media adores Isobel. They can't get enough of her." Her father patted her back. "When we spoke on the phone, you said to come with raw magick. So we have. More than enough for the recipe we discussed."

The Roach's Armor. It was an old spell passed down in the Macaslan family, and it protected the caster temporarily from death. It wasn't infallible, but it was powerful. And very traditional. Every Macaslan champion obtained the spell.

Not that it had done her predecessors much good. Isobel's family hadn't won the tournament in thirteen generations.

"I can have it ready in an hour," Reid said, "if you're willing to wait."

"We certainly are," her father answered. "You have a fascinating collection here." He scanned the rings piled carelessly on the countertop. They were distinctive—more of those oval-cut spellstones set in twisted, well-worked metal. The MacTavishes liked people to know their curses when they saw them.

After greedily examining one particular ring a moment longer, her father set it down and handed Reid their flasks of raw magick, collected from all the dearly departed of Ilvernath over the past week. Isobel unclasped her locket and handed it to him, as well. "Isobel, why don't you watch Reid craft the spell? It'll be good study for you. Unless . . . Reid, do you mind?"

"Not at all," he said swiftly, professionally.

Isobel and her father had planned for this moment—this was why they'd patronized a cursemaker for a spell in the first place. She rubbed her lips together to ensure her lipstick still looked good. She could do this.

Isobel followed Reid through a pair of black velvet curtains to a cramped workroom behind the main shop. He riffled through cabinets full of empty crystal spellstones while Isobel hovered awkwardly in the corner.

"Do you own the shop?" Isobel asked.

"I do," he responded tersely. He placed a wooden spellboard on his desk, built from a lustrous mahogany wood and engraved with a septogram. Spellboards created an energy field that directed raw magick into the crystals.

"For how long?"

"Since my father died. You should know. You were at the funeral."

Her smile faltered, but only for a moment. "Yes, I'm sorry about that," she said, though she had no memory of any of the town's specific funerals. Since her family had started dragging her to them, she'd learned to block the details out. "I've heard good things about your father, and your family."

Reid only responded with a noncommittal grunt. She edged closer, peering over his shoulder. On each point of the septogram, Reid had placed the revolting ingredients for the Roach's Armor, including a single vertebra, a molted cicada exoskeleton, a handful of thistle, a clump of iron ore, a tablespoon of grave dirt, a fly's wing, and an unearthed burial shroud. Her family made a habit of relying on the sort of spells that required resources no one else wanted to touch. Isobel's locket lay open at the spellboard's center, exposing the white crystal within.

Next, Reid popped open the corks on each of the containers of raw magick. The radiant white speckles hovered inside, still as starlight, as though not wanting to be disturbed. Carefully, he coaxed the magick out—a stroke around the mouth of the flask, a gentle word whispered so close that his breath fogged against the glass.

Gradually, the magick poured out over the septogram, a whole cluster of fireflies illuminating the otherwise dimly lit room. Once each container had been emptied, Reid leaned down and kissed the spellboard, as was common with preparing any spells or curses involving death. At once, the magick began to stir.

"I don't like people hovering over me as I work," he said curtly.

Even though Isobel had crafted enchantments countless times

herself, she was so transfixed watching him that it took her several seconds to realize that he'd spoken to her.

"You said I could watch," she said.

"You're not here to watch."

As she'd feared, her father had been overly optimistic to expect an alliance with Reid.

Still, unwilling to give up so easily—especially after her father proclaimed such confidence to the evening news—Isobel scanned the room for some other topic of conversation. Her eyes fell on a paperback at the corner of his shelves, the spine worn from excessive use.

"*A Tradition of Tragedy*," she read, fighting to keep her voice bubbly when the words left a sour taste in her mouth. "You don't see many Ilvernath locals with that."

"An Ilvernath local wrote it," Reid pointed out.

"A Grieve wrote it," she corrected. That hardly counted; the Grieve family was a joke.

"Do you disapprove of them airing Ilvernath's dirty laundry?"

Isobel knew she should be playing polite, but it was hard to rein in her opinions where that book was concerned. "It's disrespectful. And just when all the publicity settled down, the Blood Moon showed up. Now the city is crowded with even more protestors shouting at us, reporters bothering us, cursechasers gawking at us—"

"You're one to talk. I saw the show you gave out there for that reporter."

Isobel tried not to cringe. "Well, it doesn't mean I approve of us being a spectacle."

"Every twenty years, we send seven teenagers into a massacre and reward the one who comes out with the most blood on their hands," Reid said flatly, still facing his work. "You should be more concerned about us being despicable."

Isobel would never have expected to hear someone from the city's most reputable cursemaking family criticize the tournament. The MacTavishes had made a living off causing harm to others, pushing the boundaries of their country's strict cursemaking legislation. They were among the few besides the competing families who'd known about the tournament before the book's release. This might have been business to them, but it was tradition, too. Something to be proud of.

At least, that was what her father had told her last winter, when her relatives had named her champion.

What do you mean you don't want to? he'd scolded, despite her tears. *It's your duty, Isobel. So what if the media found out a little early? Finally, we have a champion who can make this family proud.*

"Then why are you making me that curse?" Isobel asked Reid, shaking away the unpleasant memory. "You know I plan to use it in the tournament."

"I never claimed not to be despicable, too."

This struck Isobel as an unsettling answer, but before she could press him further, he added, "You're not the first champion to visit me. I've already met with Carbry Darrow and Elionor Payne. Carbry's family knows more than anyone about past tournaments. Elionor delayed attending university specifically to become champion. And whoever wins the Thorburn title will have beaten scores of competitors before the tournament even starts. Yet you're the one the newspapers rave the most about. Why might that be?"

It was because after the media latched on to Isobel, her family started selling them stories. Photographs of her casting complex spells. Report cards from as far back as primary school. Even quotes from her father about what it was like to raise a gifted child.

"Because I'm capable," Isobel answered.

"Every champion announced so far has been capable."

"I'm top of my class. I'm a better spellcaster and spellmaker than any of them."

Reid didn't respond.

She tried hard to find something else to talk about, some other reason to linger in the room. A yellowed grimoire rested on the opposite end of the counter. Curious, Isobel opened it to a random page, to a recipe for a death curse called the Reaper's Embrace. She'd never heard of it before. She traced her fingers across the faded instructions, squinting as she deciphered it.

The text claimed that the curse killed its victim gradually . . . and definitively. The enchantment ranked at the highest class of all spells and curses—class ten. Isobel already owned countless mid-class death curses her family had bought for her for the tournament, but they were easily defended against with shield spells. Powerful curses were hard to come by, even for the right price.

"A locket with a spellstone embedded inside. How old-fashioned," Reid commented. "Where did you get it?"

"My mother gave it to me." It had been passed down on the other side of her family, most of whom lived in larger cities down south. Sometimes Isobel forgot that a world existed outside of Ilvernath, a world full of enchantments and stories of its own.

"A bit elegant for a Macaslan, don't you think?" He turned around and locked eyes with her. Isobel's hand froze over the page for the Reaper's Embrace, but with so much clutter in the room, Reid didn't seem to notice she'd snooped through his things.

"Tell me, princess." He sneered. Isobel stiffened at the nickname. Unlike the children of more respected tournament families, Isobel hadn't had the luxury of growing up with fairy tales. "If you won, do you really think that your family would wield high magick any better than the Lowes?"

The next time the Blairs or Thorburns call us leeches, her father had said in his usual throaty rasp, *they'll be sorry. It's our turn to taste true power again.*

"Anyone is better than the Lowes," Isobel said, dodging the question.

Reid's laugh sounded hollow. "But haven't you come here to ask me to choose *you?*"

"I did, but you won't."

"At least you Macaslans don't bullshit. I'll give you that."

Isobel had already braced herself for disappointment, yet it hurt all the same. Reid had made up his mind long before she'd set foot in his shop.

"Then if not me, who *will* you choose?" she asked.

Reid turned back around to the spellboard, apparently annoyed by her question. "Seven rotten families in an insignificant city, fighting over the most powerful magic left in the world. Why do any of you deserve it?"

Isobel didn't have an answer for him, just like she hadn't had an answer for the countless reporters who'd asked her the same question. She thought her family was rotten, too.

What have we been raising you for, if you abandon your flesh and blood the moment we need you?

"Thank you for letting me watch," Isobel said, her voice masking the sound of her ripping the Reaper's Embrace from the grimoire and slipping the page into her purse.

GAVIN GRIEVE

My family is proof that even depressing stories need a punchline.
A Tradition of Tragedy

Callista Grieve did not wear white to her wedding. She wore black, and she wore it with pride, because the silky, ashen skirts of her wedding gown proved that from that day forward, she would be a Grieve no longer.

Gavin watched her gliding down the aisle from his place at the front of the Ilvernath banquet hall, feeling tawdry and foolish in his hand-me-down suit and with his blond hair combed flat. Other members of tournament families in Ilvernath would only surrender their last name for the most valuable of wedding alliances. But Callista had spent her entire life longing for the day she could abandon hers.

Gavin couldn't blame her.

Fergus, their thirteen-year-old brother, fidgeted beside him. Gavin delivered a swift kick to the back of his calf to remind him to stop slouching. The crowd behind them wouldn't hesitate to mock their family's smallest mishap or embarrassment, and though most of the Grieves were long past caring about Ilvernath's low opinion of them, Gavin wasn't. He'd do everything in his power to make sure this wedding didn't give the town another reason to laugh at them.

The chairs were filled with Grieves and Paynes—mostly Paynes. There was a pun to be made there, but no one would have been amused. It would've been easy to tell the families apart even if they hadn't been seated on opposite sides of the banquet hall. The Grieves were a tiny, bitter bloodline, and each sat slumped in their seat while the Paynes' postures were ramrod straight.

The Grieves looked anxious. The Paynes looked disdainful. Callista looked radiant.

The groom, Roland Payne, seemed like he was a moment away from losing his lunch beneath the elaborate floral archway.

All things considered, it was one of the Grieve family's less depressing weddings.

The bride reached the end of the aisle, where Gavin's father effectively pushed her at Roland. At the end of the ceremony, Gavin kept an eye on the crowd as Callista wrapped her arms around the groom's neck and went in for a kiss. He caught a few judgmental looks from the Paynes and the thin row of other townsfolk in the back of the room, but nobody voiced their displeasure.

Light streamed in through the banquet hall windows as Callista and Roland retreated down the aisle, arm in arm. Gavin watched them go, the tension in his stocky shoulders finally easing.

Because children born of parents from two tournament families could only be named champion of one, the competing families in Ilvernath considered marriage a game, a way to engineer powerful alliances with one another in their pursuit of high magick. By marrying into another family, one spouse would forfeit their name and accept the other's. Callista was effectively abandoning ship. Because in the centuries of the tournament, no Grieve had ever won it. And Gavin's family had long since given up trying.

Gavin, on the other hand, had no choice but to care. He was the champion, mostly by default—Callista was too old, and Fergus was his mother's favorite because he wasn't embarrassed to be a Grieve. Nobody loved Gavin enough to protect him from the impending slaughter. So he'd learned long ago to rely on himself. He earned top marks in his classes and spent his weekends at the gym, training for the strength and endurance he'd need in the tournament.

He was capable of greatness. But only he could see it.

Outside the banquet hall, the weather was dreary, clouds pressing down at the edges of the horizon. After exiting with the other guests, Gavin narrowed his eyes, the muddy green of a cheap glass bottle, and gazed at the massive stone pillar that stood in the center of the square, at least three meters tall. Jagged crystals jutted out from it like teeth, with hundreds of names carved up and down its face. Every competitor in Ilvernath's history had etched their name into the Champions Pillar on the night their tournament began. Upon their death, a strike appeared through their carving.

Every single Grieve name was struck out.

That was his family's legacy: centuries of forgotten children buried facedown, as was customary with dead champions. A legacy the entire world was now intimately familiar with, thanks to *A Tradition of Tragedy*.

Gavin eyed the reporters and cursechasers who gawped at the edge of the square. They'd grown bolder each day since the arrival of the Blood Moon. At first they'd flocked to the Grieves, because the anonymous author of the book had identified themself as someone from Gavin's family. But soon the media had moved on to flashier champions, more salacious stories. Gavin, however, remained focused on the book, the details in its pages that only a member of the tournament families could've known. He'd spent the past year reading and rereading it, trying to figure out who in his family was resentful enough to put them all at risk. He still wasn't sure, but he had his suspicions, and she happened to be beaming beside her brand-new husband.

High magick wasn't just a curiosity for tourists. Common magick might've been formidable in the right hands, but high magick was the purest essence of power, the resource that had shaped so much of the world's history. Gavin had learned about it in school—the king who'd wielded it to completely annihilate a rebel army; the brave spellcasters who'd used it to quell an earthquake.

And the world had thought it was used up, *gone*.

Until now.

The morning after the book's publication, the Kendalle Parliament had summoned Gavin's parents and grandparents for questioning. They'd returned from their interrogations visibly shaken. All Gavin had managed to pry out of them was that the Prime Minister had decided against executing every member of the tournament families in order to break the curse. Not only was it already too public for such brutality, but it would mean Ilvernath's high magick could be used by anyone. And though the government didn't relish letting a bunch of child-murderers keep this power, seven families were far easier to control than the whole world.

Across the square, Elionor, the Payne champion, posed for a throng of reporters and photographers who clamored for her attention. She was a study in contrasts, with her dyed-black hair against paper-white skin and deep blue eyes.

"Elionor!" called a man on her left. "Is it true you can craft class six curses?"

"Of course I can," she said. "As can any true competitor in the tournament."

Resentment built in Gavin's throat. He could only manage class five.

"Elionor! Elionor—over here!"

The girl turned, her spellstone ear gauges glimmering in the light of a camera flash. It was a wholly unnecessary way of carrying enchantments around, although the reporters seemed to eat up Elionor's choice in edgy accessories. She was clearly making a play for Isobel Macaslan's crown as the media's favorite champion—as if public opinion would matter once the Blood Veil fell. Perhaps she thought it would help her with spellmaker sponsorships.

Nobody cared enough about Gavin to take any pictures of him. His announcement had gone public that morning, a profile in the *Ilvernath Eclipse* that had been embarrassingly sparse—declaring him as the fourth member of what the tabloids had dubbed the "Slaughter Seven." It didn't matter that he was acing his classes or that he could deadlift 140 kilos. He was still a Grieve.

He was storming down the sidewalk away from the reporters when a voice rang out from behind him.

"You," someone said brusquely. "Young Grieve."

Gavin turned. The man had peeled off from a clique of people Gavin recognized as local spellmakers. Among them was Bayard Attwater, a pale and elderly man with a pretentious monocle. There was Fang Wen, who wore an intricate spellstone pin in her long black hair. And Diana Aleshire, a woman with dark skin and a designer purse whose shop downtown rivaled the size of a department store.

Gavin knew them all well. After all, he'd visited each one of their shops, and they had all turned him away.

Gavin could craft crude spells himself, in the same way he could, theoretically, sew his own clothes. But he needed far better equipment if he wanted to stand any chance once the Blood Veil fell. The tournament lasted either three months or until only one champion remained—whichever came first. Grieves rarely lasted longer than a week. A spellmaker agreeing to support him would help solve that problem. Make him able to compete with the likes of Elionor and Isobel.

Unfortunately, no spellmaker would sponsor a Grieve.

"Yes?" Gavin said warily, but also hopefully.

"Osmand Walsh, of Walsh Spellmaking," the man said grandly, extending a hand. Gavin caught a whiff of cigar smoke and gin as he shook it. Osmand Walsh was large and ostentatiously dressed in a lavender suit, tufts of gray hair sprouting above his ears that were strategically combed over the bald spot on his skull. "You are your family's champion, are you not?"

"I am." Gavin didn't miss the mocking way he'd said *champion*.

"Then you should know," said Osmand Walsh, his pink face reddening slightly, "that there are rules about how to conduct yourself in the weeks leading up to the tournament."

"Excuse me?" Gavin was suddenly reminded of his schoolyard bullies, whose taunting had come in many forms, who had only stopped when he'd grown strong enough to curse them back.

"You cannot simply march into my shop and ask for an alliance. Our clientele expect a certain sort of experience in our store, and having you there, interrupting them? Well, you must understand the impression it leaves. No spellmaker has ever allied with your family. Do you really think we'd start now, after you've dragged our city through the mud?"

Fury boiled through Gavin. He focused on the spellstone on his left middle finger.

The Devil's Maw would glue Osmand Walsh's tongue to the bottom of his mouth, making all speech incredibly painful for a day. It would do nicely for a man who was so carelessly cruel with his words, even if Osmand would certainly curse him back.

Yet Gavin forced his fist to uncurl. He couldn't do this here, not at his sister's wedding. Winning the tournament would be its own revenge.

"Of course I understand," Gavin said, as politely as he could manage, and then stomped away. He tried to block it all out, all the people, all the noise. It was the only way he could think of to stay calm.

Which was why, when the fight broke out, it took Gavin a few seconds to realize that his little brother had been the one to start it.

He saw the telltale white glimmer of spellcasting from the corner of his eye and turned in time to see Fergus launch himself at a dark-haired Payne cousin on the mossy banquet hall steps, in full view of everyone, magick forgotten in favor of good, old-fashioned fists.

"Take it back!" Fergus hollered, gripping the lapels of the boy's suit.

"Your sister's no Payne," the other boy said, his voice dripping with scorn. "And she never will be."

Fergus tackled the Payne cousin with a wordless howl, and they tumbled onto the curb, a blur of half-cast spells and windmilling fists cleaving through the crowd. The cursechasers watched it all with abject delight, whooping and hollering as if this were a spectator sport. Several cameras flashed.

Gavin knew when this was said and done, Ilvernath would blame the Grieves—the same way they blamed them for the outside world's presence. He could see how the story would go already; a fight at a wedding, another embarrassment, another disgrace.

Unless he changed the ending.

Gavin eyed the large gold signet ring on his middle finger, set with a gaudy crystal that glowed white with common magick. All the anger of the past few minutes coursed through him as he cast the spell inside it.

It was a simple class three Hold in Place, a generic version of the trendier Freeze Frame, but it did the job. Both boys froze from the neck down, and wisps of white magick shimmered around them, suspending them in stasis.

"Hey!" snapped Fergus. His fair skin that matched Gavin's own was flushed red, and a bruise bloomed beneath his eye. "Did you do this?"

"No!" The Payne cousin glared at him. "I thought Grieves could barely even use magick."

Gavin stepped up between them and leveled his gaze on the Payne boy. "You thought wrong."

The spell took real effort—neither boy *wanted* to be restrained—but it was worth it for the reluctant respect that glimmered in their eyes. The knot in Gavin's chest loosened as Roland Payne took Callista's hand and murmured something that made her shoulders relax.

Around them, all the wedding attendees seemed to let out a collective sigh of relief, while the cursechasers seemed disappointed. Gavin cast them a disdainful glance. Most looked like typical tourists, but there was one woman among them who stood out. She wore a navy pantsuit, her black hair knotted into a low bun, and she was watching *him*. Her stare didn't feel malicious, exactly; it felt like an assessment. Gavin looked away, feeling strangely exposed.

He was about to unfreeze both boys, confident that their fistfight was over, when a member of the Thorburn family hurried over to the brawl—there was no party in Ilvernath the Thorburns weren't invited to. She was tall and muscular, with pale pink, freckly skin and chestnut brown hair tied in a long braid down her back. Briony Thorburn: a year behind him in Ilvernath's largest public secondary school. She was the captain of half their sports teams and made a point of being everyone's friend; just like the rest of her family, her reputation was so polished you could see your reflection in it. The Thorburns hadn't named their champion yet, but she was the clear favorite.

"Is there a problem?" she asked, her voice syrupy and self-assured.

That was another family trait. Thorburns loved to butt their heads in where they didn't belong.

Gavin shook his head, glaring at the expensive spellrings adorning her hands. "I have everything under control."

"Are you sure? I see no guarantee that the boys won't fight again once they're released."

The spellring on her index finger shimmered with power.

A moment later, Gavin hissed with pain as his spell was yanked away. It was a sharp, visceral sensation, like bending back a nail.

The boys shifted from side to side. They could move again, but they weren't lunging at each other. Instead, they both had the same sheepish expression on their faces.

"Whatever," muttered Fergus. "I don't care anymore, anyway."

"Yeah," echoed the Payne cousin. "Me neither."

A moment later, they scampered away to rejoin their families.

Gavin looked at Briony, whose smugness was palpable. "What did you do to them?"

She shrugged, practically yawned. "The Know Your Enemy spell I cast allowed them to see the fight from the other's perspective. They both realized they were being foolish, so they stopped. If you studied magick more closely, perhaps you'd have a more nuanced roster of spellstones to choose from."

Gavin felt a surge of irritation, one that only grew as he realized that the crowd's admiration had shifted from him to Briony.

"I'm the Grieve champion," Gavin said hotly. "I know how to use magick."

He'd been hoping for a second flash of respect. But instead, all he saw was pity.

"Well then," she murmured. "Good luck."

Gavin turned from Briony's retreating form and thought of the taunts of his schoolyard bullies, the rage on the Payne cousin's face, and most of all, the mocking disdain in Osmand Walsh's voice.

No spellmaker would ever ally with a Grieve.

Gavin couldn't win this tournament solely on his own merits. But without sponsorships, alliances, or worthwhile instruction, even he knew his prospects were hopeless.

He tilted his head up, stared into the hazy sky.

In less than two weeks, those clouds would turn the crimson color of high magick, like a red-tinged shroud draped over Ilvernath, and the tournament would begin. The Blood Veil would lighten a little bit with every champion's death, until at last, when only one remained, true day and night would return and seemingly wash all the blood away, just like that.

Gavin needed to believe none of that blood would be his own.

Briony Thorburn

The Thorburn family loves nothing as much as they love their own reflections.

A Tradition of Tragedy

The amphitheater at the edge of her family's estate always made Briony Thorburn feel like she was stepping onto a stage. Cracked stone benches rose in a circle from the mossy ground dotted with wildflowers, ivy twining around the topmost row like a shawl draped around a woman's shoulders. Normally, the seats would be filled with quarreling families, angry neighbors, and feuding couples, all waiting for the Thorburns to solve their problems.

But since the appearance of the Blood Moon three weeks prior, the amphitheater had been used for something entirely different than mediation. The Thorburn family had come together to declare a champion.

At first, eighteen cousins and one sibling had stood between Briony Thorburn and the honor of competing in the tournament. A series of physical and magickal tests had whittled them down one by one. Now her only remaining obstacles were her younger sister and a distant cousin—the former on the bench beside her, engrossed in a book, the latter behind them, looking deeply apathetic.

Today was their final test.

Briony drummed her fingers against her thighs. "Do you think *this* is the true test?" she asked Innes, her voice low. "Keep us all waiting here until we die?"

What felt like hours had passed since they'd sat down, but the council of elders, who presided over the Thorburns' preliminary contest for the title of champion, had yet to arrive. Behind the cousins, the rows of Thorburns had also grown restless, chittering nervously among themselves. Some tournament families looked alike, but hers was far too big for that. The only qualities they all shared were a love for the spotlight and a wide, charming smile.

"I told you to bring something to entertain yourself," said her younger sister.

"I did," said Briony, elbowing her. "You're here, aren't you?"

Innes smiled from behind her book. "I'm reading."

"Fine then, I'll read with you." Briony moved to peer over her sister's shoulder, but Innes twisted away. "What? Did you cast some kind of glamour spell on a romance novel again?"

"No." Innes snapped the book shut, but it was too late. Briony had glimpsed the chapter header. Hidden behind the drab-looking cover was actually *A Tradition of Tragedy*.

"You're reading that thing?" Briony couldn't believe it. She'd never bothered with the book herself, but she'd heard it was a mockery of everything their family cared about, a salacious, tawdry tell-all that relied on cheap shock value to entertain its audience. By publishing it, the Grieves had somehow found a way to sink even lower.

"There's a lot here about our history," Innes said. "The author might not care for any of us very much, but they did their research."

Briony personally had no interest in research or books. She placed far more stock in leadership and an instinct for battle, which was why she was captain of the girls' volleyball and rugby teams—the latter of which had a real shot at going to the international conference in Furugawa in November. Briony was a little disappointed that she'd be missing out on their season this fall because of the tournament. But only a little.

"It's not like all that research has helped the Grieves win anything," she pointed out.

Innes shrugged. "The Grieves aren't the only family who cares about that stuff. And the best way to build a strategy is to study what happened before."

"Or by being too strong for any of them to stand a chance against you."

Innes stared at Briony intently. Their family might not have looked alike, but the two of them did—the brown hair they'd inherited from their father, who'd died when Briony was three and Innes was two; the fair, freckled skin they got from their mother, who, in her grief, had left Ilvernath behind. She didn't take her daughters with her, and she had never come back for them.

The sisters were raised in the Thornburns' prized historic estate by a rotating cast of aunts and uncles and cousins; but mostly, they were raised on stories of the Thorburns' noble history. The ways they'd used high magick to better Ilvernath whenever they won the tournament. In these tales, the Thorburns were legends. Heroes.

Innes seemed perfectly content to live out those stories in the pages of her books. But Briony couldn't wait to carve her name into the illustrious Champions Pillar. To receive her champion's ring. She had the physical endurance and magickal training to dominate this tournament. And after she emerged victorious, the whole town—no, the whole world—would tell stories about *her*.

"There's more to every tournament than just who wins, Bri," Innes said seriously. "Every champion had a reason to compete, and they deserve to be remembered. Even if they didn't make it out alive."

Briony wasn't so sure she agreed with her. Dwelling on the generations of failed champions before her felt dangerous, a reminder that her pathway to greatness would be paved with six difficult but necessary sacrifices.

She preferred to focus on the possibilities high magick promised. She'd understood why the families had kept it secret before, but now that it wasn't, what was to stop them from using it? The Thorburns could do so much *good* with that power, not just for Ilvernath, but for everyone. When she won the tournament, she would make sure of that.

"Thorburns," called out a crisp, clear voice, and Briony blinked back into the amphitheater, where the elder council filed in one by one. The Thorburns were the only family big enough for such a governing body, which was part of why Ilvernath relied on them so much to assist with their problems. Elder Malvina, older than dust, was supported by her wife, Jasmit, as she shuffled to the podium. "We have an announcement to make."

Briony's heartbeat sped up with anticipation. Her moment had finally arrived.

"We've made the decision," Elder Jasmit announced, her voice quavering a little, "to hold the final champion's trial in private."

The crowd rumbled, confused. Briony whipped her head around to see Innes looking just as shocked as everyone else.

"Has this ever happened before?" Briony hissed.

"I doubt it. Our last trial has *always* been public."

"Why would they change it?" The Thorburns were loath to update even the most trivial traditions, let alone this one.

"I don't know." The admission that she didn't know something appeared to cause Innes physical discomfort, which would've been funny to Briony under different circumstances.

"We will present your champion when the trial is complete," said Elder Malvina. "For now, we request that our contenders come with us."

The elders shuffled away without another word. Their cousin Emmett coughed uncomfortably behind them, while Innes shifted in her seat. As always, Briony was the first to stand, the first to beckon for them both to follow her.

It didn't matter where they held the trial. The end result would be the same.

The elders led them across the grounds into a gazebo, where they held more intimate tribunals—or gossiped about their many relatives. The space was small, knotted artfully with vines in the last vestiges of their summer bloom, lined with a bench made of stone. Silencing spells cloaked the area in a suffocating net.

On a table in the gazebo's center sat a gleaming hand mirror with a spellstone embedded at the top of its frame. The mirror was the Thorburns' most prized magickal artifact. It was a replica of one of the Relics—the seven objects that fell from the sky randomly throughout the tournament, each granting the champion who claimed it three unique high magick enchantments. In the tournament, the Mirror let you spy on your opponents, answered any three questions, and cast a powerful reflecting spell to fling curses back at your enemies.

The mirror in the gazebo, although not *the* Mirror Relic, was both an homage to Thorburn family heritage and the final obstacle between Briony and her future. It was meant to test the Thorburns' fortitude and reveal their true souls. Once the tournament began, the terms of the curse forbade anyone—even the families—from interfering with the champions or entering the tournament grounds. But it was still expected that the Thorburn champion act in accordance with their values when cut off from their kin.

Briony was unconcerned. She saw no reason why her reflection in the mirror would show anything but a champion. A hero.

With her chin high, Briony slid onto the bench beside Innes, who looked lost in thought. Across from them, Emmett's skin was slick with sweat.

"Um," he whispered, the noise loud as a scream in the silence of the gazebo. "Who is she?"

Briony's head snapped up. She'd been so distracted by the mirror, she hadn't even noticed there was someone else here. The newcomer sat in the center of the elder council as if she belonged there, wearing a navy pantsuit and a thin smile. She looked to be around her mid-forties, with fair skin, black hair cinched into a perfect knot at the base of her skull, and lips stained the same crimson as the Blood Moon.

"Hello, everyone," the woman said smoothly, clutching some

kind of dossier in her lap. In her other hand, she held a steaming cup of coffee. "Thank you for being so accommodating on such short notice. For those of you who may not know, I am Agent Helen Yoo of the Kendalle Parliament's Curse Division. I'm here as a government representative to observe this year's tournament."

Briony's stomach coiled. Before that ridiculous book was published, the government hardly paid attention to a small, remote city like Ilvernath. But since its release, they'd interrogated every single one of the tournament families. Under the Curse Clause, they were protected from legal retribution for any crimes committed while bound by ancient enchantments. But the government could certainly ask questions. Briony had thought they were finished interfering, but apparently they had other ideas.

"Over the past twelve months," Agent Yoo continued, "it has come to our attention that a red moon and sky we always believed a natural phenomenon was . . . incorrectly reported to us by local authorities." She took a long, slow sip of her coffee.

"So you're here to . . . what, evaluate us? Haven't you already done that?" Briony asked. She wouldn't normally speak so boldly in front of the elders, but Agent Yoo didn't seem to mind the question. She looked at Briony thoughtfully, then lowered her coffee.

"The Lowes and I already came to an understanding about their usage of the most dangerous form of magick in the world. But sometime in the next three months, it may no longer be the Lowes who are in possession of it. So, though we must unfortunately allow the tournament to continue, we have our stipulations."

"Stipulations?" Briony echoed, trying not to sound suspicious.

"Well, you'll be pleased to know that they will do nothing but benefit your family," Agent Yoo said briskly. "I've been observing the potential champions and reporting back to my superiors at Parliament. We've decided that we would prefer the Thorburns emerge victorious this fall."

A swell of pride swept through Briony, and she couldn't suppress a grin. Of course the other families weren't as well-suited to power as they were. The government had seen what she already knew.

"The rules of the curse permit outside aid, at least before the tournament begins," Agent Yoo continued. "We are willing to use government resources to equip you with all the spells and curses you could need in order to excel once the Blood Veil falls. On two conditions. One: that you allow us to work with you and study the high magick once it is acquired, so that we can ensure it's being contained safely."

This didn't sound so bad. After all, there was so much potential in that prize. Potential that wasn't being used.

"And two," Agent Yoo said. "We get to choose your champion."

Unease flared in Briony's chest. Now she understood why they were having this trial in secret, away from the rest of the family. Because it wasn't a trial at all. The elders had weighed the pros and cons of Agent Yoo's offer, and decided it was worth taking. She looked from Innes to Emmett, who both appeared as shaken as she felt.

"We've chosen to share the truth of this situation with all three of you so that you may understand our decision fully," Elder Malvina told them, a warning in her voice. "But we will be taking certain precautions to ensure that truth doesn't leave this room."

She unfurled her wizened hand, one of the spellrings cluttered on it glowing white. Specks of magick hummed in the air, and Briony felt the gentle press of it swirling around the gazebo. A Sworn to Secrecy—at least class eight. Nothing like the cheap off-brand Pinky Promise spells she and her friends cast when they talked about their crushes.

Briony shivered. It was rare to see the elders use their power like this.

"Before we can proceed, all of you must swear right now that you will never speak of what happens here to anyone outside this room."

Of course they wouldn't want this partnership getting out. It wasn't just because their family would be upset—the tabloids would have a field day with something like this. They were vultures, all of them, swooping around the soon-to-be-dead and snapping tacky photographs. When the media had first descended, she'd thought of it as a valuable tool. One she'd even tried to use to help a friend.

The aftermath had forced her to transfer schools *and* gotten her reprimanded by her family. It was the only time she'd ever made the elder council angry, though they'd assured her that it would have no effect on the selection process. And she'd made it this far, so hopefully that was true. Maybe it was an advantage that Agent Yoo was choosing the champion—it wasn't as if she would care about all that.

"I swear," Briony said. She felt the enchantment press against her skin, then dissipate a moment later. Innes and Emmett followed suit.

Briony tried to sit still and tried even harder to stay calm. Her whole life had led up to this moment. Emmett didn't have her athleticism or skill, and Innes had never wanted to live in a story, only read about them. If Agent Yoo had been smart enough to pick the Thorburns, then she'd be smart enough to pick Briony, too.

"Very well then." Agent Yoo opened her dossier and clicked a pen absently, the spellstone inside it glowing. "After careful consideration, I've selected Innes Thorburn as your champion."

For a moment, Briony didn't register the words at all. They sank in one by one, through a lifetime of armor she'd built for herself, the affirmation that there would never be anyone better suited to this position than she was. That she was important, and everyone around her knew it.

Her body went cold and stiff; her lips moved soundlessly, her ears foggy. She couldn't bear to look at Innes's face. Instead she turned to the elders, silently pleading for intervention. For a moment, she saw her own shock and disappointment reflected in Elder Malvina's eyes. But then the old woman raised her hands and began to clap. The others joined in a moment later, if a little hesitantly.

They weren't going to protest. The shock in Briony's chest crystallized into panic. That applause belonged to *her*.

"Wait!" Briony barely recognized the sound of her own voice. It was raw, almost ugly.

"The choice is made," Elder Malvina said, her voice gentle but firm.

Briony swallowed hard as the rest of the elders turned to stare. She normally enjoyed having eyes on her, but not like this.

The elders' judgment was as absolute and impartial as the mirror that sat before them. Briony had never in her life disrespected them, and yet she had no other choice. They couldn't name Innes champion, not yet. Not when they hadn't even given her a chance to prove herself.

"But . . . the final trial," she protested. "It could've named someone else—"

"This *was* the final trial," Elder Malvina said flatly. "We agreed upon it, and we will all respect its result."

Briony wouldn't be remembered as a hero. She wouldn't be remembered at all.

"Bri." Innes's hand closed around her wrist. She knew how much Briony had wanted this. Surely she would give it to her. Surely she would say something. But all she said was, "Please. You're embarrassing yourself."

"Well then." Agent Yoo rose to her feet. "That's settled. Go and present her, as planned." As suddenly as Agent Yoo had appeared, she was gone—like she'd manifested in this place specifically to ruin Briony's life.

In the Thorburns' fairy tales, the hero's story began with a call to action. They were chosen, by fate or by circumstance, to protect those who were good and to vanquish evil.

But Briony had not been chosen at all. And now all that was left were stares and shaking heads, with faces she'd known all her life now seeming like strangers.

The greatest stranger of all was the one standing beside her, clutching her wrist. Because Innes had *stolen* this from her.

"Congratulations," Briony told her sister flatly. And as the others filed out of the gazebo to present their new champion, Briony stayed still as a stone, staring blankly at the mirror. A mirror that she knew, she *knew*, would've made the right choice.

ALISTAIR LOWE

Most associate high magick with other distant brutalities of the past: pillaging, plague, and lawlessness. But in Ilvernath, a piece of that history lingers, every bit as threatening as it once was.

A Tradition of Tragedy

Beneath the Lowe estate, there was a vault.

Its walls measured one meter thick of industry-grade steel surrounded by three meters of coarse earth, to ensure not even the smallest speck of high magick escaped. Its door was warded against spells and curses of all kinds. No one could enter who wasn't a Lowe, and even then, no one could enter without their grandmother's express permission.

Alistair had never set foot in the vault. Around sunrise that morning, he'd taken his usual seat in the family library, memorizing the map of the wilderness surrounding Ilvernath's city proper—where most of the tournament would take place. It was early in his daily study that his grandmother Marianne Lowe had appeared in the doorway with her request that he make a withdrawal.

Now he crept down the spiral staircase that descended below his home, his fingers trailing across the damp, uneven walls, nails scratching against stone. One of his spellrings glowed red to light his path until he reached the bottommost level, a small cave-like room— the sort any run-of-the-mill family might use to store treasure.

Alistair examined his reflection, cloudy and distorted in the vault's metal doors. The scarlet light of the high magick lanterns around him made his skin look smeared with blood.

The vault had no crank or keycode. Nothing but a spellstone jutting out from the steel, faintly red and pulsing like a heart. He pressed his palm against it and waited.

Nothing happened.

He hadn't expected it to. His grandmother had provided him no instructions on how to enter, and since it wasn't immediately obvious from looking at it, this meant the errand was some kind of test—his grandmother loved tests. The fall of the Blood Veil and the start of the tournament would occur in one week's time. Five families had now publicly named their champions, but still the Lowes remained silent. A thrill stirred in Alistair's chest.

Today, he would prove himself. His final test.

He studied the crude cut of the spellstone, searching for a hint to the enchantment enclosed within. But it was impossible to tell such a thing by looking at it.

This vault stored his family's hoard of high magick. It was more precious to them than anything because it secured their dominance over Ilvernath. It was what backed every one of his grandmother's demands of Ilvernath's mayor: the ban on selling *A Tradition of Tragedy* in town, the Lowes' freedom from paying taxes despite their vast fortune, the legal impunity whenever Marianne carried out a threat.

His family's motto, *Blood before all*, was engraved on the doors.

Blood—of course. This test was a question, and blood was his answer.

Alistair examined the spellstones lining each of his knuckles. He disregarded the simple ones he'd slipped on when getting dressed, meant for concentration or finding specific words in written text or making his coffee taste better—all common magick. He carried nothing on him that would cut. He didn't wear curserings in his own home. But he couldn't go back and face his grandmother empty-handed, especially not after his photograph from the Magpie had been published in the *Ilvernath Eclipse* and circulated to tabloids everywhere. Even a week later, Marianne's fury lingered in the estate's corridors, noxious and icy. Because Alistair and Hendry had left their home, gone somewhere they could've been hurt, could've made the family vulnerable.

Alistair's gaze settled on the ring on his fourth finger. He had an unpleasant idea.

It would be crude. It was difficult to make a spell do something it wasn't designed for.

But it could work.

He took off his black sweater so as not to harm it, shivering from the coldness of the cavern. Then he focused on the skin a few centimeters above his elbow, and with all the nervous focus he could muster, he cast the Page Turner.

He clenched his teeth.

Nothing happened.

"Shit." Alistair couldn't fail, not a week before the tournament. It wasn't that he was afraid of Hendry being named champion; it was that he knew his grandmother resented Alistair for being the family's best option.

I always knew you were weak, she often told Alistair. *Afraid of the very stories meant to make you stronger.*

He summoned a combination of other spells—Focus Helper, Espresso Shot, and Distractions-Be-Gone. They were all cheap, trendy sorts he'd ordered from local spellmakers in town to help him study.

With his energy and attention at a buzz-like high, Alistair summoned the Page Turner again. He screamed out in pain as a single layer of skin peeled open down his bare stomach in a long, thin line. He'd been aiming for his arm, not his abdomen—but it couldn't be helped. And even though the pain of it burned, he did not bleed.

It wasn't enough.

He screamed louder the second time, and the third. The top layers of skin had peeled back like translucent slips of paper, opening one by one like a fleshy book. By the fourth casting, when the charge in his Page Turner stone ran out, a small stream of blood burst through, dribbling down from his sternum and past his navel.

He bit his lip and, with two fingers, carefully collected the blood and smeared it on the vault's spellstone. The vault's mechanisms clicked one by one. Alistair, hand clutching his stomach to hold his flaps of shredded skin together, slipped inside.

The vault was filled with rows and rows of metal shelves that stretched from floor to ceiling. Each of them contained hundreds of glass flasks meant for storing raw magick, and the magick inside them—specks of light like the dust of stars—glowed a vicious scarlet. The volume was astounding, representing centuries of accumulated high magick.

Funny, he'd imagined it would be grander.

If Alistair lost the tournament, it didn't matter how much power his family locked in this vault. The tournament's curse prevented anyone but the winner's family from even sensing high magick; the Lowes would walk inside and see nothing but empty flasks. The use of Ilvernath's high magick would pass to the next champion's family for twenty years, until the tournament began anew. The Lowes could use it all up beforehand, of course, but they were the Lowes. They fully expected to win again.

Alistair grabbed the first flask he saw from the shelf, picked his sweater up off the floor, and slipped it back on as he made the steep climb up the stairs.

Just as he'd feared, his grandmother loomed at the top of the stairs like a monster from one of his family's bedtime stories. She narrowed her cold gray eyes, the same shade as Alistair's, as she inspected the flask of raw high magick in one hand and the way he clutched his stomach with the other.

"I have it," Alistair managed, handing her the flask. Its glass was smeared with his blood.

She reached for him, but instead of taking the magick she lifted up his sweater. He hissed with pain as the fabric brushed his wound. Though the blood had begun to clot, the skin was still peeled back and torn like crushed moth wings.

"If you carried curses on you, this wouldn't have happened," she said flatly. "Let this be a lesson to never make yourself vulnerable."

Alistair winced but said nothing. He'd completed the test but failed all the same.

"Do you even want this?" he asked, lowering the flask.

"I want you to use it to craft a Vintner's Plague." It was a petty curse by his grandmother's standards, the equivalent of a wicked hangover. But if she wanted it made with high magick, Alistair pitied the intended victim. "We're expecting guests."

An hour later, Alistair winced as Hendry cast a healing spell to sew him back together.

"You'll have a scar," Hendry said, his lips a thin, disapproving line.

Alistair shrugged. "I like scars. They make me look threatening."

Hendry snorted and set his spellstone on the desk Alistair was currently lying across, a number of papers, books, and a spellboard uncomfortably strewn out underneath him. His blood-crusted sweater rested in a heap on the office chair.

His brother flicked a different scar, on Alistair's right shoulder. "Threatening? This was from running into a wall."

Alistair rolled his eyes and sat up. He traced a finger over the new white mark running down his midsection, faded as though from an injury years old. "Thanks." He'd woken Hendry up for this—his brother was uncommonly good at healing spells. It was his only true proficiency. But Hendry never liked to be woken before noon.

Hendry peeked at the open page of the grimoire Alistair had previously been lying on. He frowned. "The Vintner's Plague? That's not Grandma's style."

Grandma's style was of the lethal variety.

"It's what she asked for," Alistair grumbled. He slid back into his seat and leaned over the grimoire.

"Is it easy to make?" Hendry peered at the recipe.

Alistair hunched over it to cover it up. "Sure," he answered. He didn't like to admit it, but he wasn't much good at spell- or cursemaking. Currently, he was guessing how much magick to use. The higher the class of an enchantment, the more magick it demanded and the fewer uses the stone could store. The Vintner's Plague should have three or four charges before it ran out.

"Why wouldn't she make it herself?"

"It's just a test. It's always a test," Alistair answered. "And I keep failing."

"Al, the standard she's holding you to . . . it's beyond that of any of the other champions. You can cast spells at a level most people never attain in their lifetimes. You've proven yourself to be more than enough."

"If it were enough, she'd stop testing me."

"She's only pushing you because . . ." Hendry bit his lip.

Alistair scoffed. His brother was going to say, *because she loves you.* But Alistair knew perfectly well his grandmother didn't love him. To her, he was a champion far before he was a grandson.

That made sense to Alistair, in a sad, practical sort of way. Maybe the other families acted differently, but they, too, primed their champions to die. Because if they sent no one, a random member of their family would die anyway. At least his grandmother didn't pretend he was anything other than useful to her.

"I know, I know. Blood before all," Alistair muttered. The brothers had taken their family motto to heart . . . at least where each other was concerned.

"Are you scared?" Hendry asked quietly, the same question he'd asked Alistair last week at the Magpie.

"No." But that wasn't entirely true.

When you grew up raised on nightmarish bedtime stories, when your family members skulked the halls of your home warning you of your death, when you spent nights lying awake and staring at the stars, waiting for the moon to burn crimson, there was never a moment when you weren't afraid.

"If dying were that bad, no one would do it," Hendry joked, grinning his usual sunlight smile.

"I'm not going to die."

"But if you don't die, you have to live with the other option."

Alistair thought of dear Aunt Alphina's grave in their backyard. The last Lowe victor had died by suicide after the tournament, four years before Alistair was born. Alistair needed to be stronger than that. He needed to pass these tests, no matter how challenging they were. He needed to survive this so he could finally imagine a life beyond this estate, to discover if he was anything other than a Lowe, the city's—and now the world's—favorite villain.

"This is something I should do alone," Alistair said, reaching for the spellboard. He placed an empty spellstone at its center and slid the grimoire closer to himself.

Hendry sighed. "I wish you didn't have to."

Later that evening, Alistair changed into a fresh black sweater. He wore the cursering carrying the Vintner's Plague, and though crafting it had earned him a stomachache and a dark bruise along his trachea, he was otherwise no worse for wear. The stone glowed garnet, like crystallized blood.

Alistair's mother met him in the main hall.

"You did nothing about your hair." Every word she spoke sounded low and eerie, like a minor chord.

"What's wrong with my hair?" He blew a disheveled brown curl out of his eye.

She frowned. "You look feral."

He grinned, imagining himself howling in the woods beyond the estate. "Good. So who are these guests?" The Lowes rarely had guests.

"You'll see." She placed a hand on his shoulder and led him down the hallway.

The Lowe manor resembled a home plucked out of a haunting fairy tale. Each hearth crackled with fire, making every piece of upholstery, every room, and every Lowe smell of smoke. Full of dark-stained pine wood and iron candelabras, it was where maidens pricked their fingers on spinning wheels, where every fruit tasted of poison and vice. The boys grew up acting out these stories. Hendry played both the princess and the knight; Alistair was always and only the dragon.

Glowering family portraits adorned every wall in the sitting room. His grandmother sat stiffly on the upholstered couch, and a group of adults stood awkwardly by the door, as if unwilling to approach her.

Hendry leaned against the back wall, their uncle and gloomy eight-year-old cousin beside him. Hendry's hair was combed and his clothes ironed. Alistair joined them and discreetly tucked in his sweater.

"Alistair, Hendry, come sit next to me," his grandmother ordered. The brothers exchanged a glance and reluctantly took a place on either side of her. She gave Hendry a tender squeeze on his arm. She gave Alistair a stern look. "These are the owners of every spell- or curseshop in town. As you two are both eligible to be named champion, they've each come to present both of you their wares."

The spell- and cursemakers eyed them nervously, clearly considering themselves to be more like hostages than guests. Alistair studied them all. Most of them were from well-known crafting families. There was a woman with dark brown skin and hair styled in elaborate braids. An old man with fair skin who wore a monocle. A young man with far too much eyeliner.

And, in the corner, a woman in a brown pantsuit who observed with obvious disdain.

"And this is Agent Helen Yoo," his grandmother introduced. "You remember when she visited last year?"

Alistair did. Agent Yoo worked for the government, in some department of the military or security or something. She and her team had nearly blasted down the Lowes' door after *A Tradition of Tragedy* revealed that the family was in possession of the most dangerous magick in the world. At first, even Marianne Lowe had been afraid. For eight centuries, it had been the silent responsibility of the winning family to use some of its high magick to keep the tournament secret, in fear of this very moment. They muddled the memories of any townspeople not directly involved.

The government might've spared them for now, but Marianne had been forced to reduce her tyrannical threats, in case the government changed its mind. Villainy in the modern age was a delicate balance.

On his part, Alistair had a vivid memory of one official confiscating the diary he kept in his underwear drawer as potential evidence. He wondered if Agent Yoo had read it and knew that Alistair had once had lewd fantasies about a bad guy named Manticore in a children's cartoon.

But when Agent Yoo fixed her gaze on him, it was serious. "Don't mind me. I'm just an observer of the tournament."

His grandmother looked like she absolutely did mind. But nevertheless, she turned back to the spell- and cursemakers. One by one, each of their "guests" placed a gift-wrapped box on the coffee table, as though this were Alistair's wedding shower.

"These spells are the best protection the Aleshire Emporium has to offer," the woman with the braids said coolly. "The Warrior's Helm can block any curse through a class nine"—Alistair very much doubted any of the champions were capable of a curse past class seven—"and the Dividing Haze can reduce the effects of a curse by half. The Behind Enemy Lines prevents someone from detecting the caster through any sense other than sight." Alistair's lips twitched into a smile, imagining someone not being able to taste him and why he would need such a thing.

"I provided an assortment of my favorite curses," the one with the eyeliner said. He had a flat, bored voice, even while standing in the lion's den. "The Inferno's Wake will burn anything within a nine-meter radius to ash. The Treacherous Tripwire pack allows you to set deadly traps that an enemy can only perceive with very close attention."

Each time a spell- or cursemaker provided their spiel, Marianne nodded and motioned for them to add their contributions to the hoard. Agent Yoo, true to her word, watched and said nothing.

"A collection of survivalist spells," the one with the monocle said. "They include basic water-cleaning spells, food replenishment, a few healing spells—"

"You own one of the largest spellmaking emporiums in town," his grandmother said tightly. "But all you've provided are cheap spells we could acquire anywhere, and with far less trouble. Where is your family's signature spellwork?"

The spellmaker paled but lifted his chin higher. "I've already given my work and my sponsorship to the Thorburn family." Their champion, whoever she was, had been named the fifth of the Slaughter Seven in the papers this morning. Alistair had no interest in learning the names of the people he was about to kill.

"I'm not naive," Marianne snapped. "Nearly all of you here have promised sponsorship to a family other than ours. I only allow it because it's meaningless."

"I will not see my daughter come here before the next tournament and grovel to your family because of your high magick." The spellmaker's words made Alistair's blood run cold. No one spoke that way to his grandmother. "I won't give you any more than I already have."

His grandmother glanced at Agent Yoo. Then, carefully, she said, "But for twenty years, the Lowes have used our high magick to keep the town's affairs in order. All we ask from you and from your *daughter . . .*" Her tone lingered threateningly on the word. ". . . is a little recompense."

The spellmaker swayed where he stood. His bulging eyes flitted from Marianne to the door.

Marianne placed a bony hand on Alistair's shoulder and squeezed. Alistair stiffened.

"If he attacks," she whispered in his ear, "so do you."

For several moments, the crowd hung in tense silence, and as though they'd heard Marianne's words, Alistair felt the eyes of everyone in the room on him. Of his mother, uncle, and cousin watching passively behind them. Of Hendry shaking his head as imperceptibly as he dared. Of the other spellmakers each taking a fearful step back.

The Lowes did not tell their children monster stories so that they could slay them.

The Lowes told them so their children would become monsters themselves.

One of the spellmaker's many rings began to glow. A moment later, a bolt of white light shaped like a stake flew toward Marianne's heart.

Startled, Agent Yoo stood up. But she reacted too slowly.

Marianne and Alistair didn't.

With a snap of Marianne's fingers, a Shark's Skin shield spell enveloped the sofa, red with high magick. The stake disintegrated and rained glittery dust onto the floor.

A second later, Alistair focused his concentration and summoned the curse he'd crafted, determined to do his grandmother proud.

The spellmaker stumbled, but he'd clearly been anticipating retaliation. He stretched out his hand and summoned a shield of his own. The walls of their house shook at the force of the spell. The chandeliers rattled. The portraits quivered. The shield shined with a light almost blinding to behold. It was one of the most powerful spells Alistair had ever seen. A class ten.

With common magick, the Vintner's Plague ranked at a six.

But high magick doubled the class of any casting.

Alistair's curse sprang out of his ring in a cloud of noxious red. It swarmed across the room, making other spellmakers throw up defenses of their own or clamber desperately out of its path. It shot through the man's shield as though tearing through parchment.

To the man's credit, he did not scream.

The color of his fair skin deepened and reddened into that of a vintage wine. The whites of his eyes wrinkled, the eyes themselves shrinking like pieces of rotten fruit. His limbs swelled, and he yanked off his spellrings as they started to strangle his bulging fingers. They clacked as they fell against the stone floor.

For a moment, the man stood silently, swaying as though he might faint. Then a cough shuddered through him, spraying out a strange, violet liquid. The juice began to trickle from his eyes and ears, then pour freely down his neck. He was leaking, shriveling. And even amid his unspeakable punishment, he raised his head and looked Alistair Lowe in the eyes. What remained in his sockets looked like peach pits.

Alistair gaped. Even with the high magick, it was merely a hangover curse. It shouldn't have managed . . . this.

Not unless he'd messed up the crafting.

Unable to help himself, Alistair leaned over the arm of the couch and threw up on the carpet.

When he finished, the man was on the ground. He wasn't dead—his chest still rose and fell with his breaths, but he was gravely and likely permanently injured. He lay pathetically in a pool of his body's juice. The room reeked of it and Alistair's vomit.

Agent Yoo knelt at the man's side, seething. "That was . . . *grotesque*. You didn't have to—"

"This man attacked me in my own home," his grandmother answered. "But I can assure you . . ." Marianne's gaze shifted to Alistair with a treacherous glare. "The curse wasn't intended to cause such harm. You could've killed yourself casting that."

Alistair wasn't quite sure he hadn't. His stomach gave another violent clench.

"I don't know what I did wrong," he rasped. If you weren't careful, spellmaking could turn volatile. Alistair was lucky he hadn't blown up the entire estate.

He thought he'd done everything to pass this test. But now, his lips still speckled with his own sick, Agent Yoo and the spellmakers looked at him not like he was a monster, but like he was just a boy. Which was so much worse.

"Thank you all for coming," his grandmother said tersely. She stood, stepped over the body, and walked out of the room, her footprints leaving a violet trail across the floor.

ISOBEL MACASLAN

Spellmakers are the silent eighth force of the tournament, and that makes them complicit, too.

A Tradition of Tragedy

Isobel paused in front of the window display of her mother's spell-shop advertising the end-of-summer sale. Cosmetic spells, one of her mother's specialties, were 50 percent off. All the spellstones were cut in marquis or princess shapes—the latest trends in Ilvernath's high-end stores. They glittered in rotating display towers, sending the afternoon light spinning in all directions.

But she hadn't stopped to admire her mother's taste.

CHILD KILLERS

The graffiti stretched across the window from top to bottom, dripping crimson paint.

Her skin prickled in alarm, and Isobel peeked over her shoulder, where the upscale shopping neighborhood paid the vandalism no mind. Why should they? It had happened countless times before, ever since Isobel had been announced as the first of the Slaughter Seven.

Isobel stepped inside and took a deep breath of the perfumed air to calm her nerves—it smelled like bubblegum. Everything within the store was designed to make you feel good. The wall of mirrors with elegant, gilded frames were spelled to give your complexion extra glow, and the neutral colors made the spellshop feel open and uncluttered. It was the total opposite of the MacTavish curseshop Isobel had visited with her father a week ago.

"Mum?" she called, setting down her purse and bookbag as she peeked into the back room. Usually her mother sat among the suede floor pillows, surrounded by a sea of empty, glimmering spellstones, wooden spellboards, and flasks filled with raw common magick. When another spellmaker released something new and trendy, her mother would hole up in this room for hours, trying to concoct a matching recipe of her own. There was a competitiveness to the indie spellmaking business. To invent new spells to catch the public's attention, to produce better versions of your competitor's products, to sell enough simple spells to support your family's favorite specialty. Her mother's was divination.

Looking at all this, the pink, the gleaming, the pretty, it was difficult to imagine her mother ever living in her father's house. Isobel's parents had divorced when she was eight years old. Isobel had memories of her mother living with them, of her mother at Macaslan gatherings with her cousins and relatives, of her parents in love with each other. The memories always felt wrong, mismatched puzzle pieces wedged forcibly together.

It was business hours, and the shop was unlocked, which meant her mother was here. She'd probably slipped to the apartment upstairs for a moment. Perhaps that was for the best. The graffiti would only upset her.

Isobel knelt behind the counter and riffled through the drawers of pre-filled spellstones. At last she found a Mess Be Gone! in a fashionable tourmaline crystal. The barcode sticker labeled it as class two.

She slipped outside and cast it on the mess. It took eight uses of the spell to clean the window completely, but the improved, sparkling storefront gave her no satisfaction. With only a handful of days remaining until the tournament, some other outraged out-of-towner would just vandalize it again.

No sooner had Isobel returned inside than two customers entered.

Isobel grimaced. Like her, they wore the green uniform of Ilvernath Prep.

"Hi, Oliver," Isobel said. "Hi, Hassan."

"Oh, it's you," Hassan said. "I didn't know you still worked for your mum. Aren't you too famous for that now?"

Like all her other friends and classmates, Hassan and Oliver had stopped talking to Isobel after *A Tradition of Tragedy* came out and Isobel was declared champion eleven months early. Despite knowing her for years, they'd decided the media attention made her fake.

"Nope. I still work part-time," she said flatly.

"Well, I have a spellstone I'd like to return," Oliver said. "It's broken or something."

Isobel's mother didn't sell broken spellstones.

"Let me look at it," Isobel said, and a funny expression crossed his face. "What?"

"It's broken, all right? I want to return—"

"If there *is* something wrong with it," which Isobel doubted, "then I'll fix it."

Reluctantly, Oliver glanced at Hassan, who was inspecting a rack of T-shirts that said support your local indie spellmaker. Then Oliver slid the crystal across the counter. It pulsed faintly with white light, so there was clearly magick inside it.

"What sort of spell is it?" Isobel asked.

"A Longer Locks," Oliver answered quietly.

Isobel frowned at Oliver's buzzcut. He didn't look like he'd used a hair-growth spell. Maybe it really was broken.

Isobel pulled out a spellboard and set the stone at the center of the septogram. Then she grabbed another Longer Locks stone from their display basket and compared the two.

"You're right. There's something wrong with this one," Isobel admitted bitterly. "It's strange. It's almost as if an eighth ingredient was . . ."

She narrowed her eyes.

"Did you tamper with this?" she asked, making Hassan look up curiously.

"O-of course not," Oliver grumbled.

"You did! You tried to adjust the spell. Once an enchantment is in a stone, it's done. You can only change it by removing the enchantment and starting over, and . . . *What kind of growth spell did you think you were making?*"

"Things are that bad with Mei?" Hassan smirked and even shot Isobel a friendly smile, which made hope swell in her chest. The three of them had never been close, but they'd gone to the same parties. Maybe after all this fame she'd never wanted, there was a chance she could go back to her old self again, after the tournament was over.

Oliver's ears burned red. "Look, just fix it, all right? I told my dad it was busted."

"Don't worry," Isobel said. "I won't tell anyone. But you should be more careful next time. You could've hurt yourself. And severed appendages are hard to reattach. Especially such . . . delicate ones."

While Hassan roared with laughter, Isobel got to work on the spell. She grabbed one of her mother's grimoires and found the Longer Locks recipe. If she could simply repeat it, that should erase whatever nonsense Oliver had done to it.

"So you're not the only named champion anymore," Oliver said. "How does that feel?"

Clearly, Isobel's and Hassan's teasing had put him in a bad mood.

"I'd rather not talk about the tournament," Isobel said uneasily.

"Did you hear what that Lowe kid did today? Blinded a man, and—"

"I heard he killed him," Hassan interjected.

"Nah, my aunt's a nurse at the hospital. Said he's still alive. But apparently, it only took the Lowe kid one curse. Pretty wicked, right? Even if it was with high magick."

Isobel had no idea what they were talking about. It sounded

like the sort of wild rumor the cursechasers in town liked yelling about.

Oliver drummed his fingers on the counter and continued, "So you know that the only chance anyone has to beat him is to form an alliance. The Lowe won't go down until it's at least three against one."

"I don't get alliances," Hassan said. "What's the point if you just kill each other in the end anyway?"

"You survive longer," Oliver said. "Didn't you read the book?"

Hassan frowned in confusion, which Isobel shared. She'd never seen Oliver read a book in their eleven years of school together. "Did you?"

"I watched that docuseries."

Isobel loathed the overdramatic docuseries, with its excessive use of punk music and its red filter, so she tuned out the rest of the boys' chatter. But Oliver's comment continued to nag at her. Champions who formed alliances historically fared better than those who did not, but even with four other champions already named, Isobel couldn't think of one who would willingly team up with her.

"So how do you want to go, Isobel?" Oliver asked, interrupting her thoughts. "The Guillotine's Gift would be a good curse, if I had a choice. Nice and quick. Though that doesn't seem like it's the Lowe kid's style—"

"You don't have to be a dick, mate," Hassan told him—a choice of words that only seemed to make Oliver angrier.

"I can't wait until the whole town shows up to *your* funeral," he hissed. "That'll be a nice change."

Ignoring him, Isobel set out the spell's seven ingredients on each point of the septogram, one at a time. Every enchantment always had seven components.

"You know, I think it would be even worse for the Macaslans to win than the Lowes. The Lowes, at least, keep to themselves. But what would the Macaslans do with that power? You know how they love funerals. Wouldn't you think they'd want to make some more?"

Isobel flexed her fingers. On her right pinky, she wore a Knock It Out self-defense curse, which she'd added to her arsenal ever since reporters had started following her to school. She wouldn't mind seeing Oliver's face when the enchantment slammed him to the floor.

But then Hassan took a weary step back from Isobel. "He does have a point," he admitted, and Isobel's rage dissolved into bitter, hopeless resentment. At the two boys. At Briony Thorburn. At her whole family.

Determined not to say anything—or worse, cry—she focused on her work. When she finished, the spellstone pulsed white, good as new.

"You're welcome," she gritted out, and the boys left without even a mumbled goodbye.

"I'm going to call his mother," said a voice behind her, and Isobel turned to face her own mother, leaning against the doorway to the shop's backroom. Honora Jackson had fair skin and curly blond hair that hung nearly to her waist, and she wore a floral ankle-length skirt. Her face, generally gleaming from a number of cosmetic spells, was unusually pale.

"How long were you standing there?" Isobel asked.

"Long enough. Can we talk?" Her mother's voice was hesitant. Lately, whenever they spoke, it ended in a screaming match.

"I'm not in the mood." Isobel swept past her, grabbed her belongings, and climbed upstairs to her mother's apartment. Her bedroom was the first on the left. It was far different from her room in her father's house, which was all brocade wallpaper and tarnished faux-gold everything and a musty smell no air freshener could mask. Her room here was clean and full of color, each of the walls a varying shade of gold and pink. This was the room where she hosted sleepovers, where she got ready for school dances. Her sanctuary.

Isobel collapsed onto her satin sheets. A moment later, the lock on her door unlatched with a loud *click*, and her mother entered.

"What did I say about the automatic lock spell on your door?" her mother asked.

Isobel hurriedly reached over to her nightstand and stuffed the pile of tabloids into the top drawer. She didn't want to admit that she'd been reading what the *Glamour Inquirer* printed about her.

"I'd rather you didn't barge into my room," Isobel grumbled.

"Yes, well, I do pay the rent." Honora perched at the edge of Isobel's bed. "I visited the Lowes today."

"*What?*" Isobel had never heard of anyone outside the Lowe family walking through their wrought iron gates. Sometimes she forgot that anyone *lived* in that house in the forest, that it was home to anything more than haunting stories.

"You don't exactly refuse an invitation from Marianne Lowe," she said flatly. "She summoned all the spell- and cursemakers in town, just as she did twenty years ago. I've lived in Ilvernath long enough to know what was expected."

"Marianne Lowe is still alive?" Isobel crinkled her nose. The stories she'd heard about that woman made her seem like she was a thousand years old.

Her mother laughed. "Unfortunately, yes. And I met the Lowe champion, the one from the newspaper. He . . ." She bit her lip.

"Alistair," Isobel said. "I've met him, too."

It was her mother's turn to be shocked. "How? Since when did the Lowes let their children see the sun?"

"It was the night his photo was taken. We were in the same pub. Is this about that rumor? That he attacked someone?"

"You already heard about that?"

"Oliver and Hassan were talking about it," Isobel said, a lump in her throat. "Why? What happened?"

"What that boy did today . . . it was horrible. Bayard Attwater went blind from it."

"He attacked Mr. Attwater?" Isobel asked, aghast. Bayard Attwater was a powerful man.

"It was dubious self-defense, but even so . . ." She took a deep breath. "I know that when the tournament begins, he won't be as strong without his access to high magick. But either way, I don't like this. He's dangerous, troubled. Promise me you won't be the one to confront him."

The fear in her mother's tone made Isobel's own nerves rattle in her stomach. But she didn't betray that. After the past month of arguments, Isobel knew better than to show her mother any weakness, lest she seize it and twist it into more reasons why Isobel shouldn't be champion. And when she wasn't fighting with Isobel about it, she was fighting with her father. It was exhausting.

"Can we not talk about the tournament?" Isobel asked, as if she were dealing with Oliver all over again. She rooted around her comforter for her CD player, eager to be alone.

"I just don't get it, Isobel," her mom said shrilly. "I really don't. You have your whole life ahead of you. A year ago, you were talking about fashion school. You didn't want anything to do with that book, or the tournament, or—"

"I changed my mind, okay?" Isobel snapped. "It's my decision."

"But it's not your decision. You're still a minor. If you need a medical operation, I agree to it. If you go on a field trip, I sign your permission slip."

They'd had this fight a dozen times. Isobel ignored her and went to work untangling her headphones.

"I still want to know what your father said to you," her mother continued. "I know how he is. I know he convinced you."

Her father's raspy voice filled her mind.

You'd abandon your own flesh and blood? After all we've done for you?

Is it because you're scared? You're too talented to be scared. The media already loves you.

Is it because you're ashamed of us?

You could win, Isobel. You know you could.

"Maybe I want to be champion," Isobel lied. "Maybe I want history to remember me for winning."

"That's how Briony used to talk, not you," her mother said, and

Isobel flinched at the mention of Briony's name, at the memory of everything Briony had done to her. She knew Briony must've been hurting since her sister was declared champion, and Isobel was glad for it. Glad Briony Thorburn had finally been denied one single thing she wanted. "When you were a baby, I didn't worry. I thought that since you'd only be sixteen, they'd pick one of your older cousins. It's not like they've paid much attention to you since your father and I split."

"They've always paid my school tuition," Isobel pointed out. "And sent me birthday presents."

"Isobel, your aunts and uncles probably didn't even know how to spell your name until last year. Your father was content with visits once a month. But suddenly, those articles came out. Suddenly, you're the famous pride and joy of the Macaslan family. They think of you as a tool to be used, not a person."

Her words stung. Maybe most of Isobel's childhood memories of her relatives were hazy recollections of diamond-studded wristwatches and cigar smoke. But at least, when the entire world had turned away from her, the Macaslans had embraced her with open arms.

But Isobel knew her mother's words were more loaded than that. Almost a decade ago, she'd caught her father using her business to siphon money into fraudulent accounts. Hence the divorce.

"They're still my family, aren't they?" Isobel countered. "Don't they have a right to use me?"

"No!" Her mother reached for her hand, but Isobel jerked it away. "No, they don't."

"So which of my cousins would you rather they use instead? Peter? Anita? Greg—"

"Any of them! Any of them other than my daughter!" When Isobel tried to shove her headphones in her ears, her mother ripped the cord away. "I'm not finished talking to you!"

A surge of pressure pressed at the back of Isobel's throat, and she didn't know if it was the urge to scream or cry.

"F-fine," she blubbered, very much settling on crying. She squeezed a faux fur pillow to her chest. "Say w-whatever you want! But you can't change anything. I'm already—"

"You aren't champion until you carve your name into the Pillar. You still have a week. You can march right back to your father's and tell him and all those bloody reporters you've changed your mind. That you don't want to do this anymore."

Isobel imagined such a scene playing out in her mind. She hated when her mother yelled at her, but her father's fury was worse.

"You think I'll d-die." Isobel's chest heaved as she tried to keep her voice steady. "You think Alistair Lowe will kill me. But he won't. I'm stronger than him."

"Let's say you are," her mother said, in the sort of hypothetical tone that made it clear she didn't believe it. "Do you really want to be a murderer? Just because it's technically legal doesn't mean—"

"No, of course not! But—"

"Then how will you do it? You'd kill Innes, Briony's little sister?"

Hot tears streamed down Isobel's face. She hated crying. She hated feeling so out of control. "Yes, I will," Isobel said. Because if there was anything the last year had taught her, it was that she was a survivor.

Her mother stood up and grabbed Isobel by the wrist. "Fine. Then we're leaving."

"What?" Isobel croaked.

"We're going to Keraktos, to stay with my sister. We'll catch a flight tonight. You'll be too far away for them to fetch you before the tournament starts."

A part of Isobel blossomed with relief. She could leave Ilvernath forever. She could start over.

But then the Macaslans would choose one of her cousins. Could she really do that to them? Doom Peter or Anita or someone else to death? She knew how gifted she was. She gave the Macaslans a true chance at winning, of attaining the power and wealth that would change their reputation, change their lives. Even if Isobel had always had her mother to retreat to, she knew as well as any of them how it felt to be treated like a stain, a disgrace.

"I'm not leaving," Isobel choked out.

"Yes, you *are*."

At first, when she started to yank Isobel out of bed, Isobel tried to squirm out of her grasp. But when her mother's sharp, manicured nails dug into her skin, Isobel summoned every ounce of concentration she had and cast the curse from the quartz ring on her pinky.

White magick leaked from the stone, seeping like an oil spill across the carpet. The power bubbled and rose, splattering against everything it could reach. At its touch, the polished chestnut wood of Isobel's nightstand began to bend and rot. The tapestries on the walls yellowed, the wallpaper around them flaking off like dried skin. With a loud, screeching groan, the floorboards warped and peeled back one by one like brittle fingernails, exposing mud and maggots below.

Her mother screamed and let go just as the Bog's Innards touched her skin. It stuck to her flesh like tar. By the time she could cast a shield spell, it had singed the ends of her hair. The smell made Isobel want to vomit.

Instead, she hugged her knees to her chest and sobbed, her bed the only untouched island in a sea of rot and filth. The class nine curse, meant to corrode defensive enchantments, had been a gift from her father when she agreed to become champion. She'd meant to save it for the tournament, but instead she'd ruined the one place the other Macaslans had never touched.

"You can't make me do anything," Isobel snapped at her mother, who'd fled into the hallway. Both of them were sobbing now. "And *none* of the other champions are strong enough to defeat me."

GAVIN GRIEVE

> A Grieve has never benefited from the tournament. For us, and
> perhaps us alone, it truly is a curse.
>
> *A Tradition of Tragedy*

While a storm raged outside, Gavin stole away to his room and hastily shut the door behind him. Thunder reverberated in his chest as he knelt at his desk, examining the quartz spellstone embedded in the bottom drawer. The spell inside—Keep Out, class five—warded the drawer from prying eyes. It was the highest-class spell he'd ever been able to craft on his own.

Thinking about crafting spellstones reminded Gavin of his disastrous conversation with Osmand Walsh and his failure to secure any spellmaker alliances. Maybe he didn't have the connections or the resources of the other tournament families. But he'd known he was going to be champion for most of his life. And that had given him one valuable commodity, at least: time.

He disabled the spell and pulled open the drawer. Inside were six file folders and a well-worn copy of *A Tradition of Tragedy*, annotated and marked with dozens of tabs. Initially, his notes had begun as research on the history of high magick and the competing families, but as the tournament had drawn closer, they'd become something different.

Dossiers. On the other possible champions.

Isobel Macaslan. Elionor Payne. Carbry Darrow. Innes Thorburn. Three potential Blairs.

And the front-runner, the champion he cared about most of all.

Gavin pulled out that file and flipped it open.

The flare of lightning outside only accentuated Alistair Lowe's vicious scowl.

Gavin had ripped out the picture from the *Ilvernath Eclipse* and clipped it to the front of the file. It was the first image he'd found of the boy—his family was deliberately reclusive. In the flash of a cursechaser's camera, Alistair Lowe looked deeply annoyed. He had an older brother, Gavin knew, and although both were technically eligible to become champion, Gavin—along with the mainstream media—was certain Alistair would be chosen. Even before the book had been published, there were rumors about Alistair whispered by the other families: his power, his wickedness, his cruelty. Spellmakers were undoubtedly begging at his feet to sponsor him.

Gavin chose not to think about the other thing the photograph proved: even in unflattering light, even scowling, Alistair Lowe was extremely good-looking. Not that it mattered.

"I'm going to kill you," Gavin said aloud, jabbing a finger into the center of the photo.

The door to his room creaked open. "What are you doing?" Fergus's high, slightly nasal voice drifted through the room.

Gavin slammed the file shut and whipped around. "I told you not to come in here."

His brother frowned. His blond hair was plastered to his forehead; behind him, a trail of wet footprints led into the hallway. "Then you should get a stronger spell on your door." Fergus's gaze darted from the weight rack in the corner to the wardrobe, filled with a row of identical T-shirts sorted by color, and finally, to the open desk drawer. "What's in there? Dirty magazines?"

"None of your business."

But Fergus, hopelessly nosy, had already darted forward and yanked out the book. His eyes widened as he flipped it open. "You've underlined practically every sentence. Gav, how many times have you read this?"

"Not enough," Gavin snapped, rising from his seat. He had four years and nine kilos of muscle on Fergus—he didn't need magick to make his brother sorry for snooping. "Now give it back."

"I don't get it. There's nothing in it we don't already know."

"Have you actually read it?"

Fergus hesitated, then shook his head. "Mum said it wasn't important."

"Well it is, because this book made the town hate us," Gavin said. "It's full of all our families' weaknesses—weaknesses I'm going to use to make sure the people who I'm about to be forced to kill don't kill me first."

Gavin despised everything the last year had brought him. It had ruined the few friendships he'd had, made the boys and girls he would've flirted with beforehand shy away from him with a combination of pity and revulsion. Nobody wanted to be around a dead boy walking.

Fergus's face flushed, and he lowered the file. "We're not forcing . . . I mean, I thought you wanted to be champion."

Gavin wasn't sure *want* was the right word. Want implied a choice he'd never been given. Becoming the Grieve champion had been more a process of elimination than anything else. Most of the time, he could convince himself he'd made this decision of his own free will, but in quiet moments, without the rain drumming down outside or Fergus's voice to fill the silence, he knew it wasn't true.

Still, it didn't matter, and there was no sense making Fergus feel guilty about it. Fergus, who was their mother's favorite, who would never understand why Gavin was so bitter, so cold. Gavin wanted to hate him. Gavin wanted to hate them all for doing this to him. But he'd decided long ago to save that hate for the tournament—meld it into a weapon at his disposal.

"I do," he said, trying to soften his voice. "You just surprised me. What do you actually want?"

"A spellstone." Fergus gestured at his wet clothes. "It's awful outside, and I'm supposed to meet Brian—"

"I'm not giving you a spellstone," Gavin said flatly. "I need every spell I have, since, as you've undoubtedly noticed, we're not exactly swimming in spellmaker alliances."

And then Fergus did something Gavin was not expecting. He smiled.

"You haven't heard. Alistair Lowe attacked a spellmaker at a meeting. Everyone who was there hates the Lowes even more now. Word is, they'll do almost anything to make sure the Lowe champion dies."

A sudden, desperate hope surged through Gavin. Never had he been more grateful that his brother was an insufferable gossip.

"Tell me which spellmakers were there," he said, a plan already churning through his mind.

If Alistair had been foolish enough to make such powerful enemies, if they were angry enough to want him dead . . . they'd want it to be a humiliating death. One that would ruin Alistair's legacy. A Grieve slaying a Lowe would be perfect.

Gavin could see how his story would end now. He just needed to make one spellmaker see it, too.

BRIONY THORBURN

The Relics—weapons powered by high magick—fall at random throughout the tournament's three-month duration. They are the Cloak, the Hammer, the Mirror, the Sword, the Medallion, the Shoes, and the Crown.

A Tradition of Tragedy

After the Thorburns' preliminary contest ended, there was traditionally a champion-crowning ceremony. It was a blowout bash in the gardens on the Thorburn estate with every possible branch of the family in attendance—and, this time around, with half of Ilvernath to boot. Tables in the main courtyard groaned with food and drink, and the afternoon sunlight shone down brightly upon the seemingly endless swarm of guests who'd come to congratulate Innes.

Briony had always loved parties, and she'd dreamed of this particular party for years. But now that it was here, she was miserable. There were two days left until the tournament, and she and Innes had barely spoken since the trial that wasn't a trial. Briony had spent every day since replaying the way the elders hadn't protested when Agent Yoo had named Innes as the champion, her own outburst, the hurt on her sister's face. The entire event had been utterly humiliating; even more so when the elders had lied to the rest of their family and declared that the mirror had deemed Briony unworthy.

All these people thought she'd failed, but really, her story had been stolen from her. And she had no idea how to get it back.

"There's been much speculation, you know. About the favorite to win this tournament."

Startled at the voice, Briony whipped around and saw a ruddy-cheeked man in a purple suit.

"I'm Osmand Walsh," he introduced. "Walsh Spellmaking."

"Briony Thorburn," Briony said automatically, shaking his clammy hand. She didn't understand why a spellmaker would bother talking to her when the new Thorburn golden child was holding court only a few steps away.

"As I was saying—this is the third tournament I've seen, and I think your family's champion could win it all." Osmand Walsh swirled his gin and tonic as he looked her up and down. "You must be proud. Did you always know it would be Innes? I hear the Thorburn family is fiercely competitive."

"Yes," Briony gritted out. "I'm very proud."

He was far from the last to approach her. Next on the gauntlet were two of her school friends, Liam and Kwame, who found her after growing bored with the garden's magickal photo booth.

"We know you really wanted to be chosen," Kwame said. "But after everything they talk about in that book, maybe it's better that you're not . . . you know . . ."

Liam gave his boyfriend's hand a warning squeeze.

"We're just glad you'll be around for fifth year," Liam said firmly. "Georgia said the rugby team has a real shot at Internationals now."

For the thousandth time, Briony mentally cursed *A Tradition of Tragedy* for letting all the world pry into where they didn't belong. As if she cared about the volleyball and rugby seasons in comparison to the true competition she'd been raised for.

"Excuse me," she told them as they began speculating about the odds of which champion would die first—both settling on Gavin Grieve. "I need to find a restroom."

She fled through the crowd and ducked behind the hedges at the edge of the yard, leaving the cheerful ruckus of the party behind her.

She wished she could confide in someone, but thanks to the Sworn to Secrecy, she couldn't tell the truth. And besides, the only people who would have understood wouldn't talk to her, anyway.

Isobel Macaslan, her best friend. Finley Blair, her boyfriend. Both different kinds of exes now. Both champions, as of Finley's announcement in the paper this morning.

A year had passed since Briony had last spoken to either of them. Since she'd messed up, and her family had made her transfer schools. She'd complied, of course. Her family was more important than anything.

Now, she realized she'd given it all up for a position she hadn't even been chosen for. And some of the most important people in her life were about to kill one another.

It didn't matter that she'd had a lifetime to get used to the idea. Now that the tournament was almost here, she simply couldn't comprehend it.

She was sniffling on a mossy bench tucked beside a fountain when a couple stumbled out of the hedges, giggling. At the sight of her, they both paused uncomfortably. Briony saw her smeared mascara and red nose through their eyes. She felt a rush of embarrassment—and fury.

She didn't think. She summoned the Helping Hand spell from the ring on her left middle finger—generally used for basic household maintenance tasks—and felt a rush of corresponding magick. A moment later, the spout unscrewed all the way. Water splashed over the sides of the fountain, dousing the couple. They shrieked and rushed away.

"Sorry," Briony muttered half-heartedly under her breath. That hadn't been a very Thorburn thing to do, even if it *had* only been a class two spell.

Then again, she didn't have to be a perfect Thorburn. Not anymore.

A chuckle emerged from the hedges behind her. "Does your family have a rule about PDA?"

Briony turned. A shape detached itself from the hedge and walked her way. He looked a few years older than her, with fair skin and dark hair that hung down past his ears. A collection of cracked spellrings dangled around his neck, and studded bracelets adorned his bony wrists.

Briony didn't like the way he was looking at her. It reminded her of the hawks that hunted the sparrows in their garden—how they wouldn't show themselves until it was too late for their prey to escape. "Who are you?"

He grinned, wide enough for her to see the glimmer of a tongue piercing. "Reid MacTavish." Briony recognized the name. A curse-maker. An important one. He should've been back in the main court-yard, one of the many offering Innes sponsorship, instead of lurking in the shadows like a goth ghost.

"Got any curses that would make everyone leave me alone?" she grumbled.

"That kind of magick doesn't seem like your family's style."

"Neither am I, apparently," Briony snapped, and immediately re-gretted it. Gossip spread faster in Ilvernath than an out-of-control curse—especially with journalists and cursechasers crawling out of every city gutter.

Sure enough, Reid looked at her curiously.

"My family always told me the ones closest to the champions took it hardest," he said. "You're her sister, aren't you? That must be dif-ficult."

Briony tried to regain control of her voice. "You have no idea."

"You're right. I don't. But aren't you proud of her? I read Thor-burns have to fight pretty hard for that champion spot. She must've really deserved it."

Not like I did. Briony forced the thought away, knowing if she clung to her resentment, it would fester. She tried to focus on anything else. The damp flagstones below her feet. The soft rustling of the garden hedges. The clear blue sky, which would soon be stained red.

"Read?" Briony repeated quietly. "You read that book didn't you?"

"Maybe. But even before that, well . . . A good cursemaker wants to know everything they possibly can about a curse like Ilvernath's. It's fascinating. A complex machine that keeps itself running with every cycle of the Blood Moon."

A machine. Briony had never thought about the tournament that way before—like each family was combined in seven interlocking mechanisms, twining together to play out the same story generation after generation.

"But that's all in the past now," Reid mused, licking his lips. "The future is subject to change—the book made sure of that."

"Curses don't change," Briony told him, then realized she hardly needed to explain that to a cursemaker. "Or at least this one doesn't."

"No, Ilvernath's curse hasn't changed. But the context has. Think about it—all the publicity, all the meddling. I wonder how it will alter the champions' strategies, or if all the journalists and curse-chasers grappling for their photos will make the curse's magick have to work harder, or break, or . . . Well, I'm sure you've thought about that, too."

He sounded almost dreamy, like he was babbling about a crush. Briony shuddered. Cursemakers had a reputation for being kind of creepy, and she was starting to understand why. Nobody should have that much love for something designed to hurt others.

But your family loves the tournament, whispered a little voice in her head. She pushed it down.

"Why are you even talking to me?" she asked. "Shouldn't you be listening to my sister give you a sales pitch for why you should grant her all your nastiest wares?"

Reid snorted. "Oh, my shop received a visit from a certain government representative last week. She had quite a lot of questions about what cursework had helped champions prevail in the past. Let's just say I have a feeling I know which family she was asking about: powerful enough to have a real shot at winning, but far easier to control than the Lowes or the Blairs. I bet your sister already has all the spellstones she could possibly need. That's probably why the government chose her as champion—she's compliant."

Briony gaped at him. She tried to speak, but the Sworn to Secrecy snagged on her vocal cords. Magick flared around her, white specks shimmering in the air.

"Interesting," Reid murmured, stepping closer to her. "So it *is* true."

"I—" Briony gasped out. "You—How—?"

Reid shrugged. "It was only a theory until just now, honestly."

Briony hadn't broken her oath, but it didn't matter. The truth was out there, and Agent Yoo's involvement could ruin the Thorburns' credibility.

"Please don't tell anyone," she said hastily, relieved to find that the words spilled freely now.

"Oh, don't worry. Your secret's safe with me. But I do wonder . . . doesn't it bother you, knowing that your family bent their traditions? The high magick belongs to your families, after all. Why help anyone else claim it?"

Yes, it did bother her, but Briony didn't want to give him the satisfaction of any more uncomfortable truths.

"My family's choices are none of your business."

"But they are *your* business," Reid said crisply. "Have fun being a good little Thorburn, then. If that's what you really want."

He left her by the fountain with a sarcastic goodbye wave. Briony watched him go, fury coursing through her. But it wasn't because of his pushy questions—it was at herself. For not being brave enough to ask those questions on her own.

Why would her family—her powerful, proud family—let one book cast aside hundreds of years of tradition?

Something was beginning to rise in Briony. Not an idea, exactly, but the beginnings of one, winking in the back of her mind like a bit of raw magick waiting to be collected and honed into something greater. She slipped out of the garden into the giant manor house that had belonged to her family for longer than anyone could remember. It was the home where she and Innes had grown up, always surrounded by relatives and yet never truly belonging with any of them. Briony rushed up the spiral staircase to her room and knelt on the woolen rug at the foot of her bed.

Copies of *A Tradition of Tragedy* had been anonymously delivered to all seven of the tournament families on the day of its release. Briony had been the one to find the package on the Thorburns' doorstep, and she'd told everyone that she'd destroyed it. They'd been pleased, and they'd had no reason to question her.

But the same curious part of her that was stirring now had secretly kept the book. She drew it out from beneath her mattress and swept off a layer of dust. The cover was lurid and distasteful: dozens of photos and portraits of previous champions, each filtered with an unforgiving red.

Briony took a deep, shuddering breath, and flipped to the first page.

ALISTAIR LOWE

The Lowes win even when no one expects it, even when another champion is deemed the strongest or the favorite. And the rest of us are left to ask how.

We never get an answer.

A Tradition of Tragedy

Alistair wandered through his memories in his dreams. In the first, he was seven years old, and his ankle was tied to his bedpost.

"They're called nightcreepers," his mother said. She had a low, melodic sort of voice, perfect for narrating stories. And the Lowes loved to tell stories, especially after dark. "They only emerge when it's pitch-black, so you can never see them." She switched off the lights in his bedroom and began to close the door with a creak.

Alistair cried and furiously tugged at the cord, which was secured with a magickal knot. "No! Don't—"

"That's what they like, you know. Darkness. They'll go for your eyes first."

"Please! I can't—"

"Good night!" she sang.

That had been the first night of Alistair's unofficial training as champion, and he'd sobbed all the way through it. Until Hendry had snuck into his room a little before dawn and helped him clean his soiled bedsheets. And reminded him that he'd need to endure these fears in order to become fearless himself.

The dream changed. This time Alistair was older, but not by much.

"Goblies are nasty creatures, always hunting for buried treasure," his mother cooed, looking down on him. He was wedged in an open grave beside the coffin of his dead father, and Alistair sputtered as his mother dropped a handful of silver coins on his face. "The coins should be enough to draw them in. And *you* should be strong enough to fend them off."

Alistair had gotten better at these tests by then, but he still panicked—though quietly—in the grave. The Lowes had sewn shiny buttons onto his sweater, and he swore every anxious pang in his chest was the claws of a goblie, searching for treasure within his flesh.

Hendry couldn't interfere with the tests—even at that age, they both knew that. But later, he'd brought Alistair a blanket. Logic told Alistair that fleece would hardly protect him from a monster, but even chained to a half-buried coffin, the blanket helped him feel safer.

As the years passed, their mother had used more than imagination to hone Alistair's resolve. She'd used magick.

"I see something! There! In the water!"

Alistair whipped around as he treaded in his family's murky black lake. A dark fin emerged from the surface, nearing him.

His mother stood on the bank, her expression approving as Alistair ignored his fear and continued swimming for the lake's center.

Hendry also watched, and it was his brother's soothing presence that helped Alistair ignore the sensation of something slimy grazing his ankle. It was Hendry who emboldened him, even though it should've been his family's lesson guiding him onward. The same lesson they were always trying to teach him.

Monsters couldn't harm you if you were a monster, too.

Alistair woke from the dream unsettled. Since it was the morning before the tournament, such nightmares felt like a bad omen. And so, as he always did when something was wrong, he decided to find his brother.

He threw on a cable-knit cardigan and ventured down the hallway. Unlike Alistair's slobbish room, curtains drawn in perpetual darkness, littered in half-read books, spellstones, and discarded knits, Hendry's was immaculate. His window faced eastward, toward the sunrise. Alistair squinted at the harshness of the daylight and found his brother's bed empty and cleanly made.

He checked Hendry's usual haunts. The kitchen smelled of roasted macadamia nuts and buttered croissants, yet the sweets hadn't beckoned Hendry for breakfast. His favorite napping spot was empty, the grass beside the tombstone of dear Aunt Alphina unbruised by the outline of Hendry's body. The music room was silent. The halls, vacant.

Maybe he's curled up somewhere else for a nap, Alistair thought. *Or maybe he's in the study practicing magick.* That seemed unlikely. Hendry avoided everything that involved getting out of bed during morning hours.

Growing increasingly uneasy, Alistair strode down the estate's maze of bleak hallways to the parlor. He didn't find his brother there, but he did find the rest of his family.

The Lowes were one of the smallest tournament families in Ilvernath, and it was especially apparent with the lone child and three adults sitting there so solemnly, dressed all in gray. Portraits of their ancestors lined the room's walls in gilded frames, so numerous and so dated that Alistair couldn't recognize all of their faces. Only the champions. Their eyes followed him wherever he roamed in the house.

Gifted, studious, he imagined those portraits whispering about him. *But remember him as a child? So afraid. So anxious. If nightmares are enough to unravel him, how will he fare when he lives in one?*

Above the stone fireplace was the portrait painted before the last tournament. His grandmother, just as stern and serious as she was now, despite being twenty years younger, was surrounded by her four children: Alistair's mother, Moira; his uncle Rowan; his aunt, Alphina, who'd won the last tournament only to hang herself several years later; and his uncle Todd, who'd died tragically not long after the portrait was commissioned.

Alistair glanced at the most recent portrait, completed barely a month earlier. Around him, his grandmother, his mother, his uncle, and his eight-year-old cousin, Hendry was the only one smiling.

Hendry was also the only one absent from this spontaneous gathering, though Hendry typically disappeared whenever there were serious discussions to be had. And, judging from each of the Lowes' somber expressions, the meeting was to be a serious one. Alistair's mouth went dry as he avoided the scrutiny of his grandmother's gaze. He wished he had his brother beside him.

"Alistair," his mother said gravely. "The Blood Moon has almost passed. The tournament starts tomorrow."

A mixture of thrill and nerves stirred in Alistair's chest. It no longer mattered how many tests he'd passed or failed, if he'd botched a curse in front of Agent Yoo. All those hours of study were worth it for this moment. Hendry had always been the favorite: more charming, more handsome, more loved. But Alistair had never been suited to that role, which was why he'd worked so tirelessly for his own.

Champion.

He lifted his chin proudly and sat down on the leather armchair across from them. The six other families had already announced their chosen, and now Alistair would officially join their ranks at last.

"Every generation, we present our champion with a gift." His mother's cold tone sounded colder than usual.

"So I *am* the champion?" Alistair tried to sound level, but his voice cracked. Something about this scene was wrong. In his fantasies about this moment, he'd envisioned pride in his mother's voice. Alistair had worked tirelessly for this. He was the perfect champion, and the perfect Lowe.

This was his moment, yet he couldn't help thinking her warmth was still reserved only for his brother.

"Don't interrupt," his grandmother snapped at him, and Alistair went rigid. Clearly, Alistair had not been entirely forgiven for the spellmaker incident. The only reason he'd escaped an underage assault charge was the tenuous claim of self-defense.

Alistair looked over his shoulder, wondering when the perfect son would arrive. Hendry would understand what this conversation meant to Alistair. Just his presence, just a smile from him would be enough to fix this very wrong moment.

His mother pulled a ring out of her pocket with a stone as dull and colorless as ash.

"It's a family heirloom," she explained. "As old as the tournament itself."

Although there were no nicks or markings on the stone, something about it did look ancient. Alistair had never seen anything like it. He would remember something so mysterious, so seemingly powerful.

"Blood before all," she murmured, that saying that had followed Alistair and Hendry their whole lives. Even as they slipped outside the manor grounds for entertainment, they knew none of it mattered. Those excursions were ventures into dreams, into a fantasy where they never truly belonged.

Their reality was the golden light of the setting sun splintering between the barren trees of their estate. It was the sound of hearths crackling and people barely breathing. It was hiding among forgotten alcoves, avoiding the cruel, disapproving faces of their family, who were always stealing Alistair away to shaded rooms and towers of books.

Alistair still remembered the moment when he realized he would become champion. He'd been eight years old, and his uncle had just assigned him reading that already exceeded Hendry's coursework, though Hendry was one year older. After hours spent locked indoors finishing it, Alistair had finally ventured outside, squinting into summer sunlight, to find his brother lying in a bed of overgrown grass and dandelions, his hair as wild as the weeds.

"It's because you're better than me," Hendry had explained, plucking a flower and holding it before his lips. "And they already know it."

Alistair had noted that Hendry's words were a little sharp.

"You know what I mean, don't you?" Hendry had asked. Then Alistair realized it wasn't bitterness in his voice—it was worry.

Alistair had stared into the forest surrounding their grounds, and thought of Ilvernath beyond it. The city he barely knew. The only horror story that was real.

The tournament.

"I do," Alistair had murmured. He hadn't known what to feel in that moment—terror or pride. The tournament was many years away.

"When you're not studying, you should come outside. Breathe some fresh air." He'd handed Alistair the flower. "I heard Mum talking about Aunt Alphina. After you win, I don't want that to happen to you."

Then Alistair blew the flower's seeds away—like a wish. Like a promise.

"It won't."

In the present, Alistair's grandmother placed a firm hand on his mother's shoulder. Somehow it seemed both a comfort and a threat, and his mother stiffened at the touch.

"Every family respects their history," Marianne said, "but the Lowes honor it. Every face on this wall has sacrificed something for the tournament."

Alistair's dread became a quiet tremble. He had listened to enough of his family's haunting stories to know how one began.

"All of my children were eligible to compete, and all were strong," his grandmother continued. Alistair had never heard her speak of the prior tournament before. "But the choice had to be made. How each would serve the family. Alphina was meant as champion. Rowan and Moira were meant to continue the line. And Todd was meant to die."

The other Lowes sat frozen. There were monstrous features in all their faces, in the cruel set of their lips and deep hollowness of their stares. They were stone, hardened from the inside out.

"Without Todd's sacrifice, Alphina wouldn't have won the tournament. Our family wouldn't be as strong as it is now."

His mother stood up, trembling, and handed Alistair the box with the ring. It was heavier than he expected, and glowing white with common—not high—magick. So he could use it during the tournament, he realized, when high magick wouldn't be available to him.

"There is a reason our champions so often prevail."

With each new word spoken, Alistair glimpsed monsters out of the corner of his vision, like shadows writhing along the walls. There were dragons and goblies, leviathans and wraiths. In every story his family told, the villains won. They crossed the lines no one else would. They struck when the hero least expected it.

"It's a powerful form of magick," his grandmother continued, "but just as a hog slain in fear will spoil its meat, a sacrifice made in fear will stain the spirit. It must be done quickly, while they are unaware."

Alistair's aspirations, his self, his world, fractured into a thousand pieces.

When he found his voice, it was a rasp. "What do you mean?"

Marianne pursed her lips impatiently. "With the sacrifice, you will be strong enough to win."

"I've always been strong enough to win." The certainty in his voice sounded false, even to him. He hadn't passed the tests—he'd hurt himself too much when he opened the vault, he'd grown sick at the sight of his own botched curse when he'd attacked that spellmaker, he'd called negative attention to the family in front of the very agent sent to spy on them.

It doesn't matter if you fail, Hendry had told him. And Alistair, naive and hopeful, had almost believed him.

"Not strong enough," Marianne replied. "Not to be *sure*."

He shot a glance at his mother, who stared numbly at the table between them.

The monsters had shrouded the room in darkness, and Alistair stood hurriedly, his head dizzy. Sick as he was, he still knew which monsters were the worst.

The ones who sat before him.

No horror story compared to this one.

The high magick in his spellrings coursed at his fingers, pulsing to his own anger and fear. For Alistair, anger and fear always went hand in hand. But even with all that fury, his voice still escaped as a whisper.

"Where is my brother?"

His grandmother nodded at the cursering, at the stone the color of ash.

"The Lamb's Sacrifice is invincible, and an invincible curse demands an unthinkable price. This is how we always win."

GAVIN GRIEVE

Since high magick has vanished from the rest of the world, many spellmakers have tried to create an alternative—to no avail.

A Tradition of Tragedy

Ilvernath looked different at night. The pedestrians wandering from shop to shop were gone, replaced by the bawdy laughter of bar patrons and the glowing signs in front of music halls and clubs. Gavin walked past the storefronts, his shoulders hunched, glaring at the mannequin hands displayed in the windows of Walsh Spellmaking. The shop had hiked up its prices with so many tourists in town. Gavin wasn't surprised. Hotel rates had tripled since the Blood Moon, as cursechasers and reporters booked up whatever rooms they could find. None seem perturbed by the idea of being trapped in Ilvernath until the tournament ended. They probably thought the Lowe champion would win in a matter of days.

Gavin ducked off the main thoroughfare down a maze of side streets barely wider than alleys. A glowing orange dragonfly beckoned him toward the MacTavishes' curseshop, the stone set into one of its antennae shimmering with magick.

Of the list of spellmakers that Fergus had given him, one was too incapacitated from Alistair Lowe's attack to be of any use, one was another champion's mother, and everyone else refused to meet with him, instead sending assistants to shoo him away. The MacTavish curseshop was Gavin's final chance.

The inside was cluttered and cramped, the opposite of the false, fussy elegance of the larger spellshops. Precarious piles of scrolls and books and baubles lay everywhere. Gavin's tall frame and broad shoulders made him feel too big for the space, but he liked it immediately. True power was knowing your store could look however you wanted and people would still come to you. His eyes lingered over a few of the curses labeled in neat script on the shelves—Ancient Arrows, Belladonna's Bane, Inferno's Wake. The MacTavishes were masters of their craft. They even had a distinctive style, oval gems in mostly grays and greens. He'd never seen another spellmaker in town dare to use a similar cut.

"Hello?" he called out. "Is anyone there?"

A rustle came from the back of the shop in response. Gavin nearly knocked over a bowl of cracked pewter rings as he whipped around. A moment later, a pair of black velvet curtains parted to reveal a boy a few years older than Gavin. His leather vest did little to hide that the black shirt beneath it was cut a fraction too low on his chest. A collection of dead magickal rings hung around his neck, each a broken, glimmering trophy to spells gone wrong. A curious choice of accessory for a cursemaker, but the MacTavishes were famously eccentric. Gavin wasn't about to walk into someone's family lair without doing a little research first.

Dark eyes, made darker by the black smudges beneath them, met his own. "Gavin Grieve. I was wondering when you'd come."

"You didn't know I would," said Gavin.

Lazily, deliberately, the spellmaker flicked his tongue ring against his teeth. "The MacTavishes have been watching the tournament, and the tournament families, for centuries. Do you think you're the first Grieve to believe we hold the salvation to your . . . unique predicament? To show up here the night before the tournament begins, begging for help?"

Anger sparked in Gavin's chest. "I'm not here to beg."

Reid drummed his fingers along the counter between them,

chipped black nail polish tapping against the varnished wood. "Then what, exactly, are you here to do?"

"You visited the Lowes, didn't you?"

Reid's face flickered with something that might have been surprise. "Yes."

"You saw how little respect they have for spellmakers. For you."

Reid shook his head. "I see what you're getting at, Grieve, and I admire your efforts. You're trying to act like this meeting doesn't matter much to you, like a starving dog that's pretending it doesn't need a meal. But you and I both know you'll be dead in a day, and I'll not be dragged down with you. Nothing personal."

Memories rushed through Gavin's mind: his mother, pouring a glass of wine as she calmly explained to him that her younger brother had been slain in the last tournament in less than an hour. Callista saying she'd been born a Grieve, but she certainly wasn't going to die as one. Osmand Walsh's smug, ruddy face. The girl he'd been seeing ignoring his calls the week after *A Tradition of Tragedy* appeared in the town bookshop, a classmate who'd been flirting with him backing off as soon as they realized who Gavin was.

Reid shifted to the side, tugging at his vest, and Gavin caught a glimpse of the book tucked inside. A worn copy of *A Tradition of Tragedy*, almost as well-read as his own. The sight of the book galvanized him. He couldn't give up yet.

"I've been reading past accounts of the tournaments for years, just like the ones in that book," Gavin said slowly. "When a Lowe doesn't win the tournament, it's usually because your family was backing the victor. Yet you don't get the credit for those wins—the champion's family does. If you chose to ally with me, and I won, I'd make sure you were remembered for it just as much as I was."

"Or we'd be remembered as the fools who chose to ally with a Grieve." Reid drew the book from his vest and placed it carelessly on the counter. "Everyone believes your family wrote this book because you've got no pride left to lose. Are you even strong enough to cast one of our curses? We don't sell spellwork to people who can't perform it."

Gavin knew a challenge when he heard one. He smiled grimly as magick shimmered in the air around his hand, then sent a wispy tendril up toward his mouth. The Silvertongue was a brand-name spellring he'd splurged on after his encounter with Briony Thorburn. One that guaranteed the person it was cast on would tell the truth. It was class five, the strongest he could make on his own.

Reid's black-lined eyes widened. "You can't be foolish enough to try and cast that spell on me. I'm warded."

"I'm not." Gavin took a deep breath, sucking the spell in. It tingled in his lungs like a hot beverage. Although he couldn't see it, he knew a line of common magick was appearing on his throat—spells where you needed to touch the recipient usually left a mark. "I cast it on *myself*. Now listen. Either you'll help me win the tournament, or I'll find a way to do it alone. Maybe I'll lose. But if this thing ends and I'm still alive, I will find you. Somewhere outside your safe, warded shop. And I'll have just watched six people die, so . . ." He shrugged, magick flowing around him. The spell made the world feel strangely distant, like he was in the middle of a flowing stream, letting the current take him where it would. "I don't think one more will weigh that heavily on my conscience."

The spellmaker sighed after Gavin's spell fizzled out. "You didn't have to enchant yourself to prove your threat was real. And I should kick you out for it regardless."

But he didn't move. His piercing clinked against his teeth again. Gavin was starting to realize that meant Reid was thinking.

"You're tough, I'll give you that," he said finally. "Stronger than I thought you were. And you'll clearly do anything to stick it to the other families."

"I will," said Gavin, unsure if the cursemaker was praising him or damning him.

Something flickered in the depths of Reid's eyes. "What if there was more to the tournament than winning it?"

Gavin frowned. "There is. There's losing. My family literally wrote the book on it."

"Hmm." Reid fiddled with *A Tradition of Tragedy*'s worn cover. "You're clearly tired of all of this. The same story over and over again. If you could change it—"

"I *can* change it," Gavin said forcefully. "I can win this tournament. But I need your help." He didn't know how much longer even his meager pride could stand this. He locked eyes with Reid, waiting nervously—until the other boy finally broke their gaze.

"I won't officially endorse you," he said, and Gavin's stomach dropped. "But I might have something to offer you. Something that will make you more powerful than any of the other champions."

Gavin felt the slightest stirrings of hope, but he wasn't foolish. No one would make an offer like that without some serious strings attached. "What's the catch?"

"It's not just any curse," Reid said gravely, leaning over the counter. "It will turn you into a vessel. Still interested?"

The shadows in the spellshop suddenly seemed darker and longer, the cluttered shelves and countertops pressing in around Gavin's field of vision. He was dimly aware of his heart ricocheting off his rib cage, of the way he'd frozen in place, stiff as a corpse.

It was a rumor spread in the back corner of a pub or in an alleyway over a shared cigarette, a story that everyone had somehow heard but no one could remember being told.

That if you knew how, you could draw raw magick from your own body to make your spells more powerful. Turn yourself into a vessel, capable of increasing the class of any spell you used—just like high magick. But with a terrible price.

Everyone who's ever used it lost their mind, the whispers said. *And then they lost their life.*

But Gavin was already lost. "I'm in."

"Then there's no time to waste," Reid said, disappearing through the velvet curtains. Gavin followed, wincing as the sudden rush of an enchantment coursed over him—some sort of teleportation spell.

The room he'd been transported to was a small, pristine space that reminded him of a physician's office, right down to the smell of antiseptic. The only hint that there was more to it was the flasks of raw magick and spellboards stacked neatly on the shining white shelves.

Reid caught Gavin's confused glance as he unfolded a cot in the corner. "Oh, the back room doesn't always look like this. This is just where we work on our more . . . experimental cases."

Gavin fought down the thought that Reid had wanted this all along. That Gavin had agreed to press the knife to his own throat.

"How exactly will this work?" he asked.

"Turning your body into a vessel requires a particular type of curse. I need to unlock your ability to access your own life force. After I'm done, you won't need to collect or store raw magick anymore—you'll be able to draw on yourself as a source for your magick, amplifying your spells. Everything you cast will be at least two or three classes higher than the original spell. It's not as strong as high magick, but no one else in the tournament will have power like it."

Gavin tensed. Reid said that he would cast a curse on Gavin, and curses were designed to cause harm. "But?"

"But every person is born with a finite amount of life magick in their bodies." Reid reached into a drawer and pulled out a syringe. "Each time you draw from your own life magick, you'll be siphoning from a well that does not refill. And if it empties completely, you'll die, whether you've won the tournament or not. It's permanent and irreversible."

There it was.

If he did this, he'd be restricting his magick usage for the rest of his life.

But if he didn't go through with it, the rest of his life would probably be a lot shorter anyway.

"You said you knew I'd come here," said Gavin. "Have you offered this to anyone else?"

Reid smiled ghoulishly. "You'll be my first attempt. I've been waiting for the perfect volunteer."

"And what makes me perfect?"

"You're desperate," Reid set the syringe down on a tray beside the cot and picked up a tattoo needle with a spellstone embedded in the hilt. "But more importantly, because I've met with almost every other champion, and found myself unimpressed. It's true, Grieve, that the other families have never respected us the way they should. Especially the Lowes. That's something I would like to change."

Perhaps the words were mere flattery, but they stoked something in Gavin, kindling a flame of approval that he hadn't felt before. Nobody believed in Gavin Grieve.

But Reid MacTavish did. He'd deemed Gavin worthy of power. It didn't matter, suddenly, if that power was dangerous, if this bargain came with strings Gavin couldn't sever.

"All right," he said. "I'm ready."

"Excellent," said Reid briskly. "Now take off your coat and face away from me—it'll be less painful if you can't see what I'm doing."

Gavin sat, his jacket bunched in his lap. He tried to focus on the shelf of raw magick flasks in front of him, each marked with a label indicating the person who'd brought them in for a commissioned cursering. He swallowed a sudden lump in his throat.

He wasn't scared. He wasn't.

Goose bumps swept across his skin as the cursemaker rolled Gavin's left sleeve up to the shoulder. He remembered the last time he'd been this close to another boy: Owen Liu, at a dive bar on the outskirts of Ilvernath, his fingertips tingling with something that wasn't magick but felt like it, with an entirely different idea of what the night would hold.

This was less fun.

"This will hurt." Reid's breath was hot on his ear.

It was Gavin's turn to smile ghoulishly. "Good."

The tip of the syringe brushed against his bicep, light as a feather. And then the pain began.

It was like nothing he'd ever felt before. Like being carved up from the inside out; like something was being ripped from him, an organ he couldn't name but one he knew he needed. Magick sizzled through him, so strong he couldn't think, couldn't breathe, and then, as he gasped for air, blotches of black began to seep through the edges of his vision.

Gavin came to, slumped over the edge of the cot, blinking tears from his eyes. The room swam around him as he sat up.

"Is it done?" he whispered.

Reid's face came into focus beside him. He looked almost . . . guilty.

"Yes," he said. "It's done."

Gavin's left arm throbbed. He turned his head toward the pain and sucked in a breath.

A tattoo of an hourglass stretched across his bicep. The top half was full, the bottom half empty in a way that felt expectant. Blood oozed from the edges of the hourglass for a moment, but then the dark lines of the tattoo seemed to suck them in. A metallic taste filled Gavin's mouth. He coughed, then grabbed a swab of gauze from the nearby table and coughed again. The white fabric came back speckled with blood.

"What did you do to me?" he croaked, dizzy.

"You shouldn't need to fill up your spellrings any longer, just make sure they're touching your skin," explained Reid. He was busily disinfecting the tattoo needle. "Each time your life magick goes into a ring, some of the grains at the top will fall. It doesn't fill up again. When the top's empty, you die. So watch yourself. Understand?"

Gavin nodded. He couldn't take his eyes off the tattoo. The ink was green and purple and blue, swirling slowly and lazily beneath his skin like a cluster of exposed veins. Not the color of any magick he'd seen before.

"I understand."

"That's a funny way to say thank you."

Gavin locked eyes with him. "I'll say thank you *after* I have proof it's made me stronger."

"Go ahead then," Reid said. "Test it."

Gavin concentrated on the spellring on his right thumb. Matchstick, a cheap knockoff of a Flicker and Flare. The light within the stone faded. Then, power coursed through him, strange and new, and he understood immediately that this magick was unlike anything he'd used before. He opened his palm, and a huge flame roared to life above it, tapering nearly up to the ceiling before flaring back down. It was far bigger and stronger than a class two spell should have been.

Gavin stared at it for a long, unblinking moment, then closed his hand into a fist, snuffing it out. A moment later, his shoulder began to ache, and the spellstone refilled itself with that same odd magick.

Gavin's life magick.

"It worked," Reid said softly. Gavin tore his gaze away from his hand to see Reid admiring his handiwork, clear pride etched across his face. "It actually worked."

"Did you think it wouldn't?" asked Gavin uneasily.

Reid shrugged. "Does it matter? You're in one piece, and your mind seems . . . well. About as fine as it was when you walked in here."

As he spoke, a throbbing pain shot through Gavin's arm. He turned his head, grimacing as he saw a few grains of sand trickle into the bottom of the hourglass.

"This better help me win the tournament," he growled.

Reid looked at him sadly. "Winning. Right. That's all you want."

"That's all there is."

Fifteen minutes later, Gavin barely remembered getting his coat on and leaving the curseshop. All he could feel was the beat of his heart, and all he could see was the dark, swirling form of the hourglass, of those grains of sand tumbling, one by one, warning him that he had done something that could not be reversed.

BRIONY THORBURN

> Seven Landmarks for seven champions . . . if everyone survives
> long enough to claim one, of course.
>
> *A Tradition of Tragedy*

The evening before the tournament, Briony Thorburn trekked out to the moors to mourn her fate.

More specifically, she'd gone to the Tower, one of the seven Landmarks scattered throughout Ilvernath's surrounding wilderness, where the tournament took place. The Landmarks were powerful strongholds, each imbued with unique high magickal enchantments. Briony had spent years honing her strategy—which Relics she would risk everything to collect, which Landmark she would claim on the tournament's first night . . .

It was a strategy that would never come to pass. Maybe she should've felt relieved about that, but all she could muster was bitter disappointment.

"The Tower," Briony read from *A Tradition of Tragedy*, one of the several books she had spread out around her. "Once twenty-one meters tall, this Landmark served as a sentry post to spot invaders."

The Tower was hardly so grand now, merely a heap of rock atop a hill of scraggly heather and tall grass. Until the Blood Veil fell tomorrow night like a crimson shroud draped over the city, each of the Landmarks would be little more than rubble, weathered down in the eight hundred years since the curse's inception. The high magick of the tournament would transform them from ruins to fortresses, as though pumpkins enchanted into carriages.

"The Landmarks surround Ilvernath at seven points . . . each powered by a pillar of high magick in its center. . . ."

Briony knew the stone the text was referring to. Jutting out from the ruins' center, the massive pillar was the only part of the Tower that retained any degree of splendor. Briony was leaning back against it now, like a broken throne.

"The Castle bears the strongest defensive enchantments. . . . The Crypt is warded against intruders. . . . The Cottage contains a collection of survival spells that—"

Wrung out from taunting herself, Briony pitched the paperback across the ruins. It splashed into a puddle, and she didn't care enough to retrieve it.

She hadn't come here to punish herself. After talking to Reid Mac-Tavish, she'd thought that reading *A Tradition of Tragedy* might make her see the tournament in a new light, help her find some sort of evidence to prove to the elders that they'd made the wrong decision letting Innes become champion.

Instead, the book only infuriated her. It twisted the heroic stories she'd been raised with into a lurid cautionary tale. According to its author, Ilvernath's curse was so abominable that it had earned itself a place among the ranks of such others as the Soul-Eaters' Curse in the sewers of Ucratsk, or the Lament of the Lost that had plagued a small town called Carsdell Springs.

Maybe it was even worse. Those curses had both eventually been broken.

"Bri!" Innes called, storming over the crest of the hill.

Perfect. Briony reached for the next closest book—*All Our Laments*—and pretended to be engrossed in a random chapter.

"What are you doing all the way out here?" Innes asked, slightly out of breath as she reached her side.

"You followed me," Briony grumbled.

"I'm worried about you! You won't talk to me. You won't even look at me. And now you're out here stalking the Landmarks—"

"You know why I'm here." Briony was ashamed of how her voice sounded—high-pitched and whiny, like a child denied a toy. "You knew how much I wanted to be champion. But they didn't even hold the last trial. They just . . . gave it to you."

"Of course I know why you're upset." Innes's tone was gentle. "But coming out here to sulk around some rocks isn't going to make you feel better."

"I'm not *sulking*."

"Well you've always described my books as torture before, so I couldn't think why else you would've stolen them," Innes teased as she pulled *A Tradition of Tragedy* out of its puddle.

Briony didn't answer, unwilling to admit why she'd sought Innes's books out.

"Look, I never thought things would go like this," Innes said, her tone suddenly serious. "I know you didn't, either."

Briony still said nothing.

"But if we don't talk about it now . . . well, we might never get the chance to. And . . ." Innes's voice cracked. "I don't care what the rest of the Thorburns say. You're the only family who matters to me."

That got Briony's attention. The other Thorburn children had parents to look out for them, but the two of them had grown up being shuffled from aunt to cousin like a pity project.

Briony had thought becoming champion would ensure that she truly belonged in her family's story. But Innes was right. Among all the Thorburns, she'd only ever belonged with her sister.

"I'm sorry I've been shitty," she said, feeling horribly guilty. "I just . . . I have no idea how to handle this."

"Neither do I," Innes admitted. "But for one more day, we can still handle it together."

She reached out and squeezed Briony's hand. Briony squeezed back, overcome. Even if what had happened to Briony wasn't fair, she would never become champion. It was time she accepted that, for Innes's sake.

"So," Briony started, flashing her most supportive smile, even if it physically hurt. "While we're out here, do you want to talk about strategy?"

"Let me guess. You think I should claim our family's Landmark," Innes said, looking at the Tower.

"In the first tournament, the Thorburn champion bided her time wisely from within the Tower, using the Mirror to spy on her enemies," Briony said, reciting the family story. "It's classic and smart. It's what . . ." She swallowed. "It's what I would do."

"It's also a little cliché. In my research, it's the same strategy almost every Thorburn chooses, and it's not like we always—or even usually—win. It's like we're stuck in a pattern."

"Well," Briony said, trying her best not to sound as irritated as she felt, "what will you do?"

"Statistically, the Crown is the best of the Relics. If I could . . . Maybe . . ." Her voice trailed off, and Briony realized tears had begun to pool in her dark brown eyes.

"Innes, are you—"

"Of course I'm not okay!" The words tumbled out of her in a sudden rush; Briony had never heard her sister talk like this, never seen her so emotional. Not even when their grandpa had died and they'd cried together at the funeral, glaring at the Macaslans across the graveyard. "I never wanted to be chosen. I collected all those books to try and find a way to save *you*, but I never found anything. And now I'm going to be part of this tournament. Bri . . . I don't want to kill anyone. And I definitely don't want to die."

The last words were uttered in a harsh, choked whisper. Innes immediately clapped her hands over her mouth.

But Briony understood now.

She was hurting. But Innes was *terrified*.

"You really don't want this?" she asked hoarsely.

"No, I don't. I've been checking my research ever since Agent Yoo chose me. There's so many curses that have been broken. I . . . I thought maybe . . ." She shook her head. "But our curse isn't like the others. Most of them have loopholes, or end conditions. Ours exists as long as the high magick that binds it together does, high magick that has been feeding on itself and getting stronger with every champion it claims."

Innes wrung her hands.

"And now it's going to claim me, too," Innes murmured.

Briony's resolve to support her sister suddenly felt a lot more complicated. If Innes didn't want this then it wasn't right. It wasn't fair that anyone would make her compete.

The story wasn't supposed to go like this. Briony and Innes shouldn't be crying in the ruins of a Landmark. They should be celebrating. Preparing. Innes drilling her on research while Briony selected the perfect arsenal of offensive and defensive spells.

But the wrong story was already unfolding. And both of them knew Innes wasn't strong enough to survive it.

"There's got to be a way," Briony said fiercely.

"Please," Innes whispered. "Don't lie to me."

Briony, rarely lost for words, had nothing left to say. Instead she tucked an arm around Innes's shoulder and pulled her little sister into an embrace. They stayed like that for a while, Innes sobbing into her shoulder, Briony staring at the ancient pillar in front of them.

"Let's go home, okay?" Innes said at last, breaking away from her. Her skin was blotchy, her mascara smeared in messy rivulets below her eyes.

"Okay." Briony returned the books to her backpack, even the one she'd chucked into a puddle, and swung it over her shoulder.

No sooner had they turned to leave the ruins behind than Briony heard voices. A moment later, three people clambered over the hill, their faces lit by the setting sun.

"What's this?" called the boy at the front of the group. His skin was dark brown, his tight black curls cropped close to his skull. "I see we're not the only ones scoping out the terrain before the tournament starts."

Briony knew that handsome, serious face far too well. Finley Blair: her ex-boyfriend. They'd only dated for a few months, but it had been intense, even volatile. It was hard for her to look at him without remembering their fight after *A Tradition of Tragedy* was published, the one that had led to their breakup.

Would you kill me to win the tournament? Finley had asked.

Maybe Briony had been a fool to answer honestly, but she and Finley had understood the reality of their relationship. Thorburns and Blairs were both loyal to their families; they wouldn't forsake them, no matter what they felt for each other.

Of course, she'd answered.

She hadn't expected the hurt that crossed Finley's face, the awful, villainous feeling that writhed in her stomach when he told her, *I guess we're not as similar as I thought.*

They hadn't spoken since. And now he was champion, and she was nothing at all. Briony wondered if he was relieved that she hadn't been chosen—or if a part of him had wanted to see what would really happen if they faced each other beneath the Blood Veil.

"Plotting to take the Tower tomorrow?" Briony asked him. "A bold move."

"We don't need this Landmark to win," said the girl standing beside Finley. Briony recognized her, too—Elionor Payne, a goth with an attitude as nasty as her scowl. The third member of their little clique was Carbry Darrow, the youngest of the champions, with fair skin, dark blond ringlets, and weak blue eyes. Based on the way both Elionor and Carbry were looking at Finley—Elionor as if asking for permission to strike, Carbry simply with awe—Briony could tell he was the one in charge. As per usual. He'd been class president for as long as she could remember.

Beside her, Innes hurriedly wiped the tears from her cheeks. Briony knew exactly what she was thinking. The tournament hadn't started yet, but this felt an awful lot like an ambush.

"What is this?" Innes asked. "You didn't just show up here at the same time as us by accident."

"Perceptive, aren't we?" Elionor's dark bangs framed her forehead in a harsh line, the spellstone gauges in her earlobes stretching halfway down her neck. She'd clearly gone to great lengths to look as threatening as possible. "We're here with an invitation for you, Thorburn."

"The Lowes won the last tournament," said Carbry. "Ilvernath is ready for a new victor. And we've agreed it should be one of the four of us."

"Why?" asked Briony. The others looked at her with mild annoyance, and Briony realized that she wasn't included in this conversation.

"No one wants the Lowes to win," said Elionor bluntly, responding anyway. "And the Grieve champion doesn't have a chance. If we work together, we can eliminate them easily."

"What about the Macaslans?"

Elionor scowled. "Vermin."

Briony's chest flared with anger, but before she could defend Isobel, Innes cleared her throat.

"So this is an alliance?"

Finley nodded. "We have resources, Innes. Work with us, and we'll protect you. We know you're loyal to your family . . ." He trailed off pointedly. Briony winced. "But that loyalty doesn't have to mean you do this alone. You're a talented spellcaster, and Elionor is strong in crafting. We'd make a great team."

Teaming up was a good idea. It would keep Innes alive longer, give her protection at least for a while. Admittedly, Briony wouldn't have sought out such a mismatched group herself. Innes was talented, certainly, but Elionor's flirtation with the press and Carbry's reputation, or rather lack thereof, didn't seem like Finley's style. Still

Finley clearly had a strategy, and it would be better for Innes than no alliance at all.

Innes's gaze had clouded over. "No thanks. I don't need your help."

"What?" Briony turned toward her sister, unable to hold her tongue. "Innes, think about this."

"I *have* thought about it," Innes said evenly. "My answer is still no."

Elionor's eyes narrowed. "Your mistake."

Elionor and Carbry both turned to leave, but Finley lingered a moment longer. He fixed his gaze intently on Innes, as though unwilling to look at Briony.

"Understand this," he said quietly. "Blairs, we have a code. We're loyal to our allies at all costs. But if you decide not to join us, I will not hesitate to cut you down."

Finley had talked about his family's code so often that Briony wasn't sure he could get through a conversation without mentioning it. Clearly, her ex hadn't changed at all.

Then Innes took a step back, and Briony realized with a stab of panic that her sister looked . . . intimidated. Weak.

She couldn't let Finley and the others leave like this. They'd target Innes the first night—she wouldn't last an hour.

"Not if she cuts you down first," Briony said coolly.

Finley finally met her eyes, and now that he did Briony saw a crack beneath his careful gaze. The longer he took her in, the more his rigid posture relaxed. "Well, I weighed my choices. I hope you're happy with yours."

Then Finley strutted away and joined his allies on the moors, the wind whipping at Elionor's dark hair as they walked the hiking trail back to town.

As soon as they were out of earshot, Briony turned to Innes. "What the hell were you thinking? An alliance would help you."

Innes's voice was distant and calm. "You need to stop speaking for me, Briony."

"But—"

"No. I know you had a way you were planning to do this. But I won't win this tournament if I use your strategies. I need to find my own path."

"You won't get the chance to do that if you don't make it through the first night."

"Trust me," Innes snapped. "I will. I'm the champion, okay? You have to accept that."

"But you don't want it—"

"It doesn't matter." Firm as her voice sounded, her expression looked broken. "I don't have a choice."

The conversation lapsed into silence, but Briony's thoughts had never been so loud. The Thorburns had made a huge mistake letting someone outside their family choose the champion.

And Innes would pay for it.

Furious and frustrated, Briony wondered if it would be Finley who killed her little sister. Or Isobel. Or the Lowe champion.

Maybe that book was right. Maybe this really was all messed up.

Briony had begun her research hoping to save her sister, but now she realized she'd been asking too small a question. She didn't just want to find some loophole to strike down Finley or Isobel on the battlefield. She didn't want the outside world hedging bets on which of these people she'd grown up with lived or died.

Innes had called the tournament a pattern. Patterns could be disrupted.

Reid had called it a machine. Machines could be broken.

Briony had only ever thought of it as a fairy tale. But even the grandest stories eventually found their ending.

And so, in the shadow of her family's Landmark, unchosen, unwanted, Briony Thorburn vowed that this ending would somehow be caused by *her*.

ISOBEL MACASLAN

To craft a death curse, blood must be given before blood can be spilled.

A Tradition of Tragedy

Ten hours before the start of the tournament, Isobel sipped her Earl Grey tea—milk, no sugar—while staring at the front page of the *Ilvernath Eclipse*. She had a lump in her throat that the tea couldn't wash down.

The complete Slaughter Seven. Six of them soon to be dead. Maybe, hopefully, at Isobel's own hand. The article included a picture of each of them, along with a list of their close family members and their accomplishments.

Like a celebration.

Like an obituary.

"They gave more space to the Payne girl," her father complained from across the table. He pushed aside the heap of accumulated dirty plates to make room for his own copy of the newspaper. "And this Blair kid—look at that polo shirt. This turning into a beauty pageant or something? What do they all have that you don't?"

"Maybe the reporters got bored of me," Isobel said numbly.

He shook his head and took a long drag of his cigarette. "All those stories were supposed to get you sponsorships. You got that head start, and then I thought, you know what? The spellmakers—they're logical people. When they see how talented you are, they'll line up at our door. But they turned their noses up at us."

He crumpled his newspaper into a ball and tossed it on the floor.

"It's probably your mother's fault. All the spellmakers are chummy with one another. If they're not sponsoring you, well, makes me think, is all."

Isobel didn't want to talk about her mother. They hadn't spoken since their last argument, and now that the Blood Veil would fall tonight, Isobel worried that she might never have a chance to again.

She shouldn't think like that, she knew. But it was hard. With each day that passed, the tournament drawing ever closer, Isobel grew more tightly wound. She'd spent months detesting the way the reporters had hounded her. Now that they had more champions to fixate on, she felt strangely discarded—a feeling she knew all too well. None of her emotions made sense.

"Mum wouldn't sabotage me," Isobel said sharply.

"You said sabotage, not me." Her dad leaned back in his chair and put his feet on the table. "Your Thorburn friend grew up well."

"That picture isn't Briony. That's her sister, Innes." Her father had never paid much attention to Isobel's friends, but she thought he'd at least recognize Briony.

"Well, that makes it easier, doesn't it?" he asked, sounding pleased.

Isobel wasn't so sure it did. No, even after Briony had betrayed her, she'd never relished the thought of facing her in the tournament. Killing her little sister, who'd always been sweet to Isobel, hardly seemed any better. And the more she stared at the newspaper, the more each of those faces felt like someone else's sister or brother, daughter or son.

Suddenly, something inside her cracked. It wasn't loud and thunderous, despite all these months of fame and terror and stress. Instead, it was quiet and small, betraying what she really was—fragile.

"I don't want to do this, Dad," she whispered, her eyes welling with tears.

"What?" He was picking food out of his teeth. He hadn't heard her.

"I don't want to do this," she said louder. "I don't want to be champion."

He snuffed his cigarette out in the ashtray. "It's a little late to back out now."

"There's still time. The champions don't carve their names into the Pillar until tonight. You could call Uncle Bart and—"

"Tell him that my daughter changed her mind? That she turned her back on all of us?" His voice rose, carrying into every narrow corner of the cluttered home, and Isobel shrank into her seat. "I knew your mother was planning something. She hasn't called in days."

"I don't want to die!" Isobel's voice trembled, but when she took deep breaths to calm herself, she felt like she was suffocating on all the cigarette smoke. "I don't want to kill anyone, either. I've *never* wanted to. I never wanted—"

"You've never wanted to be a part of this family," he accused.

"No, that wasn't what—"

"You don't get to choose the family you're born into." He stood up and stalked to the desk below the window. Its surface was covered in memorial cards, amassed over years of Ilvernath funerals. He grabbed a handful and waved them in front of her face, spewing dust into the air. "Do you know why we collect life magick?"

"Because if we don't, someone else will," Isobel answered quietly. She'd heard her father repeat those words often enough.

"Because we used to be great! One of the seven *great families* of this city! We might not be snooty like the Thorburns, or secretive like the Darrows, or powerful like the Lowes, but we kept our wealth. And our traditions." The hiss of his voice lingered on the last word. "We used to have a special respect for life and death, you know. Why do you think our champions often claim the Crypt Landmark or the Cloak Relic? It's because of history. It's because of who we *are*."

Isobel hadn't known that her family had any sort of legacy or traditions. All the Macaslan name had ever brought her was scorn, scorn she often felt they deserved.

"I know what you think of us. Everyone likes to pretend that magick is all starlight and rose petals, but it's not. You can find magick in waste. In anthills. In cadavers. It's dirty money, maybe, but it's that money that pays for your clothes, your school. You're still a Macaslan, no matter how hard you and your mother try to deny it."

He threw down the cards and jabbed his finger into her chest. She winced.

"Don't you want your family to be great again?" he asked her.

"I do, but—"

"Do you really think I'd ask this of you if I wasn't sure you'd win?"

She didn't, just like she knew that her mother hadn't sabotaged her chances of spellmaker sponsorships. Her parents might've had their disagreements with each other, but neither of them would let that get in the way of caring about her.

"But what if *I'm* not sure if I'll win?" she whispered.

"Then you clearly can't see what I see." He squeezed her shoulder comfortingly. "That you're so smart, and so talented, and stronger than I'll ever be. Maybe some of that you get from your mother." This surprised Isobel—she'd rarely heard him admit one good thing about his ex-wife. "But you know what else you are? You're a survivor. You get that from me."

Gently, he touched one of her red curls that perfectly matched his own.

"And all of that together? That's why I know you'll win."

Isobel took a deep breath, the must and smoke no longer bothering her. He was right. The media and her friends might've discarded her, but she was still the strongest champion in the tournament. And if any of the other champions could do what it took to win, then so could she.

"I need to get ready." Isobel stood up, and her father patted her cheek.

"That's my girl."

Upstairs, Isobel retreated into her bedroom. She'd selected her dress for the opening banquet weeks ago: white and sophisticated, with beautiful detailing along the sleeves. It hung in a plastic bag along her wardrobe door, and the hanger clacked against the wood as she threw the door open. She bent down, rooting around her shoes.

Wedged inside her favorite pair of heels was the piece of crumpled yellow paper she'd stolen from Reid's grimoire. The recipe for the Reaper's Embrace.

She hadn't attempted it yet because the instructions were complicated—even for her, trained by a professional spellmaker. Although the curse didn't promise instant death, it promised a certain one. And it was a class ten.

If Isobel *was* going to win this tournament for her family, then she would use every tool in her arsenal, even stealing. A class ten curse would be hellish to cast, more powerful than anything she'd ever attempted. But she was brilliant. And she was a survivor.

If she pulled this off, she would be undefeatable.

Perhaps this would be how she ended Alistair Lowe.

She rested the page on her bed and gathered her ingredients. From her duffel bag already packed for the tournament, she retrieved a wooden spellboard and set it on the floor. First, she sliced off a lock of her curls. Then she set out three flasks of collected raw magick. An empty quartz ring to store the curse. A dried chrysanthemum, removed from a jar on her nightstand.

After she laid out each of the other components, Isobel turned back to the spell. "A blood sacrifice must be given," she read. She wasn't surprised—powerful curses often demanded as much—but she couldn't find any specifications about what blood it required. She guessed her own. She furrowed her eyebrows and retrieved her letter opener from her desk drawer.

She gritted her teeth as she sliced across her upper arm, in a spot her dress would conceal tonight. Blood dripped down her skin and onto the stone.

To complete the recipe, Isobel leaned down and kissed the spell-board.

"It's done," Isobel said breathlessly. "Now to fill it . . ."

She opened the flasks of raw magick and spilled their contents over the spellboard. The particles glimmered over the septogram, white as bones.

Same as she had for Oliver, Isobel coaxed the swirling magick into the stone. Because the Reaper's Embrace was class ten, this ring could only hold a single charge.

The crystal began to pulse with faint, wispy light.

Suddenly, Isobel's stomach clenched, and her mouth filled with something hot. She bent over the spellboard and spewed blood onto the septogram.

And she didn't stop. It poured out of her with choking, shuddering heaves, seeping into her dull green carpet and staining it black. She leaned over and clutched her stomach, moaning. More blood came. More and more until everything was drenched in it, until it dribbled down her chin, dampened her hair, coated her hands.

She'd made a mistake.

Pain cleaved through Isobel's chest, followed by panic. She keeled over, her cheek pressed against the spellboard's edge. The room spun, and blood splattered more and more as she coughed.

Black and white bloomed across her vision like splotches of ink, even when she squeezed her eyes shut. The air she breathed was prickly with magick. It was more magick than she'd ever felt. Choking her.

She was supposed to be strong. She was supposed to survive.

Numbly, she prepared herself for the worst.

Then, all at once, the sensation vanished.

Isobel waited for several moments before shakily sitting up. Both her floor and her clothes were a mess. Her heart pounded, and she clutched her stomach.

She knew that cursemaking could be dangerous. She'd experienced backfire before, but never from an enchantment as powerful as this.

Hesitantly, she grasped for the cursering in the spellboard's center, the blood that coated it dripping down her hand and wrist. She smeared it away with her thumb. The light within the stone had stopped pulsing, so—if it hadn't already been obvious—she knew that her crafting attempt had been a failure.

Gasping out a sob, she threw it against the wall.

Some survivor, some *champion*, she was.

She staggered to her feet and opened her jewelry cabinet. Though most of her supplies had already been packed for the tournament, a few basic spellstones remained inside. She reached for a class one Bye Bye Tummyache spell.

But the moment before she grabbed it, she noticed something strange. There was no light inside it.

There was no light inside any of the stones in her cabinet.

No light inside any of the rings on her fingers.

She stumbled back, confused. Then she knelt in front of her duffel bag and unzipped it. Inside were clothes, a water bottle, nonperishable snacks, tampons, and—at the bottom—her magickal arsenal for the tournament: spells and curses of all sorts, flasks brimming with pre-collected raw magick.

Except the flasks were empty.

And the spell- and cursestones had gone dark.

"No," she moaned. That couldn't be possible. Magick didn't just *vanish*.

Seeking comfort, Isobel instinctively reached for her mother's locket around her neck and snapped it open. The Roach's Armor Reid had given her should've been sealed in the stone inside.

Instead . . . she saw nothing.

And that was when she realized it. The power hadn't disappeared. Her perception of magick had. She couldn't see it, couldn't sense it, couldn't use it. No spells, no curses, no anything.

Isobel pressed a hand to her mouth. She swore she could hear a funeral march in her head.

The opening ceremony began in a few hours, and she was defenseless. She'd be lucky to last the night.

She should tell her father. Even if he couldn't fix this, he could tell the family. They could find another champion. But . . .

Her chest tightened. He would think she'd done this to herself on purpose. After she'd cried to him about not wanting to be champion, after he'd accused her of being cowardly and ungrateful and ashamed of who she was, of course he would suspect sabotage.

And then both of her parents would hate her.

A small voice in Isobel's mind reminded her that was still better than being dead.

But a louder, sharper voice disagreed. For the past year, Isobel had known all too well how it felt to be hated by the people she'd once cared about. By the whole *world*.

Pushing her mother away had been Isobel's own fault. Botching the curse was, too. But she couldn't lose the only person she had left, especially not the person who believed in her more than anyone, even herself.

"Maybe this is temporary," she tried to assure herself. "Maybe it will go away on its own in a few hours."

And maybe a fairy godmother will appear and grant you three wishes.

No, if there was a way to fix this, then she had to do it on her own.

And if there wasn't, she would die.

But she'd made up her mind. If she died, then she would die a champion.

GAVIN GRIEVE

> The opening ceremony of the tournament is historically the last
> chance anyone has to sabotage a champion before the real fight-
> ing begins.
>
> *A Tradition of Tragedy*

Tonight the tournament would begin, and the seven champions would fight one another until a lone victor remained standing. So, naturally, Ilvernath had thrown a party.

Gavin could sense that tension hanging over everyone in the city's banquet hall. The way members of rival families glared at one another. The way "good luck" said with enough insincerity sounded the same as "goodbye." There was a hungry look on everyone's face—for alcohol or violence, it was all the same. The tournament banquet had always been a quiet, clandestine affair, but some reporters and onlookers had stolen their way in despite the magickal warding that supposedly blocked those not on the guest list. Flashbulbs popped and cursechasers gaped, and Gavin wondered if they'd find a way to sneak onto the grounds of the tournament, too, if grisly pictures of his death would soon be in the *Ilvernath Eclipse*. He probably wouldn't even make the front page.

Gavin kept to the back of the hall, beside the table of hors d'oeuvres tastefully arranged around portraits of the last tournament's champions. Aggravated, he stabbed a toothpick into a cheese cube from the platter beside Peter Grieve, who'd been similarly skewered with an Ancient Arrows curse. His family had wasted no time making a beeline for the open bar; his mother was already wobbling in her stilettos.

Beside his mother, Gavin caught sight of Reid MacTavish, sipping a drink. Reid caught his eye and winked, then sauntered toward him, smug as a cat with bird feathers sticking out of its mouth.

"Well, Grieve," he said. "How's my little present treating you?"

The hourglass tattoo on Gavin's bicep ached beneath his cheap suit, the same one he'd worn to Callista's wedding. Gavin hadn't used magick since the Matchstick. He didn't want to admit it, but he was frightened of what would happen when he did.

"Fine," he grunted.

"And have you given any thought to my suggestion? That there could be more to this sad little game than winning it?"

Truth be told, Gavin had utterly forgotten about that part of their conversation. He considered it now—clearly, Reid was trying to offer him another bargain. But Gavin had already turned his body into an unnatural magickal vessel in pursuit of winning the tournament. He wasn't interested in playing lab rat again.

"I know how your deals work now," he said gruffly. "Go away, Mac-Tavish."

"Your loss." Reid raised his drink in a mocking toast and melted back into the crowd.

Gavin took a deep breath to rein in his nerves, but it was difficult with so many of the other champions in the room. The faces that had once crowded his dossiers, here in real life.

Finley Blair and his crimson tie, boastfully donning the color of high magick. Elionor Payne beside him, posing for a reporter. Isobel Macaslan, her hair spilling like a bloodstain down the back of her white dress.

And in the corner, his father brandishing a glass, the amber glinting in the chandelier light. His mother lolled on his shoulder. Callista on the awkward fringes of the Payne table, paying no mind to him.

Suddenly, it was all too much for Gavin. He abandoned his plate beneath the scarlet-dyed fondue fountain next to a photograph of Alphina Lowe. Then he darted outside into the square.

Out here, the party was a bit less stifling. Small knots of people wove together in the cool evening air. Above their heads, magickal lanterns floated and gleamed in the evening sky, the spellstones inside them shining white.

Then he heard it: beyond the jazzy music spilling out from the banquet, the faint sounds of chanting.

"JUST BECAUSE YOU WIN A PRIZE
  YOU'RE NOT ABSOLVED FOR THOSE WHO DIED!"

Past the lanterns, at the edge of the city square, stood a small crowd of cursechasers. They wielded signs with angry slogans on them. Not cursechasers, after all. Even worse—protestors yelling bad poetry. They must've gathered here in some last-ditch effort to stop this generation's tournament from taking place.

There was no point in arguing about the morality of the curse. It was what it was, and Gavin wasn't going to feel guilty about wanting to survive it.

He was turning away from the yelling when someone slammed into his tattooed arm.

It hurt, and he turned to tell them so—then realized who was standing in front of him, pale and ghostlike in the glow of the lanterns.

Alistair Lowe.

He looked even crueler in person than he did in photographs, with his dark, slicked-back hair emphasizing his sharp widow's peak and the angular slant of his nose. Although he was shorter than Gavin, he still managed to look down at him. He'd only been publicly named champion that morning, yet Gavin had heard his name on nearly everyone's lips tonight.

"You almost made me spill my drink."

Gavin looked down and realized Alistair was clutching his half-empty glass as if it were a close friend.

"I'm pretty sure," Gavin said, "that you're the one who bumped into me."

Fury flitted across Alistair's face. "As if I could've missed you in that tawdry excuse for a suit."

Gavin realized Alistair was swaying back and forth, ever so slightly. He wondered what possible reason the favorite to win this tournament had for getting dead drunk right before it started.

Maybe he was just *that* certain he would win.

The thought bolstered Gavin's constantly simmering rage. This boy had everything, and he had nothing. Alistair was handsome and disdainful in his tailored gray suit, and he was looking at Gavin as if he were an ant, something not even threatening enough to step on.

Gavin leaned forward, summoning his magick. Power flooded through him, his spellring buzzing with more energy than he'd thought possible. His breaths became slightly labored, as if he were underwater, and then Alistair's arm froze.

All he'd meant to do was cast Hold in Place, but when Gavin's anger surged again, his new powers surged with it, coursing through the spellstone. Rather than Alistair freezing, the drink in Alistair's hand shattered.

Whisky and glass rained everywhere. Several shards sliced Alistair's palm, leaving a smear of blood across his skin. Dimly, Gavin registered the flash of a camera somewhere behind them.

"Oops," Gavin whispered, a rush of satisfaction coursing through him. "Looks like you spilled your own drink after all."

Alistair's eyes met his, but they didn't look rattled.

They looked lethal.

"For that," he said, each word enunciated with a careful sort of rage, "I will kill you slowly."

Gavin's tattoo started to throb again as the spellring refilled itself.

But he didn't care. Standing chest to chest with Alistair Lowe, with Alistair drunk and off-balance and himself victorious, he felt more powerful than he ever had.

"Weren't you going to do that anyway?" he asked, grinning.

Alistair let out a noise that might've been a snarl and stalked away. Gavin looked around—people were staring—and stumbled to the line of trees at the edge of the square. Here he was finally, blessedly out of sight. Even so, he heard scraps of the protestors' conversations.

"Am I the only one who thinks it's weird that most of them look alike? As a group, they're generally very . . . pale."

"Probably from them all marrying each other for a thousand years. I mean, would *you* want to wed into one of those families? Knowing this could be one of your kids someday?"

"Fair enough," the first voice murmured. "And that Darrow boy, only fifteen . . . It's unthinkable. . . ."

Gavin's tattoo pulsed with a fresh jolt of pain, and he let out a muffled curse. He tuned the voices out, shrugged off his blazer, and hastily rolled up his shirtsleeve.

The tattoo had moved again. Gavin stared at the grains of sand clumped in the bottom of the hourglass, feeling sick.

He'd drained part of his life force away just to make Alistair Lowe take him seriously. He'd mutilated himself just to make Ilvernath take him seriously.

But at least it was working.

Gavin yanked down his sleeve and stalked back inside.

ALISTAIR LOWE

High magick fell from the stars, and when we found it, we did what humans always do. We decided it was ours to claim.

A Tradition of Tragedy

Alistair sat at his family's banquet table, surrounded by those who had murdered his brother.

He was wearing his best. The gray suit, freshly pressed, was tailored perfectly to fit his slender shoulders. His dark hair was combed back, sharpening the hollows of his cheeks. The cursering holding the Lamb's Sacrifice on his fourth finger felt heavy as he clenched his fist.

After his family had told him what they'd done, Alistair had locked himself in Hendry's room and punched a hole in the wall. It'd hurt a great deal—Alistair was horribly clumsy—but he hated to see the room like that. Clean, the way Hendry had left it. Still smelling of pastries. As though his brother could stroll back in like nothing had happened.

Alistair twisted the cursering around his finger. His chest ached, as if his very heart had turned to stone and weighed down upon his lungs and bones. He didn't remember the last time he'd cried. But after a night miserably hoping this was one final, heartless test, he wasn't in the mood to shed tears.

He was in the mood to spill blood.

His mother leaned over and rested her hand on his. Her touch was ice. Alistair immediately wrenched his away, wishing he could conjure a stake and pierce it through her heart.

"I know what you're thinking, Al." His brother's nickname for him sounded crude on her lips.

"No," he said darkly. "I don't think you do."

"Hendry died for this family, for the tournament. Don't let his death be in vain."

Alistair wanted to laugh bitterly. He wanted to stand up and scream. Hendry hadn't died. He'd been murdered. His family thought that the Lamb's Sacrifice would make Alistair stronger, but without Hendry, Alistair was weaker. Without Hendry, Alistair was lost.

"You loved him," Alistair whispered. All these years, he struggled to believe her affection for Hendry had been a farce. Even the Lowes weren't that cruel.

Or maybe they'd only doted on Hendry because they'd always known his fate.

She stiffened, but her voice, as always, remained steady. "I love this family."

"And me?" He immediately regretted the question. It was too loaded, too vulnerable.

He turned away from her, fixing his attention instead on the party around them, roaring with music and raucous laughter. The banquet took place in the town's center, by its most ancient landmark, the Champions Pillar. It was a calling place to raw high magick, a central point for the seven other identical pillars that held the Landmarks together, although only the Lowes—as the last tournament's victors— could see the glittering red dust of high magick suspended in the air, winking and flickering around the party. It was beautiful. It was also hideous, a reminder of why they were gathered here tonight. This was the power the Lowes killed Hendry for, that Alistair would kill six others for.

It disgusted him.

All Alistair needed from his mother was a simple, one-word response. Instead, she gave him a question.

"Are you not this family's champion?"

Alistair stood abruptly, and his thoughts veered to the Grieve champion in the square, taking their encounter as inspiration. He flicked his wrist, and the Shatter and Break cursering burned as some of its power drained—power he'd intended to save for an opponent's bones, but instead would gladly waste on his own spite.

His mother's glass of wine shattered, merlot splattering across the white tablecloth. His grandmother, uncle, and younger cousin tsked with disdain.

All those years he'd sought to please them. Now his aspirations made him sick.

When Alistair did fight—and win—he wouldn't do it for his family. He would do it for his brother. Hendry wouldn't have wanted Alistair to die, too.

"It's funny." Alistair glared down at his mother. "For years you told me stories about monsters. But all along the monster was you."

He stormed off in the direction of the bar.

The bartender eyed Alistair warily as he approached. Even in a good mood, Alistair had a threatening look about him, like an apple likely rotten at its core. And Alistair's current mood was lethal.

"Three shots of whisky," he told the bartender, and the man immediately poured them. Alistair knocked back all three in a row, then coughed until his eyes watered.

Someone standing next to him laughed. The man wore a plum-colored shirt, and he reminded Alistair of a toadstool.

"You're the Lowe boy," the man said, spitting out his family name. "Congratulations."

For all of Alistair's life, he had been one of the Lowe boys.

It was such a little phrase to set him off, but he couldn't help it. Alistair cracked his neck and summoned the same curse. Shatter and

Break. The man's pointer finger *snapped*, his bone splitting cleanly in two.

The man wrenched his hand away and swore violently. The person beside him, a young man wearing smudges of eyeliner and a necklace of broken spellrings, bit his lip to hold back a smile.

Toadstool clutched his finger and glowered at Alistair. "Do you know who I *am*?"

Alistair raised his eyebrows. The whisky was warming him from the inside out. "Should I?"

"I'm Osmand Walsh. I was at your house that day." Alistair dimly recognized him as a spellmaker who'd cowered as he'd cast the Vintner's Plague. "You may be a Lowe, and your family has high magick *now*. But one day, you won't. Your little display made sure of that."

"What are you talking about?"

"You think that woman is just here to *observe*?" He nodded at Agent Yoo by the Thorburn table. "No, the government is here to interfere, and I say that it's high time for it. Letting the Lowes hold all that power? It's unthinkable. At least now, even if you don't die in the tournament, you'll die on somebody's pitchfork."

Because Marianne had forced Alistair through so many tests, he hadn't realized just how important that one had been. Automatically, he concealed his nerves behind a wicked grin. He might despise his family, but they had taught him his role well.

Alistair plucked the glass of beer out of the spellmaker's hands, and Toadstool blanched.

"I guess you'd better sharpen your pitchforks, gents," Alistair said, then laughed and strode away.

Alistair made for the closest exit he could find, which ended up being not an exit but a coatroom. With no attendants in sight, Alistair jumped onto the counter and nursed the ale.

Hendry would've loved a party like this. In fact, Hendry had been looking forward to this night. Something about making ladies swoon and an open bar.

Alistair drank more beer. By the time he was halfway done, he felt extremely drunk. He'd hardly eaten anything since yesterday.

If you do ever want to talk about the tournament, I'm here. I'll listen, Hendry had told him two weeks ago. Alistair had put the discussion off, not wanting to worry him, not wanting to spoil their fun. Now Alistair had no one to confess his fears to about leaving the tournament broken. Without his brother, he already was.

An awful voice inside him sneered that this was his fault. If he'd passed the Lowes' tests, if he'd truly been the villain they'd raised him to be, then they wouldn't have needed to kill Hendry.

Alistair stared into the golden liquid in his glass, searching for his salvation at the bottom. He wiped his eyes.

"What are you doing?"

He looked up and grimaced. It was Isobel Macaslan, the pretty champion he'd met at the Magpie. She wore a white dress, an antique locket necklace, and an expression of disgust.

"What does it look like I'm doing?" he sneered.

"It looks like you're cracking." She ignored him and went for the coatrack.

Alistair drained the rest of his glass and leaped off the counter. His dress shoes hit the carpet with a thud. "How did the Asp's Fang treat you?" He gave her a pitying expression. "You don't look well."

She raised her eyebrows. "You look terrible."

"I *am* terrible."

She snorted. "And drunk." Her red curls bounced as she stepped closer to him. "So, *rival*, what are you thinking about now?" She reached for his wrist, where the white remainder of her spell was merely a smudge. Alistair let her touch him, if only because he needed a distraction from his angry, sorry thoughts.

She ran a manicured finger over the kiss mark.

"Maybe you're thinking about your family's monster stories," she murmured. "The ones that still give you nightmares."

Alistair narrowed his eyes. His memory was foggy, but he'd

thought her Divining Kiss had only scratched the surface of his mind. He yanked his hand away.

"Maybe you're thinking that you have nothing to worry about, because you believe you have the entire world convinced you're going to win." She took another step toward him. She was now close enough that he could smell her perfume—peonies. Close enough that she was definitely a distraction. "Maybe you're thinking about the skirt I wore that night. I remember you liking it."

If the Macaslan was attempting a new strategy on him, it was working. His gaze drifted down to her neck, her waist. He stifled a smile, imagining his family's disdain if the paparazzi found their champion flirting with another hours before they were meant to kill each other.

"What are you doing?" he asked, like a dare. For the first time this evening, the nasty voices in his mind were quiet.

"What does it look like I'm doing?" she repeated his words from earlier. "I'm threatening you."

He cleared his throat. "Is that what this is?" Alistair was a master of threats, but even he had yet to employ this technique.

"I saw all I needed to know about you. *Rivals*." She snorted. "I have nothing to fear from you."

Alistair glanced down at his rings, cataloging what curses he had left now that he'd drained his Shatter and Break stone.

"What else did you see?" he asked her.

"Everything."

The thought of someone peering into his psyche was a terrifying notion. His grief already felt hopelessly transparent.

"And what do you see now?" he challenged, fighting to keep his voice steady. He knew that, to replicate the Divining Kiss from before, she would need to use her stores of magick. And she would need to touch him again. Those were dangerous propositions for both of them, though almost certainly more pleasantly dangerous for him.

But rather than reach for his hand again, she stepped back, putting distance between them. "A waste of magick," she said haughtily.

"Besides, I'd already guessed you were arrogant and self-destructive. Our conversation only proved it."

And then she left, leaving Alistair still drunk, still irritated, still grieving, still alone. The cold inside him rushed back all at once. Nothing ever went the way he'd envisioned it.

In the banquet hall, the music stopped, and Alistair knew what that meant. The introduction of the champions was about to begin.

ISOBEL MACASLAN

If no victor emerges after three months, then every champion dies and no family gets high magick for twenty years. That is the inherent joke in it all—if the families compete in the tournament to win magick and glory, why, then, does it feel like a punishment?

A Tradition of Tragedy

The seven champions lined up near the exit at the back of the banquet hall, heels clicking and shoes scuffing on the ancient marble floor. Isobel's heart pounded as the mayor, Vikram Anand, directed them in the proper order. Public displays of any kind made her nervous, and here she was shoulder to shoulder with the champions of every other family, preparing for a deadly tournament, and she couldn't sense a lick of magick.

Isobel examined the other champions, curious how they compared to their newspaper write-ups. Perfect, dutiful Finley Blair, of course, Isobel knew from school. . . . Gavin Grieve was larger and more muscular than she'd realized. . . .

Elionor Payne cast shifty glances behind her, then met Isobel's eyes with a sneer. . . .

Isobel averted her gaze and focused on maintaining her illusion of confidence, just as she'd done in front of Alistair. Even though she was in no danger at the banquet, she couldn't let any of the champions suspect that she'd lost her power. Otherwise, she would be the one they targeted first.

Innes Thorburn stood behind her. Her brown hair was styled in an updo that looked intricate and elegant for a girl Isobel had most often seen hunched behind the covers of a book.

"Hi, Isobel," Innes said. "How have you been?"

This seemed a bizarrely mundane question for their situation. In only a few minutes, the mayor would announce each of their names and families, and the spectators would celebrate as if six of them wouldn't die sometime in the next three months.

"I'm good," Isobel answered blandly.

Innes smiled warmly. "I always knew you'd be champion."

Isobel couldn't say the same. But she didn't have the mental energy to think about Briony—not tonight.

Innes gave Isobel a pointed look. "You don't have to pretend. Everyone thought it would be my sister."

Isobel didn't bother to correct her. But she didn't pity Innes, either. Isobel didn't know what the final Thorburn trial was, but for Innes to defeat her sister, she must've been far more capable than Ilvernath had given her credit for.

"Ah," Mayor Anand said, "the last champion is here."

Alistair Lowe staggered over, his face flushed.

The mayor pointed to the spot between Isobel and Innes, and Isobel stiffened. She'd managed to forget that, traditionally, the Macaslans directly preceded the Lowes, though she doubted any of the families remembered why.

Alistair shot her an impish smile.

He's dangerous, troubled, her mother had told her. *What that boy did today . . . it was horrible.*

Maintaining her facade of confidence, she rolled her eyes and turned away from the boy her mother thought would murder her.

The grand wooden doors opened to the chilly September evening, and the champions were immediately greeted by shouts.

"ARE THESE NOT YOUR SONS AND DAUGHTERS?
YOU HAVE RAISED THEM FOR THE SLAUGHTER!"

A hoard of protestors surrounded the mossy stone square, sectioned off by ropes and the Ilvernath police. Many carried picket signs with words and images, enchanted so that splotches of blood-red paint splattered across them, then faded, on repeat. Others wielded posters of each of the champions' faces from their headshots in the newspaper.

As Isobel spotted her picture in the hands of a stranger, a wave of nausea crashed over her. She only had to suffer through these theatrics for a bit longer. Once the sun set and the Blood Veil fell, magickal safeguards within the tournament itself would automatically prevent outside interference or trespassing on tournament grounds. Champions could only be affected by spells cast by one another, and they couldn't speak to anyone other than fellow champions or venture within the city limits. Nothing these protestors did or said would change that.

Alistair leaned closer to Isobel. "Let the show begin," he whispered, sending chills up her neck. She swatted him away, worried she'd be sick again.

Mayor Anand shouted something Isobel couldn't hear over the commotion of the protestors. Then, clearly flustered, he cast a Loudspeaker spell and called, so thunderously Isobel nearly leapt out of her skin, "GAVIN GRIEVE! Oh—Sorry—If you would all *quiet down . . .*"

Gavin strode down the steps into the courtyard while Mayor Anand read out Gavin's embarrassingly short list of accomplishments.

"Gavin is the oldest son of Boyd and Ailis Grieve. His accomplishments include skipping a grade and . . ." Mayor Anand cleared his throat awkwardly. "Well. He is seventeen years of age and in his final year at Ilvernath South Public Secondary School."

Gavin might as well have been invisible, as no one but the protestors paid him the least bit of attention. Even his family was somewhere else, crowding the bar inside.

She felt an unexpected pang of sadness for him. At least the Macaslans thought Isobel would win.

Gavin approached the massive stone that jutted out from the center of the square. In all the times that Isobel had seen the Champions Pillar, the veins of red crystals woven through it had never looked so much like blood.

When Gavin took the knife Mayor Anand offered and climbed the ladder to carve his name into the stone, the protestors only grew more raucous.

"JUST BECAUSE YOU WIN A PRIZE!"

From where she stood, Isobel could only see the Pillar's back, where a symbol was engraved—seven stars arranged in a circle. But even from here, she could spot the ring that appeared around Gavin's pinky finger when he was finished. The champion's ring, binding him to the tournament's power.

"YOU'RE NOT ABSOLVED FOR THOSE WHO DIED!"

"Finley Blair!" Mayor Anand continued, ignoring the jeers. "Finley is eighteen years old and the only child of Pamela and Abigail Blair. He has been the class president of Ilvernath Preparatory Academy for four straight years, as well as the captain of the school's fencing team. His interests include— OH, WILL YOU STOP THAT?" Mayor Anand shouted again, though it did nothing to quiet the upheaval.

Those in the courtyard clapped for Finley as he carved his name into the Champions Pillar, as they hadn't done for Gavin. After all, he was *Finley Blair*. Dedicated, charming, proud of his family in a way that Isobel could never be. But she'd come to know Finley rather well during the months he'd dated her former best friend, and she could see the stiffness in his walk and the careful calculation in his smile.

"Carbry Darrow!"

Isobel didn't pay much attention as Carbry descended the steps, tripping halfway down. All she could think was that she was next. And with the protestors' continued chants and Alistair Lowe practically breathing down her neck, she was sweating. She blotted at her forehead with the back of her hand, careful not to smudge her makeup.

"Isobel Macaslan!" Mayor Anand called.

Isobel graced the square, her gown trailing after her as she walked. The clapping grew louder and, for a moment, she could almost pretend everything was normal. She was wearing the dress she'd chosen. Her lipstick was flawless. Her impressive number of spellrings showed exactly how much power she commanded. . . .

Had commanded.

"ARE THESE NOT YOUR SONS AND DAUGHTERS?
YOU HAVE RAISED THEM FOR THE SLAUGHTER!"

Her stomach clenched. *I can't do this,* she thought with panic.

"Isobel is sixteen years old and the only child of Cormac Macaslan and Honora Jackson. Isobel is the top of her class at Ilvernath Prep and was president of the Young Spellcasters' Honor Society for two years. She works part-time at her mother's spellshop in—"

"JUST BECAUSE YOU WIN A PRIZE!"

Few of the faces around her were friendly. She frantically searched them for her father, who was smiling too wide. Isobel could practically see him pricing the value of high magick in his mind.

The rest of the mayor's speech passed in a blur, and Isobel numbly climbed the ladder up the stone pillar. There were hundreds of names carved into it, representing hundreds of champions, hundreds of victims. Isobel knew the history, of course, but seeing it all in front of her, in the countless crossed-out names Ilvernath had buried and forgotten, made a shiver shoot up her spine.

"YOU'RE NOT ABSOLVED FOR THOSE WHO DIED!"

The knife made it difficult to write in her usual perfect cursive. When she finished, her name looked as blunt and sharp as the cut she'd stitched up herself on her upper arm. Twenty years from now, when another Macaslan champion climbed the ladder to carve their name, they would see hers, haphazard and imperfect. And most likely, crossed out.

When she descended the ladder, she looked down at her hand in surprise. Normally, she would've expected to feel a tingle of accumulated magick as the ring was conjured. Instead she'd felt nothing. One minute, her pinky had been empty. The next, it was not.

The quartz was as red as rose petals, the color of the high magick they were all fighting for. Though she knew it must've glowed, she couldn't see it.

After her turn ended, Isobel shakily made her way to her family. Her father lowered his cigarette and kissed her forehead, definitely smudging her makeup.

"You were magnificent," he said.

Her mother—who would usually never stand so close to her former family—smiled stiffly from Isobel's other side. Isobel did her best to ignore them both and focus on the rest of the ceremony, otherwise she might cry.

"Alistair Lowe!" Mayor Anand announced.

The ruckus of the entire courtyard lowered to a hush, including the protestors. Ever since Alistair had nearly killed that spellmaker at the Lowe estate, he'd become the most notorious of the Slaughter Seven. Mayor Anand inched away from Alistair as he approached, like he was feral. There were no accomplishments, only a listing of family names.

"Marianne Lowe, Moira Lowe, Rowan Lowe, Marianne Lowe Jr. . . ."

Isobel frowned as the mayor finished the list. There was no mention of Alistair's brother. She glanced over at the Lowe table and realized he was absent. That seemed odd, when every other member of the family was present. She remembered him distinctly from the Magpie.

"Innes Thorburn!" the mayor continued.

Seeming to snap out of their trance, the protestors resumed their chants.

"ARE THESE NOT YOUR SONS AND DAUGHTERS?"

Tuning them out, Isobel's eyes flitted across the courtyard to the Thorburns, to Briony. Her old friend did not look like herself. Her usual cool confidence was replaced with a burning intensity as her sister carved her name into the ancient pillar. Isobel couldn't tell what emotion plagued her—embarrassment, resentment, worry? But Isobel knew Briony, and she knew what a dress like that meant. It was scandalously low-cut, with beads catching and shimmering in the light. It was an outfit meant to be seen. It was the dress of a champion.

Isobel hated Briony, in that moment. Hated her for betraying her, hated her for sulking about not being given the chance to throw her life away.

"YOU HAVE RAISED THEM FOR THE SLAUGHTER!"

"I just . . ." Her mother's voice was hoarse. "I just want you to know that I love you." She wrapped her arms around Isobel and squeezed fiercely, and tears welled in Isobel's eyes. For a moment, Isobel considered telling her mother everything, even if it was truly too late to change it now, but then her father slapped her shoulder.

"My money is on you and the Payne girl, in the end," he said. "The Lowe kid doesn't look like he has it in him, you know?"

Suddenly, it was too much to stand here, trapped in the throngs of the families, protestors, and claustrophobic, cobbled walls of Ilvernath itself. Isobel broke out of her parents' grasps and pushed her way to the courtyard's edge, to fresh air.

She hadn't realized she was walking toward Reid MacTavish until she nearly collided with him. He spilled his cocktail on his too-tight black jeans.

"Ah," Reid spoke, his voice slurred but unmistakably cold, "it's you. Princess. What a pleasure."

"I need your help," she said, her voice tight with panic as much as her wounded pride. And she hated when he called her that. "I stole a curse from you, but something went wrong as I crafted it, and I can't use magick anymore. I can't even feel it."

Reid nearly lost his balance, and he had to clasp the edge of a nearby table to steady himself. "You stole . . . a curse from me? What curse?"

"The Reaper's Embrace." Her face burned.

"That's from my family's oldest grimoire," he said, aghast. "I should've known a Macaslan would try something like that. The Reaper's Embrace isn't even a good weapon in the tournament. It's a contingency curse—it weakens the mark based on the mark's own actions. It feeds on hatred and darkness, so the victim gradually loses their life along with their innocence. Not exactly a good choice for—"

"Reid, I am *begging* you." Isobel didn't know how to make him listen to her. She had nothing to offer him.

Perhaps it was the desperation in her tone, but he sobered in both senses of the word. "Your sense for magick is blocked, and there are only two ways to fix it. You could reattempt the curse, and do it right this time. Assuming you know what you did wrong. And if you mess up again, you could die."

Isobel had no idea what her mistake had been. "What's the other option?"

"A Null and Void spell of a higher class. It'll wipe the curse clean from you."

"But the Reaper's Embrace is already class ten, and no one with high magick is going to undo it for me!"

"Then you have a problem. . . ." Reid shrugged and offered her his drink. "Here. You can have the rest."

"I . . . No thank you. I don't—" Isobel told him, moving away just as the last of the Slaughter Seven, Elionor Payne, joined her family in the crowd. The attendees applauded. The banquet was over. The champions would now have time to receive any last-minute advice from their families, and to say goodbye, before they made their final preparations for the tournament and headed to the town's limits. To wait for the sun to set and the Blood Veil to fall. To wait for the tournament to begin.

Isobel had barely an hour.

An hour to come up with a plan.

An hour to fix what she'd done wrong.

An hour to save herself.

An hour wasn't enough time.

BRIONY THORBURN

We're raised to call them champions, but I would argue there's a
better word: sacrifices.

A Tradition of Tragedy

While the families filtered out of the square, the sun was
slowly starting to bleed into the horizon, a harbinger of
the Blood Veil that would soon engulf the sky.

Briony Thorburn lingered behind in the elongated shadow of the
Champions Pillar.

She'd worn her best dress—and makeup, which she rarely
touched—but she felt awful. Dark circles rimmed her eyes, and her
stomach burned with the frustration of her own failure. She'd been
up all night poring over Innes's books, searching for clues eight hundred years of champions had missed: that the tournament's curse
could really be broken. That her sister didn't have to die.

There was still time, she told herself. Innes might not be killed
tonight.

Across the square, Reid MacTavish slunk away from a throng of
fellow spellmakers. Briony darted out of the shadows and cut him off
as he turned a corner into an alley.

"We need to talk," she said.

Reid took her in, raising his eyebrows. He smelled of liquor. Briony resented anyone who'd enjoyed the party tonight, knowing the
horror that followed it.

"Do we?" he asked.

"I did what you said. I read that book. I skimmed at least a dozen books—"

"Wow. A *dozen* books. How impressive."

He tried to brush past her, but Briony put her hand on his shoulder.

"Just because this curse has never been broken doesn't mean it can't be. I need to save my sister, and you know about curses. So you're going to tell me how to break this one."

Her words sounded like a threat. But she didn't care. Reid was the only other person who seemed to understand this, and if intimidating him was the way to get his help, so be it.

Instead of arguing with her, he seemed to snap to attention at her words. He shot a glance down the alley, as though making certain they were alone, then he steered her farther away from the reporters who still crowded the square. The dumpsters around them reeked.

"I want to help you," he told her. "But . . ."

"But what?"

"But no curse can be broken from the outside."

Briony sucked in a breath. "You're telling me I'm too late."

"I'm telling you that only a champion can end the tournament."

There was still time, then. She could find Innes. She could save herself, save them all, if only Briony could convince her.

"But how would a champion break it?" Briony pressed. "And what would happen if they did?"

Reid hesitated. In the darkness of the alley, his black clothes rendered him nearly invisible. "It's hard to say. When curses break, it's either because they're taken apart delicately, or because they're smashed to bits. Avoid the second option. It would definitely leave all the champions dead."

Briony didn't have time to waste discussing what wouldn't work. She'd thought of a thousand different false solutions over the last day. "So how do you take it apart delicately?"

"Briony . . . this is all just theory. What makes you think you can—"

"Because I have to," Briony snapped. "I mean, she—my sister—has to. Or she'll die."

"Well then." Reid licked his lips. "You'd need to dismantle the high magick that holds the tournament together, piece by piece. So you have to ask yourself, what are those pieces? They are—"

"The seven Landmarks," Briony answered quickly. "And the seven Relics."

Admiration glinted in his eyes, and for the first time in two weeks, it felt like someone was really seeing her.

"So you *have* been reading," he said. "Yes. The seven Landmarks and Relics. But also the story itself. The patterns, repeating every generation, reinforcing the magick and making it stronger."

Stories. Patterns. Clichés. That was how Innes had talked about the tournament before. Maybe Briony *could* convince her there was something to this.

"But how do you dismantle all those pieces?" she asked. "Would you have to do it all together?"

"You can safely take a curse apart piece by piece. I assume high magick works the same way."

"And if you do that, it won't collapse? What if it destabilizes everything?"

"Do you think I have all the answers?" He looked at her disdain-fully. "I've spent years studying the tournament, but I'm not from your so-called 'great' families. I'll always be on the outside. All I know is that curses last for centuries when nothing about them changes. Somehow, after all this time, the tournament has managed to stay the same. If you go back to the beginning, find its patterns, and break them, then you could destroy its very foundation. Maybe build something new. Maybe burn it all down."

Briony had more questions—a *lot* more. Maybe Reid would know the answers and maybe he wouldn't.

"I—" she started, but he shook his head.

"You need to hurry if you want to reach her."

Briony knew he was right. Innes knew the tournament and its history inside and out. There would be time for her to find the answers once it began.

"Thank you," she told him, then she raced out of the alley back to the square. Most of the guests had left, but thankfully, the Thorburn family was so massive that they were still wishing Innes good luck. They'd congregated at the edge of the square beside the forest, shaking hands with her one after the other. Briony spotted Agent Yoo in the line, saw her grip Innes's hand, and felt a rush of fury. This was all her fault.

Briony shoved to the front, stumbling in her heels. When she burst through to Innes's side, no doubt looking distraught, Innes waved the rest of their relatives away. They hesitated at first but soon dispersed, allowing the sisters this one small, final moment.

Briony seized Innes's shoulders. "There's a way," she heaved. "The tournament can be broken."

"What?" Innes blinked at her, shell-shocked.

"Reid MacTavish. He told me. The tournament is held together by high magick. There's the seven Landmarks, the seven Relics, and the story. The story that keeps repeating. If you can—"

"Bri, you're not making any sense."

"I know. I know. I'm sorry. There's still so much to figure out. But if you find the pattern within the story . . ." Briony's voice cracked with excitement as an idea came into her mind. "Like the Mirror and the Tower! The pattern! You have to—"

"*Please*," Innes choked, pushing Briony away. "Please stop. This is the last memory you'll have of me."

Briony gaped. "Stop? Innes, I'm trying to save you! I'm telling you how—"

"*Listen to yourself.*" Innes's voice spewed out in a low, furious whisper. "Is this why you showed up late to the banquet, looking frazzled? You've been chasing some fantasy? I need to go and get ready. . . ."

"No." Briony lunged in front of her to block her path. "You listen to me. You're not strong enough to win this tournament—you know you're not."

"I've trained hard," she said indignantly.

"Not as hard as the other champions. Breaking the tournament is your only chance to survive. Believe me, if I could be the one to—"

Innes barked out a laugh. "I should've known. This isn't about me—it's about *you*. Just like everything else. Our whole lives, you've been the center of attention. But now you're not. Deal with it."

There was an ugliness in Innes's voice that spoke to a feeling that had been festering deep inside. A resentment Briony had never seen before.

Her words plunged a dagger through Briony. Not just because it hurt that her sister thought of her as so selfish, but because Innes was dooming herself.

Briony couldn't watch her sister walk into a slaughter. She *couldn't*. Even if Reid's theories had offered her nothing but fragments of a solution, Briony was sure she could put the pieces together, if she were champion. She could save her sister. She could save everyone.

A feeling she couldn't name swelled in her chest. In every story her family told, the heroes won. They made the choices no one else could. They triumphed over villains even when all hope seemed lost.

And Briony Thorburn made the perfect hero.

Her gaze flickered to the periphery of the square, where the last of the guests had departed.

They were alone.

"You've never wanted this, Innes," Briony told her.

Innes lifted her chin. "But I'll do it anyway."

Briony advanced closer, forcing Innes to retreat beneath the shadow of the Champions Pillar. Hundreds of names were carved into it, but only one mattered to her right now: Innes's, glowing red near the top.

"Let me take your place. Let me be champion."

"You're delusional. I couldn't even if I wanted to. You're . . ." Innes's voice trailed off, her eyes brimming with tears.

But Briony didn't relent. "I'm right. I know I am."

"That's *enough*." Innes tried to take another step back, but her shoulder smacked against the Pillar.

If Innes wouldn't give up her title willingly for her own good—for the good of all of Ilvernath—Briony would have to take it from her. It was the only way she wouldn't spend her life regretting that she'd sent her sister to her death. And when Briony saved everyone, Innes would understand. One day, perhaps, she would even forgive her.

The crystal on her index finger began to glow.

"Maybe you're stronger than some of the other champions," Briony whispered to Innes, summoning the magick within the spellstone. "But I'm still stronger than you."

Innes flicked her wrist as she cast a spell of her own, but Briony had a head start. And she had the perfect spell, one she'd commissioned ages ago for the tournament. Briony had always had a fondness for finding a way to put a twist on something mundane. A class two Cat Nap spell could help someone get to bed at night; a class three was a popular choice for new parents trying to calm colicky infants.

Briony's was class seven, and it had a different name: the Deathly Slumber, because when used correctly, an opponent would be knocked into a coma-like state until the spell wore off hours later. They'd feel no pain, but they would be completely and utterly defenseless.

Briony watched, guilt rising in her, as Innes threw up a weak Mirror Image shield spell. If it had been strong enough, it would've rebounded the Deathly Slumber at Briony.

Instead, Briony's spell passed right through it.

As white, glimmering magick collected across her face, Innes's eyelids began to droop. But the betrayal on her face struck Briony straight in the heart. It was a look she would remember for as long as she lived.

You're the only one who matters, Innes had said.

She'd been wrong. Her sister would never forgive her.

"Briony," she croaked. "No—"

Innes stretched out a hand toward her sister, fingers clawing at the air in a last, feeble grab for magick—and then collapsed onto the flagstones.

Briony stood there for a moment, feeling ill.

"Well," she murmured to herself. "Let's finish this."

She gulped down a surge of nausea as she knelt beside her sister's unconscious body.

The champion's ring glimmered on Innes's pinky finger, its scarlet stone shining in the setting sun. They were nearly out of time.

She gripped the ring and tugged, but it did not give. She pulled harder, Innes's hand limp beneath hers, then froze. This was what Innes had meant when she'd said she couldn't give Briony the title even if she wanted to. The champion's ring couldn't be removed.

But Briony knew how powerful the Deathly Slumber was. If she left Innes there, outside the border of the tournament grounds, she would automatically forfeit her life when the Blood Veil fell. And if she dragged Innes into the boundary and left her there, even with a camouflage spell, the other champions would pick her off within minutes.

Then Innes's death would be Briony's fault.

No, she had to see this through. She'd already betrayed Innes. Already gone against her family's wishes.

There was no question—Briony needed to remove the champion's ring. And if the ring's power was what bound Innes to the tournament, maybe Briony could sever that connection.

Sever.

Briony stared at her sister's hand, bile rising in her throat a second time.

Knocking Innes unconscious was one thing. Mutilating her was another.

But it was the only option that could save her life.

"She'll understand one day," Briony whispered, mentally sorting through her spellrings. "They all will."

At least Innes would feel no pain. She laid her sister's hand out across the flagstones, carefully separating the pinky on her left hand, and summoned the Mirror Shards.

A line of white magick appeared in the air a moment later, in the approximate shape of a jagged shard of glass. Briony's brow furrowed in concentration—she'd never done something this precise before. She lowered it to just above Innes's hand, then swallowed.

It was too late to turn back now.

So Briony did not close her eyes, did not flinch, as she lowered the makeshift knife.

Blood pooled from the wound. Briony hastily cast a Healer's Touch on Innes's hand, a spell she'd only ever used for athletic injuries, then wrapped it in a strip of cloth torn from the hem of her dress.

Her sister's finger lay on the ground, a sliver of bone peeking out from the bloody flesh.

The world around Briony went fuzzy, and she took a deep breath, forcing her heartbeat to slow.

She was so close to finishing this. So close.

She gritted her teeth, picked up the finger, and slid the ring over the bone at the edge of the pinky. The digit was still warm to the touch. Briony bundled the finger in more cloth and placed it in her sister's outstretched palm.

She slid the ring onto her own pinky, and a strange warmth spread through her, tingling in her toes and fingertips. Then she stepped up to the Champions Pillar and cast the Mirror Shards again, gripping the glass so hard it cut her. With her and Innes's blood both smeared across her palm, Briony struck out Innes's name on the stone and carved her own beneath it.

Briony felt the change as soon as she finished the final letter. The ground rumbled and shook beneath her with a quaking groan. Then the evening stilled once more.

Now that it was done, she needed to take care of Innes. She fumbled through her spellrings, found a fire spell, and sent up a shower of sparks.

It would draw people to the square like a beacon. Hopefully, an experienced healer could reattach Innes's finger. Either way, it would not be long before they discovered what Briony had done.

Now she needed to get out of here, fast.

Crack.

Briony's head jerked to the source of the sound. It hadn't been loud, but it still shook Briony down to her bones. Where she had carved her name on the Champions Pillar, just at the edge of the final *n*, a crack crept down the stone. It was small, about seven or eight centimeters long, but an ominous red emanated from it, like a throbbing vein of light.

"Shit," Briony breathed. It had worked—she was a champion. But she'd done something irrevocable, something wrong.

As the Blood Veil darkened the sky above her head, Briony pushed her doubts aside and headed into the woods. She had no supplies, no enchantments but the rings on her hands, no clothes but the ones on her back. But it didn't matter.

She would be the final champion to ever carve their name into that stone.

ISOBEL MACASLAN

Someone usually dies the first night.
A Tradition of Tragedy

Isobel stood at the edge of her father's estate, on the hill overlooking the graveyard at the city limits. The cemetery was eerie and still. Even the wrought iron entrance gate swinging in the wind made no sound. It was silent except for the steady ticks of her stopwatch.

Three minutes to sunset.

Isobel unfurled the crumpled, bloodstained paper clutched in her hands. The page she'd torn from Reid's grimoire. She kept reading and rereading it, searching for a clue in the Reaper's Embrace's recipe for what she'd done wrong when she'd tried to craft the curse. But her mind couldn't focus.

You cannot die yet, she ordered herself. *You haven't been accepted to fashion school. You're still a virgin. You've never even left this damned city.*

She checked her watch. Two minutes to sunset.

What Isobel needed was more time. If she claimed one of the Landmarks, she'd have protection. She'd originally hoped to seize the Crypt and all its magickal booby traps, but the Castle had the most powerful defensive enchantments of any of them—it was effectively impenetrable. The champions could each choose their starting point at the edge of town, so Isobel didn't know where the other champions were. But the Castle was close. If she could make it there, she'd have somewhere safe to figure out how to fix her mistake.

One more minute.

Isobel tucked the scrap of paper away in her duffel bag, then fiddled with her locket. The Roach's Armor couldn't protect Isobel without her powers, but the piece of her mother brought her comfort just the same.

She wished she'd apologized to her. Now it was too late.

Her watch alarm rang, its mechanical screech slicing through the graveyard's quiet. Isobel's sweat-slicked fingers trembled as she pushed the stop button.

Overhead, red seeped across the sky like paint on a canvas. It swept up past the treeline, devouring the oranges and violets of sunset, swallowing each of the stars until they shone scarlet, as though trapped behind a window of stained glass. Soon the sky was red across every stretch of the horizon.

This was the fall of the Blood Veil, the signal of the tournament's beginning. Day and night, Ilvernath would remain a haunting crimson until all but one of the champions were dead.

Isobel turned around to see the other, inner Veil that had fallen around the city, a darker curtain stretching from land to sky. She stilled for a moment, taking in the phenomena she had only ever seen in poorly saturated photographs. The inner Veil blocked her path back into Ilvernath—and prevented any spectators from venturing onto the tournament grounds.

Starting now, she was truly cut off from the life she'd known.

Starting now, all the champions would race from town into the wilderness to claim their Landmarks.

Starting now, Isobel could be killed at any moment.

She ran.

Down the hill, past the tombstones, into the forest. Isobel had never been athletic, not like Briony, but she was too buzzed with adrenaline and panic to slow down. When she'd imagined this moment, she'd never considered the way the scarlet light would alter the landscape, how every puddle resembled a blood spill, how the briary trees took the shape of teeth. But the terror only made her run faster. The Castle was three kilometers away from her father's house—she was the closest of all the competitors. So long as no one used a Here to There spell, Isobel would get there first.

As she neared the end of the woods, the Castle loomed over the moorlands ahead, its impressive crenellated towers and surrounding barricades unrecognizable compared to the heap of moss-covered stones it had been before the Blood Veil fell. She locked her sights on the drawbridge lowered across the moat. If she was the first to cross it, the Castle would accept Isobel as its champion. And all of its protection would be hers.

The moment Isobel stepped past the edge of the tree line, a blast erupted in front of her, knocking her off her feet and onto her back. She gasped as her head smacked the dirt and the air rushed out of her lungs, then she frantically rolled over and fisted the grass, her vision spinning—red, everywhere red.

She cursed herself for hoping she'd be the first one here. Of course another champion would use Here to There or Pick Up the Pace spells to reach their Landmarks.

"You missed!" someone shouted—a girl. She wasn't speaking to Isobel. Her voice was a loaded taunt, despite the terrifying power of the explosive spell. Isobel peered up at the figure through the smoke.

Briony Thorburn, only paces away from her.

Isobel squeezed her eyes shut. That couldn't be right—she must've hit her head *hard*. But when she opened them again, it was still Briony she saw. Not her sister.

"I wasn't aiming for *you*!" a boy shouted back.

Isobel froze in the grass. The boy's words meant *her*. He'd seen her. But no matter how inexplicable Briony's appearance or how dire Isobel's situation, it didn't change her plans. She needed to make it to the Castle. She shakily backed toward the trees and crouched. If the two of them distracted each other, then she only needed to wait for her opportunity.

A blond boy sprinted across the field. It took Isobel a moment to recognize him as Gavin Grieve. An explosive spell of that magnitude didn't seem possible from the Grieve family. Where had he found such power?

As Briony whipped around, Isobel couldn't help feeling she *knew* Isobel was there, hiding behind the tree.

Ahead, Gavin had nearly reached the drawbridge. Briony swore loudly, then charged after him. Even close as Gavin was to his claim, Briony was faster. Plus, Gavin wasn't running normally. He darted in strange angles, leaping and halting, not traveling in a straight line.

Then Isobel understood.

Gavin wasn't firing those explosive spells. He was dropping them and triggering them from afar.

Isobel reached down into the grass and grabbed a stone. Then she leaped into the clearing, and, with all the strength she possessed, chucked it across the field. It landed several paces behind Gavin and about a meter in front of Briony.

And erupted upon impact.

Boom!

There was a chorus of shouts, from both Briony and Gavin. Isobel stood and examined the cloud of smoke, chest heaving. She'd acted automatically—it wasn't like her. She was impulsive without her power.

And she might've killed the closest friend she'd ever had. A girl who wasn't even supposed to be here.

All she'd been thinking was that she didn't want to give up.

Isobel trudged forward through the grass, waving the smoke away in front of her. The wind bit at her cheek, sharp enough to sting.

"Get down!"

Someone collided with her stomach and tackled her to the ground. Isobel grunted at the weight on her gut and spit out a mouthful of hair that didn't belong to her.

"Are you *mad?*" Briony hissed. "What sort of strategy is walking straight into the line of fire?" She gritted her teeth and ducked her head from something Isobel couldn't see. Gavin must've been firing curses in their direction. If Isobel still had her powers, they'd probably look like bullets of light, whizzing through the smoke toward her.

She was lucky she hadn't died.

Lucky Briony had saved her.

"The Castle . . ." Isobel choked—Briony's elbow was jutting painfully into her ribs.

There was a rumbling ahead. The sound of the drawbridge closing.

The sound of Isobel's plan crumbling.

"Is a shit reason to die," Briony finished for her. "There's a Landmark for all of us. Unless you're looking for a fight."

"All of us? But you're not a champion! You shouldn't even be able to be—"

Briony lifted her hand to reveal the glittering ring on her pinky. It fit her perfectly. Of course it did. Briony had always been the perfect champion.

But that was the Briony Thorburn who Isobel once had known. Now, in the harsh red light of the Blood Veil, Briony's skin looked sallow. The bags under her eyes were deep. And every shadow of her face had sharpened into points. She was still wearing her blue party dress, but her high heels were long gone.

She didn't look prepared. She looked desperate.

"Innes asked me to take it," she told her. "I'm stronger and better prepared. I'm the only one who—"

Briony ducked out of the way of some other magick that Isobel couldn't see. After a few moments, the cursefire must've ceased, because Briony shakily got to her feet. Isobel did as well, her pink leggings stained brown. They slipped behind the safety of the treeline, out of the Castle's line of sight.

"What's wrong with you?" Briony demanded. "Are you drunk or something?"

It occurred to Isobel that the danger was far from over. If Briony was now a champion, then the danger was right in front of her. Even if Briony had saved her life a moment ago, Isobel couldn't let her guard down.

"I've never been better," Isobel lied smoothly.

Briony nodded at her, her expression dark. "You've been hit."

Isobel ran her fingers over the stinging on her cheek, and her thumb came back coated in blood. A curse had struck her—but only grazed her, otherwise she'd certainly be feeling the effects by now. But that didn't mean it couldn't kill her, if it was a death curse. Her breath hitched in panic.

Briony's eyes widened. "You can't feel it, can you? You can't even see the cursefire. What happened to you?"

"It doesn't matter," Isobel said tightly.

"Something happened to your powers, didn't it?"

When Isobel didn't answer, Briony pressed further—she was nothing if not persistent.

"How long ago did this happen? Before the tournament? Why would your family let you compete?"

"They don't know," Isobel growled, suddenly reminded that this was the first time that she and Briony had spoken in almost a year. Since Briony had betrayed her. The one silver lining of walking into a massacre had been that she'd never have to talk to Briony again. "And if you're going to kill me, get it over with."

"I'm not going to kill you," Briony snapped. "You're defenseless."

Still suspicious, Isobel did not let her guard down. Not that there was anything she could really do to protect herself if Briony was lying.

"If I were you, I would go to whichever champion cursed you and find a way to undo it," Briony said haughtily.

Isobel wanted to laugh. She'd done this all to herself.

"That's not going to work for me," Isobel told her grimly.

"Then make it work. You're the daughter of a spellmaker, aren't you?"

It was the optimism in Briony's voice—not her words—that gave

Isobel pause. Briony shouldn't hope for Isobel's survival. They weren't any two girls, any two friends. They were two champions.

Just like Briony had always hoped they'd be.

When Isobel didn't have a response, Briony lifted her hand to Isobel's cheek. "At least let me heal you. Even if it only grazed you, it was probably a death curse. And you can't treat it yourself."

So Briony would save her life twice over, and even waste some of her magick to do it. Isobel wasn't used to this kind of charity, especially from her, but it felt foolish not to accept.

"Thank you."

Isobel didn't feel the effects of the spell, no soothing coolness or sting of stitches. But it must've worked, because after a few moments, Briony said, "It's done. But you'll have a scar."

As if Isobel cared about her vanity now.

"You can't do this alone," Briony told her. "You need someone to protect you until you get your magick back. I can do that, for old time's sake. I can be your ally."

Now Isobel did laugh. Oh, those words were rich after everything Briony had put her through. But rather than telling her so, Isobel's thoughts returned to Reid's words. Trying to repeat the recipe for the Reaper's Embrace would be like playing with explosives blindfolded. Reid had also said there was another way, that if someone else cast a Null and Void spell, it would fix her.

But it had to be a spell of a higher class, and no spell crafted from common magick went beyond class ten.

Unless that person used high magick. It would double the spell's power. It would work.

Which meant that Isobel did need an ally. And the more she thought about it, the more she realized who that ally had to be.

And that person wasn't Briony.

"Are you listening?" Briony demanded. "We could—"

"I'm sorry. I need to fix it alone."

Briony's face fell, and Isobel felt a pang of guilt. It was still hard to say no to her. Isobel had always liked Briony's rosy vision of the world, even if she didn't share it.

"Well . . . good luck," Briony said, and it sounded like she meant it. Then she turned and trudged north across the moors.

Isobel remained crouched in the trees, her heart hammering as she settled on her new plan.

The only people in Ilvernath who possessed high magick were the winners of the last tournament, and now that the tournament had begun, Alistair Lowe didn't have any access to it. But he knew more about it than any other champion. If anyone could help her, it was him.

Even if he had every reason to kill her.

She looked up to the scarlet sky. The Cave Landmark was on the opposite side of Ilvernath, isolated and menacing and carved into a mountain. Isobel had only gotten the one glimpse into Alistair's mind, but he seemed the sort of person to lurk in such a place.

And so she made her decision. She would be the princess to walk willingly into the dragon's lair, and she would beg the dragon to save her.

GAVIN GRIEVE

The most popular Landmark has always been the Castle. Claiming it is a valuable intimidation tactic.

A Tradition of Tragedy

The Castle was the largest Landmark in the tournament, with nearly impenetrable defensive enchantments and, more importantly, a significant amount of status attached to it.

And now Gavin Grieve was its king.

This was the first step to winning the tournament. To proving everyone wrong. He had handled the surprise of Briony Thorburn suddenly appearing as champion. He'd defeated Isobel Macaslan in combat. These were not small achievements, and together, they were intoxicating.

No wonder Alistair Lowe was such an arrogant bastard all the time.

Power felt *good*.

Gavin had always wondered how it would feel to claim a Landmark. Now he knew it was like being inside a great, slumbering creature that was slowly waking up. Every moment he spent there attuned him to the building. He could feel the defensive wards activating at the edges of the great stone walls; the drawbridge closing, locking him safely inside. He wouldn't even need the Perilous Pitfall spell to defend him now. If anyone was foolish enough to try to break in, he'd be able to fight them back in an instant.

He whistled a soft, jaunty tune as he explored the Castle room by room. The sound bounced off the lofted ceilings and echoed through the hallways, following him through a swanky bedchamber, a well-stocked kitchen complete with a bunch of survival spellstones and a liquor cabinet, and even a home gym, outfitted with exercise equipment that looked brand new.

It was as if the Landmark had been customized to his exact specifications. High magick was strong enough that perhaps it had been.

In the back of the Castle, behind the grand staircase, was a throne room.

It was elegant and regal—lofted ceilings, a marble tiled floor, and banners that hung beside the darkened windows, each emblazoned with a golden crown. The crown Gavin deserved.

He smiled at the ornate throne in the center of the room.

His throne.

Behind it stood a pillar identical to the one he'd carved his name into earlier that evening. The pillars were the center of every Landmark—the objects that fueled their high magick like giant spellstones. Grinning, Gavin prowled around it like a hyena. On its opposite side, also matching the Champions Pillar, was a symbol: seven stars arranged in a circle. Gavin—like all the other champions—knew the symbol represented the Relics, and he knew which star represented which one. When a Relic was about to fall, its corresponding star would glow red on each of the Landmarks' pillars.

For several minutes Gavin simply stood there, savoring his success. But then he spotted something on the pillar that hadn't been there before. A crack beneath Briony Thorburn's name. It pulsed red with high magick, as though it bled.

Interesting. Perhaps it was there because of her last-minute addition—he'd never heard of a champion taking another's place after their name had been carved into the Pillar.

But he was getting distracted. Even though he'd claimed the Castle, he didn't have time to rest.

The throne room would serve as his base of operations, which meant it was the perfect place to take stock of his weapon situation. He settled himself on the ornate seat and pulled out a pouch of spellstones. Other champions would've entered this tournament with dozens of enchantments; Gavin only had about fifteen viable options, so he needed to keep them charged.

He shook one out into his palm—the Golden Guard. His arm twinged as his life magick collected in his palm, purple and green, before coiling beneath the yellow crystal of the stone. He ignored the pain, placed it in the pocket of his rucksack, and pulled out another stone. Shrouded from Sight was next. Then Hold in Place. The Perilous Pitfall. Somewhere around the fifth stone, he realized he'd pushed himself too far.

He was panting and woozy, his arm ablaze with agony. He tried to stand and stumbled, spellstones scattering everywhere.

The walls darkened around him, and Gavin tumbled off his throne. He blacked out before he even hit the floor.

In his dream, it was two weeks after the Blood Moon, the night he'd formally been named champion. His family had told him over a bland sausage dinner, with the same bored tone they used to discuss the weather.

Later, determined to commemorate the occasion with or without his family, he'd snuck out to a pub downtown, the Magpie, a place where the bartenders didn't care about his last name and he had a high score on the pinball machine.

There had been two boys there that night, one with soft, elegantly sculpted features, the other angular and sallow, like the sun and its shadow had gone out for a drink. He hadn't caught much of their conversation, but he'd heard enough to know who he was eavesdropping on. Even before he saw the picture in the papers the next morning.

Gavin had glared at Alistair Lowe and his brother from the back of the pub and wondered what it would be like to have someone in his life like that. Someone who knew him. Someone who saw him.

Someone who would celebrate when, not if, he came home.

He awoke sprawled out on the floor, the torches lining the walls around him burning low in their sconces.

Gavin groaned and propped himself up on his elbows, his entire body aching.

He could tell from the lack of light streaming in through the windows that the sun had yet to rise. And the careful, steady heartbeat of magick in the room meant his Landmark's wards hadn't been disrupted.

But when Gavin tried to get to his feet, pain surged through his arm, sending him toppling over onto the floor. He lay there, hissing tortured breaths, until he regained his facilities enough to yank up his shirt sleeve.

His tattoo was changing again.

While he'd been unconscious, ink had seeped from the edges of the hourglass in strange, spiraling patterns. His arm throbbed where the purple and green ink bled into skin. Gavin stared at the hourglass, nausea roiling in his stomach. The top was definitely emptier than it had been the last time he'd checked.

Using his body as a vessel was supposed to make him stronger.

"Bastard," he muttered, picturing Reid MacTavish's smug face. "This isn't what I signed up for."

But deep inside, he wondered if he had. After all, he'd agreed to turn himself into a vessel for his own enchantments, even though he knew it would come with a cost.

He groaned and rolled into a fetal position on the throne room's cool marble floor. Everything was terrible, and he was tired.

He saw now how empty all his delusions of grandeur had been. Gavin might've won the Castle, but he was king of nothing at all.

For now.

He pushed himself up on shaking hands. It didn't matter how much pain he was in.

Time to venture out of the Castle and claim his kingdom.

ALISTAIR LOWE

The average length of the tournament is twelve days. The shortest in history lasted forty minutes—that victor was Sylas Lowe.

A Tradition of Tragedy

As Alistair crept through the woods in the dead of night beneath the crimson glow of the Blood Veil, still drunk, he had the strange sense that he was dreaming. He'd traversed these paths in his reveries, his dark hair tangled with leaves and bramble, his eyes glowing through the forest like a nocturnal creature. But it wasn't the trees or the cricket chirps or the scent of damp earth that gave him this feeling.

It was the fear.

Grins like goblins. Alistair's breath hitched as he spotted an unusual curl of branches on the oak in front of him. He wrapped his cardigan tighter around himself and shivered.

Pale as plague. He stepped over the narrow trickling of a creek.

Silent as spirits. He sped up his pace.

They'll tear your throat and drink your soul.

Those last words he heard in his mother's voice. As children, Alistair and Hendry had huddled by the fireplace in the living room, wrapped in their dead father's too-big flannels and listening to her stories. Back then, their mother's mood swings had been sharper, her laughs louder, her smile warmer, her cries shriller. Like Hendry, she felt everything fiercely and all at once.

But her favorite emotion was fear.

"You were both born in July, one year apart," she'd whispered. "We always left the windows open in the summer. Sometimes I wonder if that was a mistake." She'd lurched forward and grabbed Alistair by his scrawny shoulders. Even at that age, they knew he'd be their champion. And so every new haunting tale was a lesson. "Sometimes I wonder if the monsters stole one of my children away from me in the night, and his soul still haunts these forests. Sometimes . . ." She looked out the window thoughtfully. "I still hear a baby crying when I walk through those trees."

At seven years old, Alistair had been more afraid of the story than he should've been. "What if they did? What if one of us *is* a monster?" Of course, Hendry wasn't a monster. He'd always been asking about himself.

His mother had cackled. "Then one night, the monsters will return to claim you. They'll feed the human bits of your soul to the earth and drag you into their caves."

Even after the story, when she'd assured both her sons she'd only been joking, Alistair hadn't been able to shake the suspicion that he didn't belong. That one night, the monsters he feared would steal him away from his brother.

Don't be scared, he told himself in the dream. *You are one of them.*

Don't be scared, Alistair told himself in real life, walking through the woods the first night of the tournament. *What else could they take from you?*

He pulled the map out of his pocket and traced his steps. He'd selected a Landmark along the western boundary of Ilvernath—the Cave, tucked into the mountain peak that overlooked the city. It was a strong Landmark with decent defensive enchantments, but Alistair didn't care about such things. The Cave simply reminded him of a dragon's lair, and of all monsters, dragons had always been his favorite.

Soon, the incline grew steeper. The trees grew sparser. The air, thinner. As he finally left the forest behind, he let out a shaky breath of relief. He would not be claimed tonight.

A branch snapped behind him, and he whipped around, light glowing in his spellring as he summoned the Warrior's Helm. A shield surrounded him, clear but murky, like the surface of a lake. He peered through at the three figures who emerged from the darkness.

The Blair, wearing a polo shirt.

The Payne, wearing a large pair of combat boots and a bloodred grin the same color as the sky above them.

And a few steps behind them, the Darrow. Alistair couldn't see much of him besides his blond curls.

If Alistair had been of sounder mind, he would know that three champions were far more fearsome and rational than three monsters, but still, he was relieved to find their faces human. In this scenario, Alistair was the beast. Better to play a villain than a victim.

The Payne smirked. "I see you've sobered up."

"Unfortunately," he replied, though he still wasn't positive he had. "Have you come looking for a battle?"

During the last tournament, his Aunt Alphina had won in only four days. Alistair had been compared to her all his childhood, so he assumed himself equally capable. Still, the prospect of fighting three champions at once seemed risky, even for him. Nor was it his style. Unlike the Blair, he was not a chivalrous knight collecting glory on the battlefield. He was a dagger in the darkness, quiet blood spilled on nightclothes, a scream that died in your throat.

"Quite the opposite," the Blair answered. "As you can see, the three of us are working together—"

"For now," Alistair purred.

The Darrow and the Payne exchanged wary glances. Whatever reason they were here, it was clearly the Blair's idea.

"We're here to invite you to join us," the Blair said. "The Lowes and Blairs have allied in the past."

Yes, maybe once, four hundred years ago, Alistair thought.

"The Macaslan and Thorburn girls will ally together," the Darrow said with confidence. "Isobel knows Innes. She was friends with her sister."

Even if what they said *was* true, it did little to sway him. "So you're hoping for a team of four to take out . . . a single pair of champions."

He didn't know a lot about the other champions, but he did know this much—apart from him, the Macaslan was the most powerful competitor in the tournament. These champions only stood a chance four against two.

"This doesn't have to be messy," the Blair said.

Alistair rolled his eyes. Only a Blair would try to find honor in the twisted nature of the tournament. No code or rules applied now. "Why me? Shouldn't you be begging the Grieve? He seems desperate enough to agree."

The Payne raised her chin. "We're not looking for deadweight."

Alistair remembered the shattered glass earlier that night. The spell had been a blur, cast before Alistair had an opportunity to protect himself. Granted, he'd been drunk, but it still had taken skill. There was more to the Grieve champion than this town had chosen to see. Though, admittedly, Alistair had forgotten his name, too.

"I'm not interested," Alistair said. His voice slurred slightly.

"You should be," the Blair said. "We might not have the same reputation as you, but we have spells and curses that you don't, and we'd be willing to share."

"And wouldn't you worry I'd just murder you all in your sleep?" Alistair cocked his head to the side, flashing his best dragon smile. "Or were you hoping to do the same to me? Catch me when my guard is down?"

"There's no trick here, you have my word," the Blair assured him, and Alistair didn't like the tight, careful way he spoke, as though his words were a snare. The Blair made a piss-poor liar.

"I'm. Not. Interested," Alistair repeated.

The Darrow raised his hands. The Blair clenched his fist of spellrings. The Payne reached her hand forward, her jewelry glowing brighter.

"If you're not our friend, you're an enemy," the Blair warned.

"That's how I know you're full of shit. There are no friends here. Only people you kill now, and people you kill later."

Alistair still had a fair climb between him and his Landmark. Not that he had any desire to flee. He summoned the magick from one of his cursestones, and soon the air tasted of smoke.

An enchantment, white and smoldering, whizzed past him. It was a death curse of some sort, so bright it was blinding. Alistair momentarily lost his balance and stumbled back.

The Blair howled a battle cry and charged forward, and Alistair added more power to the Warrior's Helm. But within moments, his shield cracked. It wasn't the result of any curse flung at it, or his three shots of whisky. It had broken on its own, like flimsy tissue paper acting as glass.

A broken spell? Alistair thought. No, professional spellmakers didn't make mistakes like that. This could only have been sabotage. His grandmother had demanded all of Alistair's tournament enchantments from the spellmakers in town and they couldn't refuse, so this was their act of rebellion.

Suddenly, a phantom pain shot across Alistair's shoulder, extending down across his heart. He could feel his skin tearing from a curse. It wasn't a fatal wound, but he did cry out. He couldn't even tell which of them had cast it.

The Grieve wasn't the only champion Alistair had underestimated. The three of them possessed powerful curses. Alistair needed to counterattack—but how many of his had been tampered with? They could be worthless, like the shield. Or worse, they could backfire.

But he had no choice.

He squeezed his hand into a fist, channeling the magick within the ring on his third finger for the Dragon's Breath. Then he raised his fingertips to his lips, and blew. An eruption of fire burst from his mouth, as menacing and scorching as true dragon breath. The air filled with heat and smoke and crackling. Alistair stood before the wall of fire that separated him from his competitors, wondering whether to attack or retreat. Even when they launched a dowsing spell, the flames never extinguished. If anything, they continued to grow, hungry and wanting.

Alistair walked into the flames, and they parted for him and trailed at his feet like a cloak. His fingers were poised over a new curse-ring that stored the Winter's Scorch, and he licked his lips. Lethal magick surged inside him, writhing and slimy as leeches. He could almost feel teeth grazing his skin from the inside, looking to suck spirit from flesh.

The dowsing spell stopped at once, but Alistair hadn't finished casting the curse. It struggled inside him, wanting to escape. But as he stepped past the fire and into the clearing, he saw that he was alone. The others had already fled, perhaps using Here to There spells.

Unable to contain it any longer, Alistair lifted his hand and let the curse free. It spewed through the air, gray as ash, in coils and wisps through the wind. It rushed through the forest, and the trees—in only a span of moments—withered and shrank. The moisture from their trunks seeped into the earth, and they twisted like burnt pa-per. Their leaves turned brown and dropped onto the grass below. The crows within them cawed and took to the sky, leaving the ruin behind.

As he'd feared, a piece of the curse remained inside him, and Alistair groaned from a terrible pain in his stomach. A well-crafted curse wasn't supposed to have a rebound, but clearly the spellmakers had laced all of their gifts with such traps, despite his grandmother's certainty that their fear had kept them in line.

How many of his enchantments were compromised? A few of them?

All of them?

He couldn't depend on any of the spells he possessed. He would need to make his own. All the other champions had begun the night loaded with protection, weapons, and survival spells, but he was empty-handed.

Vulnerable.

After his pain lessened, Alistair wiped the spit on his lips away with his sleeve. He turned around, snapped his fingers, and the flames vanished. The night was quiet and dark once more, and he trudged his way up the mountain, to a dragon's lair to call his own.

BRIONY THORBURN

Loyalty is meaningless in the context of the tournament. But that never seems to stop people from forming alliances to prolong the inevitable.

A Tradition of Tragedy

While alone on the open moors, Briony tilted her head back just as a crimson shooting star blazed a course across the moon. A Relic was falling, quicker than she'd ever heard of. It'd been barely an hour since the tournament began, and already, one of its powerful magickal artifacts would be in play.

She had to have it.

Between her confrontation with Innes and Gavin's cursefire, nearly all of her protective spellrings were drained, leaving her effectively defenseless. She hadn't brought any supplies with her—she hadn't had the chance after she took the champion's ring. No clothes but the ones on her back. No food. No extra magick. No shoes aside from the heels she'd abandoned.

A Relic could save her life. Not only that, but claiming it would be the first step toward testing Reid's theory about using Landmarks and Relics to dismantle the tournament's curse, if only she could figure out how. She hadn't told Isobel about her plans because she'd known her old friend wouldn't believe her without proof—none of the champions would.

She twisted the champion's ring on her pinky finger. Guilt rushed through her at the thought of what she'd done to her sister, but she shoved it down as far as she could. It was done now. She was champion. And she needed to act like one if she wanted to survive the night.

The streak of crimson was truly falling now, heading deeper into the moorlands.

Briony bolted toward it, sprinting through the underbrush as fast as she could in a ripped gown and bare feet. She was running on too much adrenaline to care about any pain.

The terrain turned unpredictable, clumps of heather disguising loose earth and stones. She was on the true moorlands now, where they'd burned the terrain back hundreds of years ago to make hunting and foraging easier. The landscape that had sprung up since was partially heathlands and partially bog, a wide-open space perfect for tracking animals . . . or other champions.

The Relic crashed right in the center of it all, red light rippling outward in a neat circle. The force of its impact made Briony stumble back, squinting into a sudden flash of crimson. But she wouldn't be deterred. Wildlife fled in all directions, squealing, as Briony sprinted the remaining distance to the artifact.

The Relic had cleaved a small crater into the earth about three meters wide. It lay in the center, glimmering, a massive weapon of enchanted steel.

The Sword.

Briony's skin prickled as she stared at the three red spellstones embedded in the hilt. The Relic looked magnificent, like a prop right out of her family's stories.

Triumphantly, she reached forward to claim it.

But then a voice barked out, "Not so fast."

A clump of heather rustled across the crater. Finley emerged from the darkness, illuminated by the red light that radiated from the Relic.

He froze at the sight of her, the shock on his face so strong that it seemed to impede even his breathing. "Briony?" he choked. "How are you here?"

"Innes didn't want this." She needed to believe that wasn't a lie.

She raised her hand as if holding up a palm in surrender so that he could see the champion's ring, gleaming in the crimson light.

"This isn't possible," he rasped.

"Admit it. You were surprised when I wasn't champion."

"I was . . . I thought . . ." Finley had always been the sort to choose his words carefully, but all he managed was to take in a shaky breath and mold his face back into neutrality.

Briony had known the others would be surprised to see her, but this ran deeper than even Isobel's shock had. He looked rattled in a way she'd never seen before. And maybe that was good. Maybe that meant she could grab the Relic and get out of here.

Briony's throat tightened as she remembered that, unlike her, Finley came with backup.

"Where are your friends?" she asked, glancing over her shoulder.

Finley hesitated. "They're around." Which was enough for Briony to know they weren't exactly within shouting distance.

"So you came here alone." She stepped forward and squared her shoulders. Maybe bravado would be enough to make him back off. "Do you really want to fight me for the Sword?"

He scanned her up and down, and Briony knew what he was seeing—the ruined dress, her bare feet. "Do *you*?"

Now it was Briony's turn to hesitate. She'd let Isobel go back at the Castle, and she didn't want to hurt Finley, either. She'd entered this tournament to destroy it. So that no one else would have to die.

An idea dawned on her: foolish and dangerous, but far more appealing to her than either of them dying here. Surrendering the Relic would mean giving up this chance to prove her theory, but it might lead to more, better chances. If it worked, she would have not one other champion to sway to her cause, but three: Finley, Carbry, and Elionor. And unlike Isobel, they all could use magick.

Plus, there was history between her and Finley. That had to count for something.

"We *could* fight," Briony said slowly. "But I'd rather make a deal."

Finley's eyes narrowed, but he didn't immediately shut her down. Briony decided to consider that a victory. "What kind of deal?"

"I'll let you have the Sword. But you have to do something for me in return."

He weighed her words in silence for some time. Knowing Finley, he had entered the tournament with a detailed strategy—one that she *knew* included the Sword. But it didn't include her. And flexibility had never been Finley's strong suit.

"What do you want?" he asked suspiciously.

"I want to join your alliance."

"Why? Your sister turned us down."

"I'm not my sister," said Briony, trying not to wonder how Innes was doing, if Innes was safe.

"How do you know I won't just turn on you once I have the Sword?"

"I trust you." Briony thought back to their breakup. How much it still haunted her. Surely it haunted him, too. "You always keep your word. And I don't think you actually want to kill me."

Finley stared at her across the crater, the moors around them silent and waiting, the Blood Veil a rusty stain across the sky above. His spellrings glowed with power, but he didn't cast anything. He was still enough to be made of stone.

"Fine," he muttered, after what felt like an eternity. "I give you my word."

Briony sagged with relief. "Really?"

"If you let me have the Relic, I'll take you back to our Landmark. But I can't guarantee they'll let you stay."

It was a dangerous gamble, but it was the best she could hope for.

"All right," she said, backing away.

The moment Finley touched the hilt, the red light that shone from the spellstones embedded in the blade swirled around him, then sank into his skin. Finley raised the Sword with a triumphant smile, and

Briony's first thought was that Finley looked complete holding it, as though it was made for him.

Her second thought, as he turned toward her, was how defenseless she truly was now.

"I remember what I said when we broke up," he told her, holding his weapon high. "But I want you to know that I've changed my mind."

Briony's heart stuttered with fear. She backed away from him, cursing herself for relying on old feelings and misplaced trust.

But then Finley grinned, teeth stained crimson in the light emanating from the blade, and gestured outward to the moors.

"Now let's get going."

Briony thought about fleeing, but she had nowhere else to go. And as Finley led them through the darkness, Briony hoped that she was not a fool to follow him.

The Monastery was perched very close to the edge of the Blood Veil. During the tournament, its ruins transformed into a building of crumbled stone that looked more dilapidated than grand, even with the power of high magick coursing through it. It had been built on what was now a blanket bog, and over the centuries the building had sunk unevenly into the unstable, loamy ground beneath it. It was one of the largest Landmarks, with reasonable defensive properties, and it was the place Finley, Elionor, and Carbry had chosen as their fortress for the tournament.

Although monks had not lived there since before the first tournament transformed the Landmarks from ordinary buildings to constructions of high magick, traces of their presence remained—in the well-kept gardens out front, in the statues and fountains in the courtyard, and in the small, plain bedrooms that they had built for themselves, slotted into the walls of the building like tiny cells.

It was in one such bedroom that Briony now found herself, stripped of all her spellrings, totally defenseless as Elionor, Carbry, and Finley argued over her fate.

Briony had expected this argument, but she wasn't prepared for how long it would take: until the morning light streamed through the grimy windows. The lapsed time made fear flare in her like a well-kindled flame, fueled by far too many dangerous thoughts.

That she'd made the wrong decision, not just to trust Finley, but to enter the tournament at all. That if she died here, she would die a traitor to her family. To her sister.

"We can't trust her," Elionor complained. "She's your ex-girlfriend. She has better reason to want you dead than anyone."

"I'm right *here*." Briony was sitting on a harsh slab of stone the monks had apparently used as a bed, her back pressed against the wall. She'd hardly gotten any sleep, her head hurt, and her bare feet were disgusting. She was dying for a glass of water and a change of clothes. She was also resentful at the implication that she was a bitter ex-girlfriend—she'd never even tried to curse Finley after they broke up. "I let you imprison me. I surrendered my spellrings willingly. What more do you want me to do? Swear a Solemn Vow?"

"That wouldn't even work," Elionor said disdainfully. "The Cloak nullifies all oath spells—alliances can't rely on them."

"Well, fine," Briony grumbled. "Do you want me to beg? Plead?"

Even dehydrated, exhausted, and aching, she wasn't that desperate. Not yet.

"It would be a good start." The spellstones in Elionor's stretched-out earlobes shone threateningly, charged and ready.

They could suspect her all they liked. Her motives were pure. She wasn't just here to save her own skin; she was here to save them all. But she knew how ridiculous that sounded. Like the words of a desperate prisoner. Even if her intentions were good, even if her story was true, the truth wasn't how she would earn their trust.

She could worry about saving them all once she'd saved herself.

"Now wait a moment," said Finley sternly, looking between the two of them with moderate alarm. Since returning here, he had strapped the Sword across his back. "Briony's telling the truth. She let me have the Relic. She came here of her own volition."

"And you never asked her *why*," said Elionor, scowling at him. Briony tried not to be affronted at her tone. "It was your idea for us to throw ourselves at everyone in this tournament, asking for their help, and now someone who wasn't *in* the tournament twelve hours ago is claiming they want to join us?"

Finley sounded calm, controlled. "You and Carbry signed on to *my* plan. Briony joining us doesn't change our strategy."

"We're still supposed to be a team, Finley. You never should've brought her here without asking us first. You let your desperation for the Sword cloud your head—you chose yourself over our alliance."

Briony heard the doubt in Elionor's voice. It worried her more than the girl's anger did. If she broke up the alliance entirely, this could all go horribly wrong.

Finley sighed and rubbed his temples, then gestured toward the door. "Let's talk about this outside, okay? Just you and me."

Elionor's mouth twisted, but she nodded. They disappeared through the exit, leaving Briony and Carbry alone.

She met the other champion's watery blue eyes.

"When did you all decide to team up?" Briony asked, her voice raspy from thirst. Maybe if she could charm him, he would give her something to drink.

Carbry's tone was soft and reedy. "After Finley was chosen. He called me and Elionor that morning and asked us to join him." Briony already knew that Finley had engineered their group, but his choice of allies still struck her as strange. "You look surprised," Carbry accused.

"None of you have much in common."

"Which makes us stronger together. That's what Finley said. That my family's knowledge, his casting, and Elionor's crafting abilities would be hard to beat." He gave her a look that Briony understood. Where did she fit in with this group?

She was a strong caster, but they already had Finley for that. Which made his reasons for agreeing to her terms even more suspicious. She thought about what he'd said about changing his mind and tried to suppress a shudder.

"I'd make you stronger," she said finally, hoping her voice sounded more confident than she felt.

"Maybe. But it's also a numbers game." Carbry fidgeted uncomfortably, playing with a surprisingly fancy-looking spellring on his left forefinger. Briony hadn't realized the Darrows, a family of modest means and influence, could secure that level of spellmaker sponsorship. "Alliances of more than three are historically quite risky. I told Finley this before, when he was seeking others out—four or more makes it hard to work together for very long. I could only find a few accounts of such alliances proving fruitful."

"Accounts?" Briony echoed. He sounded like Innes. "You did your research, huh?"

"Well, yes. My family has a library filled with the winners' records of their tournaments."

"And you've read them all?"

"Of course."

"That's very impressive." Briony understood now what he'd meant by knowledge. "I bet you know everything about this tournament."

Carbry's chest puffed up a little. He looked far more confident than he had a few moments ago, his round cheeks flushed with pride. Briony wondered if anyone had ever given him a compliment before.

"If that's what all your books say, then why did you ask my sister?" Briony asked.

"That was Finley's idea, not ours."

Briony had no doubt that Finley did have a grand plan here, but she still couldn't put the pieces together. "And you just go along with his ideas?"

"It's my best chance," Carbry said solemnly. "The Darrows have only won the tournament a handful of times, and I could tell, saying goodbye to everyone last night, that they don't expect me to come back. Elionor pretends to be confident, but the Paynes don't have the greatest track record, either. It must be nice to come from a family who make your chances of winning better, not worse."

The stark honesty in his voice struck Briony hard. It reminded her of the way Isobel had always talked about her family, done everything she could to distance herself from their reputation.

She didn't blame Carbry for being frightened about what could befall him beneath the Blood Veil. But if she could end this tournament peacefully, Carbry *could* go home. They all could. And her own fear aside—that was worth fighting for.

"It's not fair," she said quietly. "Nothing about this tournament is."

"Unless you're a Lowe," Carbry grumbled.

"If you're a Lowe, it's just unfair in your favor."

Briony was uncertain how Alistair Lowe factored into her plans. She wanted to save as many people as possible, but she wasn't sure the Lowe champion would want the tournament ended. Not when his family had benefited the most from it for so many years. If nothing else, *A Tradition of Tragedy* had shown her just how much the Lowes had gained through their repeated wins.

"It doesn't have to go the way it always has," she continued, feeling emboldened. "The Lowes don't have to walk away with the prize. We could change that."

"By killing the Lowe, you mean?" Carbry sighed. "He's probably holed up somewhere, whispering sweet nothings to his death curses. We can't compete with him."

We might not have to. The words were on the tip of Briony's tongue. Carbry was clearly disillusioned by all this—maybe she could say something to him. Set him on the same path she was on.

But before she could speak, a noise rang out through the room, sharp and blaring—a tripped defense ward. Carbry rushed to the window and gazed out at the courtyard, his outstretched hand glimmering with magick.

"What is it?" Briony asked, hurrying behind him.

"Someone's come for us." Carbry's voice was hollow with fear. "The Monastery is under attack."

ALISTAIR LOWE

There's a rumor that the Lowe champions often go mad after they win. Maybe it's not the weight of their conscience—maybe it's the weight of a secret.

A Tradition of Tragedy

Alistair Lowe was brooding.

He lay in a mahogany four-poster bed, surrounded by crystals collected from spellmakers all over town. He held a particular teardrop stone up to the dim candlelight and examined it. The death curse inside from Reid MacTavish was one of the most powerful weapons he'd received, but he couldn't trust that the cursemaker hadn't tampered with it. All this magick, and he couldn't trust *any of it*.

He groaned and threw it across the room. It clunked against the damp stone walls of the Cave.

Alistair was far superior at *casting* spells than crafting them. After botching the Vintner's Plague a week ago for his grandmother, he didn't trust himself to meddle with the stone in case he accidentally blew himself up in the progress. All that effort and intimidation to amass this deadly trove, and now he lay upon it bitterly, a dragon hoarding its worthless treasure.

Of course, the collection contained a prized piece—the Lowe family's signature curse, the Lamb's Sacrifice. Not only did it annihilate anyone in close proximity, but it sucked the magick out of their bodies, leaving a withered, gray corpse and a fortune in raw magick behind. It could penetrate any common magick shield through class ten. It wasn't a guarantee—after all, one third of the Lowe champions still perished—but it was almost invincible.

But Alistair would never use it. The idea of Hendry's life magick annihilating another's . . . in some ways, it felt more despicable than Hendry's death. When Alistair pictured his brother, he thought of his dark curls, his sun-kissed complexion, how he smelled of sweets— and the Lowes had burned his body and forged a weapon from the ash. Just as they had done to Alistair his entire life.

Even if all six of the other champions allied against him, Alistair would still emerge victorious . . . and he would do it without using his brother's curse.

The enchantments of the Cave Landmark hummed, its iron candelabras rattling, its spiderwebs trilling like violin strings. Someone was outside, approaching the defensive spells.

Ignoring his mild hangover, Alistair shot out of bed and raced down the cavernous halls, an assortment of cursestones clutched in his fist. Perhaps he was right, and the other champions had come to slay him. He took a deep breath, sucking in all of the past two days of anger and grief, preparing for whatever new horror was coming his way.

He crept toward the mouth of the cavern, barely breathing. It was still nighttime outside and drizzling, the air smelling of wet earth, the red moonlight making the puddles look like blood.

"Hello?" a female voice called.

If this *was* a band of champions here to kill him, Alistair somehow doubted their battle cry would be a frazzled "hello." But he also wasn't the best at reading people.

He cleared his throat. "Um . . . who goes there?"

Those are some shitty last words, he scolded himself.

"I want to talk," the intruder said. Whoever they were, they were clever enough to see through the Landmark's enchantments. That was the Cave's unique power—it cloaked the location from prying eyes and made its entrance near impossible to find.

"Who is it?" he asked.

"Isobel Macaslan."

Isobel might've been powerful, but even for her, venturing to his lair alone was a deadly move. He had nine death curses on him, and countless more waiting in reserve.

"I'm unarmed," Isobel said. "I didn't come looking for a fight."

"Last time we spoke, you called me 'arrogant,' 'self-destructive,' and 'a waste of magick.' Forgive me if I'm not convinced."

A pause. He wondered if he'd actually frightened *I-have-nothing-to-fear-from-you* Isobel Macaslan, but then he felt the hum of the Landmark's protective enchantment grow stronger, the very earth quaking beneath his trainers. She was walking toward the mouth of the Cave.

"Get back," he warned.

"Or what?"

Alistair squeezed his cursestones tighter. He was already nauseous, and he didn't want to use them for fear of blowback. But he might not have a choice. "Or you won't take another step."

"I told you I'm unarmed," she said, then her voice rose higher, almost cracking. "*Please.*"

Alistair might not know Isobel well, but somehow he knew she didn't plead very often. He left his hiding spot and stood at the Cave's entrance—exposed, vulnerable. Oh, how his grandmother would curse his name if Alistair was slain by another champion just because he thought she was pretty.

Isobel was standing in the rain, shivering, her pink tracksuit drenched through and clinging to her skin. She hadn't even used a cheap Waterproof spell to keep herself from getting wet. Her red curls were plastered to her face and neck, and she hugged her arms to herself.

"What are you doing?" he asked, genuinely surprised. Maybe this *was* some sort of trick. Earlier that night when she'd flirted with him, she'd proven she had more tools at her disposal than simply magick. She could be trying to get in his head.

"I need your help," she said.

"Do I strike you as a generous person?"

"No, but I've seen in your head and I don't *think* you're so twisted that you'd kill an unarmed girl."

He scoffed. "You're not a girl; you're an opponent."

But the more he looked at her, the more he wondered how true that was. A cursemark scar was slashed across her left cheek, a thin line that hadn't been there at the banquet. Her lip gloss couldn't hide the chapped skin beneath it; her clothes were stained with mud.

She looked terrible, but terrible on her still looked pretty good.

Alistair flexed his fingers, readying to cast a curse, but his mouth went dry.

Hendry's voice filled his mind. *You should hear her out,* Alistair imagined he'd say. It left a sick feeling in Alistair's stomach that the only thing he had left of his brother was a cursed ring and a flimsy conscience.

He scowled and lowered the defenses of the Landmark, but threw up a fragmented Warrior's Helm to shield himself—he might be soft, but he wasn't foolish.

Isobel continued to stand outside in the rain, waiting, though the Cave's barriers had clearly fallen.

"Well, come on," he snapped.

She blinked in surprise and hurried in after him. Disheveled as she was, she still had a confidence in her walk that no rain or curse could take away.

"I don't have all day," he said in a low voice.

She wrung out her red hair, glaring at him. "I'm sorry. Were you busy plotting someone else's demise?"

"Careful. I could've been plotting *your* demise," he muttered. "I still might be." As soon as she stepped toward him, he lifted his hand, brandishing his fistful of cursestones. "In fact, you have ten seconds to explain to me why I shouldn't end you right now, *rival*."

She paled. "I think we could help each other."

"Champions standing outside my door in the rain, desperate and alone, don't seem like they could offer me anything."

"That. . . . that isn't true," she huffed.

They walked deeper into the tunnel, where it opened into the Cave's central room. It was sparsely furnished and smelled strongly of mud. The muted, flickering candlelight made the stalactites of the cavern's walls look like fangs. To the right, another hallway that Alistair had explored earlier led to a massive grotto, where the Landmark's stone pillar—less impressive and more cracked than the original—jutted out from the black lake water.

Alistair nodded for Isobel to sit at the desk.

Isobel examined the barren decor with amusement. "Do you feel like a proper monster now?" She ran her manicured fingers across the coarse, glistening stone of the Cave's walls, its edges sharp enough to cut. "Surrounded by darkness and filth?"

That seemed unfair—the claw-foot furniture and ruby velvet duvet were just to his taste.

"Yes, yes, you peered into my head," Alistair grumbled. "You must be so smug! You know everything there is to know about me! That explains why you're sitting here, entirely at my mercy." For effect, he cast a Scythe's Fall. One of the stalactites behind her cracked and fell to the ground like a guillotine's blade.

It was a foolish move to cast it. The curse's blowback knocked him painfully in the stomach, and he groaned and blinked back startled tears.

Isobel yelped as the stalactite crashed beside her feet, but rather than cower away, she watched him in confusion. "Did you just hurt yourself?"

He scowled and straightened. "A shoddy curse, that's all."

But Isobel's eyes widened. "You got your spells from all the best spellmakers in town. They wouldn't sell you faulty work by accident. . . . They must've wanted you to fail."

Alistair cursed under his breath. He couldn't let any of the other champions learn he'd been sabotaged. Which meant Isobel couldn't walk out of here alive.

Which left him in the unfortunate predicament of figuring out how to kill her without accidentally killing himself.

"Seems like I'm not the only one who needs help," she told him.

"I don't need anything," he drawled, his mind racing to come up with a solution. His gaze fell to her neck. A magickless murder, he considered. But he was hungover. And he wasn't very strong.

"But you have nothing but broken spells. And you're alone." Her words sounded more like a question than a statement.

He laughed bitterly. "I'm not tempted by companionship."

She picked up something from the floor—the teardrop cursestone he'd thrown earlier. "You know, the Macaslans and the Lowes aren't that different. I didn't have spellmakers lining up to ally with me, either."

"I don't care about a popularity contest."

"I'm not talking about popularity." She stood up from the desk, still clutching the cursestone. It was a dangerous play, and Alistair kept his hand raised, prepared to fire back at any moment. "My mother is one of the spellmakers who gave you these stones. One of the best in the town. I was trained by her *and* the Macaslans. And it seems to me that, more than anything, you need a spellmaker on your side."

This *was* Alistair's weakness, and if he didn't find a solution, soon every champion would learn of it. Every champion would try to use it against him.

The Payne, Blair, and Darrow had needed a protector. But Isobel didn't. What would she gain from this alliance?

He sent out a simple Testing the Waters, meant to assess the power of an opponent's magickal arsenal, harmless enough that he needn't worry about blowback. It roamed over Isobel's body, searching for concealed spellstones but finding none. Searching for *any* spellstones but finding none, except in the duffel bag she carried.

Any other champion would deflect such a simple spell, but Isobel gave no indication she'd even noticed it.

He took a step closer—close enough to reach for her. He cast another harmless spell: a Trick of the Light, a low-class illusion spell. A brown spider the size of an apple scurried up Isobel's mud-soaked clothes. But she didn't react, not even as it stroked a hairy leg from her lips to her chin. She didn't even blink.

"You've lost your sense for magick." Alistair let the illusion of the spider dissipate and flashed his best, wickedest smile. All of those insults she'd flung at him before, and now she truly was powerless. It must've been quite a blow to her pride to come here.

She lifted her chin higher, looking down on him even though they stood eye to eye. "Only you can help me get it back."

He was prepared to laugh—cackle, even—when her expression softened. "We could help each other," she said gently. Her tone infuriated him, the way the coldness of the Cave suddenly went warm and pleasant and *suffocating*. She was the powerless one. Not him.

His gaze found the sharpest point in the cavern wall. He could push her onto it. He knew he could.

"And if you do get it back," he snapped, "then all I'll have done is equip you in a battle where I'm the enemy."

"You've *always* been the enemy. You still are, even now." Isobel took a step back from him, as if reminded of that fact. "But with my help, you wouldn't need to lurk in your Cave, wondering who or how many had shown up to attack you. With my help, you wouldn't need to worry that every curse you cast will kill you."

"And you'll, what, stay here with me until you've either regained your sense for magick or died?" He was acquiescing—not just because of her convincing case, but because, no matter how much he tried to stoke his fury, he didn't have it in him to kill her. Not like this. "If we leave here, I'm not protecting you."

"Who said anything about leaving? It will take high magick to bring my powers back, and you're the only champion with the expertise. If you can fix my powers, then I promise you that I will, to the best of my ability, help you craft all the new weapons you need to win. And then . . ." She took a step closer again. Unlike at the banquet earlier that night, Alistair was no longer drunk, but her closeness still made him feel light-headed. He got the feeling she knew that. "When we're equal again, we can have a duel like proper rivals. The victor takes the glory, the loser dies. The sort right out of your monster stories."

She was winning him over. Maybe because she'd peered inside his head and knew how to persuade him. Maybe her clever dark eyes were persuasion enough.

"Just remember," he said, as much to himself as to her. "In those stories, the monster always wins."

ISOBEL MACASLAN

I believe the legends that magick comes from the stars, not just
for how it looks, but because of how it rejects the earth, how the
only way to capture it is a glass flask, a crystal stone. Even magick
behaves with reason.

A Tradition of Tragedy

listair had refused to answer her questions about high magick
until he had at least crafted new defensive spells, in case of
attack. And so, as the first night in Alistair's lair crept into
morning, Isobel showed Alistair how to safely dispose of a spellstone's
contents without hurting himself.

"You can't just empty the magick out if the spell is contaminated,"
Isobel told him. "You need to bury the stones. It'll cancel out the recipe entirely." It was no different from how raw magick dispersed
from a body at a funeral.

For two hours they both sat on uncomfortable ground at opposite
corners of the Cave. Alistair was hunched over, digging holes with
the handle of Isobel's hairbrush and heaping his sabotaged spell- and
cursestones inside. Though Isobel couldn't see it, she knew what the
process entailed—glittery common magick would burst from the
earth as though repelled. And it must've been working, since Alistair
kept swatting at invisible magick particles in the air, muttering angrily, and storing them in empty flasks.

The common magick wasn't the only thing Isobel couldn't see.
The Landmark itself looked no different to her than it had before the

Blood Veil fell. Its furniture was rotten and decrepit, and everything was coated in a filthy layer of dust. But knowing Alistair's taste, Isobel suspected the true version of the Cave looked no different.

While Alistair worked, Isobel clutched the torn page from Reid MacTavish's grimoire, reading out loud.

"*The Reaper's Embrace is an ancient curse, made famous by stories that have, over time, distorted its true nature—*"

"Have you ever crafted a curse?" Alistair interrupted her. He got up and stood over the bed, rubbing the dirt off his refilled curse- and spellstones and tossing them into various piles. From the hyper-practiced way he carried himself, Isobel would've assumed him a tidy person, but he left a mess behind him wherever he walked. He'd eaten two of her protein bars and thrown the wrappers on the desk. The blazer he'd worn at the banquet was discarded on the floor, still reeking of liquor.

"Of course I've crafted a curse," she snapped. "Even if it's not my mother's specialty, I'm a trained spellmaker. I've learned far more than what they teach you in school."

Plus, Isobel had heard the story of the botched curse Alistair had cast on that spellmaker, so she'd hardly be taking cursemaking advice from *him*.

"I don't pretend to be an expert." Alistair set his backpack down on the desk chair and walked over to her. He snatched the paper out of her hands. "I'm no good at . . ." He gestured vaguely at the recipe.

"Directions?"

"Sure, but I was taught by the best. I'm sure you're familiar with my grandmother's reputation."

"Of course I am."

Marianne Lowe's high magick curses were the stuff of nightmares. Even with the government watching over her shoulder, the threat of Marianne's wrath was enough to keep every spellmaker in town paying the Lowes tribute.

Although after what Alistair had done to Bayard Attwater, Isobel wasn't so sure that was true. She shuddered and tried not to think too hard about who she'd made this bargain with.

"According to her, curses aren't magick's natural state. You need to twist the power into that shape, and it will do everything it can to resist you. So you have to *mean* them. Death curses especially. If your command is weak, the curse won't work—or worse." He gave her a pointed look.

Isobel nearly rolled her eyes. *Meaning* a curse was pointless. The sort of idea a villain would fancy. Crafting enchantments was a neutral art.

But she wouldn't tell him that. She was completely powerless in the lair of the tournament's most infamous champion, alive based only on his mood swings. Survival meant swallowing her insults and forcing a smile.

"Maybe you can help, then," she said, as though she'd offered him the page he'd grabbed from her.

He scoffed. "I can't teach you how to be wicked."

He was being serious, but the words made Isobel laugh. There was a dirty joke to be found there, and she thought of the way Alistair had looked at her the night they'd met in that pub and she'd gotten a peek into his mind. And standing there, dressed in cable knits like he was visiting the library rather than competing in their bloody tournament, his features sharp in the flickering candlelight, he did look attractive.

She immediately cast the thought away. If Alistair knew any telepathic spells, then she would be an open book right now. It was an intrusive thought—nothing more.

"I think my mistake had to do with the sacrifice," she said quickly. "I didn't give the curse enough blood." It was the only part of the recipe with unclear instructions. It had to be that.

"Was it your own blood?" he asked.

"Yes."

"Maybe that's your problem."

"I should've used an animal?" That felt needlessly cruel.

"I never said that." He crumpled the paper and dropped it lazily on the ground, as though he was already bored of helping her. Then he walked away and collapsed on the bed. Isobel's nose crinkled. Cobwebs clung to the dusty headboard and pillows, but she knew Alistair saw a different version of this place. He reached for a crossword on the nightstand beside him—a funny thing to bring to a death tournament, but Isobel guessed even a Lowe needed his small comforts.

"Who else's blood should I have used?" The instructions clearly said sacrifice, so whose blood was more precious than her own? This was hardly a problem in *spell*making.

"That's what I mean about willingness to be wicked." He grinned slyly over the pages of his puzzle book. "And yes, I know I could make a joke out of that. You think I wouldn't check your thoughts to make sure you told the truth?"

Her skin heated, and she turned over her wrist, where she knew—could she see it—the mark of the Divining Kiss would be, in the shape of Alistair's lips. While she'd been distracted by the Reaper's Embrace, he'd made one of her signature spells and used it against her. She swore and bent down to pick up the discarded paper. "Stop casting spells on me."

He absentmindedly picked up a quartz discarded on the moth-eaten duvet. "Make me."

She was afraid. She was humiliated. She was angry.

And he could see all of that.

"It doesn't matter," Isobel bit out. "None of it matters. We only need to make the high magick spell."

"And where do you plan to *get* raw high magick?"

"The tournament is full of high magick. That's what holds it together. I figured you knew how."

"You're right about the tournament, but none of that power comes in raw form. The high magick in the Landmarks and the Relics is already crafted into spells and curses."

"What if we buried a Relic, like we did with your rings?" Isobel suggested.

He paused to consider her question. "The raw high magick would seep out, but we wouldn't be able to sense it. The only people who can sense it are the members of the winning tournament family, and until this tournament is over . . . that's no one."

Isobel's heart sank. "So we can wield the high magick enchantments that have already been given to us, but we can't make new ones."

"Exactly."

Without using raw high magick, it would be impossible to craft a Null and Void spell strong enough to fix her powers.

Isobel's chest fluttered with panic, but she didn't want to break down. Not here.

"Does your dragon's lair come with a shower?" she asked coolly.

Alistair nodded at another hallway, his gaze fixed on his crossword. Isobel grabbed a clean set of clothes out of her duffel bag—sneaking as many spellstones as she could into the pants' pockets—and followed the hallway to . . . not a bathroom, but a lake. The room was lined with torches, making shadows dance across the water's surface. In the center was a small island with a pillar jutting up from it, just like the Champions Pillar Isobel had carved her name into less than twenty-four hours ago. Isobel warily inspected the murky water, as though a sea serpent or other foul creature might lurk beneath.

After determining the lake to be both clean and uninhabited— and double-checking that Alistair hadn't followed her down the hallway—Isobel undressed and soaked away the accumulated mud and filth. She teased the knots out of her hair, trying to focus on the plan budding in her mind instead of her growing tidal wave of dread.

If what Alistair said about high magick was true, then she had no reason to stay with him. In fact, she needed to escape immediately. Alistair could change his mind about keeping her alive at any moment.

When she finished and dressed, Isobel slipped down the Cave toward the entrance, her heart pounding so loudly she feared Alistair could hear it. She doubted that any of the other champions had claimed the Crypt, and so she would go there, to her family's favorite Landmark. It would be perilous, especially if she encountered another champion, but it was the best chance she had.

However, as she neared the Cave's mouth, she slammed into something invisible and hard. She jolted back and rubbed her bruised forehead.

"Going somewhere?" Alistair purred from behind her.

She swore under her breath. He'd warded the entrance both ways—she couldn't escape. "I wanted some air."

"I can't have you leaving and telling the other champions about my predicament. Besides, you're still useful. You can help me craft new spells." Alistair walked away, his footsteps echoing down the cavern.

Isobel remained there for several moments longer, cursing herself for yet another terrible mistake. She had willingly made herself his prisoner. And he would dispose of her the second she failed to be of use.

She pressed a hand over her mouth, stifling a sob. Her entire body trembled, and the wave of dread seemed to crash over her, dragging her under.

But no, she couldn't let herself drown. She was a Macaslan. She was a survivor.

After collecting herself as best she could, she returned to the bedroom, where Alistair lay on the bed and scribbled something into his crossword.

"You knew what I hoped about high magick was meaningless from the start," she accused.

"I might've," he said simply.

Isobel's gaze fell on his stacks of spellstones. Even without her powers, he could use her guidance to craft truly impressive spells. But at some point, he would want weapons in addition to shields. He would want curses. And his words earlier had proven he didn't need her for that.

How long could she last until he disposed of her? A handful of days?

Swallowing a second wave of fury and humiliation, she sat on the other side of the bed. A cloud of dust plumed in the air, and she coughed.

He looked up. "What are you doing?"

"There's only one bed," she pointed out.

"Plenty of floor." His voice was strangely high.

"This bed is big enough for two people."

Before he could protest further, she slid under the duvet and pulled it to her chest, shuddering from the bed's moldy stench. This was a disgraceful, horrifying backup plan—one that definitely suited the Macaslans, willing to stoop to any low. Besides, she already knew he'd imagined this. Alistair might not realize it, but he had more than one weakness.

She leaned over and glanced at his puzzle. "The word you're looking for is 'bygone.'"

"You know, I'm sorry you don't have your powers," Alistair told her.

"Why is that?"

"Because I can't stop thinking about our duel."

Isobel sucked in a breath. Even now, he was thinking about killing her. "In an equal match, I know I'd win. I have more . . . finesse. That's the word you're looking for." She pointed at the empty vertical spot, a smug smile playing at her lips. It wasn't easy to feign confidence when she still teetered on the edge of a breakdown. But before she was an outcast, there had been a time when Isobel Macaslan was an expert flirt.

"Stop doing that." Alistair threw the crossword down and turned to her, his dark hair spilling across his gray eyes. He propped his head up on his elbow. "You wouldn't win."

"Even in a match without magick, I'd win. You're clumsy." Isobel remembered the way he'd so gracelessly flopped on the bed earlier, how often he tripped over his own feet. "Careful where you walk. When your back is turned, I might just push you into the lake."

"It's not just a *lake*," he said seriously. "It's a grotto."

She snorted. "Why are you like this? What sort of person dreams of being a monster?"

He scooted closer, so close she had the urge to slide back. But she refused to show that she was intimidated. After all, sharing the bed was supposed to be *her* power play.

"Do you want to hear a story?"

"I don't like fairy tales," Isobel told him, remembering how Reid had called her "princess."

"Oh, no. I meant a monster story." He licked his lips. "Give me your hand."

She hesitated. "How do I know you won't try the Divining Kiss again?"

"I suppose that's half the fun."

She slowly lifted her hand for him to take, hoping he couldn't feel it shake. She didn't know what she expected him to do with it. She certainly didn't expect him to lace his fingers with hers, squeezing so tightly his nails dug into her knuckles.

"Pretend our fingers are ribs," he said.

She furrowed her eyebrows. "What?"

"There's a monster that is a shadow. It slips between tree branches, or the spires of a building, or the keys of a piano. Anywhere with cracks." The entire time he spoke, Alistair didn't let go of Isobel's hand. She tried not to shiver at the coldness of his touch. "This monster is a jagged, grotesque creature, its bones jutting out in the wrong places, its very being full of cracks. It spends its life searching for ways to seal those cracks. To finally make itself whole."

"I've never heard of this monster," she said, as though that made his story less unsettling.

"As a child," Alistair continued, ignoring her, "I slept in total darkness. My mother always cut the lights, opened the windows. The more drafts, the more dark shapes in my wardrobe, the better. She was asking the monsters to come. One night, the monster grabbed me by the arm and dragged me out of my bed, pinned me high against the wall."

There was no hint of teasing in his voice. Isobel *knew* it couldn't be true, but still, her heart pounded faster.

"He unzipped my skin, layer by layer. I tried to scream but couldn't. I was too afraid as the creature gradually morphed into its solid form in front of me. Eyes gray and dark and colorless." *Like Alistair's eyes,* Isobel thought. "Its body was like the roots of a tree, all gnarled and twisted. The edges of it hung limply like ribbons, thin and translucent as flakes of skin."

He leaned even closer, bringing his voice down to a whisper. A warmness began in Isobel's stomach that felt less like fear and more like desire. She scolded herself. She shouldn't be feeling attraction during such an unnerving story—and to the very boy keeping her prisoner, no less. It was simply because they were a hair's breadth apart in a bed, the lights dimmed low, and Alistair had a smile that looked wicked in more ways than one. He was using her own moves against her . . . again.

"When I looked down," he murmured, "all of my organs lay exposed, gray like something pickled, something dead. There wasn't any blood."

Finally, he pulled his hand back. But they were still too close, and she didn't move away.

"It unzipped my face last. My sight split in two as my eyes moved apart. I could no longer see it in front of me." His eyes drifted from her chin to the top of her face, as though retracing the incision the monster had made. His gaze lingered on her lips a moment too long, then he looked up again and continued his story. "But I felt it."

One by one, he lay his fingers over hers. Gradually, they slipped in between once more, intertwining. It felt far more uncomfortable, now that she knew the context of the story.

"It fit perfectly. In between every bone, in my windpipe, in my skull. It was like something being stuffed down your throat, like pressure prying you apart from the inside."

Isobel grimaced, imagining such a feeling. She felt claustrophobic in her own skin.

"Once it is whole, it lives in its host body forever, intertwining so completely that there is no place where the human ends and monster begins."

She let go of him and pushed him hard in the chest. "You made that up."

"I did not." He inspected her neck and shoulder. "You have goose bumps."

She ignored that comment and instead challenged, "Then prove it's real."

He lifted up his sweater to expose his stomach. A long scar traced up the center, pale and pink, disappearing among tufts of hair at the bottom and his undershirt at the top.

Isobel narrowed her eyes. "Where is that scar from?"

"I'll leave it to your imagination."

Maybe Isobel's mother had been right about Alistair. Maybe he *was* unstable.

"You never answered my first question," she said. "Who dreams of being a monster?"

The corner of his lips lifted in a smile. "If you want to know all my secrets, you'll have to force them out of me." For a second time, his gaze traveled down to her lips, but now his gaze lingered. Isobel didn't need the Divining Kiss to read his mind. If they weren't champions in the same tournament, if he didn't possess magick when she did not, she might have been tempted—her own backup plan be damned.

"You know that monsters aren't real, right?" she asked.

"I wouldn't be so sure. What do you think of when you hear the word 'monster'?"

Because Isobel wasn't raised on Ilvernath's ridiculous fairy tales, her mind didn't conjure an image of a dragon or a big bad wolf. It wasn't even an image that came to mind at all.

It was a voice, rasping and sharp.

You don't get to choose the family you're born into.

She winced, instantly feeling guilty at her own thoughts.

"I'm going to sleep." She flipped to her other side, her back to him. Over the next few minutes, she closed her eyes and feigned slumber, even as she heard Alistair set his book on the nightstand and change his clothes.

It wasn't until the lights were extinguished that she realized the drowning dread she'd felt earlier was gone. She had cured a nightmare with a nightmare.

And though she didn't tell him so, Isobel realized she might have learned the secret of Alistair Lowe after all.

GAVIN GRIEVE

Champions have tried to escape the tournament by tunneling beneath the Blood Veil or piercing it with spells, but their magick is no match for its enchantment.

A Tradition of Tragedy

Swearing, Gavin turned around and picked his way across the moors. The landscape had never really made much sense to him—out here, the moorlands were like two jigsaw puzzles that had been mixed together, one muddy and sulfurous, the other brimming with plant life and animals crouching in the underbrush.

At last a crumbling stone building appeared at the bottom of an incline, a pocket of peaty bog pooling around the disintegrating stone walls. The Monastery.

The first night of the tournament generally ended in at least one slain champion. But the sky would've lightened had any one of them died, and their names would've been crossed off the pillars in the Landmarks. All seven of them had survived until morning. Which meant Gavin's next step was simple: draw first blood. Prove himself as a force to be reckoned with.

As the Monastery was the closest Landmark to the Castle, he'd decided to start there.

He could tell immediately that it was occupied. The wards glimmered crimson around the high walls, signifying at least one champion inside. At this point, he didn't care *who* they were. Between his damp shoes, his sweaty face, and his general fury about the state of his magick, he was more than ready to start a fight. It had been a painful, horrifying process to fill all his spellrings again using his own life force, but he'd done it. The pain had only made him vomit once.

Gavin stared at the Shrouded from Sight spellstone on his left hand. Before Reid had cursed him, the spell had merely behaved as basic camouflage; like a chameleon, his appearance would blend into his surroundings. At a higher class, it could even pass through some warding spells.

But when he cast the spell this time, it felt different.

His strange new magick shimmered around his hands, then swept over him, engulfing him in purple and green light. Gavin watched, astonished, as the tips of his trainers disappeared, then his fingertips, his torso, until he was entirely invisible, even to himself. He glanced down and grinned—if he squinted, he could just make out the barest outline of a shadow.

Shrouded from sight, indeed.

Gavin's tattooed arm twinged with pain, but he ignored it. He paused at the edges of the Monastery's overgrown garden. There would be wards surrounding the Landmark, even if he couldn't see them. And he didn't want to waste any magick finding them. He remembered what Isobel Macaslan had done outside the Castle, then reached down and picked up a pebble from the grass.

He threw it, and sure enough, it plunked against an unseen wall a few meters ahead, sending ripples of red light through the air.

Satisfied, he took a step forward—only for a crimson shock wave to tremble outward from his left foot. Another ward. He swore and jumped back, but he felt no lingering curse. Pain twinged through his arm and he realized his Shrouded from Sight spellring was refilling.

It hadn't just shielded him from view. It had protected him from the wards.

He grinned and faced down the unseen wall before him. Then he treaded forward and cautiously pressed his hand against it. Specks of red magick flitted away from his touch, and his fingers passed through without resistance.

Gavin vaulted over the crumbling wall and found a door, sealed shut. No matter what had happened before, he doubted he could walk through solid stone.

Adding a spell on top of Shrouded from Sight was a risky move—the energy needed to cast two different enchantments at once required a balance Gavin had never quite mastered. But he was stronger now. He could handle this.

He raised his hands in the air and cast Shatter and Break on the stone door.

His arm twinged again as the spellring refilled. Gavin gritted his teeth and held on to the spell, sending waves of magick shimmering around the stone.

A moment later, the door exploded.

Boom!

The noise reverberated around the garden. The dust dispersed, revealing a gaping hole in the wall where the door had been.

What he'd done to the door hadn't exactly been subtle. Which meant his element of surprise was officially gone.

And worse, he could see his shoes again. His concentration had broken, and the Shrouded from Sight spell had broken with it. He felt a familiar twinge in his arm, but he yanked the spellstone from his hand before it could refill. Gavin stuffed it in his pocket, swearing. He would need to conserve magick for the fight ahead.

He emerged into a courtyard at the center of the Monastery. Above him stretched a second-floor walkway, its windows made of brilliant stained glass, all the colors red-soaked by the light of the Blood Veil. The building was otherwise austerely decorated, its open spaces empty and echoing.

But more important than the courtyard were the two champions standing in the center of it, one raising a hand covered in curserings, the other drawing the largest sword Gavin had ever seen—and pointing it straight at his chest. Red light shone from the three spell-stones set into its hilt. A Relic, already claimed.

Gavin's stomach sank. He'd checked the pillar in the Castle before he'd left, but only to see if any champions' names had been struck out. It hadn't occurred to him to check the other side, too, that a Relic could've fallen so soon.

"Hello, Grieve," said Finley Blair.

"You've caught me in a bad mood," added Elionor venomously. "Killing you will cheer me up."

Gavin hadn't come here expecting to deal with high magick. But he wasn't going to run. He would show them what a Grieve could do. "I'm not the one who's dying today," Gavin said evenly.

One of the spellstones in Elionor's earlobes shimmered and she faded out of sight. A moment later, Gavin heard cursefire whistle through the air behind him. He blocked the magick just in time and whirled around to see her standing before him, looking smug. Before she could move again, he cast the Trapdoor on the flagstones beneath Elionor's feet. The ground in the courtyard was already unstable, and it caved in easily, as if it had been waiting for the opportunity. Elionor let out a surprised shout as she fell into a pit.

Thunder boomed from the exposed corridors above them, and Gavin tipped his head back to see Carbry Darrow casting a spell. Rain began to fall in the courtyard, wetting Gavin's shoulders. But Gavin had bigger things to worry about than a little bad weather. Finley was charging across the courtyard, brandishing his Sword.

"You want a fight?" Gavin murmured, summoning the Golden Guard on his right hand. It was another spellstone he'd painstakingly created himself. "You got it."

A moment later, a shield spun into the air in front of him.

Gavin's arm burned as he caught Finley's blade on the edge of his shield, but he ignored it. This was no time for weakness.

And it was all Gavin could do to stave off the might of Finley's blows. Although he was on par with Finley's physical strength, he lacked the Blairs' extensive combat training. He cursed himself silently—he'd known Finley was the captain of the fencing team. This had been a foolish idea. He blocked the Sword to the best of his ability, but he could tell he wouldn't last long.

He had to find another way to win this fight.

The last time he'd tried two spells at once, one had broken. But he had to take the risk.

Gavin parried a particularly vicious blow, then stumbled back, trying valiantly to summon Hold in Place. The shield in his hand flickered, and Finley smiled, bringing his blade down in a killing blow—only to have it freeze in midair.

Gavin seized the other boy's brief moment of confusion. He swung his failing shield to the side and knocked Finley's blade out of his hands, then tackled him, sending them both skidding across the flagstones.

Finley's head hit the ground hard as he fell, and he lolled to the side, groaning, a trickle of blood running from his mouth. Gavin knelt beside the fallen champion and clutched the cursering on his right pinky, his heart pumping in his chest.

He only had one death curse: the Revenge of the Forsaken. He'd found it in what passed for the Grieves' family heirloom storage, a single lockbox his parents kept under their bed. It caused a nasty death that split an enemy's body open from the inside out. He'd practiced it on a plum and been both revolted and delighted by the way the pink, ripe flesh had burst out from beneath the skin.

He summoned the magick in the cursestone, staring down at Finley's slack face—but nothing happened.

"Shit," Gavin murmured, clutching the cursering harder and trying again to cast it. But the pain in his arm spread up his chest and around his spine. His nerves were screaming in agony. He knew the cursering wasn't empty, but he'd spent too much magick refilling his other spellstones. He needed to learn a way to prevent his spell-rings from constantly stealing his life force.

Lightning scorched the earth beside him as he scrambled away from the champion's body. His throat went dry at the sight of Carbry crouched beside the hole Gavin had carved in the courtyard floor, hoisting Elionor out.

"Get ready to die, Grieve," Elionor snarled, stepping in front of Carbry as if to shield him.

Gavin's vision began to blur around the edges. He stumbled frantically to his feet as Elionor brandished a seemingly never-ending supply of curserings, the wares of a champion popular with Ilvernath spellmakers.

It didn't matter how much time and energy he'd spent preparing for this, or what horrible things he'd done to gain extra power. He didn't have the magickal arsenals the other champions did. Their training came from their families, not just from independent study.

And their talent—

Gavin swallowed hard. He'd always known he was talented for his age. But that wasn't enough in a fight like this, against the combined might of three champions.

To win, you had to be extraordinary. And he wasn't.

For a moment, he wanted to surrender. To let death take him the way it had always been destined to: first. But that same stubborn determination that had brought him to Reid MacTavish's curseshop refused to let him give up.

One more spell. One more. He took a deep breath and cast Trancewalker—a mild hypnosis spell, just enough to confuse an enemy while he escaped.

It worked. Elionor's and Carbry's eyes went glassy, and they both froze, looking bewildered. His arm was numb now, but his body still spasmed with the pain of refilling the spellring.

Gavin stumbled backward. He didn't care about winning anymore. He just needed to run.

But before he could move any further, another burst of cursefire peppered the cobblestones at his feet.

"Shit!" Gavin snarled, turning. How many champions were in this alliance?

Briony Thorburn appeared at the edge of the courtyard. She was still wearing the skin-tight dress she'd had on the night before, but it was absolutely filthy, beads and fabric crusted with grime. A handful of spellrings glimmered on her fingers.

"You . . ." Elionor gasped at Briony as the Trancewalker began to wear off. "You stole your spellrings back. . . . Shit, my *spell*—"

"Stand back!" Briony snapped, raising her hands in the air.

Gavin had expected to face one champion, not four. He raised his shaking hands, panic surging through him, but he knew he couldn't cast anything else. If his enchantments refilled themselves again, he'd pass out. And if he tried to take them off, he'd be defenseless.

He needed to run. *Now.*

Gavin dove through the doorway a moment before a fresh burst of cursefire rained down on the spot where he'd been standing. A curse struck his shoulder, then his back, as he bolted from the Monastery.

His journey back to the Castle was fueled by nothing but pure will. His new cursemarks burned with every step, and the pain in his arm was so excruciating that he had to fight to stay conscious.

All that kept him going was one simple thought.

This new power Reid had given him wasn't what he'd expected. It was stronger, yes, but it was warped and broken. He needed to learn how to manage it in a fight. And if he did figure out how to claw his way to victory, he would make the cursemaker pay.

ALISTAIR LOWE

The spellmakers of Ilvernath denied interviews or requests from my publisher to comment for this book. Considering how the champions must rely on them for their survival, imagine what it takes to dub one a "favorite." Imagine what it takes to turn a desperate child away.

A Tradition of Tragedy

Alistair hunched over his spellboard, all too aware of Isobel hovering beside him. He flipped through the pages of one of her mother's grimoires to a water purifying spell. It had been a week since the tournament began and, according to the Cave's pillar, no one had died. Alistair imagined that the other champions had also kept to the safety of their Landmarks, waiting for someone else to make a move.

And Alistair would have to make a move soon. The pair had depleted almost all of Isobel's basic nourishment spells, and both were tired of subsisting on her meal replacement bars and Alistair's instant noodles. The Cave, though aesthetic perfection, did admittedly lack the supplies of some of the other Landmarks.

"You need more spearmint leaves," Isobel instructed him, nodding at the pile of dried herbs on one point of the spellboard's septogram.

"I know what I'm doing." Alistair didn't care that Isobel was a trained spellmaker—he knew how to craft a class two Purify spell without her step-by-step guidance.

"I'm just showing you how to make it more effective."

Then she reached forward and grabbed the sealed vial of leaves, but it tipped in her hands, and a flurry of mint dusted over him. He coughed and spit several bits out of his mouth.

"Sorry," she said quickly. She reached down and brushed them off his sweater. Her hands found their way up as well, cleaning off his forehead and cheeks.

Alistair flushed at her touch. It was hard not to, the way her thumb lingered at the edge of his lips. And it was not the first time she'd touched him. At every opportunity, their hands or knees managed to graze. She'd wiped fallen eyelashes from his face for him to make a wish. Each night in bed, the distance between them seemed to grow smaller and smaller.

But as much as Isobel believed otherwise, Alistair was no fool. These endless, trivial instructions to prove her spellmaking expertise. These "accidental" excuses to make her seem anything other than an opponent.

He hated it.

The next time her hand brushed his, he grabbed her by the wrist. "Stop that."

"Stop what?" she asked innocently.

"You know what I mean."

"Actually, I don't." Her dark eyes seemed to peer into him, and he swallowed. But he refused to show that her petty tactics worked on him—he, the champion known to be a monster.

Plus, it was humiliating. No matter how much he wanted her flirting to be sincere, it couldn't be, not if he was the only one who could use magick. Her ploys were no more than a desperate farce.

Alistair stood up, chair scraping against the stone floor, and stalked to the other side of the room. "I've lost my appetite, and I'm tired. I'm going to bed."

"Fine. I'm tired, too." Isobel marched over to the four-poster bed and slid beneath the covers. She grabbed his crossword book from the nightstand and bit the end of his pencil. "I want to finish this puzzle, though. I don't like giving up."

"Obviously not," Alistair muttered under his breath. He sat down stiffly on the other side of the bed and stuffed a spare pillow between them.

Isobel moved it and rolled closer so he could get a better look at the book. "It's four letters. It ends in '-ust.' The clue is, 'Even the strongest of iron dissolves into . . .'"

"Lust," Alistair answered automatically and without thinking. Then he took a deep breath and growled angrily, "I meant rust."

She snorted. "Remind me again how you're supposed to be clever."

"I don't want to do a crossword. I want to go to sleep."

"It's not that late."

"You said you were tired."

"I am." She faked a yawn and scooted herself closer to him. She rested her head on his chest. "Very tired."

For a moment, his thoughts slipped. Maybe this was no farce. Isobel seemed relaxed. And she was so warm against him. He liked the way her hair looked splayed over his shirt. He liked how her hips—

No. This was too much. She would hear the pounding of his heart. She would know that Alistair was fake, that he was weak.

He siphoned a small sliver of power from the Dragon's Breath, so when he spoke, hot steam blew from his mouth. "How can you stand it?"

Isobel jerked away from the heat and sat up. "I don't know what you mean."

"Stop doing this! Stop pretending to . . . to . . . !"

Too mortified to finish his sentence, he pulled the covers away and bolted out of the bed. A Fear of the Dark spell made Alistair's shadow stretch up the Cave's walls behind him as though he loomed three times as large. The candles extinguished one by one until he and Isobel stared at each other in near blackness.

"Maybe you've forgotten who I am?" When he strode toward her, Isobel scrambled out of bed away from him. "Maybe you've forgotten what I'm capable of."

She pressed her back against the wall and asked coolly, "If you hate it so much, why have you made every excuse to stay in the Cave with me?"

She was right, but Alistair would never admit that.

"I've replenished more than enough of my supplies," he reminded her. "Which means you have exhausted your usefulness. You have no magick. You're defenseless. Nothing is stopping me from killing you right now."

His shadow slipped around her ankles and twisted up her body. She resisted, but when no amount of squirming would make the restraints budge, a look of true, unbridled terror crossed her face. It was exactly the expression that Alistair had hoped to inspire, exactly the one that he had been taught to.

The shadow wound around her neck.

But before Alistair could kill her, Hendry's voice came to him. *If you're not doing this for me, who are you doing it for?*

Alistair shuddered, even if his brother's words were only figments of his imagination. Winning the tournament had always meant returning to Hendry, playing the monstrous role his family assigned him so he could one day leave it behind entirely. But they had murdered the only person who'd never wanted Alistair to be a monster at all.

Was this really what he wanted to do? Really who he wanted to be?

He swore and cast a Flicker and Flare. The candelabras around them roared back to life.

Isobel blinked at him in the sudden brightness. She didn't move, even though she could have. The look on her face was wretched.

It filled Alistair with something uncomfortably close to shame.

"Go to sleep," he grumbled, calling off his shadow, which diminished into his natural one once more. "But no more tricks."

When Isobel didn't move, Alistair strode away himself. He slipped into bed, his back to her, and feigned sleep.

But he didn't rest, not even when she finally, reluctantly, arranged a pile of her clothes on the floor and laid down on the ground. Now his shame tasted sharp and sour.

Even if Alistair was tired of twisting himself into something cruel, he didn't know who he was otherwise. Goodness served no purpose in the tournament. And no matter what he felt for Isobel, she was still an opponent.

And it wasn't as though Isobel actually returned those feelings, anyway.

He rolled over to glance at her, to apologize. But across the room, her eyes were closed and her breathing steady. She was asleep.

It must have been tiring, being afraid all the time.

He should know.

Alistair slipped out of bed and skulked to the grotto. He lay on his back at the lake's edge, the way Hendry used to nap in the family graveyard. If Alistair had paid more attention to those tombstones or the portraits lining the estate's walls, he might've realized the sinister truth behind his family's success before it was too late.

But he hadn't.

He hated himself.

His guilt told him to let Isobel go free. His grief told him it was a blessing he had someone here, that he'd never done well alone. And his heart warned him the only one of them in true danger of being hurt was him.

It was absurd to wish for Isobel's powers back, because the moment she had them, they would become enemies once more.

I could still kill her, he assured himself. *If she had her powers back, if she threatened me, I could still do it.*

A red light broke through the darkness, a color Alistair instantly recognized as high magick. The pillar on the small island in the lake's center glowed as one of its seven stars shone red, then fell across the stone, mimicking the way a real shooting star would course through the sky.

Another Relic was falling.

Alistair touched the spellstone on the side of the wall that would grant him a closer look, and a bridge unfurled across the lake, glowing red with high magick. He crossed it hastily, checking to make sure the star glowing was the one he'd thought.

It was the fourth star, the one Alistair knew from his studies signified the Cloak. The object protected the wearer from all spells and curses crafted with common magick, and it was imbued with enchantments for silencing footsteps and camouflage. It was the strongest defensive Relic of the tournament.

His wish—a much better, desperate wish—had been granted.

He didn't need to kill Isobel. Not now . . . maybe not until the tournament's end. So long as he managed this.

Careful not to wake her, Alistair crept back to the main cavern, slipped on a number of his newly crafted spellrings, slung Isobel's empty duffel bag over his shoulder, and slunk out of his lair. An especially red star burned in the crimson night sky, a trail of light streaking behind it. Alistair sat atop his mountain and watched it fall.

He'd gotten lucky—the Relic was heading for the base of the mountain, where rocks met forest. Alistair descended and followed the path around the woods until he came upon a quarry. The Cloak glowed in a halo of red light at its rocky base, floating, waiting.

He heard a *pop!* Followed by another, and the telltale mist of common magick. Here to There spells. Alistair cursed as two other figures appeared at the opposite end of the quarry. He should've known other champions would come to claim the prize.

A curse whizzed across the night. Alistair threw up a Shark's Skin shield to block it. Then he wasted no time starting down the steep hill to the quarry's base.

And immediately slipped on a rock.

He fell, and he tumbled down the hill far faster than he could've run it. He came to a dizzy stop at the bottom, covered in bruises. He stifled a yelp of pain as he tried to push himself up. He'd injured his forearm badly, perhaps even broken it. So much attention had gone into preparing powerful spells and curses, yet he hadn't bothered to craft ones that would make up for his clumsiness.

The Cloak now hovered fifteen meters away.

He got to his feet shakily in time to dodge another curse.

"Impressive," said a voice from behind him. Alistair whipped around and faced the Blair champion's Sword—he definitely hadn't had that Relic the last time they'd run into each other. "Should we even bother killing you? Or will you fall down another cliff for us?"

Alistair didn't grace that with an answer. Instead, he cast his Dragon's Breath curse, and the darkness of the night suddenly grew impossibly bright. A rope of flames coiled around Finley's feet, spiraling up into a vortex. Alistair took a step back from the heat of it, squinting into the light.

A torrent of water doused his curse and flooded the bottom of the quarry. Alistair grimaced at his soaked-through socks and trainers and looked up to see the smug smile of a girl Alistair genuinely did not recognize. Process of elimination told him she must be the Thorburn champion, but he swore she'd looked different at the banquet.

"The Lowe champion," she murmured, stepping forward. Definitely not the same girl—this one was muscular and intimidating in a tank top and joggers, nothing like the meek-looking champion who'd carved her name into the pillar. "Wounded and alone."

Alistair fortified his Exoskeleton, a stronger version of the Shark's Skin he'd obtained from Isobel, and considered the rest of his arsenal. The Thorburn was right. He was hurt, and it was two against one. And the Blair wielded the strongest offensive Relic of the tournament, capable of cutting through any shield, bursting into flame, and inflicting wounds no magick could heal.

The smart choice was to flee back to the safety of his lair.

But his gaze flickered to the Cloak, so near his reach. He thought of Isobel's frightened face. And vowed to finish what he'd come here to do.

In times of crisis, Alistair defaulted to what he'd always known. There was one cursering in his arsenal that he hadn't needed Isobel's help to craft, one that he knew well from his childhood.

At his command the water levels rose, and the quarry began to fill. It inched up his calves, his thighs, his waist, and it transformed from clear as rain to an inky black.

"What is this?" the Blair asked sharply as the Thorburn fired another curse in Alistair's direction.

It was called the Conjurer's Nightmare. Whether it was truly a spell or a curse was a matter of opinion, but it allowed the caster to engineer a vision so vivid it fooled all of your senses. The water rising to their throats wasn't real. Its coldness, its sliminess. Every detail was the fruit of Alistair's imagination, and they were all very convincing.

As the levels rose high enough, all three champions were forced to tread water. The Thorburn frantically cast countercurses that fizzled out while the Blair strapped his Sword onto his back again.

Something splashed behind them. A tail.

The Conjurer's Nightmare was obscure and powerful, a combination proven perfect by the panic on the Thorburn's and Blair's faces. Even as the Thorburn cast spells to drain the water away, the vision ignored her. After all, the water wasn't real.

But the curse came with a vicious disadvantage. Because it was cast over a location, not a person, the caster found themselves within the center of the vision, too. And once cast, it was very hard to stop.

A line of sharp fins appeared in the water, drawing closer.

"Shit," the Blair cursed, swimming in the opposite direction.

Alistair swallowed. *You are the only real monster here,* he reminded himself. He searched and found the faint glimmer of red light at the lake's bottom.

The Cloak.

The Blair looked at him wildly. "Are you doing this?" he demanded. Alistair, after all, was helplessly treading water six meters from him.

"Finley, come on!" the Thorburn called, climbing atop the rocks. The water only continued to rise.

"But this is our chance!" He glared at Alistair. "The Lowes will *not* keep Ilvernath at their mercy."

Then the monster—the leviathan, one of his mother's favorites—reared its head from the water. Higher and higher, until it loomed nearly ten meters above them. Its eel-like face was as black as the water around it, and it opened its mouth to reveal hundreds of sharpened teeth. It let out a vicious shriek, and Alistair's fear coursed inside of him. It was his own spell. His own imagination. But he'd felt that sound rattle in his ribs; he felt the water soaking through his clothes, the duffel bag weighing him down. It felt so real.

The Blair let out a wordless noise of panic, then swam furiously for the quarry's edge.

The leviathan's head snapped in the Blair's direction, hungry and eager to have prey to chase. It bent low and lunged toward him.

Alistair seized the opportunity and dove.

He kept his eyes open as he swam, squinting into the murky light. The leviathan's enormous body swept past him as he descended lower and lower.

The Cloak hovered and glowed red at the quarry's bottom, its high magick unaffected by the spell occurring around it.

Alistair opened the duffel bag and carefully slid it over the Cloak so as not to touch it—he didn't want to accidentally claim it himself. He shivered. The water down here was dreadfully cold and frightfully still.

When he zippered the duffel bag closed, the red light was gone, and he floated in total darkness.

Until two golden eyes appeared centimeters from his.

A light coursed through the leviathan's entire body, electricity zapping through its fins. Its scaly form changed from black to a blinding white, its veins alit like a glimmering web. It opened its jaw wider than Alistair stood tall, revealing not hundreds, but *thousands* of teeth.

The monsters can't hurt you when you're a monster, too, he told himself. But his thoughts were frantic. His heart pounded. His spell, so powerfully constructed, was impossible to stop.

If he was truly a monster, then why was he so afraid?

The leviathan lurched forward and swallowed him whole.

BRIONY THORBURN

The Traitors' Tournament is only spoken about in whispers.
All seven champions refused to fight one another, believing they
could outlast the curse. They survived a month—until Cara-
wen Lowe cracked and slaughtered them all.

A Tradition of Tragedy

Briony followed Finley as they raced through the forest. Cursefire whirled through the underbrush behind them, and Briony
still felt the lingering clutches of Alistair Lowe's illusion spell.
She'd always been particularly susceptible to their effects, and right
now she couldn't stop thinking about those fins breaking the grimy
surface of the lake, the monster's leering eyes and gaping maw.

Neither of them stopped until they'd left the woods behind and
both their Pick Up the Pace spellstones were drained. Finley crouched
behind a rocky outcropping at the edge of the moorlands, and Briony joined him a moment later, both of them too winded to go any
farther without rest.

"We were two against one." Finley's voice was so soft and low that
chills crept up Briony's spine. "And we still failed."

"And now *he* has the Relic." Briony was in excellent shape, but her
heart pounded in her chest. From panic or overexertion, she could
no longer tell.

It'd been a week since the tournament began, and she'd spent all of
it patiently trying to win over her new alliance. She'd earned Carbry's
loyalty after helping fight off Gavin, but Elionor's still eluded her.

Bringing back this Relic would've strengthened their trust in her—and given Briony something to test her theory with.

She could scream. A whole week had passed and she had *nothing*.

"It's not defeat," Finley said, speaking quickly—and mostly to himself. "There are five more Relics to fall, and the Cloak won't protect him from the Sword. If we—"

"You already had the Sword, and he *still* beat us." She kicked angrily at the rocks scattered around their feet. "The Cloak will make him unstoppable."

Every moment that passed made the consequences of their loss more real. Alistair had been a brutal opponent even without high magick. Now it was only a matter of time until he hunted Isobel, or Gavin. Or came for all four of them at once.

And then everything Briony had done to Innes would be for nothing.

"It doesn't have to change the plan," Finley said. "The wait will just be a little longer. But that's okay—we have the defenses we need."

"Plan?" Briony echoed, remembering what Carbry had talked about on her first day at the Monastery. "You've been hinting at some grand strategy for the last week, but you still haven't told me what it is."

Finley peered at her with a reluctance that Briony hoped wasn't suspicion. It looked like it could be something else. "Our alliance means that we have numbers on our side, but we agreed to wait to attack until all of us have claimed a Relic. It means biding our time, but then we'll be strong enough to take everyone else out together."

Briony understood the concept of consolidating power. It made sense, and it aligned with her own plans of collecting Relics to test her theory. But there was still so much she didn't understand about breaking the tournament's curse, and she didn't want to share her own ideas with Finley without proof.

"It's a good plan, but why Carbry and Elionor?" Briony asked. "Isobel is stronger than them, and we both know it. And Elionor can be—"

"I've known Carbry for years."

"But you're not sentimental. Not when it comes to this."

Finley caught her gaze, studying her the same way he often had while they were together. Others had mistaken his patient nature for indecision, but Briony knew it meant he was waiting for the perfect moment to strike.

"They were the right choice," he murmured. Then he turned away, clearly finished with this conversation.

But Briony understood what his reluctance was now. It wasn't suspicion; it was shame.

"You picked them because they're weak," Briony said. "Because you need help to take out Isobel and Alistair, and with the Relics, the three of you could. But when you're all that's left, neither will be strong enough to defeat *you*."

Finley did not move, and even when he spoke, he sounded coolly collected. "It's a good plan."

Briony shuddered. For as well as she could read him, suddenly, she didn't feel she knew him—not this version of him, Finley Blair as champion. There was something horrifying about planning to live as allies for weeks with the very people you'd marked for easy slaughter, herself included.

But there was also something horrifying about cutting off your little sister's finger.

"What if there's a better plan?" she whispered. "One where they don't have to die?"

This tournament version of Finley may not have been the one she'd known, but she had to believe that boy was in there somewhere. There had been no joy in his voice when he discussed the reality of his plan—only resignation. They were both here to do what they had to do. She could only hope that he would be willing to align his goal with hers.

"What do you mean, that they wouldn't have to die?" he asked warily.

Briony gathered every bit of confidence she could. "I didn't become champion so I could win the tournament. I'm here to end it."

Briony recounted as much of the truth as she could manage. About the research she'd done. How she'd confronted Reid MacTavish and he'd told her there was something to the pairings of the Relics and the Landmarks—some way to dismantle the high magick that constructed the curse without hurting the people inside it.

She skirted over Innes. It was a convincing lie, that her sister had relinquished her role as champion to Briony once she heard her theory, and there was no point in telling him when he would never learn the truth. Not until she broke the tournament, at least.

"I know how it sounds," she finished. "But my family has this . . . story. About the Mirror and the Tower, how they go together. How they both sort of belong to us. And there has to be a reason that there are seven Landmarks and seven Relics, right? One of each, for each of us?"

She'd kept her gaze on Finley the whole time they'd been talking, but his expression had been impossible to read. Half his face was cloaked in shadow, the other half awash in red from the glow of the Blood Veil. The silence stretched long and taut.

"No," he said finally.

Briony's heart seemed to sink so far, it was buried in the dirt beneath her sneakers. "No? That's all you have to say?"

"It can't be possible. Our families' stories are just stories." For the first time, his voice cracked. He reached over his shoulder and squeezed the hilt of his Sword as though it was all that held him steady.

Briony knew what that crack meant—an opening. She'd gotten through to him more than he wanted to admit. "So your family has a story, too?"

"Sure," he spit out. "About how the first Blair was called into a cave in the mountains at the edge of Ilvernath and fought a dragon for the treasure it was guarding, then pulled the Sword—our Relic—out of the lake inside. A *dragon*, Briony. All you're chasing is a fairy tale."

The Sword and the Cave. Another pairing.

"Maybe there's some . . . dramatic flourish," Briony conceded. She had always been fond of a dramatic flourish or two herself. "But there could be truth in these stories, too."

"You can't just waste your time here chasing a fantasy."

"Are you so certain you're right that you'll stake Carbry's and Elionor's lives on it?" she hissed. "That you'd stake *my* life on it?"

"Of course I'm not sure!" The crack in his voice had widened, and emotion poured through—rage, fear, frustration. "I *was* sure. I had a plan. I trained for it. I was ready for it. But now how can I be certain anymore?" He glared at her, as though she had given him a curse instead of a blessing. As though he didn't *want* a way out.

"You can't," Briony said. "Not until I find proof."

"But why would you want to? A year ago you were willing to do anything to be champion, and now you're saying you want to stop all of this for good. How do I know this isn't some trick?"

"It isn't." She could assure him a hundred times over that she didn't want to kill him, but it clearly didn't matter. That old argument would always linger between them. And she had no doubt now that he'd meant it when he said he'd changed his mind. "I promise."

"I can't believe that." He reached into his pocket and pulled out a spellstone. "This is a Silvertongue. Will you let me cast it on you?"

A class five truth spell. Briony swallowed down a fresh spike of panic. If he asked her about Innes while she was under its influence, she'd tell him everything. But if she said no, she'd never win him over.

"Sure," she said, trying to sound unbothered.

Finley blew out a breath, as though he hadn't expected her to agree. "All right."

He took her hand in his. It was warm and strong, calloused from years of combat training. A shiver crept down her spine as his thumb slid across one of her knucklebones.

A moment later, the stone glowed white with common magick. Some of it seeped outward, a misty tendril that spiraled toward Briony's lips. She opened her mouth and breathed it in, wincing at the tingling feeling that passed down her throat. She could feel a mark forming there, a line cutting from just beneath her chin to her breastbone. The world felt suddenly distant. Finley's voice cut through her foggy mind a moment later.

"Do you really want to stop the tournament?"

"Yes."

"Is that why you became champion instead of your sister?"

Briony nodded. But that wasn't the whole reason. Another truth spilled out of her before she could stop it. "I . . . I knew Innes couldn't survive long enough to try this theory for herself. She's not as strong as I am."

"I see." His fingers tightened around hers. "You're willing to bet your life on a theory?"

"Yes," she said, and she meant it.

The tingling started to fade from Briony's throat. Truth spells never lasted long, even the powerful ones.

"Can I trust you?" he whispered.

Briony met his eyes. "I really hope so."

And then the tingling was gone, the Silvertongue faded away. Above them, the clouds shifted, fully illuminating Finley's face.

"Okay," he said seriously, pulling his hand away from hers. "I'll help you. For now, that's all I can promise."

She could've cried. A promise was more than she'd expected. Maybe more than she deserved.

Briony and Finley were welcomed back to the Monastery with a mixture of relief and disappointment. Elionor seemed annoyed that they'd returned empty-handed, while Carbry was happy they were alive. They recapped their night around an iron table in the main courtyard, where enchanted lanterns did little to break through the murky red glow of the Blood Veil above. Insects buzzed around them, swarms of midges with a thirst for flesh and an irritating habit of evading cursefire.

"We need a better strategy," Elionor said. "I told you we all should've gone to collect the Relic."

"And leave our Landmark undefended?" Finley shook his head. "It was too much of a risk after what happened with Gavin Grieve."

"I don't mind staying back," Carbry piped up. He'd brought some of his family's research notes to the table and was flipping through them. "The last Darrow to win the tournament did so by strategically retreating to their Landmark until the champions killed each other off—"

"You mean he hid," Elionor said. "You're stronger than your ancestor was, okay? Your Ancient Arrows alone could take someone out in one hit. I still don't understand why you didn't use it on Gavin."

Carbry's thumb ran over a large cursering on his hand, a distinctive oval-cut gem.

"I wasn't sure it would work," he said quietly. "I was worried about blowback."

Elionor rolled her eyes. "Uncle Arthur has been bragging for years that you can cast Mnemonic Device spells, and those are class eight. You're completely capable."

"You two are related?" Briony asked.

"We're cousins," answered Carbry. "Her dad is my mom's brother. He took the Payne name when he married." Then Carbry leaned forward and whispered. "Elionor's a natural blonde."

"I *will* curse you," Elionor snapped, but she sounded more annoyed than angry. "And you should stop worrying about your casting abilities. Finley and I promised to protect you."

Briony felt a rush of horror as she thought of what Finley had admitted to during their conversation. That these people, whom he treated as friends, were the ones he'd decided were easiest to kill. But would she have been any less ruthless in this tournament if her family had chosen her? She knew the answer, knew her own strategy well. Take the Tower. Ally with Isobel, if she could manage it. Corner and destroy the others, one by one.

And then stab her former best friend in the back. The thought had always felt distant to her, an inconvenient truth she kept tucked away. Now it made her sick just to think about it.

If Finley noticed her pointed stare, he purposefully ignored it.

"I agree that we miscalculated," Finley said. "We can't afford for our opponents to claim any more Relics. We need to be more aggressive. The next time one falls, we'll all go to claim it."

"I think we should act *now*," Elionor countered. "We've been waiting around for a week, and we already have a Relic. Gavin doesn't. We could take him out."

Finley gave Briony a look. Briony understood—on the way back, they'd discussed a need to prove what was going on before taking their theory to the rest of their alliance. But to do so, they'd need another Relic, and they'd need to know which Landmark to pair it with. Briony couldn't unite the Sword with the Cave while Alistair lurked inside. And neither of them wanted anyone to die unnecessarily in the meantime.

Elionor, in particular, would want proof of her theory. So Briony would be patient, no matter how much it killed her to wait. Until the next Relic fell. Until Elionor learned to trust her more.

"Gavin almost beat all four of us on our own turf," Briony said hastily. "I don't care that he's a Grieve. We need to take him seriously as a threat, and that means waiting and sticking to the plan."

"I'm okay with that," Carbry said.

"So three of us are voting for this plan?" Briony asked.

Elionor frowned at all of them. "We came here to fight. We have to remember that."

"We do," Finley said quickly. "And you *know* I value that about you.

But I bet Carbry's research says that nobody's won this tournament by just charging in without thinking about it."

"Um, actually, there was a Thorburn a hundred and sixty years ago . . ."

Finley frowned at Carbry, who quieted. He reminded Briony so much of Innes in that moment, from all the times Briony would cut her off when she got overexcited about her research. It made her heart hurt.

"It's settled," Finley said firmly.

Briony was surprised by how much she liked the idea of the four of them fixing the tournament together. She already had Finley on her side. Maybe it wouldn't be so hard to convince the others to join her.

If I can get them to tell me their stories, if we can recover another Relic, we can test this theory for real, Briony thought, looking around at the allies she'd found. *I just need more time.*

An image rushed into her head of Innes lying on the ground, unconscious. Of the way her sister's severed finger had felt in her hand, the bone glinting at the edge as she yanked off the champion's ring. She would make that sacrifice worth it. She had to.

ISOBEL MACASLAN

Just like the Landmarks, the Relics come with unique pros and cons. For example, the Cloak allows its wearer to be shielded from all harm, but it makes it more difficult to cast offensive magic.

A Tradition of Tragedy

Isobel was woken in the middle of the night by Alistair looming over her.

She shrieked and yanked up a fistful of the T-shirt she'd used as a blanket, as though it would be enough to protect her from a gruesome death.

But rather than kill her, Alistair tossed her duffel bag onto her lap. "It's yours. Take it." He was pale—paler than usual. And he held his left arm limply at his side, bruised purple.

Isobel suspiciously unzipped the bag, certain this was some sort of trick. Inside was something soft, silky, and white, but it wasn't until she pulled it out that she realized what it was.

"The Cloak?" she asked, stricken. She didn't understand.

"The one and only," he said dryly. "It's invincible. And it's yours." He stalked over to his desk, where he rummaged through the loose crystals for a particular spellstone. Then he leaned against the wall, his lips a thin line, and began to heal his arm. Isobel realized it was broken.

Why would Alistair, who had her entirely at his mercy, give her something that undermined all the power he held against her? With the Cloak, Isobel would be protected from all common magick spells and curses, including his own.

"What happened?" she asked quietly.

He shuddered. "I had to fight off the Thorburn and the Blair for it. But I won."

"Are they . . . ?" Her heart clenched, thinking of Briony. She didn't even realize Briony was working with Finley now, though she supposed she shouldn't be surprised.

Alistair shook his head. "No. I didn't kill them."

But he looked shaken, and he'd clearly been hurt.

For her sake.

"Why did you do it?" Because no matter how much she tried, Isobel couldn't reconcile the image of Alistair, wounded and shivering, with the one who had almost murdered her hours before.

"Because I hate the way you look at me," he spat. "Like I'm a monster."

"Aren't you?" Isobel had learned that Alistair wasn't invulnerable, but the role of the dragon was one he'd fashioned for himself. One he wanted.

"Obviously, I'm not a very good monster." He reached for another healing spellstone, having entirely drained his first.

Unsure how to respond, she pulled the Cloak over herself and fastened its three spellstone clasps—no doubt pulsing with the vibrant red of high magick, if only she could see it. The tension in her shoulders eased for the first time since she'd lost her powers. With this, she was safe. It was the most priceless gift she'd ever received.

When Alistair finished, he wordlessly dumped his own pile of clothes onto the cavern floor.

"You can take the bed," he said.

"Um, thanks." It looked just as disgusting to Isobel as the floor, but at least it was comfortable. She slid beneath the moth-eaten covers and watched him bundle a cardigan into a pillow.

The silence was so complete that she could hear her own heart hammering against her ribs. It had been easier to spend time with Alistair when she believed seducing him was merely part of her strategy. Because with every touch, with every breathless look, she had noticed things about him other than his cruelty, things she'd tried to ignore.

He *was* clever. Even if he'd needed her instruction in his spellmaking, he asked the right questions and was quick to see the pattern in its details. He was rigidly self-disciplined when it came to studies—oftentimes he sat down in the morning to craft spells and remained there for hours, until Isobel's own mind had grown exhausted. She liked his eyes, dark and gray. The sort of eyes meant to be admired in candlelight.

She would need to rethink her opinion of him. She would need to rethink everything.

"What are we?" she asked.

He paused for several moments before finally answering, "Champions."

It was only a kinder way of saying enemies.

"We had a deal." Isobel would help him craft new spells and curses, and Alistair would help her get her powers back. But he'd already risked his life to bring her the Cloak, and she hadn't asked for that.

"I'm sorry for frightening you earlier. Now that you have that, you can leave any time you wish."

But Isobel didn't think it wise to go. She already knew that Carbry Darrow, Elionor Payne, and Finley Blair had formed an alliance. If Alistair had faced Briony tonight as well, then she'd probably joined them. Even if Isobel regained her powers, she had far better odds of defeating a group of four with an alliance herself. Two against four was hardly a winning match, but she and Alistair were stronger than all of them.

"We should be allies," Isobel told him.

"Alliances only put off the inevitable."

"Four against one is suicide."

"Well, it's not four against two if I'm the only one fighting."

"It won't be. Not if I get my powers back." As if that would be so simple. As if she hadn't spent the past week agonizing over the question of what had gone wrong with the Reaper's Embrace.

Alistair sat up and turned to her. Isobel's breath hitched from the intensity in his gaze. Now that she had the Cloak, the two of them were on more equal ground. But somehow, she was still losing her balance.

"If you make a mistake, you could die."

"I'll die if I don't get my powers back," she pointed out. "The Cloak can't protect me forever."

"You don't even know what went wrong."

"It was the sacrifice. I'm sure of it. Sure enough, at least."

He jumped to his feet. "If you had the Mirror, you would have your answer. You would know for certain."

Isobel considered this, intrigued. The Mirror was one of the remaining five Relics that had yet to fall. It gave its user the answers to any three questions, as well as the ability to spy on opponents.

"I could ask it how I messed up," Isobel said breathlessly.

Her hopes rose at the thought of getting her powers back. She wouldn't have to continue hiding in this haunting, repulsive cave. She could stop hating herself for her mistake. She would march down this mountain, once again the most powerful champion of the tournament, and she would . . .

She would try to kill them all—kill them before they killed her.

She swallowed. This past week, she'd been so focused on convincing Alistair not to murder her that she had put off thoughts of all the reasons she hadn't wanted to be a champion in the first place.

"The only problem . . ." Alistair said, his gaze fixed away from hers even as he leaned against the post at the foot of the bed. Cobwebs clung to the wood above his hair, forming an unsightly crown in the candlelight. ". . . is that there are still eleven weeks left. That's a lot of time waiting for the Mirror to fall. With . . . me."

His voice caught on the last word, and Isobel realized that even if Alistair had known her flirting had been theatrics, it had clearly made an impression on him. He sounded almost wounded.

Even though he'd said he was sorry, even though he'd given her the Cloak, he was the one who'd terrorized her. She didn't have to apologize for hurting his feelings when she'd only been trying to survive.

That's all this is, she told herself. *A performance.*

So why did her cheeks warm at the thought of eleven weeks alone in this Cave with Alistair Lowe?

Forcing her voice into nonchalance, she said, "I hope your crossword book lasts us until then."

He laughed loudly, as though the moment before, he'd been holding his breath. "Not the way you plow through it."

"The other champions won't wait for that long," Isobel pointed out. She was surprised they'd already waited *this* long.

"The Cave is the second strongest defensive Landmark in—"

"But if one of them claims the Crown, then all the Landmarks will weaken. Or if the Medallion falls, that can void other Relic and Landmark claims—"

"Then I'll defeat them, all right?" he said fiercely. "It's nothing I haven't trained for."

Alistair might've been clever and powerful, but even he would be outmatched against a gang of champions armed with Relics.

But he sounded confident, and he was a Lowe. Maybe he really had trained to overcome all odds.

"Can I ask you something?" Isobel whispered.

"Sure."

"Did you always want to be champion?"

"Yes," he answered matter-of-factly.

"Oh." Isobel squeezed the sheets in her fist, thinking of her father. Maybe he'd been right. Maybe Isobel really had originally turned her back on her family's legacy, on honor.

"I know how that makes me sound," he said quickly, misinterpreting her response. "It wasn't that I was eager to put myself in danger or kill a bunch of people. But . . ." His voice hardened. "All my life, we were told it was all that mattered. That we all had our roles to play."

"By 'we,' do you mean you and your brother? He was with you at the Magpie, wasn't he?"

For a moment, something sharp passed over his features, and she worried that she'd upset him somehow. "You don't have to—I was being personal—"

"No, it's fine." His Adam's apple bobbed as he swallowed. Then he asked, his voice strained, "What about you? I assume because you were named champion so early, you must've wanted it—being famous and all."

She laughed bitterly, remembering the first time she'd been approached by a journalist on her walk to school. The way she'd felt nauseous when he'd called her a champion. The way Briony had smiled. Even after a year, the memories felt raw and fresh.

"All of that was a mistake." Her voice trembled. "I didn't ask to be a celebrity. If it wasn't for . . ." For her best friend. For her family. But she didn't want to get into that. "It wasn't supposed to be like that."

Alistair's voice was surprisingly gentle when he asked, "So you didn't want to be champion?"

"No," Isobel answered, even though it felt like admitting something terrible. "I didn't. I . . . still don't. Sometimes, when I close my eyes, I can pretend that it isn't real. That I'm still in my bed at home." In the room that Isobel had wasted a spell to ruin, just because she'd been angry and scared.

Suddenly, the candles in the room snuffed out all at once, pitching them from the already dim candlelight into total blackness. It took her a second to realize that he'd extinguished them with a spell, for her. So she couldn't see where she truly was. But she could still smell it—the rot, the mold, the damp, earthy odor of the cave walls.

"You want to know something funny?" he asked. "In a choice between staying here or going home, I'd still choose here. With you."

Isobel didn't think that was funny, and a dozen questions about the Lowes itched on her tongue, if the truth did justice to the wicked rumors whispered around Ilvernath.

But rather than pry, she said, "You don't have to sleep on the floor. I know it's uncomfortable."

"I think I owe you more than a night on the floor."

"You broke your arm tonight. It'll be stiff, even if you healed it. I don't want my ally wounded."

She knew, after all the ways she'd flirted with him before, that any invitation could be misconstrued. Especially in a bed with little space between them, entirely in the dark.

But there was no misconstruing the way her stomach somersaulted when she felt the mattress shift as he sat down. When he lay beside her and a warmth like fire spread through her from her head to her toes.

Nothing good would come of this.

This was Alistair Lowe, she reminded herself. The one everyone had declared her greatest rival. The boy her mother had warned her about.

After they'd slain all the other champions—her ex-best friend among them—it would only be the two of them left. Maybe that would be months from now. Maybe it would be days. But that was what this alliance led up to. Not a kiss stolen in the dark, or a priceless gift given without being asked.

A duel.

Sobered, Isobel turned so her back was to him. Several minutes had passed, and Alistair hadn't moved. She wasn't even sure if he was still awake.

"Tell me a monster story," she whispered.

He stirred, then drowsily, he murmured, "Have you ever heard of a nightcreeper?"

"I haven't."

"They're drawn to places with complete darkness because their bodies are made of shadow." Isobel noted the complete darkness around them and slid deeper beneath the blankets. "They can see in the darkness no better than you can, but their eyes are burned away by the faintest of light. That's what they search for—eyes. New ones that don't scorch in the daylight, that they can pluck out and use to replace their own. So they can finally feast outside."

Isobel's dread receded, her real fears replaced by make-believe ones. When she did fall asleep, she didn't dream of Briony's demise. She didn't dream of how it would feel to kiss Alistair or to curse him. She dreamed of fears that, for once, felt surmountable.

GAVIN GRIEVE

One of my earliest memories is of watching my family put money on our own champion dying first. They were correct.

A Tradition of Tragedy

It took a week for the wounds Gavin had sustained at the Monastery to heal. His body no longer felt like his own, did not behave in ways he recognized. He hid all his spellrings in a dresser drawer and slept for days, feverishly sweating through his T-shirts, until he became lucid enough to feel paranoid.

When he finally felt well enough, he left the protection of the Castle and set off across the moorlands. It would take him ages to reach his destination without a Here to There spell, but he wouldn't waste more magick than was absolutely necessary. Not until he could find some way to stop his spellrings from automatically draining his life force.

It made no sense, marching toward Ilvernath proper. No champion could enter it during the tournament. The Blood Veil had an eye at its center, above the Champions Pillar, that blocked them off from the city—and blocked the city off from them. Nobody could leave or enter for the few months the tournament was in place, a reality that the winning family used to wipe away from the townsfolk's memories once it was all finished.

But after Gavin had used Shrouded from Sight to pass through the Monastery wards, he realized his new power didn't behave by the regular rules of magick. So maybe this was a rule he could break, too.

It wasn't long before the barrier that divided the tournament grounds and the rest of Ilvernath appeared in his line of sight, shooting up through the trees. A translucent wall that pulsed red with high magick—the inner Blood Veil. Up close, it was almost beautiful, specks of crimson swirling together like shimmering oil paint.

Gavin cast the Shrouded from Sight spell, and his body vanished from view, same as at the Monastery. A moment later, his arm ached as the spellring refilled.

Feeling foolish, Gavin stretched his hand toward the inner Blood Veil. But as his fingers brushed against the high magick, he found it strangely tactile, like clay. He closed a hand around it experimentally, and the high magick let him grab it, let him tug it to the side.

For the first time in a week, he felt powerful again.

He clawed at the barrier until it tore open, then—one arm and leg at a time—he clambered through it. He stumbled as he regained his balance on the sidewalk on the other side. He'd barely had a chance to take in the city that he never thought he'd see again when he spotted a group of people gathered at the edge of the barrier. A camera flash confirmed his suspicions—reporters.

Panic surged through him, but thanks to his Shrouded from Sight spell, the reporters looked right through him. They continued their gawking, unaware that a champion watched from only half a dozen meters away.

"I'm on location in the infamous Ilvernath," one journalist said to a video camera. "I know our viewers are eager for updates, but so far, a week has passed without change or news of the tournament. The Blood Veil remains as red as ever, and our Champions Pillar correspondent tells us none of the names of the Slaughter Seven have been crossed out yet."

Vultures. Gavin tuned them out and faced the gash he had torn in the barrier. With two hands, he gripped its edges and yanked them shut, and the high magick knitted itself back together. He couldn't risk leaving an entrance for them to go through. The last thing he wanted were reporters on the front lines of the tournament.

This shouldn't have been possible. But if he could mess with the very fabric of the tournament itself—well, it made Gavin wonder what else he could do.

He took a deep breath and started resolutely down the road into Ilvernath proper, the buildings etched like silhouettes against the scarlet gloom of the sky. It was evening now, and most of Ilvernath had retired to their homes or hotel rooms. The few faces he passed didn't notice him thanks to his spell, although it never stopped being unnerving watching people come toward him.

He wove through the cobbled streets until he found MacTavish Cursemakers. Though the shop was closed, he peered through the window to spot Reid inside, hunched over a spellboard and focused on his work.

Gavin released his spell and pounded on the door.

Reid glanced up and locked eyes with Gavin, but he didn't look as shocked to see him as he should have. It was unnerving.

"Grieve," Reid purred as he let him in.

Gavin frowned. "We need to talk."

"The tattoo must be working, if you can come into town."

"So you knew. What else can I do?" His voice grew sharp with pent-up frustration. "My magick is out of control, and it's going to get me killed."

"You asked for my help," said Reid, looking moderately bored. "I gave it to you. We were both there."

"You didn't tell me it would do *this*," snapped Gavin, yanking up his sleeve.

His entire arm now pulsed with a sickly purple and green light. The magick twined through his veins from wrist to shoulder, his muscles and tendons bulging, and the sand piled at the bottom of the hourglass was about a quarter full. Healing the curses that Elionor Payne had cast on him had cost him more magick—more life—than he wanted to think about.

Reid froze for a moment, staring intently at Gavin's arm. "I turned your body into a vessel to siphon out powerful raw magick. Did you think using it would be fun? There's a reason it's taboo."

"I don't care about that," Gavin said brusquely. "You said my life magick would automatically refill my spellrings, but you didn't mention I wouldn't be able to stop it. I can't use more than a few at a time without basically passing out."

"I wondered if that would happen. I guess that once you start to draw on your own life force to fuel spells, it's hard to turn it off."

"Well, you'd better tell me there's a way."

Reid fixed him with a pitying look. "Have you tried just . . . not wearing spellrings?"

"And being totally pathetic in battle?"

"Pathetic is better than dead."

"No, pathetic *leads* to dead." Gavin scowled. "Why didn't you warn me this might happen?"

"Would you have chosen not to go through with it if I had?"

His words made Gavin pause.

The truth was, he'd come to the MacTavish curseshop out of desperation. He would've agreed to anything. There was no price too high. No line he wouldn't cross.

"No," he said hoarsely. "I would've done it anyway."

Reid's smile was a little smug, and a little sad. "Then why are you complaining?"

The hourglass pulsed painfully on Gavin's shoulder. He didn't have an answer. Instead, he opted for another question.

"How is it even possible that I'm here?"

"I'm not completely sure," Reid answered. "But my best guess is that because you're working with something that's not exactly common magick, not exactly high magick, the tournament's curse doesn't know what to do with you. You're bending its rules."

Gavin contemplated this. He was still confused about how it had interfered with the rules of the tournament. It seemed inconsistent. He'd managed to claim a Landmark; he'd carved his name into the Pillar and received a champion's ring. But he could speak to someone other than a competitor. He could pass through the barrier.

Holy shit. He could pass through the barrier.

"Do you think I could run?" he asked Reid. "Just . . . leave the tournament completely?"

He had never before considered that he could find a way out of this. The shreds of hope within him felt painful—he hadn't even known they were still there. He'd forgotten how to feel like there was anything in his future aside from bloodshed.

"Maybe," Reid said carefully. "But if it worked, there's a chance that would automatically forfeit your spot in the tournament, and then . . . well, the enchantment would take someone else."

Gavin pushed his hope back down. There was only one other Grieve of tournament age: his little brother. Gavin might not have wished himself a champion in the tournament, but he didn't want Fergus to die in his stead.

"So then what's the point of any of this?" he muttered, feeling foolish for hoping at all. "My magick is stronger, sure, but I have so much less of it than anyone else."

"You came here because you didn't want to be like the rest of your family. Isn't that the point?"

His words reawakened the reasons Gavin had made this bargain at all. To make himself powerful enough to stand a fighting chance. If that meant swallowing more pride and being careful about managing his spellrings, so be it. The other champions wouldn't be able to laugh at him if they were dead.

There was nothing else for him here. He took a deep breath and turned to leave, but like the last time he visited Reid's shop, that same row of curserings on the shelves caught his eye. They didn't just look similar to him now—they looked *familiar*. He was pretty sure he'd seen one of those distinctive MacTavish rings in the tournament, but he couldn't remember who it had belonged to.

"You didn't help any other champions," he said abruptly, turning back. "Did you?"

Reid dragged his gaze up to him. "None of the other champions who came to me, no."

That was carefully worded. Maybe because Reid remembered that Gavin carried a truth spell on him, although Gavin didn't want to waste magick on that. It didn't seem worth pressing the issue by asking, either. But Gavin trusted his gut. And his gut said something was strange about all of this.

"All right then." Gavin did his best to copy Alistair Lowe's threatening smile. "Well, now that I know I can visit you . . . I suppose I might have to take advantage of that again."

Reid's smile was equally barbed. "I look forward to it."

As Gavin passed through the barrier and trekked back to the Castle, bleeding away precious power on yet another Shrouded from Sight, he couldn't shake the feeling that Reid was studying him instead of helping him. Like a rat in a cage.

Maybe the cursemaker and those reporters clustered outside the Blood Veil weren't so different after all.

Briony Thorburn

The tournament has only failed once, when several champions
eluded one another for the full three months. And so they all perished. Seven dead champions. And unlike every other tournament, their deaths meant nothing—the high magick they had
fought for remained inaccessible to every family until the Blood
Veil fell again.

A Tradition of Tragedy

Briony Thorburn was trying to craft an Overcharge.

She sat in the middle of the courtyard, glaring at the spellboard she'd spread across the iron table. Waiting for the next
Relic to fall was excruciating, and trying to replenish her spellstone
arsenal was her only real distraction. She'd brought almost no
enchantments into the tournament, and although Finley and Carbry
had both been kind enough to lend her some, she still needed more.

Good thing the Monastery had come with a fair amount of empty
spellstones. Or at least it would've been a good thing if Briony was
a gifted spellmaker. Casting had always been her strong suit—she'd
suffered through her crafting lessons at school only because she'd
known she would need to use them here.

"Okay, okay," she grumbled, arranging the components for the
spell on the points of a septogram. Some moss, some rocks, a burnt
match, a dead midge, a screw, a vial of rainwater, a sliver of petrified
wood. The instructions for the spell sat beside her, scrawled in a nearly
illegible scribble. Briony had successfully crafted some class three and

four spells, but she needed stronger offensive spellwork. The Overcharge at class seven would round out her arsenal nicely—it was a curse that would give its focal targets a nasty electric shock, leaving them incapacitated and perhaps a little singed. But the last three times she'd tried to make it had been miserable failures, as evidenced by the cracked spellstones scattered around the table. Her hand hurt from the blood she kept spilling from her palm to finish the curse.

She only had one more flask of raw magick. This needed to work.

Briony's gaze strayed to the papers that cluttered the far side of the table. Carbry had left them behind and gone to grab some dinner. There was a map of Ilvernath with a bunch of notes scribbled on it, the edges held down by several thick, ancient-looking books. He and Elionor had been strategizing about how they could breach the Castle, since that was Gavin Grieve's sanctum.

Thinking of Elionor reminded her that these spellmaking instructions for the Overcharge were hers, that she was *very* good at crafting. Briony had watched her spellwork over the last week and a half. It was almost on par with Isobel's.

She frowned and glanced back at the septogram, the spellstone, and her remaining flask of magick. Then she swallowed her pride and went to go get help.

"Well, of course it's not working." Elionor took Briony's seat and began fussing with the components of the spell. "You're trying to craft a class seven Overcharge, right?"

"Right." Briony hovered uncomfortably in front of Carbry's mess, trying not to feel patronized.

"Your components are incorrect. You need pine needles instead of moss, and then you need to rearrange them like this. . . ." She swapped around ingredients on the spellboard, then nodded. "There."

"Oh," Briony said, feeling foolish. Elionor's scrawl had been difficult to decipher. "Thanks."

"You could've figured this out on your own if you'd just read the instructions more carefully. Instead, you wasted three flasks of raw magick."

"I'm sorry." Briony could feel her cheeks flushing. "But you don't have to be so hard on me. Carbry makes mistakes all the time, and you don't get mad at him—"

"Because he's a child," Elionor said fiercely. "I saw you in that fight with Gavin. You can cast almost anything, but you should understand how your equipment is made if you want to use it properly. There's more to this than just flinging spells at your opponents."

Briony was truly baffled by this outburst. "Are you complimenting me or insulting me?"

"Forget it. I'll just do it myself."

One by one, Elionor arranged the ingredients on the seven points of the septogram. Then she placed the empty spellstone in the exact center, nodding with satisfaction.

"Precision in all things," Elionor murmured, her spellstones shining in her ears. Briony had the distinct sense that she was talking to herself. She hadn't wanted Elionor to do this for her, but apparently she wasn't getting a choice.

She sighed and looked back at Carbry's papers. The map of Ilvernath flapped in the evening breeze; she smoothed it down.

And froze.

She'd seen maps of the Landmarks before, of course. All the champions had. But with the Champions Pillar in the center like that . . .

She looked at the spellboard, where Elionor was coaxing raw magick from the flask. The ingredients laid out in their neat little corners. And it came to Briony all at once, a sudden burst of understanding. She couldn't believe she'd never seen it before.

"It's a spellboard," she whispered. "This entire tournament is a giant spellboard."

Elionor looked up from her work, frowning. "What?"

Briony hadn't realized she'd spoken aloud. In the time she'd been thinking, Elionor had nearly finished crafting the curse. The Overcharge spellstone, a plain white crystal, now glowed with magick.

"I— Nothing," she said quickly, but Elionor's eyes narrowed.

"Didn't sound like nothing to me," she said, reaching for Briony's hand. "Here. You need to give it blood."

She looked a little too happy as she slashed Briony's palm open, another painful gash to match the ones Briony had given herself.

Unease pulsed in Briony's stomach as she bandaged up the wound. Elionor was skeptical of her. She knew that. She needed proof to have any hope of making her understand.

But . . . Elionor knew a lot about spellmaking. And she could already tell that the other champion wasn't going to let go of this, not without some kind of explanation.

Briony tugged out the map of the tournament and spread it beside the spellboard. "Look at this. The spellboard and our tournament grounds are structured exactly the same way. A septogram . . ." She gestured toward the Landmarks. "And a cursestone at its center." She jabbed her finger at the Champions Pillar.

Elionor stared at the map and the spellboard, then looked up at Briony. "Well, yeah. My family's known that for ages. The basic curse structure is repeated across the tournament grounds. Because it's a curse. Which I'm kind of concerned you didn't know until just now."

"Of course I know it's a curse." Briony glared at her.

"Well then, what's your point?"

"My point is that you need more than a spellboard and a stone to craft a curse. You need ingredients, and a sacrifice. We're the sacrifice, obviously." Briony picked up one of the twigs and waved it dramatically in the air for emphasis. "But we've got the ingredients, too."

Elionor frowned. "A curse's ingredients wouldn't stick around for hundreds of years. That's ridiculous."

"Then how can you explain the Relics?"

Elionor straightened up, her eyes wide. For the first time, Briony felt as if she were seeing her as an equal instead of a nuisance.

"But . . . ingredients have to go in a specific order for a spell to work," she said softly.

Briony reached over and picked up the Overcharge. Her family had plenty of good spellwork, so she could tell immediately this curse was well-crafted.

"They *do* have an order," she said. "Relics go with specific Landmarks. Doesn't your family have a story about it? I know mine does. Finley's, too."

"So he knows about this." Elionor's voice was flat. "About your . . . theories."

"Yeah, he knows. But that isn't what matters. Don't you understand what this means? You know about spellmaking. You know that the only way to break a curse is to undo each piece of it. If we put the right ingredients at the right points of the septogram, we can do that."

Elionor's hands were curled tightly around the edge of the table. Briony could tell before Elionor said a word that she didn't believe her, that whatever moment of vulnerability she'd had was long gone.

"You can't even craft a class seven Overcharge." Elionor sneered. "What makes you think you could break a curse that's held for longer than anyone can remember?"

"I don't know if I can," Briony said. "But I have to try. Don't you want to save everyone?"

"I don't need to be saved." Elionor's face was flushed with frustration. There was a heaviness to her words, like she had spoken them before. "Each of us champions understood what we were sacrificing when we carved our name into the Pillar. But clearly you didn't."

"I *do* understand sacrifice." Briony thought again of the champion's ring on her finger, what she'd done to take it. Elionor might've said "us champions," excluding her, but Briony had earned her place here. She was still putting her life on the line. She was as much a champion as any of them. "I gave up everything to take my sister's spot. Not because I wanted to win. But because I was willing to bet my life on saving others."

"So bet *your* life, not ours." Elionor swept her hands out, gesturing at the courtyard around them. "I don't want your ridiculous idealism and half-baked theories poisoning my alliance."

"Your alliance?" Briony's temper flared. "Your alliance is a death trap. All you're going to do is pick off the others, and then whoever's strongest will kill the rest."

"You think I don't know that?" Elionor snorted. "Finley's plan is transparent, but I don't care. It's my plan, too. My crafting skill is far greater than his. Without that Sword, I can take him and Carbry out. Especially once I have a Relic of my own."

"Finley's plan has changed," Briony snapped. "He believes me. And if the four of us work together, if we share each of our families' stories, we might actually be able to end this."

But Elionor just shook her head. "You're just drawing out the inevitable. Six of us will die. One of us will live. If you can't accept that, you don't belong here."

Briony grabbed the map again, then waved it in Elionor's face. "Carbry clearly cares about this stuff, too. Why don't we talk to him about it? Put it to a vote?"

Elionor slapped the paper away. "We are *not* giving him false hope."

Briony was ready to go tell the others about it anyway when red light splashed across the table. Both of them whipped around to face the pillar and watched silently as the sixth star streaked down the ancient stone in a straight line.

Briony's heart leapt. The sixth star meant *her* Relic. The Mirror.

It was perfect. It was fate. It was time for Briony to prove she *was* the hero of this story.

"You don't have to believe me yet," Briony said. "But we're going to get this Relic. And then I'm going to prove you wrong."

ALISTAIR LOWE

What is a happily ever after to the child is a nightmare to the monster.

A Tradition of Tragedy

The evening the sixth star of the pillar shone red, all Alistair felt was disappointment.

Another week had passed since Alistair had given Isobel the Cloak, and in the darkness of the Cave, time managed to slip by unnoticed, its passage marked only by their diminishing supply of processed food.

And now the Mirror was falling, exactly as they'd hoped.

But foolishly, selfishly, Alistair would've traded it for one more night with Isobel. So they could keep pretending to be in any horror story other than their own.

"You don't have to come," he told her as she slipped on her mud-stained trainers.

"Of course I do," Isobel said. "You're not lugging around the duffel bag this time. All the champions will want the Mirror—our best strategy is me coming along and touching it first."

Alistair knew this. They'd rehearsed the strategy many times, but Alistair still didn't like it. Isobel might've been protected from common magick while wearing the Cloak, but the Blair's Sword used high magick.

Outside, the wind howled, making the Cave's defensive enchantments thrum. Alistair's skin prickled, and like he always did, he crept toward the entrance. He needed to know his wards had held. He needed to check—

Isobel squeezed his shoulder, and he jolted. "Don't you dare leave without me."

"I wasn't going to," he said. "But promise me—if we encounter trouble, you run. No matter what."

Something between sadness and resolve crossed her face, and Alistair noticed that, for the first time since she'd arrived in the Cave, her hands glittered with spellrings. "I can't run anymore. I need the Mirror."

Without the Mirror, Isobel would likely kill herself trying to get her powers back, and that would undermine all the other plans Alistair had spent the past week brewing.

"Are you all right?" she asked him suddenly. "You're jumpier than usual, and you haven't been sleeping."

"I've never been better."

He strode toward the Cave's exit, where the Blood Veil washed the darkness in harsh crimson. At this elevation, he could spot Ilvernath in the distance.

It had all felt so important, once. Being champion, his family's high magick, his grandmother's approval.

His mother had told Alistair to ensure that his brother hadn't died in vain, but the weight of that death was on *her* shoulders, not his. When she killed Hendry, she'd lost both her sons.

Which was why, once Isobel got her magick back, once they were the only two champions remaining, Alistair would ensure she won their "duel." He had nothing to go back to in Ilvernath, not anymore. But she did.

The red streak of the falling star ripped through the sky, headed for the forest.

The two wordlessly descended the mountain and entered the trees. The night was quiet and chilled, and though October had certainly changed the leaves into an array of rich autumnal color, amid the tournament, they and the rest of the landscape wore scarlet.

Alistair marveled at how severe everything looked when illuminated by the Blood Veil. His hands had gone sallow. Even Isobel's soft features had sharpened, and the whites of her eyes were dull and pink.

"Why are you stopping?" Isobel asked.

"Because it looks like it'll fall right around here." Alistair pointed at the comet-like streak in the sky directly above them. "So now we wait."

Quickly, he cast several spells over the surrounding area to muffle the sound of their voices and shield them from long-distance curses. The pair might've been the first to arrive, but he was certain other champions were soon to follow.

An owl hooted behind him and, instinctively, Alistair cast a Guillotine's Gift. A branch severed from a nearby tree and crashed—soundlessly, thanks to his wards—to the grass. He whipped around, his heart pounding.

"Al," Isobel said sharply.

She'd unknowingly used his brother's nickname for him. It made his heart clench, an unwelcome feeling when he'd rather his heart just stop altogether.

Realizing the threat had been nonexistent, he took a step back from her, pressing himself even more firmly against the tree. But while distracted in his thoughts, his foot snagged on a root and he slipped. He caught himself on a branch, swearing.

"What are you thinking about?" Isobel asked, her concern obvious in her voice.

"What does it look like I'm thinking about?" he shot back. "The others could arrive any moment." He mentally combed through his spell collection for more defensive enchantments, but even with eight, ten, *twenty*, the Sword could cut through them. He'd faced the Blair champion with the Relic once already, but that didn't mean—

"You need a distraction," Isobel told him.

"Now is *not* the time for a distraction."

"Okay. That was a bad choice of word. What you need is to relax." She took a step closer, backing him into a nearby tree. His heart picked up even faster. "Five letters. A mathematical symbol. Think fast."

Alistair wracked his brain for the answer. He normally did crosswords when he was bored, when he had nothing else to think about. But right now he had a thousand thoughts competing for focus in his mind. The peony smell of Isobel's perfume. The fact that he'd never brought anyone into the woods other than his brother. How even with all his enchantments, he still felt exposed. Vulnerable. Weak.

"Power?" Alistair guessed, unsure if that even made sense.

She smirked. "What an Alistair Lowe answer. I *meant* 'equal.' You can't read my thoughts. I can't read yours."

Thank everything for that, Alistair thought, skimming the silhouette of her lips, her neck, her waist in the dark. He was pretty sure she'd yell at him if she could still read his mind. For what he was thinking about her. For what he was thinking about giving up.

"It's about to become real, isn't it?" she asked, her voice suddenly gentle.

The Relics fell randomly, at any time, in any order, and even if Isobel desperately needed that second Relic, it was hard for Alistair to view its quick fall as anything other than bad luck. That time was all he had, and it wasn't enough to make Isobel like him after she'd spent so long afraid of him. To figure out who he was without his monster stories. Without his brother.

"It is," Alistair agreed.

"You have that expression," Isobel said warily.

Alistair clenched his hand into a fist. "Like murder?"

"No, not this time," she murmured.

He swallowed, knowing that if everything truly did change tonight, he might never have his chance again. "I really am sorry for how I . . . for who I am."

"I like who you are more than who you pretend to be." Then she reached out and took his hand, interlocking her fingers with his. He didn't know if she was still playing games with him. He didn't think so, but he didn't care. The hope that flared in his chest felt better than anything had in a long time.

Alistair's logic told him that this was a terrible, dangerous idea. Even with his protective spells surrounding them, they weren't invincible.

Her lips hovered a breath away from his own. Her free hand found its way around his neck, teasing the dark curls behind his ears.

In a war between logic and wickedness, his wickedness always won. And so Alistair's free hand slid down the small of her back, pulling her closer to him. There were no rules to the tournament, other than victory and death, but this still felt like breaking one.

Snap! A twig cracked somewhere behind them, and Alistair twisted around Isobel so she was protected behind him. The branches around them moved in an eerie, dreadful wind.

"Did you hear that?" he hissed.

Isobel nodded and put a finger to her lips.

The two of them stood there frozen for several moments. Footsteps came toward them, loud from the sound of dried leaves crushed beneath shoes. Alistair swallowed.

"We know you're out there!" a voice called, one Alistair recognized as the Blair.

A light shone through the trees, dim and ghostly. Two silhouettes drew closer. Both carried a flashlight. The Blair also carried the Sword, which he swiped through the air as though slicing through thickets. Panic seized Alistair by the throat. This was exactly what he'd been afraid of. That he would—

The Sword struck his enchantments, and they shattered with a cacophonous crash. Alistair forced himself to lower his hands. Because of the Cloak, Isobel was camouflaged to anyone she wished. So he needed to look like he was alone.

"Look who finally emerged from hiding," the Payne sneered at Alistair. "You should've accepted our offer when you had the chance. We're far more powerful than you ever gave us credit for."

"Why isn't he wearing the Cloak?" the Blair asked, his voice low.

The Payne narrowed her eyes. She scanned the clearing, and Alistair heard Isobel suck in her breath beside him.

"So you took an ally after all," she said.

The Blair's eyes widened. "Isobel? Is she—"

"I don't know what you're talking about," Alistair cut in, trying to keep his voice steady despite the panicked pace of his heart. "I work alone."

The Blair shined his flashlight toward them, making Alistair squint. "The Cloak doesn't camouflage your shadow, Isobel."

Alistair cursed under his breath. He'd overlooked that detail.

The Payne smirked. "You're not that scary," she told Alistair. And to Isobel, sighting her shadow: "And you're not that smart. Not smart enough to keep the reporters' attention, anyway."

Alistair didn't want Isobel drawn into this fray. He leaned toward her and whispered, "I'll distract them. You go after the Mirror once it touches down."

Isobel dropped his hand, but she hesitated instead of racing off through the trees.

Alistair would not let her foil her one chance to get her sense for magick back, not for him. He shoved her out of the way and cast the Dragon's Breath.

As the ravaging flames tore through the forest air, Isobel finally took off into the darkness.

Relief washed over him. Maybe she would reach the Mirror. Maybe she would hide. What mattered to him was that she was safe.

The Blair turned to follow her, but Alistair cast a Blockade spell. Bramble and roots erupted from the earth, obstructing the Blair's path.

The Payne growled and shot another curse at Alistair. Alistair managed to deflect it with another Shark's Skin, only for the Blair to shatter that as well.

"You'd let her escape?" The Payne girl advanced, shooting out new curses with every step. Alistair was rapidly running low on defensive spells. "How *noble* of you."

It was not in Alistair's nature to be noble. Three weeks ago, if he'd known how un-Alistair-like he would behave during the tournament, he would've been shocked. All his life, he'd thought Aunt Alphina had been overcome by the horror of the tournament, and so he'd vowed to be too cruel, too monstrous for guilt.

Now he understood. The greater horror was returning home, where your loved ones no longer waited for you.

Maybe that newfound nobility would be his downfall.

But he didn't want to die here, not yet. Maybe Isobel *would* get her powers back tonight, and everything would change. But if the two of them did see this through to the end, if they were the last ones left standing, then they would also have time. It was all he had left to hope for. To fight for.

Alistair gritted his teeth as the Sword shattered his last defensive spell. Debris littered the ground from every curse Alistair had sent at them, yet both the Payne and the Blair still stood. Sweaty and scraped and burned, but standing.

"Face it," the Blair said, moving forward. Behind him, the Payne smiled viciously. "You won't win this. Our allies will reach the Relic before Isobel."

Maybe so, but still, Alistair sent out a curse—the Forest's Hunger. The trees surrounding them bent low, their branches reaching forward like hands. It was not a deadly attack, but it was time-consuming and irritating. While the Blair whacked at the branches with the Sword and the Payne deflected many with a shield, Alistair turned and ran through the trees, in the opposite direction of the falling Mirror—now minutes from touching down.

He wanted to draw them as far away from Isobel as possible,

but he didn't run for long. After half a kilometer, he collided with a tree.

"Fuck," he growled, clutching his throbbing knee. He should've known this was where nobility would get him.

It was too dark to see clearly, but shining any sort of light would alert the two other champions to where he'd gone. He stepped forward, and a pain shot up from his knee into his spine. He stumbled and groaned.

Someone laughed behind him, high-pitched and girlish. Alistair turned, hands raised, as the Payne stepped around a thornbush, her cheek dripping blood where his branches had cut her. Alistair winced as he leaned on his injured leg. He was in no condition to run, which meant his only option was to fight.

The Payne must've sensed this, too, because she smiled widely and said, "I could play this game all night."

Alistair held his breath as he waited for the Blair to appear, but the Payne remained alone. Maybe he'd gone after Isobel. The thought of his Sword left Alistair's stomach in knots.

Alistair tried to think of a way to overpower the Payne. He had a few stronger curses at his disposal, but only a few.

He cast a Chimera's Bite, which she deflected with yet another of her seemingly endless supply of high-class shields. He cast a Dragon's Breath, then a Basilisk's Gaze. The dark of the forest around them came alive with bright flashes of light. One of Alistair's curses succeeded in tearing through her shield, sinking fangs into the Payne's neck until she screamed. One of her curses knocked into Alistair's knee like a hammer, and even over his own scream, he *heard* the sound of his bone shattering.

He crumpled. The radiating pain made him delirious, and he grappled to stand as she approached. The next curse he shot whizzed far off its mark and burned a hole straight through the heart of a tree. The Payne laughed as she stood before him.

"Any last words?" she asked.

He didn't have anything left to say. No more spells or curses or plans.

Except for one.

The Lamb's Sacrifice.

He clenched his fist, feeling its power course through the stone ring. He would rather die than use his brother's death to kill another, even if it meant his own survival.

Maybe that made him noble after all.

"Just get it over with," he said, his voice catching only slightly.

She lunged forward. Alistair swatted at her arm to block her, but as soon as he did, pain burst in his abdomen. He looked down to find a red stain spreading across his lower stomach where her curse had struck him. He coughed, and blood spurted from his lips.

"I always wanted to be the one to kill you," she said smugly.

Alistair clutched at his stomach. His palm was hot and wet with blood. His other hand was braced against the oak tree beside him, fingernails digging into the coarse bark as he swallowed down the pain.

Trembling, he reached into his pocket where he'd stowed a few healing spells, but she shoved him to the ground. He groaned, his head smacking the dirt.

Even dizzy from loss of blood, Alistair was not without tricks. While she knelt beside him and rifled through his clothes for every spellstone he had left, he swiftly slid off the ring with the Lamb's Sacrifice and tucked it into the sleeve of his sweater.

Then with one last, shuddering breath, he closed his eyes and went limp.

He felt the Payne rip the last of the spellrings from his fingers, and after she finished, she lifted his chin up and whispered, "Beg."

She made a far better villain than he did.

When he didn't respond, she laughed. "You didn't live up to your stories, did you?"

She fumbled for his pulse, and panic flared in Alistair's chest.

A loud crash rang out beyond the trees. The Mirror had fallen—

and close. Elionor's grip on his arm loosened. After a moment's hesitation, she rose to her feet and rushed away.

Once she was long gone, Alistair finally felt safe enough to breathe. She hadn't had the chance to finish him off, but her negligence wouldn't stop him from bleeding out. His stomach continued to throb in violent pulses, and the world smelled sharp and metallic.

He had more spellstones in the Cave. If he could make it there . . .

Propped on his elbows, he tried to drag himself through the dirt to his last chance at life, but the pain made him cry out. He collapsed, breathless, into the grass.

Just as Alistair's eyes began to droop, his brother sat down beside him, ashy and gray like a dried flower. "I knew I'd find you in the forest."

Alistair felt no shock at seeing Hendry, even if he was merely a hallucination. Only relief. Alistair leaned his head back as though pressing into a pillow instead of earth, shaking off what had been a terrible dream.

"No place I'd rather die," Alistair mumbled, his voice lulled and groggy.

Hendry looked up at the crimson night sky. "I don't think you're meant to rest quite yet."

Alistair disagreed. He didn't deserve to live, having failed Hendry.

"And you?" Alistair asked. Hendry wore the same clothes as he had at the Magpie, though the gray tint to his skin made him look ghostly in comparison to the charcoal color of his T-shirt. "Are you here? Or are you gone?"

"If I was gone, could I be here talking to you?"

Alistair wanted to frown at him—he hated questions answered with questions—but his consciousness was giving out. When he reached out for his brother's hand, his fingers intertwined with bramble.

ISOBEL MACASLAN

I was never a contender for champion, but I still used to have nightmares of it, as a child. Of my name carved in stone and struck
through. Of the inescapable red sky. Of dying violently.

A Tradition of Tragedy

Isobel sprinted through the trees.

As five, ten, fifteen minutes ticked by, she stole glances at the
night sky, where the falling star drew closer. It was still impossible
to discern where in the forest it would land. She ducked beneath
branches and listened for the sound of Finley or Elionor approaching, but she only heard crickets.

He's more powerful than they are, she thought frantically. *And he's
faced them before.*

A thunderous boom swept across the forest as the Mirror touched
down, not far from where Isobel stood. She raced toward it, then skid-
ded to a halt at the edge of a clearing, where the Mirror floated in
the center. It was small, with an ornate gold handle embedded with
three spellstones, and if Isobel had her powers, she knew it would glow
with the typical red luster of high magick.

Just as she prepared to run toward it, another figure entered the
clearing.

Elionor Payne.

You need to beat her there, Isobel screamed internally to herself.
But one question was louder, filling her with dread. *What happened to
Alistair and Finley?*

Isobel froze. Elionor didn't see her—not only was the Cloak camouflaging all but Isobel's shadow, but Elionor's gaze was locked on the Mirror. But as Elionor neared, Isobel saw dark stains across her clothes and scarlet smeared across her skin. Blood. And by the way Elionor strutted, it was not she who was wounded.

Alistair.

Isobel tried to convince herself she was wrong, that it might be Finley's blood, but she knew Alistair wouldn't have let Elionor go after the Mirror unless he didn't have a choice. And now *she* had a choice: leave him behind and grab the Mirror, or save him the way he'd tried to save her.

Isobel ran. Not toward the Mirror—but away from it, back toward Alistair.

When she swore she was close, she slowed down her pace and squinted through the dark thickets of trees, wishing she had her magick to cast some sort of light. It was deathly silent except for the crickets.

"Al?" she whispered again. "Al?"

She tripped over a root and reached for the closest tree to catch herself. But when she turned around, she realized it was no root.

It was a body.

Alistair slouched at the base of an oak tree, his head slumped over. He didn't move. His already pale skin was several shades paler. One of his hands clutched at his stomach, and Isobel saw he was hurt, just like she'd feared. Alistair had protected her. He'd faced the other champions to secure the Cloak, and she'd rewarded him by abandoning him to be injured—maybe even killed.

"Don't be dead," she whispered. She fell to her knees beside him and lifted his head. His eyes were closed. She felt for his pulse. "Don't die on me, Al."

She grasped Alistair's hand. He winced and groaned something unintelligible, reaching forward.

"What is it?" she croaked out, relieved that he was still cognizant enough to communicate.

"Blood," he rasped. "You needed . . . blood." Alistair lifted his hand, and his palm was coated with crimson. Isobel's heart filled with dread. Whatever curse or weapon had struck him had cut deep into his abdomen.

"Please tell me this was a curse and not the Sword," she said. If it was the Sword, no magick would heal it.

Alistair coughed. "A curse. Class . . . eight, at least."

Isobel hadn't even realized Elionor was capable of casting a class eight curse. Maybe all those cheap ploys Elionor had made for media attention really had paid off. Must've been nice.

Isobel riffled through her pockets and dumped out every spellstone she had. She'd brought them in case she got her powers back before they returned to the Cave.

"H-here. Some of these have to be healing spells." She shoved a tourmaline into his hand, wishing she could sense the magick inside it. "I think this one—"

"Don't worry about me. Just use the blood."

She was nearly certain it'd been the sacrifice that had ruined the Reaper's Embrace. But a blood sacrifice could mean a hundred things—it didn't have to mean *this*. It didn't have to mean a gift given by someone with little left to give, someone who Isobel wanted and cared about far more than she should. And being wrong was a deadly risk.

Maybe Alistair *was* right. Maybe this was Isobel's only chance.

But she didn't care. There had to be a way to save herself that didn't doom him. "We can worry about my powers later." She shoved more spellstones into his hands. "You need to heal yourself—"

"I can't." He let them fall from his grasp. "I can't . . ."

Isobel didn't know whether to believe him. It was true that casting required perfect concentration, but Alistair was gifted at casting—a prodigy, even. She suspected that he was only being stubborn, that he was trying to save *her*.

"Hurry." Alistair lifted open one eye, but cringed as though it hurt to do so. "They're still looking for you."

For *her*. Not him. That meant they thought Alistair was already gone.

She pressed her hands to his wound, desperately wishing she knew more about first aid, but he pushed her away.

"A class ten curse requires a great sacrifice," he said seriously. He coughed again, and a bit of blood dribbled onto his chin.

"You don't know that."

"I know that you didn't get to the Mirror in time. Otherwise ... you wouldn't be here."

"That isn't true. And I swear, if you don't fucking heal yourself this very moment, I'll ... I'll ..." But when Isobel tried to give him the spellstones for a third time, she noticed his hand had gone slack. He'd lost consciousness.

"No, no," she said frantically. Without her ability to heal him, he was going to die.

Isobel felt reality the same way she felt her father's hand squeezing her shoulder. She'd answered countless interview questions about what she expected the tournament to be like, yet for almost a year, the idea of it all felt distant. Even the past two weeks seemed shrouded in the hazy fog of a dream.

Now, it was real. The cold of the night. Her knees pressed into the pebbles and damp earth. Her senses on alert for the smallest movement in the trees, the faintest rustle of bramble or leaves. The smell of autumn and blood and her own sweat. The crimson cast of everything, like her own terror superimposed on the world.

Frantically, she reached into her duffel bag and grabbed her spellboard.

"Are you happy now, you terrible excuse for a rival?" she choked, tears blurring her vision. "You better hope this kills me because otherwise, I will heal you and then torture you in ways even your twisted mind can't imagine."

Isobel rushed through her work. She sliced off another lock of her hair, laid out the dried chrysanthemum and other ingredients across the septogram, the single white quartz at the center. Her hands trembled with each movement, remembering the disaster that had occurred the first time she'd attempted this. The phantom taste of blood lingered in her mouth.

Swallowing her urge to be sick, she dipped two fingers in Alistair's wound and smeared it across the board.

She squeezed her eyes shut, partially to focus, partially to avoid looking at Alistair. She couldn't hear him breathing. The longer she waited, the more she began to sense the presence of raw magick around her. The magick tucked within the bushes tickled the hairs at the back of her neck.

After waiting long enough, she finally leaned down and gave the bloody spellboard a kiss.

A burning sensation coursed through her eyes, and she stifled a scream and squeezed them even tighter. It felt like her retinas were being scorched away.

Reid had warned her that attempting to fix her powers could kill her.

The pain was so intense. Her breath came in rapid gasps, and she collapsed on the ground beside Alistair, her palms pressed against her closed eyes.

Then, after what felt like hours, a cooling sensation passed through her. When she opened her eyes, she saw the magick glowing in the flasks scattered around her on the grass. She saw the white pulse of light in every stone, waiting for her.

Without pausing to celebrate her victory, she grabbed each of her healing spellstones and tore at Alistair's sweater and undershirt. She gasped when she exposed the wound, his flesh split open and brimming with blood. Swallowing her dread, she pressed her hand to it, and in her other, she squeezed a Healer's Touch spellstone.

She cast it once, twice, three times, until all its magick had depleted. The blood stopped flowing. Still, the wound didn't close. She moved on to the next stone.

And the next one.

"Come on, Al."

And the next.

And the next.

Finally the wound closed, and his broken patella was mostly re-set, but she had exhausted the stones and Alistair hadn't opened his eyes. Clutching his hand, Isobel rested her cheek against his chest, listening for a pulse. At first, all she heard was the noise of forest crickets and owls. Then she finally made out his heartbeat—faint but there—and far beyond, the sound of approaching footsteps. Probably Finley and Elionor returning to finish her, too.

"Seven letters," she whispered to Alistair. "To endure."

"Survive," she heard him rasp. She almost thought she'd imagined it at first, but then she lifted her head and realized his eyes were open, watching her. He let out a wheezy breath, then he smiled. She realized she'd never seen Alistair smile in a way that wasn't meant to be a threat. "Hello, rival," he whispered.

The footsteps running toward them grew louder. With her free hand, Isobel reached for her curserings, ready to face reality at last.

"When I say it," Isobel told him, "you run."

Briony Thorburn

The youngest champion on record to win the tournament was fourteen-year-old Callum Thorburn. The Thorburns consider it an achievement, when really, it's a tragedy.

A Tradition of Tragedy

There had been no real time to prepare once the Relic started falling. Briony could only hope all four of them were ready to carry out the strategy they'd worked on for the past week, despite her and Elionor's fight. As soon as the sixth star shone red, all that had been forgotten anyway—Briony had left almost immediately to retrieve the Mirror, while the other three began their own preparations.

Elionor and Finley planned to head off would-be attackers coming from the mountains, while Carbry moved toward the Castle to deal with Gavin Grieve. Briony was heading straight for the Relic, but it wasn't falling on the trajectory she'd expected. Instead of the moorlands, it fell in the forest, closer to where Finley and Elionor had gone.

She trekked closer to the area where the scraggly underbrush became wood again, trying to follow the red light. A Pick Up the Pace spell made a five-kilometer sprint feel like half the distance. This wasn't like the Sword, which had basically dropped into her lap, or the Cloak, which had been easy to follow. She was only sure she was heading in the right direction when cursefire whizzed above her head.

She jerked backward and threw up one of the cheap shields she'd crafted, holding it alongside her speed spell as two boys tumbled into the clearing beside her, mid-battle.

She recognized Carbry's face first. His blond curls were slicked back with sweat, his expression intensely focused. He raised a hand and arrows glimmered in the air.

The second boy snorted, then cast a countercurse. A surge of power crackled through the air, a shimmering net that destroyed the arrows everywhere it touched.

Briony didn't understand how the hell Gavin Grieve had gotten so strong—but the magick worked on her, too, dissolving her shield *and* the Pick Up the Pace spell. Both of their heads swung to look at her. Gavin raised a warning hand.

"Here." Briony darted to Carbry's side. "Let me help."

But the look on his face was not relieved. It was hostile. "Get away from me," he snarled, backing into the trees.

"What?" Briony gasped. "Why?"

"You attacked Elionor. Don't try to pretend you didn't."

Briony gaped at him. "What are you talking about?"

"She told us everything. How you turned on her as soon as you saw the Relic. How you ran away to take it for yourself."

"I didn't. I followed the plan. Our plan—"

"You're a good liar," Carbry said, with that false bravado she now knew was just a front for fear. "But you can stop now. We know who you really are."

Briony had a sudden flash of the betrayal on Innes's face; the warmth of her pinky finger as Briony slid off the champion's ring.

"Carbry," she said. "Come on—I'm—We're *allies*."

Carbry glared at her, his blue eyes glistening with tears. "I really thought I could trust you."

She put the missing pieces of the night together, a deadly puzzle. How Elionor hadn't believed her, but had let her leave first anyway to reach the Relic. How her absence must have allowed Elionor to craft whatever narrative suited her to make the boys believe Briony had betrayed them.

Briony couldn't let this be the way their alliance ended. She had given up too much to forge it.

"I don't want to hurt you," Briony told him. "I swear."

"So you're not allied anymore?" Gavin asked. Briony had almost forgotten he was there. Instead of running or casting a spell of his own, he watched them as though this were a spectator sport. She noticed that he wore very few spellrings—three to her and Carbry's ten. "Interesting."

Carbry scowled at him. "I'll kill you both. I—I know I can."

Before Carbry could good make on his threat, Gavin rolled his eyes and summoned a curse of his own. Carbry froze a moment later, his face contorted in a rictus of rage. Through the light of the Blood Veil, he looked unrecognizably grotesque, his teeth stained an unnatural pink.

A sudden pain swept across Gavin's face, and he stumbled. Carbry shook off the effects of Gavin's curse a moment later, then, seizing the opportunity, he charged toward him and cast another spell.

This one landed. Dark green vines sprang from the underbrush and wound around Gavin's ankles.

Gavin fell to his knees, choking and gasping as as more vines sprung from the underbrush and coiled around his throat. Briony realized that this was her chance. The boys were distracted. She could run back into the forest and search for the Mirror in some vain hope that the other champions hadn't already found it.

But if she did that, Gavin Grieve would die.

Briony didn't care for Gavin at all, didn't even know him, but she still believed she could save him. Save them all.

She cast the Mirror Shards. The vines dissipated as soon as her magick touched them. Gavin clawed at his throat where the vines had been, only to find himself grasping at air. He stared at her, shocked, then bolted into the woods as Carbry turned accusatorially toward her. Of course Gavin was running away—she should've done so, too, while she'd had the chance.

She still didn't want to hurt Carbry. She didn't want to hurt anyone. Briony sucked in a breath.

"Please don't make me do this." The Deathly Slumber on her finger glowed white, ready for her to cast it. "I know we can figure this out. If you just listen to me—"

"No! I've listened to you enough. Elionor's right, this alliance was never going to last forever. And I can't just hide in the Monastery until everyone else is dead."

The fear in his eyes, the stubbornness in his expression—it reminded her so much of Innes when she'd attacked her.

Briony had cast the Deathly Slumber then, too. But this time . . . this time, she hesitated.

Carbry didn't.

The oval ring Briony had noticed back at the Monastery began to glow. Giant arrows formed in the air around Carbry, glinting threateningly as they pointed at her.

Briony gasped, panicked, and threw up the Mirror Image spell. A wall of shimmering white magick appeared in front of her as the arrows surged forward. They battered against her shield, but it held, absorbing his magick. Relief stirred in her chest.

And then the spell did what it was designed to do. The part of the enchantment Innes hadn't had time to finish when she was trying to defend herself against Briony.

It flung the curse back at him.

Arrows formed again, but this time they were pointed at Carbry. Briony could feel the force of power behind them, much more than she'd anticipated. This curse was easily class eight—and she was a far stronger spellcaster than Carbry.

Panic built in her chest as she tried to pull back the enchantment. But it was too late. The arrows were already flying across the clearing.

Carbry barely had time to suck in his breath before they found their target. His arms, his legs—his throat. He fell to his knees, letting out the most horrible sound Briony had ever heard.

It was a scream that made the world stand still. A harsh, piercing cry of pain and desperation. Briony cried out in horror as the last few arrows struck his face. Carbry's scream cut out abruptly, and he keeled over backward.

Briony rushed to him, knelt, and peered at his face. The sight before her left her nauseous. Two arrows protruded from his eyes. Another had struck the center of his throat. Blood dribbled from the wound; it glistened at the edges of his lips, pooled in the hollows of his face like drops of water. There was so much of it. Too much. She reached helplessly for his hand, slick with crimson, and gripped it as hard as she could.

"I'm so sorry," she whimpered. "Carbry, I'm so sorry—"

"Tell . . ." he rasped, "I love . . ."

And then he said nothing at all. His hand went limp in hers as she gazed at his mutilated face. She knew Carbry was gone when his champion's ring began to shimmer, then dissolved into flecks of red light.

She'd killed him. She'd *killed* him. And she understood in that one, awful moment that no matter how hard she'd tried to prepare herself for this, no matter what she'd said to Finley, there was nothing heroic about taking someone's life.

"Hey." Gavin's voice was sharp. Briony turned to realize he was kneeling beside her, extending a hand. His voice sounded very far away. "You need to get up."

Briony realized, dimly, that she was shaking. She thought he had run away, but here he was, looking at her with clear concern. Maybe it was a trap, but even if that was true, she was too shocked to do anything except take his hand and pull herself up.

Her fingers were sticky with blood and grime. Carbry's body lay before her, twisted in agony. She and Elionor had encouraged him to try that curse, to be crueler than his ancestors. Cruel enough to kill.

Like he'd been trained to do. Like they all had.

"Of course not." She folded her shaking arms around herself. "I've never killed anyone before."

"It was his curse." Gavin opened his hand, and Briony realized he had the ring Carbry had been wearing. It sat in his palm, smeared with blood—just like Innes's champion's ring had been. Briony felt a rush of wooziness as he continued to speak. "This is . . . strong spellwork. It would've killed you if you hadn't stopped it."

"No!" The word burst furiously from Briony's throat. "I'm not supposed to kill everyone. I'm supposed to save them."

Gavin frowned. "Did you read different tournament rules than I did?"

Briony let out a shrill laugh. "Fine then, kill me. Go ahead. Try and chase down the Relic we're all looking for."

"I thought about it. But it doesn't make sense. The other champions are all working together. An alliance will get us through the night."

Before she could respond, her name rang out from the hill behind them.

"Briony!"

She whipped around. Finley Blair was advancing down the hill. He looked utterly disheveled, his sleeve torn, a cursemark glowing on his cheek.

"You're alive," he said, gasping for breath. "Are you wounded?"

"No," Briony murmured. "Why do you care? Didn't Elionor tell you I betrayed her?"

"I didn't believe her." His voice was ragged. "I knew you wouldn't turn on us."

Briony sagged with relief. But then Finley's gaze flickered behind her shoulder—and went gravely still.

She knew what he had seen: Carbry's body.

"No," he murmured. "Grieve, did you kill him?"

Beside her, Gavin choked out a laugh. "It wasn't me, man."

Briony watched Finley's face move through grief and disbelief and despair all at once. And when he spoke again, she had already steeled herself for what he was going to say.

"Did you do this?"

Briony thought of the Mirror she'd come here for. Of Carbry's blood, still warm against her skin. Elionor had tugged them apart—but it was Briony who had broken their alliance for good. With the one thing she'd come here to prevent: a murder.

"He attacked me," she whispered. "It was an accident."

"An accident?" He looked at Carbry's mess of a body. The pain on Finley's face broke something inside of her—and worse, how quickly he molded his face into his usual impassivity. "I suppose this was inevitable, wasn't it?"

"No, Finley. You heard what I said under that truth spell. Please, you have to believe me—"

"I did believe you!" Finley's voice shook. "I came here to help you. I broke all my rules for you, and now . . ."

He raised his Sword, and Briony realized she had no energy left to fight. No words she could say that would make him listen.

Part of her wanted to let him end it, here and now. At least then it would be over. But she would die a disgrace. Whatever shreds of her pride remained tugged at her, urging her to run.

"Come on," she said to Gavin, and then she turned and bolted into the forest. A moment later, footsteps crashed through the underbrush behind her. She could only hope they were Gavin's.

Everything was a horrible, muddled tangle in her mind. The pain on Finley's face. The bloody ring in Gavin's palm. All the betrayal and confusion that had brought her to this moment.

And overlaying all of it, waiting every time she blinked, was the image of those arrows deep in Carbry's eyes.

She had killed him for a prize she didn't even want to win.

Above them, the Blood Veil changed. The harsh crimson of the sky lessened slightly, a muted scarlet. But it did nothing to lighten the bloodstains on her hands.

ALISTAIR LOWE

Ilvernath drivers take a detour to avoid the Lowe estate. I don't
think they even dwell on the reason anymore. It's just a habit.
                                    A Tradition of Tragedy

When Alistair regained lucidity, he was still sprawled out
in that same spot below the oak tree. A cool wind blew
over his exposed stomach, and he moved a shaking hand
to cover his skin. To his surprise, the mortal wound the Payne had
dealt him was just another scar.

Isobel stood over him. She wore crystal spellrings on every finger,
and her Cloak billowed out behind her, almost haunting.

"When I say it," Isobel murmured, "you run."

Alistair attempted to push himself up, but his strength gave out.
"Joke's on you," he said mirthlessly. "I can't get up."

Isobel shot him an exasperated look. The footsteps approached
through the forest, and Isobel readied to attack.

"Elionor!" she called. Alistair realized Elionor was probably the
Payne's name. "If you take a step closer, you'll wish you—"

"It's not Elionor," choked a female voice. The Thorburn stepped
through the trees, her hands up in surrender, and behind her, the
Grieve.

Kill them, a voice in Alistair's mind whispered, his Lowe instinct.
There was no more perfect opportunity for Isobel to strike.

But as much as Alistair liked to win, the thought left him more
fatigued than exhilarated. It wasn't that he cared about the Thorburn's

or the Grieve's fates—he didn't even know their names—but their deaths would only bring Alistair closer to the truth: once he and Isobel defeated all of their competitors, there could only be one person to leave the tournament alive.

And even if he'd evaded death for now, he still wouldn't let it be him.

"What the fuck happened to you?" the Grieve growled, looking at Alistair as though the sight of him bloodied and vulnerable personally offended him. The thought of a Grieve seeing him like this offended Alistair, too.

"You're working with the Grieve now, too?" Isobel asked the Thorburn.

The Grieve opened his mouth to argue, but the Thorburn quickly cut him off. "I'm not with that alliance anymore. The two of us are alone."

Alistair looked up and realized, for the first time, the Blood Veil had paled slightly. One of the champions was dead.

"Why should I believe you?" Isobel asked.

"I was betrayed. Carbry attacked me, but Gavin and I . . ." The Thorburn looked down at her blood-crusted hands and shuddered. "We both ran. We didn't mean to find you, but maybe it was a good thing we did."

Isobel's gaze shot toward the sky. "Carbry Darrow is dead?"

Briony nodded gravely.

Alistair, for many reasons, didn't like the idea of expanding their group of two to four. He didn't trust the Grieve or the Thorburn. And he'd already made his plans for the end of the tournament. New alliances were only more complications.

Isobel took a deep breath and relaxed her stance. "You saved me before, Briony. Consider it a favor returned." But the sharp edge to her voice made it clear she wasn't happy about it.

The Thorburn's—Briony's—eyes shifted to the Grieve, then slowly back to Isobel. "Him, too," she murmured, almost as an afterthought.

The Grieve nodded, though his expression looked more murderous than pleading. "Yes. Me, too."

Isobel pursed her lips. "Fine. But where will we all go?"

"We could go back to the lair," Alistair suggested, seeing that he was outnumbered. At least then they'd all be in his Landmark, which answered to him. Plus, his belongings were still there, and he needed them, now that Elionor had stolen every stone he'd had.

Except one.

"You call your Landmark your lair?" Alistair heard the Grieve ask, but he wasn't paying attention. He reached into his sweater sleeve and pulled out the Lamb's Sacrifice. He slid it back on with a relieved sigh. In this small way, he still had his brother.

"The Cave is too small for all of us," Isobel said, and Alistair realized that Isobel was different now that she had her powers back. She was more confident, already the unspoken leader of the group. "You claimed the Castle, didn't you? Take us there."

The Grieve didn't respond right away. Instead, his gaze settled on Alistair—more specifically, on the blood covering Alistair's torn shirt. His face contorted into something cold, a look Alistair knew well. The Thorburn might've shared some sort of bond with Isobel, but Alistair had trouble believing the Grieve was loyal to anyone. Even if Isobel protected him for the time being at Briony's request, if he saw an opportunity, he would strike.

"Fine," the Grieve said flatly. "I'll lead us there."

"I know the way," Isobel replied, shoving her spellstones littering the ground back into her pockets. One ring in particular—a white quartz—she slipped onto the chain of her necklace, beside her locket. Alistair realized it must've contained the finished recipe for Reaper's Embrace, though she hadn't charged it with magick yet. "You can help Alistair walk."

Before Alistair could be offended, she shot him a pointed look. One that told him she didn't trust the Grieve, either. Although Alistair appreciated the idea of keeping one's enemies close, he wasn't keen to wrap his arm around the Grieve's shoulder and depend on him for support. Alistair might not have died, but his leg was still in bad shape and he was unarmed. And he didn't like the way the Grieve looked at him, as though committing each of Alistair's weaknesses to memory.

Isobel strode ahead, and the Thorburn hurried after her. Alistair dimly heard pieces of their conversation.

"So you have it back?" Briony murmured.

Isobel nodded. "Yes. Did you—?"

"I didn't tell a soul."

As they talked, the Grieve walked over to him and held out his hand. Alistair ignored it and pulled himself up with the help of a tree branch.

"How are you feeling?" the Grieve asked. From anyone else, the question would've seemed considerate. From the Grieve, it sounded like a threat.

"Like murder," Alistair answered.

He took several steps forward, then tripped. He wasn't sure if it was his own clumsiness or the weakness in his injured leg. The Grieve approached him like he was a wild animal, then he hesitantly slipped his muscular arm around Alistair's waist. Alistair instantly tensed.

"Will you let me help you?" the Grieve asked with exasperation.

"Should I? Isobel owes the Thorburn a favor. What reason do *you* have to be spared?"

"It's my Castle."

"You're still deadweight."

The Grieve let go of Alistair, and Alistair crumpled gracelessly in the dirt. "Crawl there, Lair."

"Fuck yourself, Castle."

Alistair grimaced, not expecting the Grieve to actually run off through the trees. He cursed again and staggered back up. It took a considerable amount of strength—and an even more considerable amount of pain—but Alistair quickened his pace until he caught up with the others. They'd reached the end of the forest. In the distance, the Castle looked like a shadow cast across the moor, black ivy stretching across black rock. Alistair half expected lightning to flash behind its tower or a banshee's scream to pierce the night.

Isobel studied the ground hesitantly. "Are there still landmines?"

"No," the Grieve answered, striding forward, leading the way.

The three followed him across the moat bridge and into the fortress. The Castle was famously impenetrable to everything other than the Crown, a Relic which had yet to fall. It meant the four were safe . . . at least, to attacks from the outside.

As Alistair limped over the threshold, the moat's drawbridge closed behind him with a foreboding thud.

ISOBEL MACASLAN

The only thing worse than making another champion your enemy is making them a friend.

A Tradition of Tragedy

The interior of the Castle was grand—golden trim lining elegant crown molding, glass chandeliers in every room, and regal carpets sweeping down the hallways. It was impossible to enter it and feel anything less than royal.

"What a dump," Alistair muttered behind her, probably just to earn a scowl from Gavin.

Gleaming suits of armor lined the corridor, with swords or axes clenched in metal fists. Isobel caught her reflection against a polished chest plate, her hair wild and tangled, the dried mud crusted against her clothes.

She almost didn't recognize herself. The Cloak trailed behind her like the train of a gown, and her spellstones glittered on each finger—the Reaper's Embrace now included among them, ready to be filled with magick.

She looked like a champion.

She looked *good*.

"We should spend the night replenishing our supplies. Grieve, do you have raw magick stored here?" Isobel asked.

Gavin's eyes widened. Then he quickly cleared his throat. "That's not your concern."

Alistair scoffed. "You're useless, aren't you?"

"I'm not the one who nearly got himself killed."

Alistair's and Gavin's eyes both flickered to the weapons along the walls, then toward each other, as though daring the other to strike.

"Go ahead," Gavin murmured. "You're on my turf now, Lowe."

Isobel grimaced, trying to come up with a plan before the boys decided to sport those decorative suits of armor in a duel. But Briony spoke first—typical.

"I say we go collect our own," she declared.

"Now?" Alistair asked haggardly. Wincing with every step and favoring his right leg, he looked in no condition to venture outside.

"You can stay here," Briony said.

"With *him?*" Alistair looked at Gavin, aghast.

"We agreed to play nice, didn't we?" Briony asked. "For the night?"

Isobel didn't like the idea of abandoning Alistair with Gavin. But truthfully, the events of the day had left an uneasy feeling in her stomach. Alistair had nearly sacrificed everything for her, and as much as she cared for him, as much as she was grateful, it worried her that he'd act so recklessly. Two weeks spent in the Cave's seclusion had let them forget the reality of their circumstances. Maybe it was better if they separated for the time being, for both of their sakes. Playing pretend would only get them hurt.

"If we're going to be allies, even temporary ones, we need to use our time to our advantage," Isobel said. "That means we can't take a break to rest. And since Grieve is unwilling to share his raw magick . . ." Gavin stiffened and frowned at the floor. "The rest of us need to replenish our supplies."

"I don't have any raw magick, all right?" Gavin muttered.

Alistair's grin was wicked. "I *knew* it."

"So it's decided—Briony and I will go." Isobel didn't relish the idea of alone time with Briony, but it couldn't be helped. "Gavin can defend the Castle, and Alistair can rest. Hopefully we don't meet Elionor and Finley along the way, but if we do . . ."

"I don't want to go looking for another battle," Briony murmured. "Not tonight."

"Didn't Elionor and Finley betray you?" Gavin asked. "I'd want to kill them if I were you."

"It's just that . . ." Briony's voice grew taut, and she swallowed.

Isobel stared at Briony—at the filth splattered across her palms, at the tremor in her hand, at Carbry's crusted blood.

Briony was cracking, Isobel realized. It was hard to believe after the years her former friend had spent dreaming of the tournament but, clearly, the grisly reality had not been kind to her.

Isobel would be lying if she claimed it didn't give her a rush of satisfaction.

"It's just that," Briony continued, sounding increasingly frazzled, "I don't want to fight them because I think there's a chance that all of us—including Finley and Elionor—can make it out of this tournament alive."

Isobel frowned. Briony's state of mind was worse than she'd thought.

"What are you talking about?" she asked. Out of the corner of her eye, she saw Alistair and Gavin exchange wary glances. They must've thought Briony's words were as absurd as she did.

"This tournament is a curse," Briony continued. "And curses can be broken."

"The tournament isn't an ordinary curse, Bri." The gentleness in her tone surprised even her. "It's ancient. Powerful."

"Just think about it. If we—"

"You're not the first person to consider that. But every champion who got it in their head that the tournament could be broken failed. And *died*."

"But that's because they got it wrong. There are—"

"And you have it right because . . . ?"

"Just listen to me," Briony huffed, her voice rising, amplified by the lofted ceilings and echoing stone. Isobel struggled to contain her shock. Briony truly believed what she was saying. "Haven't you ever looked at a map of Ilvernath and thought it strange that there are seven Landmarks, arranged in a circle? That's because they don't make a circle. They make a septogram, and the Champions Pillar is at the center."

Isobel had never thought of the city that way, but she supposed it made sense. Even so, she didn't see how drawing a star over the map changed anything.

Seeming to take everyone's silence as encouragement, Briony continued, "When our ancestors cast this curse, they made the Landmarks the board. And the Relics were the ingredients. That means, if we arrange the board as it was originally, we can destroy the curse altogether."

"You mean, put a Relic in each Landmark?" Gavin asked, sounding as skeptical as Isobel felt. "This curse has lasted eight hundred years. That's definitely been done before. If only by accident."

"It can't just be any Relic in any Landmark," Briony said. "I talked to a spellmaker who had the same theory—that buried in the tournament's history, every family has a story. About a Landmark and Relic their champions favor. A pattern."

Isobel remembered what her father had told her about the Macaslans once having a special connection to death, which was why their champions usually favored the Crypt and the Cloak.

Not that it proved anything. Every old lineage had stories.

Briony shot the others a triumphant grin. "Don't you see? I've found a way to save *all* of us."

But it wasn't just the logic that bothered Isobel. There was something in Briony's expression, something proud and eager and *familiar*. Unwanted, unbidden, memories flared behind her eyes like a camera flash.

* * *

"What the *hell*?" Isobel had breathed, halting in front of her locker.

Pages torn out from the Macaslan chapter in *A Tradition of Tragedy* had been taped over the entire door. Spray-painted vertically across them, in big red letters, was the word "LEECH," and a rancid smell leaked out of the locker's slits, as though someone had slipped a Rotten Egg curse inside.

Beside her, Briony stormed forward and ripped every paper down. She crumpled the wad of them in her fist. "It's been weeks. You'd think everyone would be over it by now."

This was far from the first vandalism Isobel had experienced since that book was released last month. But it *was* the first time anyone had targeted her at school.

Isobel glanced down the corridor to Briony's own locker—untouched.

"It's not about the book," Isobel murmured, shrinking under the stares of the other students who walked past. "It's because of my family." It wasn't enough that the Macaslans had amassed a fortune through deplorable means. Now they could add murder to their list of sins, too.

"That's bullshit. You're nothing like them. You barely even talk to your dad." Then Briony cast a Matchstick spell, dropping the heap of papers and letting them burn on the linoleum floor.

Isobel lurched back, not wanting to be burned. "What are you doing? You'll get us in trouble." It was Isobel who deserved to be outraged, not her. And Briony's tone when she talked about Isobel's dad bothered her. Just because she didn't always live with her dad didn't mean he wasn't still her father.

But Briony only stamped the flames out with her loafer. Soot stained her Ilvernath Prep uniform. "They shouldn't treat you like this. You're capable of so much, and now all of them know you're part of something special. Something great."

Isobel changed the subject, as she always did whenever Briony described the tournament as a fairy tale instead of a curse.

"They'll stop eventually," she said, tugging Briony along to class. But the stench of the curse followed her for the rest of the day, no matter how often she spritzed the air with peony perfume.

A week later, Isobel peeked from behind a school bus to make sure the reporter who'd just accosted them was out of sight.

"I-I don't understand," she stuttered. "Why would that journalist think that I was a champion?"

Beside her, Briony grinned and lightly punched her shoulder. "Because you're obviously your family's best choice. You could probably teach our spellmaking course. You'd be better than Mr. Flannagan."

"But the reporter didn't make it sound like a rumor." Dread churned in Isobel's stomach as they hurried inside the building. The hallway seemed narrower than before, her classmates' whispers rising to a fever pitch. "He said 'announced as champion.' Why would he—?"

She was cut off by the screech of the loudspeaker, requesting that Isobel Macaslan visit the dean of students. Immediately.

"Do you want to explain this?" the dean demanded, waving that morning's edition of the *Ilvernath Eclipse*. "Or why every journalist in Kendalle is calling my office, asking the school for a quote?"

That was when Isobel saw the headline: "ISOBEL MACASLAN FIRST TO BE NAMED 'CHAMPION' IN ILVERNATH'S DEATH CURSE." She snatched the paper and flipped through the six-page article, her chest so tight she could barely breathe. At first, she assumed it was a sadistic prank, fabricated by the city's media to draw more tourists. But the research was sickeningly thorough. The photograph of her winning a gold ribbon at last year's Spellmaking Fair. Her spring semester report card. An anonymous source detailing Isobel's "high achiever" and "perfectionist" personality.

"I can't go back to class," she croaked, and when she looked back at the dean, she wanted to scream at the pity on his face.

An hour later, her mother picked her up from school. Isobel didn't return for a week. She'd hoped in that time, the paparazzi who camped outside her parents' houses would grow bored and move on.

But it only got worse.

Her classmates' gossip, already emboldened from the book, grew increasingly vicious.

"The Blood Moon isn't supposed to be until next year. She's *that* excited."

"No surprise from the Macaslans."

"Attention-seeking bitch."

The hate mail came next. Strangers across the city, the country, even the *world* had written to her to tell her that they thought she was brave. Or that her whole family was despicable. Or that they looked forward to the day she died.

"No, no. Listen to this," Briony read to her one weekend, clutching a copy of the *Glamour Inquirer* and lying beside her on Isobel's pink duvet. "'With such an impressive list of accomplishments, we can't help wondering if Macaslan is exactly the one to rival the future Lowe champion, whose family won the prior generation's tournament.'"

"How am I supposed to be happy about that?" Isobel snapped, burying her face in her pillow.

"Don't you see? Now that the world sees how amazing a champion you are, they don't care about your family. They only care about *you*."

"But I don't want them to care about me! I've never even wanted to *be* champion!"

For several moments, Briony only stared at her—as though Isobel were a stranger.

"What do you mean you don't want to be champion?" she asked carefully. "You've always wanted—"

"No, *you've* always wanted." Isobel's face burned. She'd never been brave enough to admit this to Briony, but after so many lies about her had circulated around the world, at least there would be no more lies in their friendship. "I don't want to die! I certainly don't want to hurt *you*. And now this . . ." She yanked the tabloid from Briony's grasp and chucked it across the room. "This tournament has already ruined my life."

Instead of consoling her, Briony swung her feet off the bed, backing away like Isobel was poison. "I can't believe you right now."

"You're leaving? What's so bad about what I said?"

"I—You . . ." Briony's face contorted with anger. "You were going to be just another Macaslan champion, but now you're not. Now you're the *first* champion. Now you're the Lowe's rival. Now everyone is impressed by you—spellmakers, cursemakers, reporters. I *saved* you."

Briony had been the anonymous source who'd contacted the newspapers. Isobel felt foolish for not realizing it before. Of course Briony, who had barely faced a tenth of the vitriol Isobel had, would decide that Isobel needed a hero to save her from her family.

And Briony *always* got to be the hero.

They'd screamed at each other after that. Briony had cried. At one point, both of them had resorted to petty cursefire, leaving Isobel with a magickal breakout and a nasty headache.

And somehow, their fight wasn't the worst part of Isobel's evening.

The worst part was when her father had gathered the other Macaslans together and gleefully quoted Isobel that same article. When they decided that she would formally be their champion.

"This is nonsense, Briony," Isobel snapped in the Castle, so loudly that Alistair tripped and smacked into a suit of armor along the wall. "Save us? Where have I heard you talk about saving people before?"

Briony flinched. "This isn't—"

"If you felt this way, then why did you kill Carbry?"

Isobel hadn't been absolutely certain it was Briony who killed him, but Briony, not Gavin, was the one with blood on her hands. And the horrified look on her face confirmed it.

"It was self-defense," Briony whispered. Tears welled in her eyes, and for a heartbeat, Isobel really did feel like she was back in her bedroom, having the same argument with her best friend. But Briony Thorburn had destroyed her life. She didn't get to cry. "Look, I'm not asking you to believe me, if you can't right now. Elionor didn't. But I am asking for time to prove my theory. I only need to match one Relic to the right Landmark to prove the curse *can* be unraveled."

Her eyes flickered to Isobel's Cloak, and Isobel squeezed it tighter around herself. She wasn't willing to give up something so powerful just to soothe Briony's feelings. Briony might've saved her life, but Isobel was returning that favor by sparing her tonight. She didn't owe Briony any more than that.

"Elionor and Finley won't wait for you to test your theory," Isobel told her coolly. "While you're searching for these perfect combinations, they'll attack."

"The Castle is impenetrable without the Crown," Briony said. "We'll be safe here. And they'll be safe out there."

Isobel picked at the dried blood beneath her fingernails—Alistair's blood. She was covered in it, and she kept replaying the moment when she'd thought he'd died. The night air cold, his hands colder. The only sound her own voice pleading in the dark.

And Alistair wasn't even the boy who had died tonight.

She didn't believe Briony, didn't trust Briony. But more than her own grudge, Isobel couldn't keep living in a fantasy. She had never wanted to be champion, but she was now. They all were.

Isobel would do what it took to survive. And in the tournament, the only way to survive was to win.

"Look," Briony breathed, "if there's even a chance, don't we owe it to ourselves to try to save one another? To end the curse?"

Briony glanced desperately toward the boys, clearly looking for backup. But Gavin stared at his shoes, while Alistair checked his reflection in a helm mounted on the wall, licked his hand, and rubbed the grime off his cheek.

"We've agreed to a truce for tonight," Isobel told her. "But Alistair and I aren't staying."

To her right, she felt Alistair's gaze on her, but his expression was clouded, and he didn't voice any disagreement.

"You have to stay," Briony gasped. "I need help to test my theory. Everyone else already abandoned me."

"Did they? Or did you lie to them, betray them, and ruin their lives, too?"

Briony blinked back the last of her tears. "So that's it, then? You'll just go back to plotting to kill everyone? To kill me?"

Her expression was so ugly that for the first time, Isobel was grateful to be a Macaslan. Had she not scrubbed every hateful piece of graffiti off of her mother's shop, had she not joined her family to collect the magick at each funeral, then seeing that disdain on her best friend's face might've broken her.

"I don't want to kill you," Isobel murmured. "I never did, and I still don't."

"Then I can make it easy for you. If you help me and I turn out to be wrong about breaking the curse, then you won't have to hunt me down—any of you. I-I'll forfeit myself."

Behind Briony, Gavin snorted. "You say that now. But once it all turns out to be bullshit, I have a feeling you'll change your mind."

"I won't," Briony said firmly.

Isobel wasn't so sure. Briony had already proved herself to be a liar.

"Then prove you mean it," Isobel said coolly. "I'll craft a Truth or Treachery." It was an unbreakable truth spell, class nine. If Briony attempted to lie while under its influence, she would perish. And then Isobel would not be the one forced to deal Briony a killing blow— Briony would deliver it to herself.

That did not make it less cruel. But the more the fantasy of the Cave faded and reality settled in, the more Isobel realized she had a capacity for cruelty after all. She could steal a recipe from an heirloom grimoire. She could seduce a boy who was otherwise an enemy. And when it came down to it, she could see her best friend dead.

Briony stared at her as though seeing Isobel for the first time.

"All right." She hiked up her chin. "I'll do it."

A heavy, awkward silence fell over the corridor. Isobel did her best to ignore it and focus on picking the last of the dried blood from her nails.

Alistair cleared his throat and turned to Gavin. "Does this Landmark have a wine cellar?"

"No," Gavin answered flatly.

"Not much of a castle then, is it?"

"It does have a liquor cabinet. And a dungeon."

Alistair smirked. "I never say no to either."

"Of course you don't."

The boys disappeared around the corner, and Isobel could hear the echoes of Gavin cursing down the hall.

"I'll go find us some more raw magick in the courtyard," Isobel said. "I'll need a lot to craft the oath."

Before she could follow after the boys, Briony leaned close to her and whispered, "You know, no matter what you might want to believe, you make a perfect champion."

GAVIN GRIEVE

My family does not tell those who marry into our line the truth
about our curse until after the wedding. It makes for a miserable
honeymoon.

A Tradition of Tragedy

The Castle had been Gavin's sanctum for the past few weeks.
As long as he was within its walls, he was safe.

Until tonight, when he'd been forced to open the gates and
willingly let his archenemy inside.

Gavin couldn't stop seeing the Landmark through Alistair's eyes,
in all its gaudy glory. Everything he'd been proud of felt cheap now,
gold paint and lacquer slapped over rubble and ruins, even though it
had been enchanted exactly to his taste.

"Very impressive," Alistair drawled, patting the mahogany arm
of the throne. Isobel had returned from her errand with a flask of
raw magick for each of them, then left to find a spare bedroom. To
Gavin's great surprise, Alistair hadn't followed her. Which meant
Gavin was stuck with his taunting. "Did the Castle give you kingly
clothes, too, so you could play dress-up while sitting on your throne?
Maybe a powdered wig?"

"At least I have a throne," said Gavin tersely. "Weren't you squat-
ting in a cave?"

"The Cave is actually quite cozy." Alistair tilted his head. His widow's peak made the angles of his face look even more pronounced. "It
has a lovely four-poster bed. A grotto. And quite the view."

"So . . . you had furniture. Not sure that's worth bragging about."

Alistair's lip curled. "Because you have so much to boast of? Seems to me Briony Thorburn's the only reason you're still alive right now."

Gavin didn't want to admit it, but Alistair was right. When Briony had convinced Isobel and Alistair to protect her, she'd somehow gotten Gavin included in a two-for-one deal.

Still, Gavin wasn't happy that she'd offered up his Landmark like it was some kind of bed-and-breakfast. Her theories about ending the tournament for good were delusional.

But there was one thing she'd said that had stuck with him. *I talked to a spellmaker who had the same theory.*

Gavin thought of the ring in his pocket, the one he'd taken off Carbry Darrow's body. He was willing to bet his life that both that fancy cursestone and Briony's harebrained theories came from Reid MacTavish. And if Reid had messed with at least three of the champions, counting Gavin . . . then what did he want from this tournament? What was his game? Gavin was determined to figure it out. But unlike Briony, he wouldn't be foolish enough to share his suspicions.

"If you're going to try and kill me, just do it, okay?" Gavin said brusquely.

Alistair let out what seemed to be a deliberately dramatic sigh. "I wouldn't have allied with you for the night if I was going to kill you."

Alistair surveyed the throne room with visible distaste. When his gaze fell on the pillar, something dark crossed his expression. Gavin realized he was looking at Carbry's name, struck out.

But then Alistair reached his hand forward, and his fingers traced a crack along the edge of the stone. It curled inward, like a piece of a broken heart. "That wasn't there before." His words sounded like a question. "I saw a crack on my own pillar, but now there's two. Is it supposed to do that?"

Gavin didn't know the answer, but he didn't want to admit that. "Don't start saying that you think Briony is onto something."

Alistair pursed his lips and said nothing.

Gavin could go to bed. It had been an exhausting day. But he would be a fool to waste an opportunity like this—one night of guaranteed peace with Alistair Lowe. One night to find the monster's weakness.

Gavin looked at Alistair's blood-crusted knuckles. Other than his champion's ring, he only wore one more, a plain yet finely crafted piece, with a stone the color of ash.

"Well, you've got raw magick now," Gavin said, trying to sound casual. "Don't you need to craft some spells?"

Alistair stared at his fingers, as if just now remembering why they were so bloodied and empty. He clenched his fists, then, after a pause, shrugged. Completely unfazed by his near encounter with death. Gavin didn't know why he was even surprised.

"I'm not the only one. You're only wearing three?"

"Some of us don't need ten spellrings to fight." Gavin stuffed his hands into his pockets. Suddenly, convincing Alistair to stay here and replenish his supplies seemed a little foolish. He didn't want Alistair to ask questions about his own magick.

"Or you don't have ten spellrings," Alistair said pointedly. Gavin flushed with embarrassment, but it was better Alistair think him lacking in supplies than learn the real reason he wore so few. "So what happened to that liquor cabinet we were discussing?"

Gavin detested liquor thanks to his parents, but if drinking meant he'd get to study his opponent, then so be it.

"It's full," he answered.

Alistair smiled. "Perfect."

The boys made their way to the dining hall and seated themselves at the impressive round stone table, each clutching a bottle of golden liquid so coated in dust that their fingerprints left streaks across the glass.

Alistair popped the cork on his and took a heavy swig. He made a revolted face. "What is this?"

Gavin sniffed his uneasily. It smelled . . . like alcohol. "Beer?" he guessed.

"I think it's mead." Despite being apparently disgusted, Alistair drank again.

Two spellboards sat in front of them, littered with empty spell-stones. Gavin fiddled with his stones, making a bogus show of inspecting them each closely. He kept most of them in his pockets these days, only swapping out the few he felt he most needed. It wasn't worth the risk of them constantly draining him. Alistair, meanwhile, coaxed the raw magick out of his flasks. You were supposed to draw it out gently, but Alistair reserved that treatment for the mead bottle, instead shaking the flask like a broken Magic 8-Ball.

Gavin watched him take yet another generous gulp. "Aren't you worried about what will happen if you let your guard down?"

Alistair's smile was sallow in the harsh filter of the Blood Veil through the windows, his teeth feral and pointed. The red was a little weaker now that Briony had killed Carbry.

Gavin thought of the boy's corpse and shuddered. He'd never given much thought to how it would look when someone died. Now he realized it was more intimate, more *messy*, than he had anticipated. As he'd watched Carbry collapse to the ground, the life leaking out of him, Gavin had realized he could feel the boy's life magick draining away—a cloud of white that dissipated into the air. It had felt . . . familiar.

Life magick was only supposed to come out of bodies when they were buried.

"Really, Grieve," Alistair purred, his voice lingering on the last word with obvious disdain. "What could I possibly have to be afraid of?"

"I have a first name, you know."

Alistair's gaze dropped to the spellboard.

"You don't know my name, do you?" Gavin demanded, humiliated. Isobel and Briony had both said it in Alistair's earshot.

"Maybe I like calling you Grieve."

Face flushing in anger, Gavin actually lifted the mead bottle to his lips and drank.

He immediately coughed, feeling the acidic sweetness burn its way down his throat.

"You know," drawled Alistair, "I thought the Grieves were famous for handling their liquor."

"I don't really drink," Gavin mumbled. *Because of that reputation,* he didn't say.

"Too bad. It's fun." Alistair took another sip, for emphasis.

If Gavin's archenemy wanted to underestimate him, refused to even learn his name, that was fine. He could use that to his advantage, until the perfect opportunity presented itself. And then, for the first and last time, Alistair would see what he was truly capable of.

"Well then," Gavin said, raising his mead bottle in the air. "To fun?"

Alistair's laugh sounded like he hadn't used it in years. "Why not?" He knocked his own bottle against Gavin's. "You know, I almost hope you poisoned this."

And with that, he drank deeply.

Gavin pretended to drink with him, a strange realization creeping through him.

He'd always known Alistair was dangerous. But he'd never had the chance to see how sad he was. It was unmistakable, in the lines of his profile, in the way his hand desperately gripped the bottle.

What right did he have to be sad?

"You know, in my research," Gavin said, unable to keep the bite from his voice, "I saw that Lowes usually claim the Castle. But you didn't even try."

Briony had said something about patterns. Gavin agreed with her; champions from certain families did gravitate toward specific Relics and Landmarks. But he'd studied the history of the families extensively. If there was a way to break this curse, he would've seen a hint of it by now.

"I don't need a fancy Landmark for people to know I'm a threat," said Alistair, smirking. "The most dangerous monsters are the ones who sneak up on you. Haven't you heard the stories?"

"My family doesn't really tell stories. We don't have any good ones."

The words rang out starkly across the room. Gavin hadn't meant to be so honest, but when he looked at Alistair, his brow was furrowed in thought.

Gavin was unfathomably grateful for that. Hatred or apathy, he could handle.

Pity would've been too much to bear.

"My mother used to tell me a bedtime story about changelings," Alistair said hoarsely. "They'd switch a human baby out for one of their own. The child would be almost human, but not quite. They'd be more dangerous. Wilder. Stranger. And then, one day, the monsters would come back to claim their own, to bring them to their caverns below the earth."

Alistair changed when he told stories. His voice took on a reverent, eager quality, and his face looked more like a boy's, a boy with wistful eyes and a wry, gentle curl to his lips. It didn't matter that the words he spoke were frightening—Gavin could have listened to him talk like this for hours.

"What about the human baby?" Gavin asked, trying not to let his fascination show. "What happened to them?"

Alistair smiled ghoulishly. "The changeling would slit their throat and feast on all the magick inside."

"What kind of a bedtime story is that?" Gavin shivered, thinking about the deal he'd made, the way he'd mutilated his own body's magick.

"Not all bedtime stories have happy endings."

"But your family are winners. Shouldn't all your stories have happy endings?"

"The Lowes win because they're monsters," Alistair said bitterly, coaxing raw magick into a spellring. "And we play our parts very well. We know who we're supposed to be."

The boy beside him was not what Gavin had expected, not the menace who'd nearly killed an elderly spellmaker, not the brash champion from the Magpie. He tried to remind himself that Alistair would always be a Lowe, and Gavin couldn't—wouldn't—let himself feel anything but hatred for him. Not when it was too easy to wonder if it had ever really been hatred at all.

"No, it's a choice to be a monster." The words came out more sharply than Gavin intended them to. "You could have the town eating out of your hand if you wanted. Your family decided to make them fear you. I wish I'd had that kind of choice."

"I have fewer choices than you think," said Alistair, quietly, dangerously. "And your family chose their reputation. They chose to give up centuries ago."

Gavin bristled. "I'm not my family. And I haven't given up."

"I've noticed." Alistair eyed him appraisingly.

Gavin felt a rush of pride, then a rush of annoyance that he *wanted* Alistair's approval. He liked to think of himself as good at being alone, or at least accustomed to it. But one conversation with his supposed mortal enemy and his guard was already down. Was he really this desperate for validation?

Or was it just because that attention was coming from Alistair Lowe?

Gavin tried to picture himself standing over Alistair's body, watching the life drain from his eyes. Tried to believe that was what he wanted. But as he sat there, beside the mead he refused to drink, he couldn't avoid the newfound knowledge that Alistair was more boy than monster—despite how much both of them pretended otherwise.

ALISTAIR LOWE

Per old superstitions, a champion's body is always buried face-down. If they attempt to claw their way from their graves to seek vengeance, they will only dig deeper into the earth.

A Tradition of Tragedy

Alistair was torn between two harrowing options: to go to bed or to keep drinking. Isobel and Briony had disappeared somewhere—more than likely, they'd fallen asleep. He was still surprised Isobel had agreed to indulge Briony's fantasies about ending the tournament. It wasn't like her, but he didn't know the girls' history.

"Fantasies" seemed the right word for it. When their ancestors had devised the tournament's curse, they had not engineered it to be broken.

Even so, foolish, useless hope burned in his stomach. He'd hoped the alcohol would douse it—the hope and every other sorry thing he felt. Instead, it all burned twice as strong.

The Grieve was sitting beside him, still horrifyingly sober. He'd been casting Alistair grave expressions all evening as he hunched over his spellboard, as though worried Alistair might kill him . . . or like he was plotting to kill Alistair himself.

Alistair would like to see him try.

He reached for the Grieve's bottle and shook it emphatically.

"What are you doing?" the Grieve asked.

"I've made my decision," Alistair declared. "I'm going to get you drunk."

The Grieve smirked. "I'd like to see you try."

Alistair frowned at the echoing of his thoughts. His gaze flickered down to his wrist, for any mark of the Divining Kiss, but found none. He and the Grieve were just equally combative.

Alistair grabbed a handful of freshly filled spellstones from his pile and scattered them across the table.

The Grieve narrowed his eyes suspiciously. "What are those for?"

Alistair reached for a rose quartz and held it up to the light. "A game, of course."

"Is this the part where the Lowe plays with their victims before they kill them?"

"Relax, Grieve. It's just gambling."

The Grieve leaned back in his chair and crossed his arms, emphasizing his bulky frame. He smiled smugly. "Instead of bets, we could fight with fists. A drink for every hit landed."

"You'd like that, wouldn't you?" Alistair had been beaten up quite enough tonight. "How about something more equal? I don't know you. You don't know me. If we both commit to honesty, whenever the other guesses something right about us, we sip. And we bet our stones."

"That sounds like a quick way to get drunk. *And* lose your spells."

"You assume you know me, then."

"Fine." The Grieve shrugged and raised one of his spellstones. "It's a class five."

Alistair tossed a class five Shark's Skin in the pot.

"You're wicked and childish," the Grieve said, "and your family has probably been priming you to become champion since before you can remember. You've never been anything but strong. You take that for granted."

Alistair didn't wince as he raised the glass to his lips and slid the Grieve his spellstone as prize. "Fair enough."

And so they played.

It was an easy distraction from the many things plaguing Alistair's mind. Like the thought of Isobel sleeping somewhere else in the Castle, how she'd abandoned him the moment they left the lair, how he clearly wanted her more than she wanted him. He wondered how pathetic that made him.

He was also trying to avoid thinking about his brother, especially after hallucinating him in the forest. But it wasn't working. He thought about their pinball game in the Magpie. About the times Hendry had stolen pastries for Alistair and left them among his books. The night the boys had snuck into town for a carnival—how Alistair had sloshed cider all over his clothes, how Hendry had eaten three funnel cakes and thrown up in a dunk tank, how Alistair had found a worm in his caramel apple, how Hendry had charmed one of the volunteers so much in the kissing booth that she'd given him his money back.

Now every fleeting happy memory was a wound. He should know. He'd already been mortally wounded once tonight.

Alistair offered up a class six Dragon's Breath that he'd just set into a golden band.

"You're rotten at school, but your parents still insist you're bright," Alistair guessed. "But it has nothing to do with that, bright or not. You just stopped trying a long time ago."

"I'm at the top of my class," the Grieve said dryly. "And I'd be surprised if my parents even knew that."

"Another champion who hates his parents. It's becoming a cliché. Hating your family doesn't make you better than them."

Even though he had no reason to, Alistair took another sip.

The Grieve's gaze had a piercing edge, like he was trying to peel back Alistair's layers one by one. He grimaced as he swallowed. Alistair had noticed he favored one of his arms—maybe he'd been cursed during his own fight that evening. "You can keep your stone and call it even. I do hate my parents. But I know you weren't really talking about me."

They continued playing. He was more proficient at this game than Alistair had expected, which irritated him.

Alistair reached for the bottle. "I guess I'll need more, then."

The Grieve slid another of Alistair's spellstones from the pot to his collection, which, despite all their time sitting here, he'd somehow made no progress in filling with magick. Probably because he was focused on absolutely obliterating Alistair in this game. He'd guessed a baffling amount of information on him, and apart from some class eight curse called Revenge of the Forsaken—the Grieve had literally pouted when he'd taken it—Alistair had won little, and his newly crafted hoard was quickly diminishing. With most of his possessions still in the Cave, Alistair obviously needed enough spells and curses to defend himself, but he was struggling to care. After all, each one of the other boy's answers gave Alistair another excuse to drain his glass.

"You think Briony's theory is horseshit," Alistair said.

Alistair had hoped the Grieve would take the bait and discuss it— Alistair still burned with the need to discuss it—but instead, the boy only smiled and took a sip.

"The last Lowe champion won after only four days," the Grieve said. "I bet that eats at you."

"Like even the idea of a Grieve winning eats at you."

"If Isobel wasn't protecting you, you would've died tonight." The Grieve's words were slurred. "You might be a Lowe, but you're not special. Finley could've gutted you." He glanced, once again, at the suits of armor. "Or I could have."

I always wanted to be the one who killed you, Elionor had told him after she'd cursed him. And she was hardly the only one. All of Ilvernath had likely stared at the lightening Blood Veil and hoped it had been Alistair who'd died.

"Is that what you want? To fight me?" Alistair asked quietly. He stood up, and his balance veered slightly. "You could still lose the tournament, but at least . . . at least you'd have *that*, right? At least you killed the Lowe."

The Grieve tipped his bottle to the side, as if lightly surprised he'd made so much progress. "Yeah. At least I would have that."

"Should I be afraid of you, then?"

"I thought we weren't asking questions."

"I'm not sure we're still playing."

"But I have a question, and if you answer it, then I promise not to kill you before the sun rises." The Grieve's threat sounded real, like he believed he could actually kill him. And maybe he could. If Alistair was weak enough to let Hendry die, then maybe he was weak enough to lose to a Grieve, too.

Now furious enough to consider a fight, Alistair grunted. "Fine. Ask your question."

The Grieve leaned forward, and when he looked at Alistair, he looked at his throat.

"That ring on your fourth finger—it's the only one you were wearing earlier, besides your champion's ring. It's a curse, isn't it? A powerful one."

Alistair stiffened, all the anger seeping out of him. He could ask him about anything . . . anything but that. When he squeezed his eyes shut, he stood at the edge of his family's estate. The forest in front of him was eerily quiet, the house behind him quieter.

"It must be powerful. It's clearly the most precious stone you have," the Grieve said. "So what was sacrificed to grant you that?"

Alistair stared at the bottom of his bottle, though there was nothing left inside it.

The Grieve could insult him, could fight him, but he couldn't force him to say it.

But he needed to say it. He needed to lift the weight off his soul, even if the Grieve was the only one there to listen.

"My brother," he rasped. The words tasted like ash on his tongue.

The other boy's expression hardened, just as Alistair had known it would. The Lowes had always been the undisputed villains of their town's ancient, bloodstained story, and now the Grieve knew for certain—all those tales were deserved.

"That's despicable." The Grieve stood up, his chair screeching across the stone floor. "So that's how the Lowes win, is it? They seclude themselves in their estate and secretly sacrifice whoever they deem weakest to ensure their victory?"

Alistair didn't reply. A part of him knew that his family didn't deserve Alistair taking their punches for them. Another part knew he should. All his life, the secret had been right in front of him. In the portraits. In the graveyard. And he hadn't seen it.

Hendry's blood was on Alistair's hands, too.

"What does the curse even do?" the Grieve asked.

"It ignores defensive enchantments and drains the life magick of anyone in a fifteen-meter radius." The thought of Hendry's life magick so mutilated left a sick feeling in Alistair's stomach.

In several strides, the Grieve reached over, grabbed Alistair by the collar of his sweater, and yanked him up, close enough for Alistair to smell the liquor on his breath. Even as broken as he was, Alistair felt a rush of fear. "So why hide in this Castle? Why protect Isobel? You're just going to kill us all, in the end."

Alistair opened his mouth to correct him, but stopped himself. The Grieve's green eyes burned with a feverish intensity, with how badly he wanted to kill him. And even if it meant he tried this very moment, Alistair would still rather he think of him as a villain than as pathetic.

The Grieve yanked Alistair harder, causing him to stumble, and Alistair steadied himself by gripping the edge of the table.

"I promised myself I wouldn't use it," Alistair said. He didn't know why he bothered—it wasn't like he would ever seem anything less than a monster to the Grieve. But he couldn't stand the thought of anyone thinking he'd played a willing role in Hendry's murder.

"I don't believe you," the Grieve spat.

"I mean it," Alistair said. "I won't win using my brother's death."

"Then prove it."

Alistair's eyebrows furrowed. "How?"

"Bury it."

He stiffened. If he buried the ring, the enchantment inside it would dissipate. To bury the ring would be the ultimate rebellion against his family.

It was an idea he should have had ages ago, he realized. The moment his family had given it to him, Alistair should've buried it in Hendry's favorite spot in the graveyard, should've mourned him properly. Alistair could delude himself into thinking he hadn't had time between the shock and the tournament, but really, Alistair hadn't wanted to say goodbye.

"Fine," he whispered. The other boy's expression softened. He clearly hadn't expected Alistair to agree. But he didn't back down now, either; he led Alistair to an isolated courtyard in the center of the Castle.

Without using magick, Alistair knelt on the ground and clumsily dug into the earth with his hands. His fingers were quickly coated in dirt, caking underneath his nails. He pulled up grass and roots, removing the worms and beetles squirming beneath, and created a hole.

He slid the ring off his finger.

Nearly a minute of silence passed. Part of him wanted to cry, but he was too proud, too drunk, too embarrassed to do so in front of the Grieve. Instead, he pictured the faces of his family—all those who had played a part in Hendry's death.

And he cursed them as he dropped the ashen ring into the dirt.

He covered it and patted the earth back down, bracing himself for the magick to release. But there was nothing besides a phantom aroma of pastries wafting through the air. Maybe the curse was so strong, it would take longer to undo itself.

"You did it," the Grieve said in disbelief.

Alistair stood, keeping his face downcast. "I'm going to bed." He walked toward the courtyard's exit back into the Castle, his chest tangled into knots of everything except regret. He'd made the right decision. He just wished he'd been good enough to come to it on his own.

"Alistair," the Grieve called. "Wait."

Alistair turned around. "What?" he snapped. "Do you have other demands to make of me? Or are you going to kill me like you obviously dream of?"

Even with the iciness in Alistair's voice, the Grieve didn't avert his eyes. "I'm sorry," he said softly.

"Winners aren't sorry, Grieve," Alistair said, then he whipped around. Before he disappeared down the hallway, he glimpsed something flickering in the corner of his vision: crimson specks of high magick in the courtyard air, like smoke wisping in wind. The spell finally dissipating, he thought. But the raw magick in the air should have been white, not red, and when he turned to see it properly, the magick was gone.

ISOBEL MACASLAN

Supposedly, the Blood Veil shields the tournament from outside influence, but I believe it simply allows us to avoid looking too closely at what's going on inside.

A Tradition of Tragedy

In the early red sky of morning, Isobel lay in bed and studied the cursering that dangled on her necklace beside her locket.

Reid had warned her that the Reaper's Embrace wasn't appropriate for the tournament. It fated a person for death rather than delivering it, ensuring that every wrongdoing they committed was a step closer to the grave. If Isobel had known that ahead of time, she would never have risked her life to craft it.

But now that she had, she could only behold the stone in awe—it held the most powerful curse she'd ever possessed.

It was time to fill it.

No sooner had she dressed and placed the ring at the center of her spellboard than someone knocked on her door.

"Come in," Isobel said.

It was Alistair. "Good. You're awake." He seemed paler than usual, perhaps even a little green. He cast nervous glances at the hallway behind him before slipping inside and closing the door. "We need to talk about your friend's tournament-breaking theory. Did you already craft the Truth or Treachery?"

"We're far from friends," Isobel said tightly.

"Okay, but did you already craft it?"

There was something strangely tight about his tone that she didn't understand.

"Not yet," she replied carefully. "Why?"

Alistair didn't respond. Instead, he sat beside her while she worked. She emptied the flasks of raw magick she'd collected last night over the spellboard. Because the Reaper's Embrace was a class ten, it required a huge amount of magick, almost everything she had. The shimmering particles swirled in a cloud over the septogram, funneling into the ring.

"I know Briony said we could stay here," Alistair finally answered, "but I don't trust the Grieve, and this is his Landmark."

Isobel tried to guess what might've happened last night after she'd gone to bed. Briony had also retreated to one of the bedrooms, leaving the boys to their own devices. Maybe something had happened between Gavin and Alistair, a threat, an argument. If Alistair was determined not to trust him, then Isobel wouldn't, either. She'd preferred their alliance when it was just the two of them anyway.

"What should we do?" Isobel asked.

Alistair gazed at her intently, and her stomach fluttered in a way that was both terribly distracting and terribly pleasant. Last night, Isobel had committed to being a proper champion, and proper champions did not feel like this about other ones—not even their allies. It was foolish. It was dangerous. And as harshly as Isobel had scolded Briony for chasing fairy tales, a part of her still desperately wanted to return to the Cave with Alistair. To see how far these feelings could take them. To pretend their story was anything other than a tragic one.

Alistair rested his hand on Isobel's, intertwining his fingers with hers. And before he even spoke, the word "yes" was already formed on her lips.

"What if Briony's right?" Alistair asked.

Isobel stiffened. That wasn't what she'd expected him to say.

"If she *is*, it would be . . . we would be . . ." The ghost of an expression crossed his face. Because Isobel had never seen it on him, it took her several moments to recognize it. Hope.

She squeezed his hand tight enough for him to wince. "Al. It's just a fantasy." The more she dwelled on it, the more she realized it should've been no surprise that Briony had fallen victim to such notions. It wasn't good enough for Briony to just be a champion—she had to be better than all of them. The hero she'd always dreamed of.

"Haven't we always been living a fantasy?" he murmured.

Alistair had nearly sacrificed himself for her in the forest. She had kissed a spellboard coated in his blood. She had used every healing spellstone she had to drag him back to the living.

But Isobel couldn't hide from the truth any longer. When it came to the tournament, none of that mattered.

They would not have a happy ending.

"We promised to duel each other when I got my powers back," Isobel reminded him. She pressed her thumb to where the white scar of her spell had once stained his skin. It was gone now. So was hers.

"I won't duel you," he said seriously. "My plans have changed."

"Then what *is* your plan?"

He pulled his hand away from hers and looked down. Isobel's chest tightened.

"Your plan is to wait this out until it's just us. To make me kill you, because you can't bring yourself to kill me, isn't it?" Her voice came out scathing, but she had *healed* him. She'd held his body in her arms. She'd pleaded for him to come back to her.

And he expected her to kill him without a fight?

They weren't supposed to care like this. He was supposed to be her rival. But he wasn't the same person she'd met that night in the Magpie. And neither was she.

"If Briony is right, then we could break the tournament." Alistair's voice cracked. "We could both—"

"You're deluding yourself," she snapped. "*Both* of you are. Both of *us* are."

He looked away from her, a muscle in his jaw twitching. "Isn't it better to have hope?"

No, not for her. Isobel might not have ever called the Macaslan estate her home, but she had still been raised on a legacy of corpses and filth and rot, scavenging in the most revolting places for magick so her family could thrive. And in a choice between an ugly reality and a pretty delusion, Isobel would always choose the truth.

"But this hope is *empty,*" she said. "Why can't you understand that?"

Alistair held out his hand again.

"You have your powers back. Find the answers yourself."

Isobel reluctantly reached forward and took it. One of her spell-stones glimmered, and the Divining Kiss's familiar mark of lips appeared on his wrist.

Alistair's most recent thoughts swept through her mind. She saw the face she recognized from the Magpie—Alistair's brother. His anger and his grief coursed through her like a current, and as dozens of scenes passed—the somber faces of his family, pastries and pinball, a terrible curse within a gifted ring—the force of them all threatened to drown her. She could nearly feel the dirt under his fingernails as he buried the ring and all that it meant.

And then she saw herself. Even though their conversation had left his thoughts tangled and uncertain, he had opened himself so willingly to her spell that she wasn't prepared for how much she would find. She saw a self-destructive plan that made her furious. She saw desires that made her blush. It was all so twisted together, these wants to live and this willingness to die . . . until the moment Briony had given Alistair hope.

In front of them, the last of the magick siphoned into the Reaper's Embrace. The stone pulsed slowly, like a heartbeat edging toward death.

"I want to live," he said firmly. "I want us *both* to live. If you want to leave, then go. But I'll stay. And, I think, so will you."

"I'm sorry about your brother," she murmured. After the countless funerals she'd attended, she should've seen the grief in him before, recognized it for what it was. "But I can't risk everything I've worked for because of some desperate plan."

"Then what's the point, if you're resigned to being hopeless?" Alistair bit out his words, sounding cruel and threatening even though Isobel didn't think he meant to. "Why even put off the inevitable? Let's have our duel now."

This time, when he reached for her, Isobel was too shocked to flinch away. He grabbed the cursestone from the board's center and pressed it to his own throat, the Reaper's Embrace pale and shimmering against his skin.

Her eyes widened, and she snatched the ring back. Only minutes ago, she had marveled at the power of the curse, but she would *not* use it on him. Not the boy who had sacrificed himself so she could make it.

When she didn't cast an enchantment, Alistair said, "I don't understand what you're waiting for."

Maybe Isobel should go. She could hunt down Elionor and Finley alone, while the others played make-believe.

But even if it was inevitable, Isobel couldn't bring herself to hurt Alistair. She knew the way he cared for her, and she never wanted him to see her as a villain.

She slid the Reaper's Embrace back onto her necklace chain, and at the center of the spellboard, she placed a new stone—the one for the Truth and Treachery.

"I'll stay, for now," she murmured.

But their fantasy was gone.

Briony Thorburn

The most common look on the face of a dead champion—the
ones that still have faces, anyway—is surprise.

A Tradition of Tragedy

B riony knew now how it felt to be held together by nothing but
magick and stories.

How it felt to come apart.

Last night, she had lain awake for a long time, staring through the
window at the weakened red sky, imagining a trail of bloody footprints
that led to Carbry's body. It was easy to think about it in absolutes:
her life or his. No other choice, no other way.

But Briony could picture a dozen other paths the night could've
taken, ones that could've led to peace, or ones that could have ended
her life instead of his. She'd thought taking Innes's place was worth
it for something greater, but instead she had wound up scared and
isolated, crouching like a mouse in the dark.

She must have passed out eventually, as she woke to muted daylight streaming through the window. The bedchamber she'd chosen
was a love letter to ostentatious interior design; gold lacquer dripped
down the walls and adorned every piece of furniture. Briony snorted
back a laugh at a portrait of Gavin that hung on the wall beside her,
wearing a crown. She wasn't sure if the Castle had conjured it or if
Gavin had spelled it himself.

"Subtle," she muttered, hauling a blanket around her shoulders and
padding out of bed.

Briony's clothes from the night before were covered in bloodied grime, and they'd belonged to Elionor anyway. Briony wanted nothing more to do with them. She ransacked the wardrobe for an outfit that wasn't completely ridiculous and wound up in a pair of jogging trousers that cinched at the ankles and a gray T-shirt clearly meant for Gavin's physique, not hers. It would have to do.

She found Isobel in the dining hall, scowling at a spellstone in her hand. The Cloak was draped around her shoulders, the three clasps glowing with high magick.

"Good, you're here," she said brusquely. "I've just finished the Truth or Treachery."

Briony winced. "Right. That."

It hurt to know that Isobel couldn't trust her unless she put her life on the line. As if she hadn't put her life on the line just to take Innes's place.

"Do you want to wait for everyone else?"

"I don't care about the boys," Isobel said tiredly.

Briony raised an eyebrow. "I find that *very* hard to believe. I saw the way Alistair looks at you."

Isobel flinched, even though Briony had only meant to tease her, but her old friend's voice came out surprisingly raw. "It isn't like that."

"I thought he was only here because of you."

"Maybe he came here for me. But he stayed because of *you*. Your . . . idea. Breaking this tournament, for good."

Her voice dripped with disdain. Clearly, she still didn't believe anything Briony had told her. Not after everything that had happened between them.

Briony had only had good intentions when she'd called those journalists. When she'd sent them Isobel's information. She'd only wanted to give her friend a fighting edge that previous Macaslan champions had lacked.

Briony wished she could tell Isobel that it had cost her, too. Her own family had come down hard on her once they'd realized Briony had created a paparazzi darling who wasn't a Thorburn. They'd forced her to transfer schools and end all contact with Isobel—as if Isobel had any interest in talking to her anymore.

But words obviously weren't enough for Isobel. This spell felt like the only chance she had left to win her over.

"Go on," Briony said. "Cast it."

Isobel clutched the Truth or Treachery in her hand. It pulsed as fast as Briony's own heart, and she sucked in her breath when Isobel grabbed her hand, just like Finley had with the Silvertongue. But this felt different—Isobel's gaze was hostile as her grip tightened. Their matching champion's rings pressed painfully against each other, and Isobel paused for several moments, her gaze lingering on Briony's pinky.

Briony knew, in a sudden, horrible rush, that Isobel wasn't just going to ask her about her cursebreaking theories.

She was going to ask about Innes. And once the spell was cast, Briony wouldn't be able to lie.

Briony ripped her hand away. "Wait."

"What?" Isobel asked warily.

"I—I need to tell you something, and I don't want to do it because of the spell."

Isobel's words were slow and cold. "What did you *do?*"

Briony winced—from Isobel's complete lack of surprise, from the pain of what she was about to confess. But something inside her had been breaking since the moment she saw Carbry's body. No, since the moment she'd picked up that ring and slid it on her finger. She had cracked just like the Champions Pillar. And even though she knew a confession would not absolve what she'd done, she needed to lift the burden from her shoulders before it could be lifted for her.

"Innes didn't give me the title of champion," Briony whispered. "I stole it."

Again, Isobel did not look surprised. "How? I watched Innes carve her name into the Pillar."

"I took her ring." Briony didn't have to explain that she'd taken the finger with it. Isobel knew those rings could not be removed. And as horror spread across Isobel's face, Briony whimpered, "I-Innes would've died if I hadn't. I was only trying to save her."

"Like you saved me when you forced me to become champion?" Isobel advanced on her, gripping the Truth or Treachery spellstone. "Face it, Briony. The only person you care about is yourself."

"That isn't true. If I'd only cared about myself, I would've sent those reporters information about *me*. Made it impossible for my family to pick anyone but me as champion."

"Well, I wish you had. Why the fuck didn't you do that?"

Briony hesitated. She'd thought about this dozens of times since Innes had been chosen over her.

"I couldn't believe they would choose anyone else," she said finally.

"Of course you couldn't," Isobel sneered.

Briony swallowed her anger. Swallowed her pride. After everything that had happened, she didn't want to lose this flimsy alliance, too. Even though part of her feared it was already gone. The Isobel she had known wasn't the girl standing before her, hardened by a year of training and media attention. She was sharper. Bolder. Crueler.

"I'm sorry, Iso," Briony said. The nickname made her old friend tense up. "I really am. I thought you wanted this, too. And I regret doing that to you. Every day."

For a moment, Isobel seemed to waver. "I . . . I don't know how I could ever forgive you."

"I'm not asking for forgiveness," Briony said. "I just want you to help me stop this. Cast your spell on me. I'm ready. You'll see I'm not lying about ending the tournament. Then I can make it right. We can both walk out of here. And none of that stuff will matter anymore."

For a moment, Isobel stared at the amethyst spellstone in her hand, still glowing white. Then she shook her head and tucked it into her pocket.

"I don't care if you think you're telling the truth," she said. "You still made me champion. You still killed Carbry."

"I didn't mean to kill Carbry," she spoke into the broken silence. Her words echoed off the stone walls, the high ceilings. *I didn't mean, I didn't mean, I didn't mean*—It sounded less convincing every time. "When he attacked me, I rebounded his enchantment back at him. I didn't know it was a death curse."

"Even so," said Isobel, "That doesn't change what you've done. You don't get to erase the impact of your choices by justifying them with some slim chance that it might lead to things changing for the better."

"I'm not trying to erase anything. I'm going to be a hero. I'm going to save everyone—"

"You're the only champion with a kill. You're so determined to make this tournament about you. So much that you forced yourself in where you didn't belong. So much that you don't care who gets in your way, or what happens to them if they do. No one in here is a hero—least of all *you*."

It was rare Briony didn't have something to say, but she was at a loss for words right now. Because she couldn't refute any of Isobel's points. And because there was a new thought forming in her mind, or maybe a very old thought, one that she couldn't ignore any longer.

This tournament wasn't a place for heroes. It never had been. All the grand deeds her family had celebrated had been bloodshed just like this. And they could call it what they wanted, but Briony knew what they really were.

Villains. All of them.

A noise rang out through the room, and Briony turned to see the door opening. Gavin Grieve stood there, looking pleased.

"Well hello," he said, licking his lips. "Are we turning on each other already?"

GAVIN GRIEVE

When high magick was plentiful, and the world was ruled by grand, violent gestures, this tournament must not have seemed so horrifying.

A Tradition of Tragedy

When Gavin stumbled on Briony and Isobel's argument, he was relieved. This—betrayal, threats, secrets—was a language he understood. And it signified an end to the bizarre events of the past twelve hours, where he'd let three other champions talk him into an alliance that went against all his instincts of self-preservation.

"You were spying on us!" Briony said, brows drawn with indignation.

"It's fair game," Gavin said calmly. "If you wanted to have a private conversation, you should've used a soundproofing spell."

Gavin had expected this alliance to turn on him at any moment—the only reason it hadn't, he'd assumed, was because they were inside his Landmark. But drinking last night with Alistair, things had gotten all muddled.

He could've tried to kill Alistair Lowe a dozen times. When he was drunk. When he buried the ring. When Gavin woke up this morning and found Alistair curled up on the leather couch in the study, a throw draped over him, an embroidered pillow beneath his head. His expression was cruel even in his sleep.

But Gavin hadn't. He told himself that he was just being practical, that it had nothing to do with their conversation. He couldn't believe the Lowes killed their own, and yet, at the same time, he could. It was all there, in the rumors, in their tiny numbers, in the way they kept their secrets locked up tight.

Knowing the truth about Alistair should've made him believe he was even more of a monster.

But he had seen Alistair and his brother that night in the Magpie. He'd watched him carefully when he'd buried the ring. And he'd believed his grief. This morning, Gavin had woken up to the feeling of life magick seeping from the ground, from the place where Hendry Lowe had been laid to rest. It had been a grim reminder of the night before.

After Gavin had learned the truth of the Lowes, he'd decided to let Alistair live, for as long as this alliance lasted. But since Isobel and Briony had started arguing, he had a feeling that wasn't going to be long.

"What did you hear?" Briony demanded.

"It doesn't matter what he heard," Isobel said to Briony. "The entire town must know what you did by now."

"They won't care when I fix everything."

"I don't think you will." Isobel turned toward Gavin, assessing him as if she was truly looking at him for the first time. "Do you believe her, Gavin? Do you think she can end the tournament?"

Gavin saw the opportunity in Isobel's question. Briony had broken the pattern of their alliance. Proven herself to be the weakest link in their chain. And with that sort of destabilization came a chance to take control of the situation.

"The tournament has existed far longer than we have," Gavin said. "If there really was a way to end it, it would've happened already."

Briony scowled at him, but Isobel looked gratified.

"Don't you want to end this?" Briony asked.

The idea in and of itself was, of course, appealing. But even if the possibility of breaking the tournament didn't strike Gavin as utterly ludicrous, then it wouldn't be his win. He knew Isobel had seen that, too—that Briony wasn't trying to work with them as allies. She was trying to use them to further her own glory, just as she had at Callista's wedding.

"Not really, not when you'd just take all the credit for it," Gavin said. "I won't be the sidekick in your story."

"You'd rather perish than help me?" Briony's voice shook. "Don't you understand that this is life or death?"

"Oh, I understand." Gavin mentally sorted through his carefully selected spellrings. "I think you're the only person here who doesn't."

Briony's eyes widened, and an enchantment shimmered around her outstretched fingers. "Do you really want to fight here?"

"It's my Landmark." Gavin waved a hand, and the wards around the room tightened; everywhere, from the rafters to the doors, would be impermeable to her. If she wanted to leave this room, she'd have to go through him. "I like my chances."

Briony sent a curse spiraling toward him. He blocked it, and his arm throbbed as the Shark's Skin refilled. But he advanced anyway. Now was not the time to look weak. He had new enchantments from his game with Alistair the night before, and he was ready to use them.

Isobel stepped between them, the Cloak draped around her shoulders. "Stop. It doesn't make sense to hurt each other."

Gavin hesitated—she had the Cloak's defensive high magick. If she sided with Briony, he couldn't take them both down.

Seeming to share his thoughts, Briony relaxed her shoulders. "Good. We can still talk this out."

Isobel glanced from Briony to Gavin, and Gavin held his breath, waiting. Isobel had told them to stop fighting, but nothing about her expression reminded Gavin of a mediator. It was calculating. She was making a choice, and Gavin braced himself, knowing it wouldn't be him.

But then Isobel murmured, so low Gavin almost missed it, "I'm sorry."

Isobel turned to Briony and cast her curse.

The wooden beams above them sagged, suddenly corroding; the walls and floor began to creak and groan. Gavin stumbled backward, struggling for purchase, but the table had decayed, too, leaving dark brown rot behind. Tendrils of muck squirmed through the floor, wrapping around Briony's legs, then pulling her down.

Briony yelled with pain as the floor collapsed beneath her, but it didn't pull her in all the way. Just enough to coat her body in that awful, rotting mud, as if Isobel had disemboweled his Landmark. When the grime touched Briony's face, she fell silent, eyes rolling into the back of her head. Her entire body went limp.

Gavin wondered warily if Isobel would go for him next. After that disgusting curse, he didn't put it past her. But she didn't summon any more magick—she just looked at Briony sadly.

"She'll wake up eventually," Isobel said quietly. "And she'll be furious."

"You didn't kill her?"

"I don't want to."

Gavin frowned, considering the scene before him. He wished she'd found a way to do this that hadn't destroyed his dining hall, but the mess before him was the least of his concerns.

Isobel had betrayed her friend, but that didn't mean she'd chosen him—she'd merely stopped them from fighting. If he seized this moment and killed Briony, he'd lose any chance at this strange new alliance. And the truth was, Gavin was realizing he couldn't win this tournament alone. Not with his flawed, mutilated magick that gave out when he needed it most.

He had to handle this right.

To make things all the more confusing, Alistair Lowe burst in through the door. He took in the scene before him, his eyes swiveling toward Gavin.

"What did you do, Grieve?" he asked, his voice accusatory, but Isobel was already speaking.

"I'm the one who cursed her," she said wearily. "She's not dead, but . . . I couldn't trust her to work with us."

"Shit." Alistair ran a hand through his hair, looking rattled. "I thought you were willing to hear her out. I thought you agreed to *stay*—"

"I did," Isobel said. "And I will, if we become what we should've been calling ourselves last night—an alliance. But I'm done pretending there's a way to end the tournament, and I'm done listening to Briony claim she has noble reasons. Either we fight together or we fight each other, but there's no sane option where we don't fight at all."

Gavin understood. Alistair would go where Isobel went. And Isobel might not have been willing to kill Briony outright, but she still saw her as a liability.

This morning, Gavin had dismissed the alliance as foolish, but now he saw the merit in it. Both Isobel and Alistair were strong, and it was in Gavin's best interest that he remain part of it as long as possible. But if that left Briony at their mercy and Alistair and Isobel a pair, Gavin was the odd one out. He'd need to find a way to disrupt that.

"So leave Briony here," Gavin said. They both turned toward him, as if surprised to find he was still there. "The three of us will go after Finley and Elionor together."

Alistair's face turned a slight shade of green. He didn't want this. But he looked to Isobel, waiting for her response.

Isobel nodded, and Gavin could hardly believe his success. A Grieve, on equal footing with a Macaslan and a Lowe. "Fine," she said. "Let's start preparing."

She motioned for the two of them to follow, and they did, Alistair's face grim, Gavin trying not to smile. Because he was already concocting the next steps of his plan.

Once Isobel's and Alistair's usefulness to him had expired, he could kill Briony and pin her death on Alistair. That would turn Isobel against him and make them kill each other.

Leaving Gavin to take his crown.

Alistair Lowe

Even high magick has its limits: it can't bring back the people who died for it.

A Tradition of Tragedy

In a number of ways, the Castle Landmark reminded Alistair of the Lowe estate. Every time he turned a corner, he swore he caught a glimpse of Hendry disappearing through an archway, or a view of him from beyond a gothic window. As Alistair discreetly hurried down the hallways, the suits of armor watched him with all the cruel judgment of his family's portraits.

A pitiful excuse for a Lowe champion, he heard them whisper.

And they were right. Alistair had buried what was left of Hendry, even if it had meant sacrificing the curse that could've led to his victory. And while Isobel and the Grieve plotted upstairs amid a pile of curse-rings, Alistair snuck off to do the least Lowe thing imaginable.

His heart hammered as he descended into the bowels of the Castle, remembering the time he'd visited the vault at home. Several monster stories crept into his mind, and his own imagination clawed at him in the darkness. The worst of them was the scent of pastries, a tinge of sweetness among the gloom. Phantom high magic winked in the corners of his vision. He could almost hear Hendry's laughter in the quiet of the stairwell.

Maybe that was what this was. Maybe he was losing his mind.

By the time he reached the dungeons, his whole body trembled. He shivered even as he sweated.

A swift Skeleton Key spell opened the lock with a click. The iron door swung open, revealing Briony Thorburn in the cell's corner, awake and with her knees hugged to her chest. At least they'd let her clean up a little. That curse had been rancid.

"Did they send you to kill me?" she asked him.

"Not exactly."

"Then they're leaving to kill Finley and Elionor, and this is my last chance to reconsider." Her voice was painfully matter-of-fact when what Alistair needed, more than anything, was faith. Alistair had spent so long avoiding being good that he wasn't sure he knew how.

"I'm setting you free, Briony," he said, his voice cracking.

Briony's eyes narrowed. "I'm not a fool."

"No, the fool is probably me." He sighed and took a step back, allowing her a path to the door. Then he tossed her a leather pouch. She opened it and pulled out one of her own spellrings in surprise. "Leave, because I won't fight them, even to help you escape."

Briony gaped at him, as though still unable to reconcile his reputation with who he really was. "But they'll fight you, once they learn what you did."

Alistair shrugged with false confidence. Isobel might not have killed him this morning when he'd pressed her cursering to his throat, but then he'd only been a disappointment—not a liability, not a threat. Alistair had hoped that by letting her use the Divining Kiss, she'd understand his true feelings. That he hadn't been strong enough to save Hendry. That he didn't want to live in the kind of world where brothers had to be sacrificed, where two people who cared for each other were forced to be enemies. He'd wanted her to see that he'd give anything for this chance, no matter how unlikely it was.

Instead, Isobel hadn't even been willing to try.

"Maybe I'm damning myself," he murmured to Briony. "But I also think I'm saving myself."

"So you believe me?" Alistair didn't know Briony, but there was something comforting in seeing the expression on a stranger's face perfectly reflect his own. Maybe what Briony also needed, more than anything else, was faith.

"Stories have always had a way of burying themselves inside me," he told her honestly. "The good and the bad."

"And which is mine?"

Alistair didn't delude himself into thinking Briony's theories would ensure a happy ending to this story, but he knew with certainty it wasn't a story the Lowes would tell.

"Good," he said firmly.

She sighed. "I don't think so."

But Alistair was sure. Even with her long hair tangled, her nails caked with dirt, Briony still looked like a hero.

"Well," he said. "I'm letting you out anyway."

"I don't deserve it." Still, Briony stood up and slipped on the first of her spellrings. "Will you come with me?"

Alistair's nails were also brown with dirt. His hair was greasy. His sweater was torn and stained where Elionor's curse had struck him in the gut. Even he knew, no matter how much good he did, he would always look like a villain. He would always be a Lowe. Isobel had proved that he couldn't convince anyone of anything.

"I have to stay behind," he told her. "The Castle is a Lowe favorite—I know the wards will only trip if someone comes in, not if someone goes out. And since they'll still think you're here, it'll give you a head start to go find your allies. They both have Relics, don't they?"

"Allies," she murmured. "I . . . I'm not sure I have those anymore."

"You have one," he said quietly.

Her lips quirked into something resembling a smile. "I'll do my best to convince them. Well, convince Finley. I don't think Elionor can be swayed."

Alistair thought of the night before—what he could remember of it, anyway. The Payne definitely hadn't seemed like the easily convinced type.

"Can you test your theory before there's a battle?" he asked.

Isobel and the Grieve were preparing to leave in only a few hours, and Alistair didn't know how to stop them.

"Probably not," Briony said darkly. "But I'll try."

The only way Alistair could protect Isobel and the Grieve was to be on the battlefield beside them. But the moment they realized what he'd done, he would be their enemy, too.

"Then hurry," he choked.

Briony walked to the stairwell, then she turned around. "Thank you," she told him, before fleeing up the stairs.

Left alone in the dungeon, Alistair's monster stories returned to him. Shadows danced in the corners of his vision, and he glimpsed a familiar, ghostly silhouette.

"Can the tournament really be broken?" he whispered to Hendry. He knew it was only his imagination, his grief, but it still felt good to ask his brother for advice. Whenever Alistair got carried away with a story, Hendry had always been the one armed with reason.

But the shadows didn't answer, and as Alistair climbed back up to the Castle, all he heard was his brother's laugh.

Briony Thorburn

The Blairs who've won the tournament have almost always done
so through an alliance.

A Tradition of Tragedy

The sunlight on the moors shone more brightly than Briony had
grown accustomed to over the past several weeks. She'd cast
the Compass Rose a little while ago, a tracking spell she'd bor-
rowed at the Monastery that required something of the person she
was looking for. Finley had lent her a spellring, and that was enough
for it to work—a line of silvery white had looped around her wrist
and shot off into the distance. She followed it across the rugged landscape, her stomach churning.

Isobel had betrayed her. Alistair had freed her. And even though
Briony had taken her spellrings and fled, she couldn't shake Isobel's words back in the Castle. But Alistair was counting on her, and
she didn't want the risk he'd taken to be in vain. So she soldiered onward, trying to push her fears away.

Her senses flared with warning, a shiver running down her spine.
The spell changed a moment later, and a second line of magick
wrapped around her wrist.

Finley Blair appeared at the crest of a distant hill. Silver stretched
between them, binding them with a cord of magick. Briony watched
him approach. Something inside her withered as he coiled his finger
around the edge of the spell and snapped it in two. There was no
emotion on his face at all.

Briony hoped he could see the honesty on hers.

"I don't want to fight you," she said quietly.

Finley's hand clenched around the hilt of his sheathed Sword—then released it, his head bowing slightly as he closed the distance between them. They stopped less than a meter apart. Briony felt exposed out here in such a large, open space. Nowhere to run, even though she'd brought this confrontation upon herself.

"So it was all a trick," he said matter-of-factly, as though he had already made up his mind. "You only allied with us until the Relic you wanted fell."

"That's not what happened," Briony said. "I told you the truth. I want to end the tournament. Elionor manipulated me, then made it look like I betrayed you."

"How can I possibly believe that?"

"Your truth spell—"

"I don't care what you *meant* to do." Finley's neutral expression wavered. "I care about what actually happened. You told me there was a chance Carbry wouldn't have to die, and then you killed him yourself."

"His death curse rebounded off my shield." Her words called up the image of those arrows. The way his hand had gone limp in hers. She shuddered. "It isn't the same."

Finley hesitated, but then he shook his head. "He's still dead because of you."

Alistair had claimed Briony's story was a good one. And Briony wanted to believe him, the same way she wanted to believe that Carbry's death was because Elionor had betrayed her.

But Alistair didn't know her. And the people who did had judged her differently.

Briony thought of the rage on Isobel's face. *You forced me to become champion.*

Thought of Innes falling to the ground. *Briony—no—*

Of Carbry— *I really thought I could trust you.*

Finley tightened his grip on the Sword's hilt and asked, "So is this why you wanted us to find each other? To see which of us is next?"

"No. *No.*" Her voice was so low it sounded like a moan. "Nothing has changed. I still . . ."

But that was a lie. Everything had changed. Two weeks had passed since the tournament began, and all Briony had to show for it was a death she hadn't meant to happen. A friend who would forever hate her, a sister who would never forgive her. A theory held together by nothing except how desperately she wanted to be right.

No one in here is a hero, Isobel had snarled at her. *Least of all you.*

"I'm still prepared to win this tournament, whatever it takes," Finley told her, and Briony could not help thinking of how far both of them had taken those words. This tournament had made the unimaginable their reality. "I was ready to kill—or die. But now what you've told me is in my head, and I can't let it go. I can't let *you* . . ." He swallowed. "I just need to know if there's a chance of stopping this. I need to know what I'm supposed to do."

Briony was taken aback by the vulnerability in his words. Finley had always defined himself by his family's code, by clear standards of right and wrong. There was nobility in being a champion, in claiming victory no matter what violence or betrayal it took to get there. Her theory hadn't given him hope—it had given him doubt.

In the tournament, the surest way to lose your life was to lose your conviction.

"I wish I had an answer for you, but I *don't.*" Briony's voice shook with guilt. "I—I thought I could change the tournament. Save everyone. But all I've really done is destroy people I care about. Innes should've been the champion, and I took it from her. I . . . I attacked her and cut her finger off. My own *sister.* And I really thought it would be worth it if I could fix things. But a part of me wasn't doing it for her, or for any of you. I was doing it for myself. I thought I belonged in this story, but I never did. So maybe it's time to take myself out of it."

Giving Alistair a silent apology for the hope he'd mistakenly placed in her, she yanked off her spellrings one by one, letting them tumble to the ground. The Compass Rose. The Mirror Shards. The Healer's Touch. The Deathly Slumber. Finley didn't say a word, only watched, his face solemn. When only her stolen champion's ring was left, she knelt on the ground before him, then tipped her head up to meet his eyes.

"I forfeit," she whispered. "You need an answer, but I don't have one. So I'm giving you a way out. You told me you changed your mind about whether you could kill me or not. Well. Here's your chance."

She bowed her head and closed her eyes.

The only sounds were her own breathing, shallow and quick as a rabbit's, and the scrape of Finley drawing his sword. He knew the whole truth of her now. Every awful, guilty part.

The edge of the Sword brushed her exposed neck, the steel cool against her skin. It hovered there for a long, long moment, and Briony waited for him to pull it away and bring it down in one great strike. She tried not to think about how much it would hurt.

But when the steel moved away from her neck, so did Finley.

"Look at me." His voice was gruff.

She opened her eyes to see him staring at her intently, his face silhouetted by the brightness of the red-stained sun. He had returned the Sword to its leather strap.

The air between them thickened, not with magick, but with something else. Something that felt both dangerous and important. Briony had never seen Finley look at her with that much emotion before, not even when they broke up. Like he was frustrated. Like he was furious.

At last, he spoke. "Do you know how the Blairs choose their champion?"

Briony shook her head, unsure what that had to do with anything.

"All of the eligible candidates train their entire lives, and growing up, we were told there was a test to choose the champion," Finley explained. "And so my cousins and I waited, and waited. Until the tournament was days away, and the adults hadn't said a word.

"And that's when I realized. Our champion isn't selected—our champion volunteers. Whether or not they're the strongest doesn't matter. What matters is that they're mentally prepared and willing, no matter the outcome. Our code is simple: honor, valor, integrity. A champion who chooses this is one prepared to uphold all three of our family's values in life—and in the tournament."

"So you volunteered to protect your family," she whispered.

"Yes. And no. I volunteered because I wanted to do my family proud. But I wouldn't have volunteered if the Thorburns had named you champion instead of Innes."

Briony remembered the way he'd looked at her when the Landmarks were still ruins. When she was still the champion's sister. "You didn't want to fight me."

"Of *course* not. I never changed my mind. And then when I saw you here that first night . . ." It was now *his* voice that shook. "I won't kill you. Why the hell would you ask me to?"

Briony hadn't thought she could possibly feel worse, but she did.

"So you've done some fucked-up things to get here—I won't pretend that my strategy was ever noble, either. But I'm realizing that nothing about the tournament is good, and my family's code of honor will never make up for that. I think it's time to write my own rules. To find my own way to make things right."

Then he held out a hand.

"Come on," he said. "Get up."

She took it, then rose hesitantly to her feet. They were very close now. She could see the remnants of a few faded cursemarks against his skin, the dried blood still crusted to the collar of his polo shirt.

"I want to make things right, too," she said.

"Then don't give me your guilt. You need to take responsibility for yourself and the people you've hurt." Finley paused, and he didn't need to add that he was one of them. "If you really mean what you say, then you won't surrender. You won't give up."

He wasn't giving her an ending. But he wasn't giving her a new beginning, either.

"Then what happens now?" Briony asked.

"The two of us finish what you started. No matter what it makes us to our families—heroes, villains. I don't care. And I don't think you do anymore, either."

Briony felt a gratitude beyond measure well up inside of her. She would no longer be adrift. She would find a new way forward, and she wouldn't have to find it alone.

"So you . . . you want to go back to the Monastery?" she asked.

But Finley shook his head. "Elionor told me what you said about the septogram, and that she didn't care. I don't think the others will believe you, either. Not without indisputable proof."

Briony eyed the Sword on Finley's back. Just minutes ago, it had rested against her neck. And now it could be the first step to all of their salvation.

"Well, I know how you can get that proof," Briony said. "Alistair has left the Cave unattended. He's at the Castle. And you've got the Sword."

Something ignited in Finley's eyes. Determination. His gaze moved past her to the mountains beyond them, where the Cave was hidden. And then he turned back toward her.

"Then let's go," he said.

Briony nodded, then knelt to collect her spellrings. She knew the truth about herself now. She had caused so much pain, so much damage. And she'd been trying to end the tournament for the wrong reasons. But if she and Finley could prove this was real, maybe, just maybe, she could find the right ones.

ISOBEL MACASLAN

Our families kept this secret for centuries. Seems to me that means, on some level, we all know that what we've been doing is wrong.

A Tradition of Tragedy

For several heartbeats after the drawbridge lowered to the earth, no one moved.

Isobel tightened the Cloak over her shoulders.

Gavin cracked his neck.

Alistair hovered behind them, dark and noiseless as a shadow.

Gavin was the first to stride over the bridge. Though Carbry's death had lightened the effect of the Blood Veil, the difference was slight, and Gavin in particular did not wear the scarlet-tinged day well. Every shadow of his cheekbones and jawline seemed starker, any softness in his face washed out. His cool blond hair looked almost colorless.

"I've been to the Monastery before," Gavin boasted. "I know its weak points."

"Do you think they'll hide?" Isobel asked.

"It'll be more fun if they do."

Isobel cringed. They were doing what had to be done, but there was no fun in it.

"Our only problem is their two Relics," Gavin continued. "We'll need to be quick on the offensive. We can't give Finley time to coun-terattack."

His words made Isobel's chest tighten. Ever since she had been named champion, she'd imagined what it would look like, what it would feel like, to strike down her friends. Because with friends like Briony, golden child of the Thorburn family, and Finley, the obvious Blair favorite, she'd always known it would be asked of her.

But even the months of anticipation hadn't prepared her for how it would feel to lose everyone she cared about in the span of hours. Finley, unsuspecting of their attack. Alistair, who wanted a version of her that had never been real to begin with. Briony, who'd fashioned herself into some sort of hero when she had more blood on her hands than any of them.

It all left Isobel with rage and bitterness so strong that, even without the Blood Veil, her vision would still be colored red.

Though the Monastery was also located on the moorlands, it was a long journey, made longer by the silence draped over the group. The only sounds were their footsteps and the hem of the Cloak brushing against the brittle heather. Isobel mentally recited her curses and spells, trying to decide if any of her enchantments would be weakened by the Cloak's magick, which hindered her from casting strong offensive spells. Strategizing distracted her from her nerves. From Alistair's cool presence behind her, not beside her.

"There it is," Gavin said, indicating a gothic stone structure swathed in vines. Its spires stretched like daggers toward the crimson sun. "They must've fixed the doors. But I made easy work of them last time."

Isobel stepped aside so that Gavin could cast his spell. His brows knitted in concentration, and the door quivered on its iron hinges. Isobel and Alistair backed farther away, braced for a blast. But after several moments of struggling, Gavin dropped his hands, flushed.

"They've changed the wards since last time." He shot a furious look at Alistair. "Just going to stand there, are you?"

Wordlessly, Alistair cast a spell of his own. A white blade of wind sliced through the air and struck the door's padlock. Rather than cutting it, the blade snapped. It wasn't strong enough.

After that, all three of them tried for several minutes—without success. Gavin cursed and dropped his arms.

"It's impossible!" He seethed. "Is this you?" he shot at Alistair.

Isobel gritted her teeth. Her Skeleton Key spell had been a higher class than the Scythe's Fall Alistair had used. Contrary to what Gavin believed, Alistair was not the only formidable champion here.

"How could it be me?" Alistair answered flatly.

"You don't want this. I can tell."

"If I hadn't wanted to come, I wouldn't have."

Gavin advanced toward Alistair. He was so much bigger than him in comparison, taller, broader. Alistair might've been a Lowe, but Gavin cast a shadow twice as long and twice as dark. Though Gavin was on their side—for now—Isobel wondered if it'd been a mistake to bring him along.

"Don't waste your magick," she warned him, knowing Gavin wouldn't listen to simple reason. Her words earned her a scathing look from Alistair. And even she knew how they sounded—raspy and cold, like her father.

"Prove it, then," Gavin spat at Alistair, ignoring her. "*You* do it."

"How do you expect me to do that when both of us couldn't open it together?" he asked.

"I didn't say to open it. All we need is for Elionor and Finley to come out." Gavin took a last step forward so that they stood chest to chest, as though determined to intimidate him. But judging from the cool disdain in Alistair's eyes, it wasn't working. "Elionor nearly killed you. Don't you want revenge?"

Isobel considered casting a curse to stop Gavin, and her hand even reached for the Reaper's Embrace dangling from her necklace. But then she stopped. Gavin was the only other one among them not spouting nonsense about breaking the curse. No matter how resentful or furious she felt, she didn't know if she could face the rest of the tournament if she was the only one with the sense to fight in it.

But what did that make her? A survivor, definitely. A winner, maybe. But also something worse. And it scared her.

"You know what I think, Grieve?" Alistair countered. "You're just upset that I'm not the villain you imagined I would be. Slaying me was supposed to be your ultimate act of victory. But I'm not your monster. Or your trophy."

"You're still my enemy," Gavin growled.

Alistair smirked. "Then attack me."

Gavin's spellrings glittered, and Isobel leaped between them.

"I'll do it," Isobel said quickly. "I'll make them come out."

Even though her words were designed to form a truce, her stance said otherwise. She'd reacted instinctively, thoughtlessly—her gaze leveled in warning at Gavin, Alistair protectively behind her. It seemed that in a choice between her mind and her heart, somehow her heart still won.

That scared her, too.

Gavin stared her down. "How?"

"By making them open the door for us," Isobel answered.

She reached her hand out. She'd learned this curse from Alistair while they were in the Cave. It was called Dragon's Breath, a very Lowe sort of name. If it worked, Elionor and Finley would have no choice but to flee, like termites being fumigated from their nest.

Isobel summoned the curse, and the magick spiraled around her fingertips. A flame burst forth in the air. What began as little more than the flicker of a candle grew and grew until it took on a life of its own. The fire slithered around her, so bright she needed to squint, so scorching it hurt to breathe.

As the flames soared out in front of her, the jaws of the dragon opened wide and soared through the door of the Monastery. The fire spread throughout the Landmark, and within moments, each of the spires were engulfed.

For the next few minutes, none of them spoke. No one had charged through the doors, and Isobel wondered with a mixture of horror and relief if she had burned the other champions inside, if it would be so easy. But the Blood Veil remained unchanged, so they waited.

"A class eight? Nine?" Gavin asked, sounding begrudgingly impressed. "I guess the papers didn't lie about you."

"That curse is a family favorite," Alistair told her darkly. "You cast it better than I ever could."

Isobel had seen enough of his mind to know his words were not a compliment.

At last, the door to the Monastery burst open. Elionor collapsed at its threshold, her skin coated in a layer of soot. She coughed and sputtered into the grass. Then she crawled, pathetically, to their feet.

Gavin grabbed her by her shirt and wrenched her up.

"I guess I'll do the honors," he said, and cast the curse.

Elionor grinned as she shoved something gleaming into its path— the Mirror. The curse rebounded off the glass and shot up, between them, into the sky, grazing Gavin's cheek as it blazed past.

Gavin screamed . . . and then fell unconscious to the ground, blood pouring down his face.

BRIONY THORBURN

Theoretically, at least, this curse can be broken. But sacrifice makes any curse grow stronger, and few curses in history have been given this much blood.

A Tradition of Tragedy

The Cave was carved into the mountains at the edge of Ilvernath. It was a jagged gash in the stone, plain and unassuming, and the wards around it camouflaged it even further. Briony didn't understand why a Lowe would gravitate toward something so humble, so hidden. But then, there was clearly a lot she didn't understand about Alistair.

She checked the Blood Veil as she and Finley crept closer, but it hadn't weakened. Which meant that all the other champions were alive—for now.

"These are strong defensive spells," she commented.

Finley stared into the darkness. "It's nothing we can't handle."

They walked into the Cave together, the three spellrings set into the Sword's hilt gleaming red as the darkness swallowed them whole. A few spells activated at the entrance, but Finley's Sword swiped through them easily, high magick dissipating the ropes of spellwork designed to block out any intruders.

The Cave would only respond to Alistair, and since he wasn't here, their sole source of illumination was the dull glow of the Sword. Until, after a minute of walking, Briony found a candelabra, mostly by bumping into the rock formation it was sitting on.

A quick Flicker and Flare spell set it alight. She raised it in the air, feeling a little ridiculous, to survey the space that Alistair Lowe had described as his lair. Apparently he'd meant that literally. The main area of the Cave was one large room: a four-poster bed sat along the far wall, spellstones spilling from the blankets down onto the floor beyond it like a dragon's hoard. Clothes were piled on the edge of the covers and rumpled on the ground. Everything was coated in a thin layer of dust, and cobwebs hung like tapestries from the damp walls.

"It's filthy in here," Briony said.

"It isn't supposed to be, according to Blair lore," Finley said. "But Landmarks tailor themselves to their champion's taste."

Briony snorted. Lucky for Isobel that she wouldn't have been able to see any of the magick while she stayed here, but she had to question Alistair's judgment. Nothing like some decorative dead cockroaches to put someone in the mood.

Briony met Finley's eyes, hoping he would also crack a smile. But he only stared grimly around the Cave. He'd been civil to her as they trekked here, but it was clear he hadn't forgiven her.

"There's a hallway in the back of the cavern that should lead to the lake . . . There!" Finley gestured with his blade toward a narrow passageway that led farther into the bowels of the mountain. "That must be it."

Finley's family lore was right. The passageway opened to reveal a lake with a craggy rock protruding from the water: the pillar.

Briony set the candelabra on the ground and cast her Flicker and Flare spell again, fully draining her ring to send orbs of light to hover around the edges of the cavern. Now that it was illuminated, she could see the pillar stood on a small island in the center of the lake.

She walked to the edge of the water and gazed down at both of their indistinct reflections. Finley's form turned to stare at hers, expectant even in the muddled ripples at the shoreline. "Now what?"

This needed to work. She'd sacrificed too much for it to fail. But the truth was . . . Briony wasn't sure what to do next. It clearly wasn't enough to just have the Relic and the Landmark in the same place at the same time. If that were the case, the curse would've crumbled ages ago.

They had to do something to cancel out the magick that existed in both of them. Nullify the curse.

"If a Relic counts as an ingredient," she began, "and the pillar counts as the point on a septogram—the very heart of the Landmark—then we need to get over to that island." That, at least, she was sure of.

"And then do what?"

"I don't know. But we can figure it out."

"All right." He frowned at the lake. "If the Lowe champion was living here, he must've had a way to access this pillar. Hang on." He walked to the wall, where one of Briony's lights glinted off something embedded in the rock. Briony realized it was a spellstone the moment before Finley touched it.

Crimson magick swirled from it, spiraling outward into a thin, rickety bridge leading straight to the island.

"I knew it," he said, grinning with relief. "Let's go."

They moved across single file, the Sword slung across Finley's back. Briony let him go first because he'd insisted, chivalrous fool that he was. The moment she set foot on the island, the bridge shimmered once, as if taunting them, then disappeared.

Beside her, Finley stared at the pillar with an odd expression on his face.

"Are you okay?" she asked.

He shook his head, as if trying to clear away a fog. "I just . . . It's strange to feel so close to my family's story."

Briony understood the feeling. She'd felt it when she'd visited the Tower, even if it had merely been in ruins at the time.

"Okay," she said. "In your family's story, the champion is on this island, right? And then . . . a hand emerges from the water and gives them the Sword?"

"Yeah." Finley pulled the Sword from his scabbard and knelt at the edge of the lake, the flat of it balanced perfectly in his palms. "Seems to me like the thing that would make the most sense would be to . . . give it back?"

"But what about the pillar? It's the anchor of all of this, right? Putting the Sword in the water won't do anything to hurt it."

"I don't know. We came all this way. We have to try *something*—" Finley broke off and turned appraisingly toward the pillar. He raised the Sword and touched the tip of the blade to the rock. The air around them seemed to shift, sending a gust of wind outward from where the metal met stone—and then a spell erupted from the pillar, throwing him back. The Sword clattered out of his grasp and slid to the edge of the lake.

"Finley!" Briony rushed over to where he lay halfway in the water, dazed. "Are you okay?"

He nodded, chest heaving as he rose into a sitting position. Above them, the ceiling shuddered.

"The pillar is defending itself," he said. "That must mean we can destroy it with the Relic, right?"

Briony nodded, hope swelling in her. "Right."

But when she turned to grab the Sword, the ceiling rumbled again. Something silver clattered onto the ground at her feet. She scrambled away from it, gaping at a Sword identical to the one lying nearby.

Briony tipped her head back, dread coursing through her. Where there had once been a cluster of stalactites glittered dozens of copycat Swords. She lunged for the real one, but Finley pushed her out of the way. The two of them toppled back into the dirt as a shower of blades fell where her body had been a moment ago.

"Shit!" Briony clambered up. "Maybe if we use the water as cover—"

"Briony." Finley's voice was raw with horror. "Look."

Briony turned, confused, to realize that Finley had dipped a finger in the lake. When he drew it out, it was coated in crimson. The smell of copper wafted from the trail of red that spread through the water—red that was not only high magick, but—

"Blood," she croaked. Tendrils of crimson reached out and spun through the lake, a sharp, metallic smell rising around them. She clambered backward, struggling not to vomit.

"We have to stop this." Her voice came out strangled. "We have to destroy that pillar."

Above them, another blade fell from the ceiling, the point aimed directly at Finley's skull.

This time it was Briony's turn to lunge for him. She slammed into his side, sending them both toppling into the lake of blood. The copycat Sword clattered onto the island behind them.

The sensation of sinking was the most horrifying thing Briony had ever experienced, a dozen times more gruesome than the illusion curse Alistair had cast on them at the quarry. The blood was warm and viscous, clotting around her flailing hands and sucking her down into it. Her eyes were squeezed shut, but her mouth had opened during the fall. She clamped it shut—too late. The taste of metal flooded her nostrils and her throat, and the sticky texture coated her tongue. She clawed upward, desperate for air, until at last she broke the surface.

When she opened her eyes, blood smeared her vision. It was in her nostrils, her ears, matted in her hair. She tried to breathe, but coughed up crimson instead. Just like Carbry had—

"Briony." Finley's voice rang out beside her, hoarse with panic. A moment later, his arm gripped her waist beneath the surface, pulling her toward him. She sagged with relief—he was okay. Red stained his face and hair, pooled in the hollows of his throat. "You're alive."

Behind him, Swords were still raining down from the ceiling, some splashing into the lake beside them, others piling around the pillar. There was no way to tell which one was the real Relic.

Briony nodded and wrapped an arm around his neck. There was so much blood, too much, and for a moment she was back in the forest, staring at Carbry's body. She saw the arrows protruding from his eyes, heard the rasp of his final words, and then she was clutching Innes's finger, that sliver of bone still protruding from the end.

"No," she choked, her guilt as strong and viscous in her throat as the taste of copper. Her free hand clawed desperately at the blood, trying to keep them both afloat. "This lake . . . I . . ."

"It's an illusion," Finley whispered. "It's not real, Bri. It's not actually blood."

Above them, the ceiling rumbled again, a fresh round of Swords falling into the lake. Panic surged through her, but she remembered what Finley had said. *If you really wanted to make things right, then you wouldn't surrender.*

She could use this guilt, this fear, as fuel to do better instead of sinking even lower.

She took a deep breath, trembling, then let go of Finley and swam closer to the pillar. Red light flared inside, the outer stone going translucent. The Landmark wasn't casting this enchantment—the pillar was. Which gave her hope that destroying it with the Relic would theoretically stop the spell.

"You're right," she breathed. They were treading blood side by side now. "We need to focus on finding the real Sword and stabbing it into the pillar. Do you have any spellwork that could do that?"

"The Blade of Truth should dispel illusions."

"Then I'll cover you with Mirror Image," Briony said, a plan crystallizing in her mind. "That should give you enough time to destroy it."

"Sounds good to me."

"Perfect. Let's go fuck this curse up."

Finley chuckled in response. Briony was surprised to find that he could still be amused by her bravado. She knew he hadn't forgiven her yet—but someday, maybe, he could.

Briony wanted him to know that he'd made a good decision.

That she would do everything in her power to help him end all of this before anyone else got hurt. The words that came to her were not that promise—but they were the right words, all the same.

"I never could have killed you," she whispered.

"I know." His voice felt like a spell of its own, a Compass Rose thrumming between them like a lifeline. "I've always known. I'm just not so sure that you did."

The island was a lot smaller than Briony remembered when she hauled herself back onto the rocky shoreline. The blood or water or whatever it truly was had begun to rise. If they didn't hurry, the whole cavern would flood. She crawled over to the pillar, kicking Swords out of the way, then reached for her Mirror Image spellring. The same spell that had hurt Carbry and Innes. She took a deep breath, the stench of copper nearly making her gag, and cast it.

A moment later, a dome of white light appeared above her and Finley's head. Blades fell from the ceiling, but where they hit the light, they rebounded, windmilling across the cavern. Briony felt the force of each of the Swords, but she held the shield steady, kneeling at the shoreline, her arms outstretched and eyes watering from the effort.

"I can see it," Finley gasped, a spell of his own shimmering around him. "I know which one is real."

"Go!" Briony urged. "I'll cover you."

He clawed his way up onto the island, stumbling through a pile of Swords, and emerged a few moments later with one that looked like all the others. Above them, the ceiling quaked yet again. But now, instead of Swords, rocks began to fall.

"Hurry!" she screamed.

He nodded, panting, then turned and buried the Sword deep within one of the glowing red veins in the pillar.

Immediately, the Swords on the ground vanished. The smell of blood disappeared. Briony stared at the water, gaping as the color bled away until it was an ordinary lake again. Finley had been right.

It had all been an illusion. But her relief was short-lived as the cavern ceiling shook again, rocks raining down as the magick failed.

"Come on!" Briony shouted to Finley. "The whole thing's coming down!"

High magick thrummed through the cavern, red light bouncing off the walls; Briony dove into the water and clawed against the current back toward shore. Finley was only half a stroke behind her as they swam to the lake's edge. They scrambled back to the shoreline, panting and soaking wet, but there was no time to stop. Briony rose to her feet to the backdrop of deep rumbling emanating from the Cave around them, the walls, the floor, the ceiling.

On what remained of the island, water lapped at the halfway point of the pillar, the entire Sword glowing the same deep red as the crevice Finley had plunged it into. Briony took one last look at those three spellstones winking in the darkness, then turned to follow Finley as he bolted toward the passageway.

She was grateful for all the time she'd spent on the rugby field and the volleyball court as the walls of the passageway shook around them. She could narrow her focus, keep her footing, think only of getting through this as fast as possible. Briony rushed back into the main part of the Cave a moment before the passageway collapsed, sprinting past the four-poster bed. Light had appeared up ahead at the mouth of the tunnel that led outside, but the ground shuddered below her, then quaked, sending her sprawling onto the floor.

"Shit!" Briony rolled over and pressed her palms flat on the ground, struggling to get her bearings. She could hear rocks smashing into the cavern floor behind her.

"Briony!" Finley grabbed her hand and yanked her upward. "Come on. We have to get out of here."

They half ran, half scrambled their way out of the Cave together, until at last the light of day flooded around them and they were standing at the peak of the mountain.

Behind them, the mouth of the cavern quivered—then collapsed in a small avalanche, rocks piling over the entrance.

The two of them sat on the ground, soaking wet and utterly exhausted.

"The Landmark," Briony croaked out at last. "It's destroyed. Do you still feel a connection to the Relic?"

"No. The Sword's power is gone," Finley said. "They canceled each other out. Just like you said they would."

She turned toward him, and adrenaline surged through her at seeing the hope on his face. She hadn't known what would happen when they united the Landmark and the Relic. Now she knew for certain they could break each piece of the septogram, one by one, until the tournament was destroyed just as the Cave and the Sword had been.

It didn't erase the harm she'd caused. But at least, at last, she'd done something right.

Beside her, Finley cast a quick heat spell that dried out their clothes and hair. The blood had been an illusion, but the smell of it lingered in Briony's throat all the same.

"Thank you," she murmured as Finley tucked the spellstone away. "You believed me, even though you had every reason not to."

"I never could've lived with myself knowing that there was a way to stop this, even a hypothetical one, and not trying it."

"Well. It's not so hypothetical anymore."

Briony gave Finley a hesitant smile, feeling gratified when he returned it. She couldn't help the way her heart rattled in her chest when she looked at him, how his touch had been comforting even in the midst of unfathomable horror.

But that moment in the Cave had surely been just that. A moment.

Pushing aside her feelings, she said, "Let's go end this." Briony thought of a world in twenty years where a Blood Moon did not rise. Where for the first time in centuries, the seven families of Ilvernath could choose a story free of slaughter.

GAVIN GRIEVE

The bodies of the victims lie there for however long the tournament lasts, left to rot.

A Tradition of Tragedy

Gavin dreamed he languished at the bottom of a pit. Strands
of purple and green snared around his wrists, his calves, his
abdomen, taking over his body the way they'd already taken
over his arm. He screamed in pain as they pinned him to the ground.
Thrashed his head from side to side as the veins crawled up his face.
Even if he hadn't yet consumed the last of his life magick, his body
couldn't stop the magick from consuming him.

And then something brushed against his cheek. He was unaccus-
tomed to physical affection, and this touch felt like electricity against
his skin. Like a rope thrown down to him from a world above, one
where he wouldn't be in agony anymore. He tried to move his arm
and found he could, then his leg, and suddenly the magick receded.

"Gavin?" a voice asked, with what Gavin guessed was genuine concern. He'd never heard it before.

His eyes opened. There was a face hovering over his own, a hand
cupped around his cheek. Alistair Lowe's widow's peak and deep gray
eyes. Alistair Lowe's surprisingly soft palm. The fact that Gavin had
found that momentarily *comforting* was somehow worse than the fact
that he'd been on the verge of death.

"Don't touch me!" Gavin scrambled away from Alistair, trying not to show his immense embarrassment. His shirt and pants were stained where he'd hit the ground, his temples throbbing with pain. Whatever healing spell Alistair had cast on him wasn't finished, but Gavin couldn't let Alistair get that close to him again.

Not if it meant Alistair might see what Gavin had done to himself. To his magick.

"You're welcome," Alistair muttered, and after what had happened between them last night, Gavin almost felt sorry.

"I thought you didn't know my name," Gavin accused.

Alistair rolled his eyes. "*Yes*, I know your name, you absolute gremlin." Then his eyes widened, fixed on something behind Gavin. In an instant, a shield spell sprang around the two of them, and without asking Gavin's permission, Alistair grabbed him by the hand and yanked him to his feet.

A curse struck the shield. Dizzy, still clutching his tattooed arm, Gavin whipped around. He'd been so distracted by Alistair and his magick that he'd forgotten Elionor reflecting his spell at him and knocking him out.

Several paces away, Isobel had backed Elionor against what remained of the stone wall of the Monastery, while the flames continued to rage farther back in the Landmark. Elionor's chest heaved. Her black clothes were covered in soot and grime, the bags under her eyes purple and puffy. But the Mirror, still clenched in her right hand, rebounded Isobel's curses back at her.

"Where's Finley?" Gavin asked. They'd expected to find both of them here.

Isobel gritted her teeth, focused on the battle. "He's gone."

Gavin swore under his breath. But at least they'd slay one champion this morning. He cast the Chimera's Bite—another Alistair cursestone—on Elionor while she was trying to defend against Isobel. She blocked it, but not fast enough—a gash appeared on her arm, a cursemark glowing around it. A rush of satisfaction welled in him when he realized he, a Grieve, had managed to draw blood from every champion. Gavin remembered Carbry, gasping in panic when Gavin breached the Monastery; Briony and Isobel fleeing from his cursefire on the moors; Alistair's glass shattering in his hand; and Finley scrambling for his Sword.

The ground beneath his feet tremored, and he accidentally slammed into Alistair's side, breaking Alistair's concentration and making the shield fall.

"What's going on?" Isobel asked.

"I don't—" Alistair began, but then the sky above them flickered— red to white and back again. So fast that had Gavin blinked, he would've missed it.

The quaking stopped, and for several heartbeats, all four of them were still. Elionor had fallen to her knees. Isobel was braced, as though waiting for the earth to shake again. Alistair gaped openmouthed at the sky.

Taking advantage of their distraction, Gavin shoved Alistair out of his way. He didn't have Revenge of the Forsaken anymore, but he'd taken a different death curse from Alistair, the Guillotine's Gift, and he aimed it at Elionor. It fell through the air, a blade of white. Elionor dove out of the way. A gash sliced across her neck, but she'd avoided the full brunt of the curse. She gasped, trembling, and her grip on the Mirror loosened as she stumbled.

Ignoring the pain in his arm, Gavin lunged forward and wrestled the Mirror out of Elionor's grasp. He overpowered her easily, then stumbled backward, clutching the handle in his fist. It was useless to him right now, but if Gavin was the one to kill Elionor, the owner-ship of the Mirror would transfer to him.

Elionor, still bleeding on the ground beside them, stiffened as Gavin readied himself to cast the curse again, this time aiming for her throat.

But before he could, Alistair grabbed him by the shoulder and wrenched him around. Gavin stifled a scream as his tattoo throbbed beneath Alistair's grasp.

"Stop," Alistair breathed. "Both of you—you can't go through with this. Not if there's a chance that Briony could be right."

"What are you doing?" Isobel asked, as though she hadn't heard him right. Gavin wasn't sure he had, either.

Alistair jabbed his finger at the sky. "You saw what happened to the Blood Veil. You felt the ground shake. What do you think that was?"

"How could that be Briony?" Gavin asked. "She's still locked in—"

"Because I . . ." Alistair swallowed. "I set her free."

"You did *what?*" Isobel seethed.

"Just because it's always been this way doesn't mean there's no hope. It could change. We could change it."

Alistair's anguish was visible and real, and the idea that Alistair didn't want bloodshed but Gavin did infuriated him. His entire life, his role had been written for him. A Grieve. A loser. A dead boy walking. And Gavin might've wanted to change his story, but the Lowe champion, the enemy, shouldn't want to. He didn't deserve to. Slaying Alistair had always been the ultimate prize, and Gavin had not spent his life battling his conscience and fear into submission for Alistair to take away everything that prize had meant to him.

"Alistair," Isobel murmured. "You can't run from the tournament."

"Am I the only one who saw what happened to the sky?" he growled. "Have either of you ever heard of anything like that before?"

Beneath him, Elionor let out a hacking cough and spit a mouthful of blood onto the grass. "Don't tell me that Briony got to you, too? Pathetic."

A dark expression crossed Alistair's face. Gavin preferred it.

"Get out of the way, Lowe," Gavin threatened. "Or I'll cast your own curse on you."

"Don't do this," Isobel breathed, and Gavin struggled to tell who she was talking to—Alistair or him.

Gavin knew it was a bad idea to curse Alistair, especially if it made an enemy of Isobel, too. His magick had already come close to consuming him once. And Gavin couldn't survive this tournament alone.

"If you're not going to fight with us," he spat at Alistair, "then you're not part of this alliance."

Alistair glanced to Isobel, trying to gauge her reaction.

"Please don't make me," she said softly. "I don't want to fight you. But what you're doing . . . You're not giving me a choice."

Alistair swayed a moment, as though dizzy. "Fine," he said tightly. "But there's always a choice."

And then he turned on his heel and walked away, clearly daring them to attack him.

Isobel had turned a faint shade of green, but Gavin refused to lose his focus. He took a threatening step closer to Elionor, who was curled into a ball on the ground in front of the Monastery. It was time to show Ilvernath—show the whole world—what he was capable of.

But before he could, Elionor uncurled and launched herself at Gavin, her lips bared in a snarl as she reached for the Mirror. She missed, but as Gavin lunged out of her path, her hand struck his arm instead. He growled like a wounded animal as agony bulleted through his nerves from his shoulder to his fingertips. He fell, and the Mirror fell beside him. Groaning, Gavin rolled over and reached for it.

But Elionor got to it first. She snatched it up and loomed over him. "Now it's only two on one. Or one and a half," she purred, smiling wickedly at Gavin. "I like those odds."

ALISTAIR LOWE

Victor or not, a Lowe has never left the tournament without killing someone.

A Tradition of Tragedy

After abandoning the battle, Alistair walked wherever his feet chose to carry him. Because his familiarity with Ilvernath began and ended with the pub district, he was lost until the forest path approached the edge of town. In the distance, a translucent wall of crimson light separated the grounds of the tournament from Ilvernath proper, impenetrable to champions entering or townsfolk leaving.

A dead end.

He sighed and slumped against a tree, unsure where to go, unsure if he truly wanted to leave Isobel behind, unsure who he was supposed to be anymore.

Through the red field, he spotted the Champions Pillar in the square outside the banquet hall. How ironic that, as he fled from the tournament, he was drawn back here, to the place where it had started.

He thought of Carbry Darrow's crossed-out name compared to the dozens of Lowe names. Something burned in him knowing that his was included among them. He didn't want this anymore. Not his family, not this story. Briony's plan seemed like the only way to escape from it, but no one else believed her. No one else even *wanted* to.

He'd never felt more hopeless.

His gaze found something strange on the Pillar—another crack. Not just the ones beside Briony's name and at its base, like he had noticed on the matching pillars in the Cave and the Castle. But a third. It trailed up the length of the stone like a vein and pulsed with light.

Maybe it is breaking, Alistair thought. After the Blood Veil had flickered earlier, it was the only explanation that made sense, even if it happened to be the one he wanted.

As though in answer, a cool wind blew from the west, caressing the hairs on the back of his neck.

Alistair, whispered a voice from nowhere. Chills crept up his spine, and he dug his fingernails into his thighs, his stomach filling with dread. The voice was a rasp, as unsettling as trees scratching against window glass, or the howl of a wolf in the distance.

You really are losing it, he thought to himself. Just like Aunt Alphina.

"Alistair!" a different voice called through the trees behind him. He recognized it as Isobel's. She'd run after him, but for what? To kiss him? To kill him? His hope and dread tangled into something indistinguishable from each other.

"Alistair! Alistair, run!"

A death curse tore through the courtyard toward him, and he saw a flash of blond hair between the trees. Alistair scrambled out of the curse's path, skirting the high magick wall, then he tripped and fell. He threw his arms out, expecting to crash into the town's magickal force field, but instead he fell through it, onto the edge of the square.

Behind him, an ancient oak split down the middle, its bark unwinding like skin being flayed layer by layer.

His thoughts spun in dizzying shock. Alistair looked up to see who had cast the curse, still astonished that he'd passed through the Blood Veil . . . when another chill swept over him.

Alistair, the voice whispered again from nowhere.

He whipped his head around, but there was no monster—only Gavin. He stood in front of the hole Alistair had made in the Blood

Veil—a messy thing, as if someone had torn a scrap of paper. The other boy walked through it, then glared at Alistair with a wild look in his eyes.

"Y-you," Alistair stuttered. "I—How did I—"

"You just left us behind," Gavin told him, seething, somehow unbothered by the fact that the Blood Veil had torn. "I didn't think you actually would."

"So you're going to kill me?" Alistair asked from the ground.

"I wasn't aiming at you," he growled.

Alistair got up and turned to see Elionor several meters away in the forest, the Mirror clutched in her hand. When he'd left the Monastery, he thought he was leaving her to die. The Payne must have been tougher than he thought, to have faced down both Gavin and Isobel.

Elionor stared at the two boys through the Veil with wide eyes, then peered at the hole, the Mirror dropping to her side. She looked as shocked as Alistair felt.

"How did you do that?" she asked.

"The Veil has been messed up for a while," Gavin said. Then he motioned for Elionor to come closer. "Well? What are you waiting for? Come get us."

Elionor reached forward and tore a gash in the Veil with her long fingernails. She stepped through it with a nasty smile on her face, but before she could reach them or cast a curse, Isobel appeared through the trees. "Me first."

"I'm not taking requests," Elionor hissed.

Isobel's eyes briefly found Alistair's, the shield of scarlet between them, and for a moment she froze. Alistair didn't know why the barrier around town would tear and let them inside, but if something was wrong with the tournament's curse, that proved it was not indestructible, that Briony was right and it could be broken. Finally, Isobel would have to see that.

Alistair's mouth was dry. "We shouldn't be able to . . ."

But Isobel turned back to Elionor.

And Alistair realized that what had happened between them in the Cave really had been a fantasy. They were too different. Alistair had spent his entire life fashioning himself out of the glamour and allure of stories. Isobel couldn't even see that their own story was fraying at the seams. And she probably never would.

"Let's finish this," Isobel told Elionor coolly, stepping through the hole the other champion had torn.

The Mirror's and Cloak's defensive powers made them a good match for each other. A flurry of curses shot through the air in brilliant flashes of white and red.

As Alistair staggered away from them, farther into the square, the air in the courtyard trembled. A strong gust of wind blew his hair into his eyes, strewed fallen leaves across the streets, whistled between the creaky shutters. Flurries like snowflakes swept past them, except it wasn't snow. They were dull and lifeless as ash, like pieces of burnt paper wafting into the evening light, and they were red like dried flecks of blood.

"Is this raw high magick?" Gavin asked, his eyes wide.

Alistair knew a lot about high magick. Like common magick, it was perceived as a glimmer, like pieces of glitter suspended in the breeze. The scarlet color might've been right, but it wasn't supposed to look like decay.

The back-and-forth curses between Elionor and Isobel stopped.

"What is this?" Elionor called, her voice high-pitched and frightened. "Did you do this?"

"I didn't," Isobel answered. Though panting from their fight, her face had gone ghostly pale.

Monsters aren't real, Alistair told himself desperately. In that moment, he was locked in his childhood bedroom with the window open and his mother's warnings creeping in his mind. He was in the lake waiting for the leviathan's approach. He was trapped in the woods, buried alive, locked in the darkness.

"Alistair," that voice whispered again, this time louder. And clearer.

"What was that?" Gavin asked. The two boys took several nervous steps backward, colliding with each other. They braced themselves, back to back. The Champions Pillar loomed over them.

Alistair swallowed. He had no answer.

The doors to the banquet hall flung open. The lights of the building were off, leaving only darkness.

"Grins like goblins," the voice murmured. "Pale as plague and silent as spirits."

Alistair stiffened. He knew that voice.

A silhouette appeared in the shadows.

"They'll tear your throat and drink your soul."

The figure stepped forward into the red daylight. He tilted his head to the side, his curls falling lazily over his eyes. His fair skin was tanned and freckled from afternoons spent napping outdoors, his cheeks sunken but otherwise rosy with life. His expression was caught in a smile—as it always was—but it wasn't as bright a smile as it had been before.

A scar was etched across his neck. Deep. Red. Lethal.

"Al," Hendry Lowe said hoarsely, "it's me."

A tremor shot through Alistair, quaking in his heart.

Except for the scar, his brother looked just as he'd last seen him, only two weeks prior. He even wore the same clothes he had that day the spellmakers visited—a gray sweater and dark-washed jeans.

"But you're . . ." His voice trailed off, his mouth gone dry.

"You're the other Lowe, aren't you? You shouldn't be able to interfere," Elionor told him, anxiously eyeing his scar. "It shouldn't be possible."

But Alistair didn't care what was possible. He felt like the other half of his heart, of his soul, had been delivered to him once again. He was four, his brother's arms wrapped around his shaking shoulders during a tumultuous thunderstorm. He was eight, playing the dragon who fought the knight, laughing as he dodged his brother's halfhearted blows. He was sixteen and they were drunkenly stumbling out of their favorite pub, arm in arm.

Hendry seemed equally shaken and relieved to see him. But as he turned his head to assess the others around them, something strange happened. A streak of red high magick appeared as he moved, as though there was a lag in his image. As though he was made up of magick and illusion and nothing more.

Alistair felt a hand squeezing his shoulder. Gavin. He shrugged him off and took a step closer to Hendry. He had to touch his brother; he had to know if he was real.

"He's dead, Al," Isobel said from a few paces away. "First the Blood Veil, now this. This isn't—"

"What the fuck do you mean he's *dead*?" Elionor asked.

"Dead as in brutally murdered," Gavin shot back. "As in not waking up. That kind of dead."

Alistair winced at that, feeling more unsure than ever. "Is one of you doing this, then?" Alistair croaked. "Is this a spell?" He climbed the mossy stone steps of the banquet hall until he stood before his brother. The streak of lagging red light appeared again as Hendry threw his arms around him.

His touch was solid. His touch was as real as anything.

All the events of the past two weeks unwound inside Alistair. The game played with Gavin over shared drinks. The nights spent with Isobel in the Cave. The horrible morning his family had gathered together to name him champion.

"I'm here," Hendry said softly. "It's me."

"Do you remember . . ." Alistair swallowed. "Do you remember what happened?"

Hendry lifted his hand to his neck, the light of red magick once against streaking behind him as he moved. "I remember all of it."

"I'm so sorry," Alistair said, his words cracking. "Are you . . . are you okay?" It was a ridiculous question. Of course none of this was okay. After a childhood spent listening to tragic tales, none had scarred Alistair as deeply as this one. He stared at the mark on his brother's throat, where their grandmother had torn it open and extracted his life magick.

"I am now," Hendry responded, and gradually, his face lit up into another smile.

A curse, white as bone, flashed in his peripheral vision. Alistair reacted instantly, stepping protectively in front of Hendry and throwing up an Exoskeleton to deflect its path. His heart hammered with a fear so strong it threatened to consume him. He'd lost Hendry once—he couldn't lose him again.

He searched wildly for the caster and saw it had been Elionor, braced for battle once more at the courtyard's edge. The whites of her eyes were bloodshot. Her long black hair was plastered to her skin with sweat, her shoulders heaving in exertion from such a powerful curse. One Alistair could only assume was meant to kill.

"What are you doing?" Alistair growled. "Hendry isn't a champion."

"Then he shouldn't be allowed to interfere! And from the sound of it, he shouldn't even be alive," she countered. "I don't know how you did it, but I'm not surprised that the Lowes would cheat. Don't you have enough of an advantage already?"

Elionor was half right. The Lowes might not have intended to break the rules, but the rules *were* breaking.

Alistair's gaze flickered briefly to the Champions Pillar, to its three cracks.

"You buried the ring," Gavin said from the bottom of the steps. "You buried the ring with the curse made from Hendry's sacrifice. In an area full of high magick. And look at him—he goes all red when he moves."

Alistair knew that magick left a body during burial, but that was a body. Surely this couldn't be the same. Surely this couldn't be some . . . some *trick*.

Beside him, Hendry took a deep, shuddering breath. "I feel real," he rasped but even he didn't sound certain.

But Alistair was sure. He had to be sure. He had never needed anything as much as he needed this.

"If you attack again," Alistair warned Elionor, "I'll fight back."

"Al . . ." Hendry said warily. Alistair quickly fished in his pocket and withdrew a handful of extra spellstones. Hendry had never been a fighter, but Alistair thrust them into his hands anyway. He was about to tell Hendry to take them and run, but instead, Hendry squeezed them tight. "I'm not leaving you. I don't want you to fight alone—I never did."

Elionor took a wide-eyed, nervous step back, assessing them both. The wind in the courtyard continued to whistle, and the dark, overcast sky went darker still. Both Isobel and Gavin seemed frozen.

Then Elionor raised her hand, fist clenched for battle, and cast another curse.

GAVIN GRIEVE

The only place where Grieve champions are immortalized is in
a drinking song.

A Tradition of Tragedy

Everything had gone bad and nonsensical so quickly, Gavin had
no idea how to process it. He struggled to accept the sight before him: Hendry Lowe was back from the dead, but altered.
A photographic negative of Alistair, as if the brothers had swapped
roles—Alistair was now the sun, and Hendry the shadow.

Beside him, Elionor Payne cast a barrage of curses, but they
weren't meant for Gavin anymore. Instead they spiraled toward
the brothers standing on the mossy steps, the magick white and
glimmering. Alistair desperately raced to conjure shields, but he
was too slow—one flew past, and Hendry cringed as the curse
struck him in the chest. Rather than harming him, the curse unraveled into red wisps of smoke. Elionor's face went stark white
with fear.

Hendry trembled as he raised his hand to his neck, to his scar, as
though he'd felt a phantom pain there. "I guess you can't cast a death
curse on me. Since I'm already dead."

Even though Hendry sounded more haggard than anything, as he
started down the stairs, Gavin automatically stepped back.

"That's . . . not . . . possible," Elionor ground out, visibly shaken.

Hendry's expression was grim and shadowed. "It shouldn't be,
should it?"

Though Hendry might've trembled earlier, no one was shaking more than Alistair. His eyes were pink from the cast of the Blood Veil, making him look wild. His chest shuddered with every breath as he fixed a ruthless gaze on Elionor. It was the sort of look that made Gavin's own heart stutter with fear.

Gavin wasn't sure who he was supposed to be cursing anymore. Elionor believed the Lowes had cheated, but Gavin had seen Alistair bury the ring. And he'd seen Alistair's shock at the sight of his brother. Whatever had happened, he didn't think it was intentional. But it didn't change the fact that the tournament still demanded blood.

Still, Gavin didn't attack. If two of his enemies wanted to kill each other, he wouldn't stop them.

"If you try to hurt Hendry again," Alistair warned Elionor, his voice cracking, "I'll kill you. I swear it." Gavin believed him.

"This doesn't make sense." Isobel strode between Elionor and Alistair, the Cloak around her shoulders shielding her from any curses they might cast. "Al, I know this isn't a trick. But your brother can't be here."

"I won't leave him," Hendry cut in.

"And I won't let him," Alistair added.

"You can't honestly mean you're fine with this," Elionor spat at Isobel. "Why should the Lowes get *two* champions?"

However Hendry had come to be here, Gavin didn't consider him a champion. Every awful rumor had always been about Alistair—Alistair's wickedness, Alistair's talent. He didn't know what that made Hendry, but Elionor was treating them like equals, when one was clearly the greater threat.

"That isn't what—"

But Elionor didn't wait for Isobel to finish. She cast a curse, the fumes of it hissing and spiraling in every direction. It deflected off from Isobel's Cloak, ricocheting into the banquet hall, blasting through the stone exterior. Isobel and the brothers lunged out of the path of the falling rubble, while Gavin hastily threw up a Shark's Skin as cover. When the clouds of dust and gravel settled, Gavin saw Alistair stumbling to his feet, a limp left wrist dangling at his side. There was no mercy on his face at all.

Alistair tilted his head, his widow's peak slicing his face in two, and drew a hand out of his pocket. Clenched in his fist was the cursestone he'd taken from Gavin the night before.

"Thanks for this, Grieve," he breathed, and then he cast the Revenge of the Forsaken before Gavin even had the chance to understand what he meant.

Elionor's torso broke apart in a spray of splintered bone and mangled flesh. Blood splattered everywhere as her body caved inward on itself and she collapsed onto the stone. Gavin gasped and stumbled back, his vision coated in red. When he'd scrubbed the worst of it away, he was rewarded by the sight of Elionor's ruined rib cage. Her intestines had been shredded. Crimson leaked through the remnants of her black clothing, pooling around his feet.

She'd been dead the moment the curse touched her. Dead before she hit the ground. And because it was Gavin's cursestone, he knew what that death entailed. He knew exactly how difficult it was to cast it so well, so effectively. It was something he'd never been able to manage.

An awful sound grated to Gavin's left. He jerked his head toward it. The Champions Pillar was glowing brighter than it had just a moment ago, a crimson line now etched through Elionor's name.

Gavin shuddered and looked back at the others. Isobel was silent, pale as a sheet.

Elionor's arm was flung out to the side, her fingers just centimeters away from Gavin's bloodied boots. Her eyes were sightless and glassy, mouth open in something between horror and surprise. He could see a slight shimmer of white gathering around her mouth, her nose, her ears. Her life magick, dissipating into the air.

He felt a tug toward it. A physical pull. And instead of hovering aimlessly in the air, the magick drifted toward him. Like it wanted him to take it.

Gavin reached forward, gasping as a tendril wound around his hand—and sank *into his skin*. The ever-present pain in his arm lessened slightly, but he could not process what this meant. Not while staring down at the horror of what Alistair had done. The whole courtyard smelled of copper and bile.

He raised his eyes from Elionor Payne's corpse to Alistair Lowe's cruel face, now accentuated with a thin misting of blood. "You didn't have to kill her like *that*," Gavin rasped.

Alistair examined the body with a horrified stare, as though this act surprised even him—no matter if it had been in defense of his brother.

Gavin had told himself that Alistair Lowe was callous. Brutal. Wicked. He'd been wrong about all of those things. But his biggest mistake had been not in what he'd learned, but what he'd forgotten: Alistair Lowe, first and foremost, was dangerous.

Above them, the sky let out a great, wide groan—and then, like a miracle, daylight streamed through for a moment, like an eye opening. Everyone gasped, squinting into the light.

As quickly as it came it was gone, red stitching the sky back together. But the high magick around them felt . . . different. A *crack* sounded from the Champions Pillar, and Gavin whipped his head around, wondering who else had died. But instead of crossing out a name, a gash appeared on its other side, across the carving of the moon and the line of seven stars. Crimson light spilled through the cracks, identical to the light that hovered around Hendry.

"What just happened?" asked Gavin. The sky hadn't done that when Carbry died, but now it had happened twice in one morning.

But everyone else looked just as confused as he did.

"I don't like this," Isobel said, stepping away from the body. "I've never heard of the Pillar cracking when champions die."

"This is the fourth crack," Gavin pointed out. "But only two champions are dead."

"Or the tournament really is breaking," Alistair said.

Gavin instinctively opened his mouth to disagree, but he couldn't find the words. They were outside tournament grounds, after all. He circled the Pillar and examined its cracks, three on its front side and one on its back. He didn't know what it meant. He didn't know what Hendry's inexplicable resurrection meant. After his years studying the stories of the tournament, nothing in his files or in *A Tradition of Tragedy* had prepared him for when the story veered off course.

Before either he or Isobel could respond, footsteps thudded from behind them.

Gavin turned.

Briony's dark hair swirled behind her as she walked toward them with Finley Blair.

Gavin had seen Briony Thorburn kill a champion less than twelve hours ago. The look on her face then was nowhere near as frightening as the one he saw now, because she didn't look defeated. She looked triumphant.

"What are you doing here?" he asked warily. He barely knew who his allies were anymore, but he doubted Briony and Finley were among them.

Briony bared her teeth in a victorious smile. "We figured it out. We know how to break the curse."

BRIONY THORBURN

The only part about the tournament that makes it a fairy tale is
that it's definitely gone on ever after.

A Tradition of Tragedy

B riony swayed as she saw Elionor's mangled corpse, a heap of
tattered strips of black fabric and flesh.

She and Finley had come to save her—to save everyone. But
they were too late. The courtyard was in ruins. One of them was
dead. And Gavin was drenched in blood.

Somehow, impossibly, the tracking spell Finley had cast on Elionor
had led them into town, behind the inner part of the Blood Veil. And
even more impossibly, a boy stood beside Alistair at the top of the
stairs to the banquet hall. A boy who did not belong.

"Who are you?" Briony's voice cracked with confusion and horror.
They shouldn't be here. And they shouldn't be able to interact with
anyone but the champions.

"I'm Hendry," the boy said. As he shifted, the image of him lagged.
There was a red glow of high magick around him, only visible as he
moved, like a projection that could not keep up with his form. "I'm
Alistair's brother."

"But . . . how?" she asked.

Before Hendry could respond, Finley rushed over to kneel beside Elionor's broken form. The way he forced his expression from
anguish to neutrality made Briony's heart ache. This was not the
first bloodied body of one of his allies that he had found.

"Who did this to her?" she demanded.

For a long while, no one answered. Then Alistair, without meeting her gaze, croaked, "Guilty."

Briony took a step back, unable to understand. Alistair had set her free. He'd believed her.

"Why did you kill her?" she asked. "I thought we were agreed. We've proven that we can break this curse. Finley and I united the Sword and the Cave. They're both gone now—and the tournament is changing."

"Oh, come on," Gavin said, pausing to push back his blood-soaked hair. "I don't see any proof—"

"You must've seen the Blood Veil flicker. We did that."

"That was you?" Isobel's voice was raspy with disbelief.

"It was," Finley said, turning away from Elionor's body to stare at all of them. "Briony is telling the truth. The curse *will* break if we can repeat this on the other Landmarks. And then no one else will have to die like this. Ever."

Briony watched this information pass over all their faces. Isobel looked shaken, her gaze fixed on Elionor's blood pooling between the cracks in the cobblestones. Alistair looked relieved. Gavin's shoulders were tense, his broad frame hunched, like he could not separate his mind from the battle.

But it was Hendry who spoke. "Is that why I'm here?"

"Maybe," Briony answered. "Maybe as the tournament breaks, so do some of its rules. Maybe we could all interact with our families now, if we tried."

The thought made her swallow. Hard.

"I think we're all more concerned with figuring out why he isn't dead," Gavin said.

"Dead?" Briony echoed.

Hendry stretched his head up and pulled down his collar, revealing a gruesome red gash stretching across his neck. Briony instantly recoiled, disturbed.

"I watched you bury the ring in the Castle last night," Gavin said.

"I buried it to release its magic," Alistair snapped. "How could that reverse—"

"I don't think that's what you did," Briony said, trying to think all of this through. "If the high magick of the curse is falling apart, then maybe . . . maybe when the magick in the ring dispersed inside the Castle Landmark, it got sucked into the magick of the tournament. And when that magick unraveled a little more, it produced Hendry. Like a side effect."

Alistair rubbed one of his bloodshot eyes, then peered at the Champions Pillar. He looked utterly wretched. "When I buried the ring, there were two cracks. Both on its front, with the names. And now there's four—three on its front, one on its back."

The Pillar had cracked when Briony had slid the ring off Innes's finger. She hadn't realized it had happened three times more.

"The last one just happened now," Alistair continued. "On the back. The side with the stars. That one's from what you did, isn't it?"

"So it was already breaking?" Finley asked, furrowing his brow. "That . . . that can't be right. We united the Sword with the Cave. What else could be breaking it?"

Briony remembered, with a sudden, sickening rush, the other words that Reid had told her the night of the tournament's beginning. Words that, in her hurry and panic, she had ignored.

"There must be two ways to break the tournament, just like there are two ways to drain the enchantment from a cursestone," Briony spoke, bile rising in her throat. "You can take it apart safely, matching each Relic to each Landmark one by one. Or you can do it the other way."

"The cursestone breaks." Isobel breathed. "And everything inside it is destroyed."

"So we could all die?" Finley's voice hitched just the slightest bit. "Everyone who's left?"

"I . . . I think so." Briony shuddered. "I didn't know any of this was real until an hour ago."

Finley still looked shaken, but he nodded. "I guess it makes sense that this would be dangerous. But we need to do everything we can to make sure that doesn't happen."

"We will," Briony said firmly.

Isobel stalked to the Champions Pillar and examined it with the focused gaze of a spellmaker. "The side with the stars represents the safe way to dismantle the curse, the way Finley and Briony started when . . . when they united the Sword with the Cave."

Even though Isobel didn't look at Briony as she spoke, Briony still felt a rush of relief and pride at her words. Isobel finally believed her.

Isobel traced her hand over the side with the names of every champion, past and present. "I think this side represents the dangerous way of breaking the tournament. This is the way that's been breaking since it started. This is what brought Hendry back."

"Fantastic," Gavin said dryly. "That's the side with three cracks."

"But we have no idea what's causing those cracks," Finley pointed out.

Briony's stomach churned with trepidation as she looked from face to face. She remembered how polished all of them had looked the last time they'd been here, in their banquet finery. Now they were covered in blood and bruises, cursemarks glowing on their limbs and faces, Elionor's body lying only a meter away.

"It doesn't matter what's causing them," Briony said, "because we have a plan that will work. All we have to do is repeat what Finley and I just did, pairing Landmarks and Relics before the enchantment unravels completely."

"Wait a moment," Alistair murmured. His icy tone was nothing like the nervous boy who'd set her free only hours before. "You said Hendry is caught in the high magick that makes up the tournament. So if we break the tournament, what happens to him?"

Hendry rested a hand on Alistair's arm. Briony stared grimly at the trail of shimmering high magick that moved alongside him. If the tournament ended, Hendry would probably go with it.

But before she could find the words to tell him that, her gaze trailed back to Elionor's corpse. Alistair had never explained why he had killed her, but Briony could see the answer now. It was in the splatters of Elionor's blood across his face. In his threatening stance as he braced himself in front of Hendry.

Gavin was the one who answered, after a long, uncomfortable silence. "Hendry would go back to being dead, is what would happen."

"There has to be another way," Alistair shot back. "We'll figure out another way."

"With what time?" Briony asked. "The tournament is collapsing as we speak."

"You both said that you don't know what's causing those other cracks. We shouldn't—"

"I don't want you to die, Al," Hendry told him. "I don't want you all to die trying to save me."

Alistair didn't look like he'd even heard him. His gaze was focused on Briony and Finley, warning, pleading. "All I'm asking for is more time."

"The way you gave Elionor time?" Finley gestured from Elionor's body to the holes in the Blood Veil, the cracks in the Pillar. "We don't *have* time. We need to act as fast as possible, if the magick really is unraveling."

Briony felt a twinge of guilt at the anguish on Alistair's face. But he'd chosen to kill Elionor. And he was choosing his brother's life over all of theirs.

"You're right," Briony said. "We should get started right away. We'll take the Cloak to its Landmark, and—"

"The Relics fall randomly over the course of the whole tournament!" Alistair shouted. "That's another ten weeks! How can you say you don't have time?"

"If the tournament doesn't collapse, it'll end. It always ends after three months, even if there's no winner," Isobel said softly. "Which means Hendry will be gone then, too. I'm so sorry. He'll end with the tournament either way."

"You don't know that," Alistair growled. "There's a thousand reasons that might not be true. The rules are breaking. There's high magick in Ilvernath, even after the tournament ends—"

"So what you're saying is that you won't help us break it at all," Briony said. "Because breaking it could make him disappear."

"I . . . I . . ." Alistair clearly didn't know what to say.

"And if you don't plan on surviving the tournament by breaking it, then the only way out is to win it," Finley said, a warning note in his voice.

Alistair no longer looked at any of them, only at his brother.

"I've made my choice," he spoke. "If breaking the tournament means losing Hendry, then I'd rather fight."

The wind wailed as it blew through the courtyard, whisking blood-tipped leaves into the air and scattering them aside.

None of the champions moved. Only their gazes darted between one another, assessing who was friend and who was foe.

Alistair attacked first.

He held nothing back. One, two, three curses fired across the courtyard, forcing Briony and Finley to throw up shield spells in less than a heartbeat. The power of the curses collided with her Mirror Image in moments, but it was too powerful for the spell to absorb. Instead, they splintered her protective magic and left deep craters beside their feet. Briony didn't have any option but to return fire.

Then another spell struck Briony hard in the side. She gasped. Ice seeped up the cracks between her fingers, and her breath fogged the air around her. For a moment, she couldn't move. Then the ice shattered, the spell failing, and she whipped to the right where Isobel stood.

"Why are you cursing me?" Briony demanded.

"I won't hurt you. *Either* of you," Isobel snapped. "But you both need to stop before someone else dies."

"Tell that to your boyfriend," Briony said.

At that, another ice-blue spell shot in Briony's direction, but before it could reach her, it sputtered out and struck the cobblestones. Isobel swore and shrugged off her Cloak. Then she cast the same spell again, this time at Alistair. It was stronger without the Cloak draining her offensive magick, but Alistair still deflected it.

Hendry, armed with spellstones Alistair had given him, cast a haphazard flurry of defensive barriers, all of which either Briony or Finley blew through with each new curse they cast. Only Gavin had staggered out of the range of battle, clutching his arm as though wounded, with a look in his eyes like he didn't know which side he would even fight for.

Something flashed in the corner of Briony's vision, and she whirled, ready to throw up a shield. But it wasn't a curse.

It was a camera.

Horror crept through her as she made out a crowd of paparazzi, crouched eagerly at the edge of the courtyard. In the rush of everything, Briony had forgotten the most dangerous part of breaking the tournament rules: this wasn't private anymore. The lightening of the Blood Veil had surely drawn attention, and now this fight would be splashed on the front page of tomorrow's tabloids.

"Hey," Briony croaked out, trying to gesture to the other champions. "We're being watched—"

A curse hit the ground, and roots burst from the earth at Finley's feet. Finley lunged out of the way before they could reach for him, then rushed over to her side.

"Look," Briony breathed, gesturing to the cameras.

"Shit," Finley muttered. "We have to take this fight back behind the Blood Veil."

Another curse whizzed past them, so close it singed a piece of her hair.

Briony grimaced. "I'm not sure we have a choice."

So this was Alistair's notorious strength. This was who Briony had gained as an enemy and lost as a potential ally, a potential friend.

But Briony had made the right decision, she was certain. She was fighting for a real cause, not a lost one. Her gaze turned to Isobel, who was blocking Alistair's latest bout of cursefire with polished precision.

"You can still stop this!" Isobel called. "You—"

"Isobel Macaslan!" one of the paparazzi called. They'd drawn closer now, emboldened despite the cursefire. "Look over here! Let us get your good side!"

Isobel turned, shock on her face as she beheld the row of cameras.

"No," she moaned, looking haunted. "Not now."

Her shields faltered, just for a moment. But that was all it took.

A curse struck Isobel in the center of the chest, right above her rib cage. Magick seeped through the fabric of her dress, lighter and more sinister than blood.

Briony watched, horrified, as Isobel gasped and reached a trembling hand toward the wound—and then collapsed onto the mossy ground beneath her. Her eyes were still open. Her hand clutched at the dirt.

Across from her, Alistair looked utterly shocked.

"No," he gasped. "I wasn't firing at . . ."

But Briony had no time to listen to him.

The cameras were still flashing, the paparazzi crawling toward them like a swarm of maggots. All Briony could think about was Isobel's body as tomorrow's headline news. She'd already forced her friend in front of those cameras once. She wouldn't let it happen again.

"Get away from her," Briony snarled, at the paparazzi, at Alistair, calling upon every spellring she could. Two spells, three spells—it didn't matter. She was strong enough to cast them all.

Magick spread from her hands, tendrils of white curling around her. Mirror Shards. The Deathly Slumber. And the spell Elionor had crafted for her, the one that had helped her realize this tournament was a septogram—the Overcharge.

"You want a story?" Briony called out, stepping between Isobel's body and the camera flashes. She locked eyes with the nearest reporter, a young man only a few years older than herself. He looked utterly terrified. "You want to know what this curse really does to us? I'll show you."

Briony let the magick go, sending ripples of power in all directions. Glass shards spiraled toward the paparazzi, smashing their camera lenses and slicing bloody gashes in their flesh. Those that weren't hit fell to the ground, fast asleep. But Briony wasn't done.

She smiled and let Overcharge free.

Crackling electricity rose around her, coiled taut, then spiraled outward in a neat circle. Every single camera in her sight line sputtered and sizzled, sparks rising pathetically into the air.

There would be no pictures of this moment.

She stared around at the paparazzi—either passed out on the ground or retreating, frightened. At Gavin and Finley, watching her with expressions she couldn't read.

And then she turned to look at the Lowe brothers, still standing on the front steps.

"Isobel was right. No more fighting," Briony said, in her best team captain voice. "Not today."

To her surprise, Alistair was nodding before she'd even finished speaking.

"Please," he said, starting forward. "I didn't mean— I— Please let me try to heal her."

Briony hesitated. But then she gazed into Alistair's face, and saw grief and fear and—love. Or at least something close to it.

"Can you help her?" she asked.

"I don't know," Alistair whispered. "But I have to try."

Briony understood suddenly that both of them were only trying to save the people they cared about, in the only ways they knew how.

"Okay," she said. And stepped aside.

ISOBEL MACASLAN

Do not judge the champions too harshly. Survival could make villains of any of us.

A Tradition of Tragedy

The last time a death curse had touched Isobel, it'd been a graze. A trace of white against her cheekbone, as though a chalk mark had been drawn on her face. And even that, though barely perceptible, was enough to prove deadly. Had Briony not healed it, Isobel's body would still lay untouched on the moors.

She choked as this new one struck her, her hand grasping at her chest. For a brief moment, the world around her ceased. The pain . . . the pain was burning. It was agony. It tore the air from her lungs and pierced into her skin, a thousand needles gouging into flesh and bone and marrow. Searching for the heart within. To end her entirely.

The world went cold. Isobel shivered as she collapsed onto the ground, cheek pressed against damp, mossy cobblestones. There wasn't enough life in her to let out a scream.

She tried to stretch her arm forward, but she didn't move at all. Her heart clenched. She felt so cold it hurt, like skin pressed too long against ice, from the inside out. A cage of frost was closing around her heart and gradually shrinking, tightening.

Then her fingers finally found it.

The locket.

For weeks, Isobel had been so focused on the other enchantment that dangled from the necklace that she had forgotten the original one: the greatest gift that her family had given her, on the day she and her father went to visit Reid MacTavish.

Life.

She barely had the strength to cast the spell, but as the world around her numbed, she focused everything she had left into the magick.

The Roach's Armor seeped out of the locket, a swarm of magick skittering across her skin. She felt it everywhere. In the grooves between her fingers and toes. At the edges of her ears, beetle-like legs and antennae grazing her eyes.

Crawling and cramming their way down her throat.

For several heartbeats, she couldn't move. She couldn't breathe. She could only panic.

But then all at once, the sensation stilled. Isobel's eyes flew open as she coughed out a sticky violet tar and gasped as new air burst into her lungs, as the curse slowly drained from her body.

Alistair Lowe knelt beside her, grabbed her by the shoulders, and took her in his arms. Behind him, the others hovered. And beyond them, a dozen members of the paparazzi or cursechasers lay unconscious, scattered limply across the courtyard. A welcome sight.

"Is she alive?" Briony asked, starting forward. Finley put a firm hand on her shoulder and whispered something to her that Isobel couldn't make out.

Gavin grimaced. "She looks . . ."

"I'm fine." Isobel coughed, unsure if that was a lie. She felt cold— very cold.

Alistair's eyes widened, and he squeezed Isobel tighter. A part of her was comforted by his touch. But another part couldn't shake the image of Hendry Lowe watching from only paces away, his expression grave.

"Did you cure her?" Briony asked.

Alistair shook his head. "She saved herself."

Isobel frowned and searched Alistair's pleading expression. She was reminded of only the day before, when Alistair lay dying on the forest floor and still used his life to save hers. Even though his brother had risen from the dead, what Isobel found hardest to believe was that Alistair had tried to kill her, even if by mistake.

It was her own fault. For almost a year, she'd been so resentful of Briony, of her parents, of the world, that she'd let that bitterness fester. She'd let it chase away any hope she had. She'd let it ruin everything she'd touched. All in the name of survival.

Even if the Roach's Armor had halted the curse, she had no idea if she'd been cured. Her heartbeat was so weak and slow she could barely feel it. So, clearly, no amount of coldness or cruelty had ever been worth it.

She lifted her hand and ran it down his cheek. "You weren't ever the monster in this story, Al," she said softly.

"Then who am I?" he asked.

Not long ago, Alistair had told her that he always had a choice.

Isobel grabbed Alistair's hand and cast the Divining Kiss. Alistair's thoughts spilled into her mind. She saw the panic when his curse had struck her. She saw the events of the past several hours, how he'd freed Briony.

And then she saw something much bigger, draped across all his other thoughts like a shroud. His grief. All he'd wanted since the tournament began was his brother back. What he felt for her was a mere candle flame beside that longing, that uncertainty, that hopelessness. It didn't matter if the tournament was breaking or not, if Isobel loved him or not. No one could take Alistair's brother from him a second time. He would rather die with Hendry than lose him again.

And Briony wouldn't back down, not after being proven right.

Those were her options:

A friend who'd betrayed her when she needed her most.

Or the boy she cared about, who hadn't wanted to be the villain in this story.

Alistair had been right. Isobel always did have a choice, and no matter how heartbreaking, the choice was still clear.

Hendry put a steady hand on his brother's shoulder—meant to comfort or persuade, Isobel couldn't tell. But Alistair didn't let her go. Not yet.

Too much had happened too quickly for Isobel to know if she was truly dying. All she knew was that there was a chance that many of them could survive, a real chance.

And Isobel Macaslan might hate herself for it, but she was a survivor.

"I don't know," she whispered to him. "But the story ends here."

She let out a sob as she grabbed Alistair's collar in her fist and pulled him toward her. His lips pressed against hers, and she felt him stiffen in surprise. For a moment, they both froze. His breath was hot against her skin, and he tasted of her tears. Then his arm slid tighter around her, pulling her close as though she might be stolen away like so much else in his life. Isobel felt the Divining Kiss's chalice tip over, and a thousand of her own thoughts from the past two weeks were laid bare to him, all her desires to match his own. As Reid's curse coursed up her throat from its ring, Alistair was too distracted amid Isobel's tangled emotions to notice what she had done.

Suddenly, the kiss tasted of decay.

Alistair's eyes went wide, but before he could react more, he was yanked away from her as the ghostly white of the Reaper's Embrace seeped across his fingertips. He took shaky breaths as though any one could be his last.

Isobel collided painfully with the ground as Hendry let out a hoarse whisper. "What did you *do*?"

In this story, the princess slayed the dragon.

"Isobel!" Briony shouted. Suddenly, the other three were at her side, grabbing at her, pulling her away.

The last thing Isobel saw before the Here to There spell sparked was the fury in Alistair's eyes, and she knew she'd made the right choice. Their story had never been destined for a happy ending.

GAVIN GRIEVE

Every dead champion deserved to be more than a name crossed out on a pillar.

A Tradition of Tragedy

With two champions dead, the scarlet of the Blood Veil had weakened again, and the blue of the afternoon sky behind it had rendered Ilvernath a deep, reddish purple.

And Ilvernath had noticed. Pedestrians crowded the streets—residents, cursechasers, reporters alike. They pointed overhead and whispered, rumors about Elionor Payne's death already spreading through the city's gossip network like wildfire.

None of these onlookers noticed a blood-soaked Gavin Grieve stalking the streets beside them. He grimaced as he fought to maintain his Shrouded from Sight spell despite the throbbing pain in his right arm. Even through the thin cotton of his T-shirt, he could feel his veins bulging from his skin, pulsing with magick.

The others had tried to get Gavin to join them, but he'd declined. He wanted no part in Reid MacTavish's manipulations or Briony and Finley's heroic delusions. From now on, it was back to basics. Back to relying on the only person he could trust: himself.

Gavin made for a row of shiny storefronts, all the spellshops that had turned him away just a few weeks ago. He paused before the gleaming window display of Walsh Spellmaking Emporium. His face was still splattered with Elionor Payne's blood.

Elionor was part of the reason he was here, she and Carbry

Darrow. When they'd died, their life magick had been drawn to him, and ever since, he'd been chewing on an idea. That Gavin could refill his hourglass, not with his own life magick, but with someone else's.

And now that all the tournament's rules were breaking . . . his options for acquiring that life magick had gotten a lot more interesting.

The shop bell tinkled merrily as Gavin trudged inside, and the cashier glanced toward the door. Their brow furrowed as they realized that no one was there.

"That's odd," the cashier murmured.

"Who is it?" called out a thin, reedy voice. A moment later, Osmand Walsh emerged from the back room, his cheeks slightly flushed, smoothing down the folds of the same purple suit he'd worn when he'd mocked Gavin at his sister's wedding.

Gavin waved a hand, unmasking himself to Osmand Walsh alone, smiling at the look of panic that crossed the spellmaker's face.

"Surprised to see me?" he asked smugly.

Then, before the man could so much as blink, Gavin grasped him by his lapels and cast a Here to There spell. Another gift from Alistair Lowe.

They landed in the Castle dungeons.

They were nothing like the rest of the Landmark. The dank stone walls were coated with filth and rot, the packed dirt floors littered with animal bones and cast-off bits of manacles and chains.

Osmand was a powerful man, a respected spellmaker. But he was so startled by his ghastly new surroundings and Gavin's wicked smile that he only managed a rough, terrified, "H-How?"

A rush of satisfaction swept through Gavin. Osmand had made a fool of Gavin in front of half of Ilvernath. It was fitting, then, that his only purpose now would be ensuring that Gavin was never laughed at again.

For a moment, Gavin's thoughts veered to Alistair. Was this how he'd felt when he'd turned on them? When he'd proven to be exactly the monster that Gavin had always suspected? The exhilaration of knowing there was no turning back, and yet beneath it all, a trace of doubt?

No. Alistair didn't doubt anything, and neither would Gavin.

Before Osmand Walsh could truly gather his bearings, Gavin cast Trancewalker on him. His eyes went glassy, and he slumped against the wall, frozen beside a pool of murky water that had dripped from the ceiling. His purple suit dampened with muck.

The spellmaker was so far gone that he did not move when Gavin searched around the floor for something sharp. He found a cast-off sliver of iron and pressed it thoughtfully against the spellmaker's throat.

He had never killed a person before.

He was pretty sure he wouldn't have to. Not yet.

He lowered his makeshift weapon to Osmand's collarbone and pressed it gently against the spellmaker's skin, smiling as a line of blood welled up against his flesh. He waited, staring impatiently at the wound, until a curl of white emerged. Life magick. Gavin reached a hand forward, letting it sink into his arm. Immediately, the pain of his magick being drained began to fade away. He gasped with relief.

The most difficult part was not going too far—he didn't want to kill the man, not when he had so much life left to give him. So he forced himself to stop after just a few precious seconds, quickly stepping back. The spellmaker slumped to the ground, unconscious.

When Gavin looked down at his arm, he was glowing purple and green from the inside out.

His skin shimmered for a moment, and Gavin saw himself reflected in a pool of cloudy water, his skin turned to scales, his tongue forked and flickering like a snake's. *I am a monster now,* he thought, *a changeling*—but it was just his imagination, an intrusive image from one of Alistair's stories. In a blink, his skin returned to normal. All that was left was the original tattoo on his arm. Sand had begun to trickle in the opposite direction, from the bottom of the glass back to the top.

All the rules were breaking, but Gavin hadn't lost sight of his original goal.

Victory in the tournament, however he had to achieve it.

And he already knew which champion he would strike down first, now that Isobel's curse had provided him with a perfect opportunity.

Gavin reached into his pocket and pulled out the Mirror he had snatched from Elionor's body. When he stared into it, the face he saw reflected was not his own—it was pale and pointed, dark hair swooping back into a widow's peak.

As Elionor's killer, the Mirror belonged to Alistair Lowe, and it showed only his image. But Gavin had it now.

He stared at his rival for several moments, picturing how sweet it would feel when Gavin drained every bit of life from his cruel face.

BRIONY THORBURN

Next time the Blood Moon rises and the tournament begins, it won't just be Ilvernath watching.

A Tradition of Tragedy

R eid MacTavish had not seemed particularly surprised when three champions showed up on his front stoop. He'd handled them with an efficiency that felt almost practiced—invited them in, set up a woozy Isobel in his back room, and cast extra wards across the front windows in case of wandering paparazzi. Isobel had quickly fallen into a deep slumber. Reid had said that she'd wake up soon, that her body needed time to process what it had been put through, but Briony knew her stomach would be in knots until it actually happened.

Gavin Grieve had refused to come with them. He'd told them he was done with alliances before vanishing into thin air, and Briony was too exhausted to chase him down. She hoped he'd see reason, but she was no longer trying to force everyone to her side.

Her and Finley's purpose here was twofold. Because surely the best cursemaker in town could help Isobel, and, now that they could pass through the Blood Veil, she and Finley had a chance to get more information from him about the tournament itself.

"So," Finley said to Reid. "You helped Briony develop this theory?"

"I did, yes." They'd convened in the main room of the shop,

crammed between the shelves of expensive curses and the cabinets brimming with trinkets and ingredients. Everything smelled of incense and herbs. "And you two really managed to pair a Relic and a Landmark?"

"The Sword and the Cave," Finley answered. "So we know that if we can do that six more times, we'll successfully drain the enchantment. But we're worried that . . . isn't all that's happening."

"Oh?" Reid leaned forward, interest glimmering in his eyes.

"Remember what you told me at the banquet?" Briony asked. "About how there are two ways to break the tournament? How do we know if the second way . . . I mean . . ." She swallowed, then held up her hand. The champion's ring on her pinky glimmered red and gold in the cobweb-coated lights above them. "When I took this from Innes, the Champions Pillar cracked. When Finley and I collapsed the Cave, it cracked again—but on a different side, the star side. We think that star side means we're doing it right. And the side with the names . . ."

She trailed off, feeling sick.

Reid's hand closed around one of the broken cursestones around his neck. They were dull and cracked. Dead. "You're worried it's going to implode completely."

"Yes," she choked.

"There are already three cracks on the side with names," Finley said solemnly. "We need to know how to prevent more."

"Hmm," Reid said. "The tournament's curse feeds on itself. Not just blood or high magick—but the repeated story. For centuries, it has been accustomed to a pattern. But you've all been changing it, as Briony did when she took Innes's place. Those other two cracks must come from champions behaving in ways that deviate in extremes from the way this story has always been told."

Briony thought of the paparazzi swarming their fight. Of Hendry standing next to Alistair, red flickering around him. So much had gone haywire—it was impossible to tell what events had been big enough to crack the pillars.

Briony slumped against a nearby cabinet, crossing her arms in frustration. "It's like it's punishing us for trying to break it."

Reid's gaze was intensely focused. A thistle plant on a shelf above him caught the light, casting a strange, many-pronged shadow across his cheek like a grotesque cursemark. "I think that's exactly what it's doing."

"How many cracks until it's destroyed?" she asked.

"Probably seven. Same as the Landmarks and the Relics."

"Okay," Finley murmured. He kept turning a spellstone in his hand, over and over. Briony recognized it as one of Elionor's. "So we have to pair up the rest of the Relics and Landmarks as fast as we can. We need to figure out what happened to the Mirror. And we'll need to learn the other families' stories, starting with Isobel's, of course . . ."

He was making his own rules. A new plan. Just like he'd said he would. Briony inhaled a deep, shaky breath. It had only been two weeks of the tournament—they still had two and a half months for other Relics to fall. But at the rate the tournament was already collapsing, it wouldn't last that long.

Still, she couldn't let the odds break her. They were already closer than any champion had been before.

"We need to figure out which pairings are right," she said firmly. "So we can do this as quickly as possible once they fall. Reid, would you be willing to help us with that?"

"Of course," Reid said. "You'll need me. I know more about curses than any of you."

Briony felt a twinge of unease at the eagerness in his voice. After all this time, all her questions, she'd never actually asked him *why* he wanted to be part of this, if there was a reason other than his own fascination with his trade. But before she could get the words out, a noise sounded from outside the shop. Briony jerked her head up. Paparazzi crowded the windows, peeking through the cracks in the shades, mumbling to one another. And *they* didn't have broken cameras.

"Damn it," she muttered. "They found us already."

Finley's shoulders locked, braced for another battle. "The wards ran out already?"

"They must be stronger than I thought," Reid said, waving his hand dismissively. Then he gestured toward the velvet curtains behind him. "Don't worry. You go to the back. I'll handle it. There's a fire exit behind one of the cabinets that you can take to avoid them."

He strolled confidently to the door. Briony and Finley hastily retreated behind the black velvet curtains to the back room.

To Briony's surprise, Isobel was awake again. She was sitting up on her cot, shivering a little, gazing around her cluttered surroundings with wide eyes. At the sight of Briony, she sighed in relief.

"Where are we?" she asked, at the same time that Briony gasped, "You're alive."

"We're at Reid MacTavish's curseshop," Finley told her. "We figured you needed help."

Isobel took a breath so deep Briony could practically hear her bones creak. "I feel okay, actually. Just a bit strange. But . . . I guess that's to be expected. I survived a death curse."

"Which Alistair cast on you," Briony pointed out. Then, unable to contain her curiosity, she added, "Right before you . . . kissed him."

Isobel's voice trembled. "I didn't just kiss him, Briony. I cursed him."

Briony jolted back in shock. She didn't have to ask what kind of curse. She remembered the way Alistair had pulled away from Isobel. The horror on his face. "But we're going to break the tournament. You shouldn't have—"

"You saw the state he was in when his brother showed up. You know how powerful he is. He'll do everything he can to stop us from breaking the tournament. And so . . . I had to make a decision."

Isobel had chosen her side. Even after betrayals, and fights, and a year estranged. Briony swallowed down a grateful lump in her throat. This was no time to cry.

"So he's already dead?" Briony whispered.

"Not yet. It's a very slow death, but he won't be able to stop it. And I don't regret it. It was what I had to do."

Even if Isobel's words sounded resolute, the expression on her face told Briony otherwise. She bit her lip, red splotches breaking out over her cheeks. Casting that curse on Alistair must've ripped her apart.

"I'm sorry," Briony said. She'd apologized before, at the Castle, but it felt different now. "For everything you've had to do. If I hadn't made you become champion, you wouldn't need to deal with this at all."

"I know," Isobel said, so softly that Briony barely heard it. "I'm sorry, too. That I didn't believe you about ending the tournament for good."

Briony wanted to ask if they were okay now. If maybe they could be friends again. But Isobel had just escaped death by the most narrow of margins. Had betrayed a boy who clearly meant a lot to her. Briony and Isobel's tattered friendship could wait.

"Will you come with us?" Briony asked.

Isobel tried to rise from her cot, but her face paled even further, and she collapsed back down. "Um. I don't think I can. Not yet."

"Then we'll wait for you," Briony said quickly. But Finley coughed, and Briony turned to see that he had moved a cabinet aside. A door was open now, revealing a back alley.

"The reporters," he said urgently. "Reid bought us time so that we could leave, remember?"

He was right. But she didn't want to abandon Isobel, even if Reid could keep the paparazzi at bay.

"Go," Isobel urged. "I'll meet up with you later."

Briony pulled out her Compass Rose spellstone and pressed it into Isobel's palm. "So that you can find us."

"Thanks." Isobel smiled weakly. "Now go. I'll be fine."

Outside, the sky was visibly lighter due to Elionor's death. Blue and red bled together to make a ghastly purple, washing the cobblestones and the buildings in an odd violet glow. Briony and Finley fled through the backstreets of Ilvernath proper, using the little spellwork they had left to camouflage themselves until they slipped out the inner Blood Veil. It still felt unnatural to simply walk through that translucent redness.

"If the inner Blood Veil is broken, then it's only a matter of time before the tournament grounds are swarming with reporters and cursechasers," Finley said, as they trekked through the underbrush. Neither of them had any desire to return to the Monastery ruins, so they were headed for the mountains. For the Tower.

"And Agent Yoo," Briony said gravely. "I don't think the government's going to like any of this." Briony couldn't tell Finley that the government wanted to study their high magick, thanks to that Sworn to Secrecy spell. But he was nodding anyway.

"I don't think so, either," Finley agreed. "They want to be able to control this curse. But that doesn't change what we have to do."

They were approaching the mountains now, near the spot where they'd paired the Sword and the Cave. It had only happened hours ago, but it felt like days. Briony couldn't wait to see the glorious spire of the Tower appear above the trees—couldn't wait to refill her spellrings and finally get some sleep. Finley walked in front of her, still holding Elionor's spellstone. She knew he needed to rest, too. It had been a long, horrible day.

And then a voice rang out from behind her. "Briony."

A voice that had filled her with comfort for the last seventeen years, but now it filled her with guilt.

Briony whipped around, barely breathing, and stared into Innes's wide, accusatory gaze. It was only an illusion, magick shimmering at the edges of her sister's form. But the sight of her was still gutting.

On some level, Briony had known this moment was coming as soon as she and Finley had landed in the town square and she'd realized how broken everything had become.

But that didn't mean she was ready for it.

"I'll be at the Tower tomorrow." Innes's voice was cold. She looked older and more severe, her dark hair chopped to just below her chin. Her left hand was encased in a glove, while her right hand bristled with spellrings. "If you still care about me at all, you'll meet me there. The two of us need to talk."

A moment later, the illusion spell flickered and disappeared.

It had been magick, nothing more. But that didn't matter—Innes's message had been clear.

Her family—and maybe every family—knew what Briony had done to become champion. Thanks to the pillar, they knew what she and the others had done to the tournament since.

And their reckoning was coming.

ISOBEL MACASLAN

I didn't write this book for entertainment. I wrote it to tell the truth. Somebody has to.

A Tradition of Tragedy

Isobel was cold. Her heart did not beat. Her lungs did not breathe. Exhaustion weighed on her eyelids, but despite waking up a half hour before, the thought of sleeping again frightened her. She had never felt this weak, this tired. And she worried that, if she drifted off once more, she might never wake up again.

She shivered beneath Reid MacTavish's flannel blanket and tugged it closer. Briony and Finley had left, so she was alone with the cursemaker in the back room of his shop.

"What's wrong with me?" she whispered. "Am I still dying?"

"Not exactly," Reid told her. He leaned forward and weaved his fingers around the chain of her necklace. The two trinkets that hung there, the locket and the cursering, clattered together. "The Roach's Armor staves off death, but it isn't a spell—otherwise, your family would have commissioned it from a spellmaker, not from me."

"It's a curse," Isobel said, feeling foolish for not realizing it before. She'd always thought that her father had patronized Reid that day as an excuse for Isobel to ask him to sponsor her, not because the Roach's Armor required a cursemaker. "But I watched you craft it. You never gave a sacrifice."

"No. You paid the sacrifice when you cast it."

Isobel's hand instinctively crept to her chest, to her heart. She hadn't wanted to worry Briony when she'd spoken to her, but the stillness . . . the cold . . . Whatever had happened to Isobel, it scared her.

"So what is it?" she asked, her voice weak.

"The Roach's Armor takes a different toll on each person. How do you feel?"

"Terrible. Like a . . ." She swallowed. "Like a corpse." She took a deep breath, but it was only out of habit. Her body did not need the air. "Why didn't you tell me when you crafted it?"

"I assumed you knew. It's your family's enchantment, isn't it?"

Isobel turned away, pressing her cheek into the pillow. She might've spent more time with the Macaslans since they named her champion, but prior to that, it wasn't as though she'd known them well. It felt shameful to admit that, though. After the world had turned on her, Isobel had so badly wanted to belong somewhere, and her father's family had welcomed her. It was why her father could always use them to twist her so easily—because she'd always known that if she turned her back on them, then they would undoubtedly turn their backs on her.

Instead of answering, she only asked, "Is it permanent?"

"I don't know. It could get better. It could also get worse."

Isobel didn't want to consider that, so she asked about a different curse, instead. "How long will Alistair have?"

"The Reaper's Embrace kills you a little more for each wrong committed. So for Alistair Lowe . . ." Reid shrugged. "I'd give him a few days."

That wasn't fair. No matter what the world thought of Alistair, he wasn't a monster.

"Oh, don't look so glum. It was his curse that almost killed you, after all," Reid said. "But I have to say . . . I'm impressed that you solved your little problem. The Reaper's Embrace requires a heavy sacrifice to craft. How did you manage it?"

Isobel shuddered at the memory, not even a day old. She'd saved him only to kill him.

"Alistair," she said hoarsely.

Oddly, a smile crept up Reid's face. "That must be it. The second crack. When Alistair sacrificed himself for another champion's magic, he unwound part of the pattern."

Isobel had heard Briony mention something about the tournament's patterns and the curse, but she still didn't understand Reid's words. And more so, she didn't understand the glimmer of eagerness in his eyes. He scooted his chair closer to her bedside.

"Tell me about how it happened," he urged, his voice high-pitched and excited.

But Isobel didn't want to relive that scene. "I'd rather not."

"I'm helping Briony and Finley solve this," he said, sounding frustrated. "That means I need to be informed. And I know more about this curse than anybody."

Isobel narrowed her eyes. She had made a mistake—a terrible mistake—not to believe Briony. But even if Briony trusted Reid, Isobel wasn't sure she did. The look on his face was hostile and greedy, the sort her father wore whenever he spoke about her as champion.

She nervously eyed the door, suddenly wishing Briony and Finley hadn't left her alone after all.

"Even if you are a cursemaker," Isobel said stiffly, "I don't see how you could know more about the tournament than us or our families. How could you? We're the ones inside it."

Reid leaned closer. So close Isobel could smell the sage in his cologne, could make out a faint scar beneath his eye, razor thin and years old. Isobel wasn't threatened by someone just because they wore cheap eyeliner and black clothes, but her breath hitched all the same.

"I *have* been inside it. Who do you think hinted to Briony that the tournament could be broken?" he asked, and his tone made Isobel's skin crawl. "Who do you think made a Grieve so powerful? Who gave you the idea to go seek out Alistair Lowe? The Null and Void spell never would have worked, you know, princess."

Isobel's already cold blood ran colder. He'd tricked her? He'd led her to Alistair?

She glanced at the spellrings on her hand. But the few enchantments she had left wouldn't hold against the arsenal of an accomplished cursemaker. Not in a real fight.

And so, deftly, she reached forward and took Reid's hand. He jolted, surprised by the touch, but before he could pull his hand away, the magick of the Divining Kiss had already seeped out of its spellring. It was her final charge before she would need to refill it; the spellstone flickered, then dimmed. Reid stiffened as white lips appeared on the inside of his wrist, in the shape of Isobel's own.

A handful of Reid's thoughts from the past few minutes tumbled into Isobel's mind, one after the other. And with them, the secrets he'd withheld.

Then Isobel's otherwise still heart gave a terrified clench. She wrenched her hand back and slid as far from the cursemaker as she could. She needed to flee. She needed to warn Briony and Finley. All the champions were in danger, and not because of one another.

"You wrote the book," she hissed. "It wasn't a Grieve. It was you. Why?"

Reid's expression turned furious. He grabbed her by the forearm and yanked her forward, his nails digging into her skin. Isobel considered screaming for help, but she sensed a shield spell descending over the room, locking the two of them inside behind the black velvet curtains. She had a terrible feeling only one of them would make it out.

"Because when the tournament collapses and the rest of you die," Reid growled, "the high magick your families have hoarded for so long will be visible to *everyone*. And I will be the one who controls it."

ALISTAIR LOWE

I think, deep down, some people don't want their stories to have
happy endings.

A Tradition of Tragedy

As the boys approached, a chilling breeze tore through the October morning, and the wrought iron gates of the Lowe estate creaked open to welcome them home.

The first boy took a deep breath and squinted up at the sun as though he hadn't seen it in a long time. It was on a morning like this one that he'd been betrayed, and after, there had been nothing but the dark.

The second boy shivered at the reminder of his days in this place, of hours spent sequestered in its shadowy alcoves. Every arduous lesson, every haunting story was intended to shape him into a deadly weapon.

When the two brothers—the discarded and the broken—returned home, they did so with cursestones in their pockets and wrath in their hearts.

But as they crossed the gate, Alistair Lowe hesitated.

"Are you sure?" Hendry breathed.

Alistair had never been more sure of anything. All his childhood spent in terror over the nightmares threatening to torture him or devour him or take him away, and he had never realized the greatest evil was *within* this estate, not outside it.

The nightmares had not taught him to fear the dark.

The nightmares had taught him to become it.

The magick of the tournament was ancient and binding, yet Alistair, a champion, walked freely onto his family's grounds. The fabric of it all was breaking.

But if the tournament ended, then Hendry would, too.

"I am," Alistair answered. "But it's still your choice. You don't have to."

Hendry looked coolly at the bleak estate. "I need to see them. I need to hear them tell me why."

"But you know why."

Hendry sighed. "I guess I need to hear it, anyway."

Even at the entrance to their home, Alistair couldn't imagine facing their family, either. When he'd resigned himself to dying in the tournament, he had thought he'd never have to see them again.

In one hand, he clutched the front page of the *Ilvernath Eclipse*. But his hand did not look normal. The fingertips had gone white as frost, the symptom of a curse that killed its victims slowly rather than all at once. And it would certainly kill him—Alistair had helped Isobel study the curse enough to understand its power.

Most of the page was taken up by a massive photograph. Alistair on his knees, Isobel limp and half dead in his arms, their lips locked in a kiss. Briony's spell had missed someone's camera. They must've been delighted when they developed their film and saw their next headline waiting for them.

He crumpled the newspaper in his fist, a surge of emotions coursing through him: loss, fear—and, strongest of all—betrayal. Alistair had nearly given his life for Isobel to perfect this curse, to save her. Never had he suspected he would be its victim.

Alistair tossed the trash aside and forced himself to look away from his encroaching death sentence. "You're back . . ." He swallowed. "But soon I'll be gone."

"I won't let you die." Hendry rested his hand on Alistair's shoulder and squeezed.

But I let you die, Alistair thought guiltily.

No, he corrected himself. He wasn't to blame for what had happened to Hendry. But the people who *were* waited, unsuspecting, inside.

"Are you sure that's what you want to do?" Alistair asked. "Talk?"

Hendry took too long to answer. When Alistair turned, Hendry's cheeks were wet. And as he moved to wipe the tears away, a red streak of high magick lagged behind his arm.

"No," Hendry whispered.

"Then I say we don't."

Alistair stormed ahead of his brother, down the paths both of them knew so well. He sang under his breath while he walked.

Grins like goblins.

They approached the front door. It was twice their height, made of gnarled wood like the twisted roots of an oak tree, with faces carved into the knots. All of their mouths were open in a silent scream.

Pale as plague and silent as spirits.

They crept into the foyer. Portraits of Lowes past lined the walls, and Hendry conjured a knife and stabbed it into the closest one, right into their grandmother's painted face. He sliced the enchanted blade down like the streak of a claw, tearing through the images of their mother and uncles and dear, departed Aunt Alphina.

They'll tear your throat and drink your soul.

The brothers found a shadowy figure alone in the sitting room, in the exact same spot she'd been when she'd presented Alistair the family's gift. She screamed so loud the murder of crows outside the door cawed and took flight.

Alistair Lowe smiled, and the white of the Reaper's Embrace crept a little farther up his skin. By the end of the morning, his hand was stained white with sins and red with blood.

Every tale of the Lowe family was deserved.

Acknowledgments

All of Us Villains began as a passion project between two best friends in the summer of 2017, but since then, so many others have assisted us in making this campy, twisty death tournament novel what it is today.

First, our agents, Kelly Sonnack and Whitney Ross—thank you so much for all of the enthusiasm, guidance, and hard work you've put into this book. We've become a four-person team over the last few years, and we couldn't be happier to be collaborating with you both.

Next, thank you to the marvelous crew at Tor Teen, including Ali Fisher, our editor, whose excellent notes, calls, and insights cut straight to the bloody heart of this story and brought it to life; Devi Pillai, our advocate and cheerleader from the beginning; Melissa Frain, who first saw the potential in Ilvernath (and its nefarious cast of characters); and Kristin Temple, whose savvy support keeps us on the ball. We're also extremely grateful to Saraciea Fennell and Giselle Gonzalez, publicists extraordinaire, and Anthony Parisi, whose creativity and innovative ideas have consistently blown us away. Thanks as well to Fritz Foy, Tom Doherty, Isa Caban, Andrew King, Eileen Lawrence, Sarah Reidy, Lucille Rettino, Melanie Sanders, Jim Kapp, and Heather Saunders.

Thank you to Gillian Redfearn and to all of Gollancz for bringing this book to the other side of the pond.

Thank you to Amanda, Melody, Grace, and Margaux, our early readers who provided invaluable feedback in making our villainous characters and world come to life. To the Cult, including Kat, Janella, Mara, Axie, Meg, Akshaya, Maddy, Erin, Tara, Katy, Ashley, Claribel, and Alex—thank you for cheering us on from the start. And to Rory—thank you for being the kind of friend who always understands.

Thank you to Will Staehle and Lesley Worrell for designing a beautiful cover and jacket.

To Ben and Trevor, thank you for listening to us gush about this story for four straight years.

And last, most especially, thank you to each of our readers. It's your excitement and support that made this book—and all our books—possible. We can't wait for you to read the sequel . . . but you should know by now that villains tend to get what they deserve. ☺

CREDITS

Christine Herman, Amanda Foody, and Gollancz would like to thank everyone at Orion who worked on the publication of *All of Us Villains* in the UK.

Editorial
Aine Feeney
Gillian Redfearn

Editorial Management
Charlie Panayiotou
Jane Hughes

Audio
Paul Stark
Jake Alderson

Contracts
Anne Goddard
Tamara Morriss

Design
Nick Shah
Joanna Ridley
Nick May
Helen Ewing
Clare Sivell

Finance
Nick Gibson
Jasdip Nandra
Afeera Ahmed
Elizabeth Beaumont
Sue Baker

Marketing
Lucy Cameron

Production
Paul Hussey
Fiona McIntosh

Publicity
Will O'Mullane

Operations
Jo Jacobs
Sharon Willis

Sales

Jen Wilson
Victoria Laws
Esther Waters
Rachael Hum
Anna Egelstaff
Frances Doyle
Ben Goddard
Georgina Cutler
Barbara Ronan
Andrew Hally
Dominic Smith

Maggy Park
Linda McGregor
Sinead White
Jemimah James
Rachel Jones
Jack Dennison
Nigel Andrews
Ian Williamson
Julia Benson
Declan Kyle
Robert Mackenzie

ABOUT GOLLANCZ

Gollancz is the oldest SF publishing imprint in the world. Since being founded in 1927 Gollancz has continued to publish a focused selection of bestselling and award-winning authors. The front-list includes **Ben Aaronovitch**, **Joe Abercrombie**, **Charlaine Harris**, **Joanne Harris**, **Joe Hill**, **Alastair Reynolds**, **Patrick Rothfuss**, **Nalini Singh** and **Brandon Sanderson**.

As one of the largest Science Fiction and Fantasy imprints in the UK it is no surprise we have one of the most extensive backlists in the world. Find high-quality SF on Gateway written by such authors as **Philip K. Dick**, **Ursula Le Guin**, **Connie Willis**, **Sir Arthur C. Clarke**, **Pat Cadigan**, **Michael Moorcock** and **George R.R. Martin**.

We also have a strand of publishing in translation, which includes French, Polish and Russian authors. Gollancz is home to more award-winning authors than any other imprint, with names including **Aliette de Bodard**, **M. John Harrison**, **Paul McAuley**, **Sarah Pinborough**, **Pierre Pevel**, **Justina Robson** and many more.

The SF Gateway
More than 3,000 classic, rare and previously out-of-print SF novels at your fingertips.
www.sfgateway.com

The Gollancz Blog
Bringing you news from our worlds to yours. Stories, interviews, articles and exclusive extracts just for you!
www.gollancz.co.uk

GOLLANCZ
LONDON